I0707579

Special Envoy 2

IN SERVICE TO HER COUNTRY

Special Envoy 2 – In Service to Her Country

Published by
M. J. Simms-Maddox, Inc. ~ P. O. Box 1966 ~ Salisbury, NC 28145-1966 US
https://www.mjsimmsmaddoxinc.com (a.k.a. https://www.novelsbymj.com)

ISBN: 979-8-9863089-1-3 Hardcover
ISBN: 979-8-9863089-5-1 Paperback
ISBN: 979-8-9863089-4-4 eBook

Library of Congress Control Number: 2024900323

Logo Design by John Simms

Special Envoy 2
IN SERVICE TO
HER COUNTRY

Priscilla Journeys into War-Torn Former Yugoslavia

M. J. Simms-Maddox, Ph.D.

M. J. Simms-Maddox, Inc. Salisbury, NC US

ALSO BY M. J. SIMMS-MADDOX

THE PRISCILLA SERIES
Priscilla Engaging in the Game of Politics

Mystery in Harare: Priscilla's Journey into Southern Africa

Three Metal Pellets

Special Envoy: Priscilla Journeys into Arab Islamic Territory, classic edition
Special Envoy 1: Priscilla Journeys into Arab Islamic Territory

The Mysterious Affair at the Met:
Priscilla Plays in High Cotton in the World of Highly Valued Works of Art
Originally published by M. J. Simms-Maddox, Inc. June 1, 2021
Republished by Austin Macauley Publishers LLC, January 5, 2024
Republished by Citi of Books, Inc., December 4, 2024

Nonfiction
A Handbook for Emerging and Seasoned Authors:
An Insider's Step-by-Step Approach to Becoming
A Successful Indie Book Author and Publisher

Creative Writing and Self-Publishing Your Way

Book Reviews
Maqoma – The Legend of a Great Xhosa Warrior

Forewords
Can't Complain: God Is Good to Me

Contents

IN SERVICE TO HER COUNTRY

1

THAT LITTLE RASCAL IS RIDING TOO LOW

Priscilla J. Austin-Bernhardt—nicknamed "PJ," "Missy," or "Miss Prissy" whenever she got beyond herself—gazed out the massive, mullioned windows on the second floor of her bedroom on the palatial Bernhardt estate. It was the winter of 1991, and one would have thought she admired the scenery of the snow-capped forest and rolling hills reaching out into the horizon and beyond. Instead, she focused on her ever-enlarged belly bump. Oh, how she complained.

Her attention shifted as she gazed upon the falling snow, reflecting on growing up in the Snowbelt of western New York. Priscilla loved the cold and snow. But on this cold, snowy day, she was at her in-laws' in Bow Lake, and she did not like being there—not in the least.

The Bernhardt estate was situated amid a picturesque one hundred acres in the undulating New Hampshire hills of Tarrytown. Most people called it "Bow Lake," after the beautiful lake meandering through the property. The estate was one among 1,100 properties belonging to a handful of wealthy landowners, of whom the Bernhardts were atop the heap.

One of two highways to the estate led to spacious woodlands, where neighbors across the county were allowed access, particularly during winter and summer. Given the plentiful wildlife, including deer, ducks, pheasants, and other animals, the Bernhardts granted limited access to hunters. They also provided staff to monitor hunting and other weaponry sports to avert accidents. Depending on the season, some skied on the bunny slopes while others skated on the shimmering ice-covered lake. Yet others took advantage of the short summers and camped, hiked, swam, and picnicked. There was also helicopter surveillance, all of this and more, at no cost to the visiting neighbors.

Priscilla's father-in-law was the esteemed entrepreneur-turned-financier Emerson C. Bernhardt II, called "Father" by family and close friends. The Bernhardts amassed their fortune from their Lebanese-based olive oil export business and, more recently, a winery and Father's finance expertise. When Father visited England in the early 1940s, he met and married Lady Chelsea, the daughter of a British duke, whose family was land-rich but capital-poor. The couple settled in America, where Emerson's father, Emerson C. Bernhardt I, called "Poppa," and his wife Marlena had already emigrated and built a home in Bow Lake. Over time, Lady Chelsea graciously assumed the role once played by her mother-in-law, who had initially hosted fundraising projects, particularly for children's charities, which were almost always held on the property, regardless of the season. To say the Bernhardts were generous with their bounty would put it mildly.

All of that and more, Priscilla would eventually learn about the family she had married into one year ago. But as things stood, she had yet to realize the significance of her marriage to the son of the wealthiest man in New Hampshire, actually one of the wealthiest in America.

Save for the secret life she led, Priscilla's marriage into the lap of luxury was no small feat. Nevertheless, she likened her background to that of an ordinary woman. But there was nothing ordinary about Priscilla. Of diverse ancestry, she was Black American with British on her father's side and Irish on her mother's. Moreover, she would be the first to boast of Choctaw on her father's side and Cherokee on her mother's. From a working-class turned middle-class, her father, the late Reverend James Nelson Austin, had groomed her for a life he could never have. A life he never imagined. Priscilla was a daughter who had been raised like a son to go after her heart's desire, and her race and gender might be problematic for some, but blessings for her. Along the way, she earned a Ph.D. in political science, taught political science at Florida A&M University, served as a legislative aide in the Ohio Senate, operated her own public relations firm with offices in Columbus, Ohio, and Manhattan, and served as the CEO of the Bernhardt Foundation for Boarding Schools for Zimbabwean and South African Girls—lest one forgets her highly recognized persona. But Priscilla lived a double life, which was not on her résumé but about which her acquaintances had their suspicions.

This was Priscilla's first winter at the Bernhardt estate. Although she could not participate in sports because of her pregnancy, she learned that Bow Lake was known as a winter wonderland throughout Merrimack County. Among Lady Chelsea's favorite charities, disadvantaged youngsters with physical and mental disabilities were particularly welcomed. Their favorite sports included making snow angels, horse sledding, ice skating, snowboarding, snow tubing, and amateur

10

skiing on the bunny slopes. Older visitors enjoyed watching the children entertain themselves, and when they grew tired and cold, they could warm up in one of the well-appointed cabins on the property.

As Priscilla watched the snowfall, she felt a deep yearning for the freedom she had lost. The desire to run to the stables, mount Mystique, her favorite horse, and trot along the lake was overwhelming. She missed the exhilaration of riding, sledding, snow tubing, and skiing on the bunny slopes. But her obstetrician's caution had stripped her of these joys, leaving her feeling confined and restricted.

She missed other pastimes she had been warned against, such as eating whatever she wanted and smoking her long brown cigarettes; her brand of choice was More. Acutely aware of the danger of smoking during pregnancy, it was one of her weaknesses.

Add dressing as she pleased to the ever-growing list of things she missed because Melissa, her assistant, had dutifully replaced her stylish black pinstriped pantsuits, bespoke Oscar de la Renta gowns, and well-worn blue jeans and safari shorts with matronly maternity wear of elasticized skirts, slacks, and tops. The loss of her identity, as reflected in her wardrobe, added to her growing discomfort and dissatisfaction.

Sometimes, she thought, *Melissa was too efficient.*

Priscilla detested her new wardrobe as much as she detested her weight gain. The changes in her body, a result of her pregnancy, were a constant reminder of her loss of control and her growing discomfort.

Since her pregnancy also caused her hormones to fluctuate, one never knew when her mood would shift as, on this day, it shifted from exceptionally pleasant and happy to be pregnant to exceptionally annoying and irascible. Nor was she pleased that she and her darling husband Carlton were having their first child at Bow Lake; she would rather have it be at their Harlem brownstone.

She remembered insisting to her mother-in-law, "I know not to run up and down the stairs."

But to no avail. Lady Chelsea had made a stronger argument with Carlton.

"That's all well and good," she had said to her son. "But what happens if PJ falls or has some other mishap, and no one else is home to assist her?"

Priscilla had interpreted her mother-in-law's remarks as a slant on the predominantly Black, crime-infested Harlem neighborhood where she and Carlton lived. But Lady Chelsea had no way of knowing their neighbors had taken a liking to Priscilla, notably their appreciation for her kindness to young Jules McCorkle and later his mother, Mamie, who struggled with narcotics addiction.

"Besides," Lady Chelsea continued, "Ramses and I, as well as Nanny Hettie and Mavis, are all familiar with childbirth. We know what to do." The lady of the house referred to Hettie and her second-in-charge, Mavis. Hettie and Mavis had moved with the Bernhardts from England to the States. At nearly seventy years of age, Hettie was short and thick but still energetic and sharp. She had been Carlton and his older sister Arvana's nanny. Like Ramses was Carlton's surrogate father, Hettie was his surrogate mother. Everybody who was anybody knew that much about the Bernhardts of Bow Lake. As such, although Lady Chelsea was Carlton's doting mother, Hettie had raised him and Arvana, and she would do likewise for Carlton and Priscilla's child.

Bored and restless, Priscilla dressed in her woolen coat, hat, gloves, and boots and went for a walk on the snow-covered grounds of the estate. Ten minutes later, Ramses caught up with her. Although he pretended to be out for his daily walk, he was keeping an eye on her. Priscilla was four months pregnant, and he did not want her to be alone in the woods if she slipped and fell.

An adoptive member of the family, Ramses was a proud Egyptian who was still spry and handsome in his early seventies. Bronze-complexioned, medium built, and though only five feet eight, he was taller than Priscilla's five feet four inches. Ramses was the son of a concierge at a hotel frequented by the Bernhardts during Poppa and Marlena's early Egyptian visits. His father had consented to allow Poppa to take him to America when he noticed how close Ramses and Emerson II were. He also knew Ramses would have far more opportunities in the States than in Egypt. As the years went on, the two young men became like brothers. Eventually, Ramses, who was five years older, became Emerson II's surrogate father and later performed the same role with Emerson II's son Carlton.

Priscilla was in a bad mood. Frowning, she said, "Uncle Ramses, how the devil do other women do this? I've never been so miserable in all my life." She pulled at her twisted locks of hair, which had grown long during her pregnancy.

Her unhappiness was glaring, so Ramses reverted to his prediction about her baby's gender: "That little rascal is riding too low to be a girl. For sure, it's a boy."

He's been saying that for weeks now. Perhaps it was an old wives' tale or an Egyptian myth, Priscilla did not know, but she hated it every time he said it. She called Ramses "Uncle" because he reminded her of a favorite uncle in Indianapolis, Harold Austin, her father Nelson's youngest brother.

As Ramses listened to Priscilla fussing, he said, "Oh, Miss Prissy, I've never seen you so resplendent." He chanced to touch her hair and continued. "And your hair. I love your new look. These long-twisted locks suit you. And look how your eyes sparkle."

Priscilla looked much younger than her thirty-eight years. She wore a tan complexion, which paled early in her pregnancy because she spent so much time indoors. But her light brown hair had grown long, which she now wore pulled back from her face. Back when she renovated her Harlem brownstone, she began wearing her natural hair after observing Black women wearing theirs in Afros, braids, twisted locks, dreadlocks, cornrows, and the like. Though she loved the look of dreadlocks, she had decided on twisted locks instead. Some women even shaved their heads, but Priscilla was not that bold.

Otherwise, the only noticeable change in her appearance was the large belly bump.

Priscilla kept fussing, even after Ramses had complimented her.

"Uncle Ramses! *Who* and *what* are you going on about?"

"Miss Prissy! Surely, you know there is nothing as beautiful as a woman carrying a new life. Why, when God created woman, He made her exclusively the creator of life, the most precious gift in all His creation."

Priscilla felt ashamed, even somewhat disrespectful, for complaining about her pregnancy.

"Oh, Uncle Ramses!" she pouted. But then she said, "Bless you."

From then on, whenever she felt out of sorts, and there were many such times, she remembered that her pregnancy was "the most precious gift in all of God's creations," and the thought calmed her.

Yet, she felt isolated from her family and friends. Her girlfriends Julia, Macy, and Laverne rarely visited because of the distance, and when they did, their conversations were awkward. None of Priscilla's friends had children, so their talks almost always centered around their work or their social life, which Priscilla no longer had. Oh, how she missed her life outside Bow Lake. So, she was glad Ramses had joined her on her walk. They could not have grown closer.

As it so happened and unbeknownst to the expectant mother, the higher-ups in the American government were discussing the details of their special agent's impending secret mission. She would be called back "into service to her country" when she least expected it.

2

THE TIDE HAS TURNED

While the sage Egyptian imparted words of wisdom to Priscilla in Bow Lake, New Hampshire, three higher-ups in the American government—the president, the Joint Chiefs of Staff chairman, and the Central Intelligence Agency director—met in the Oval Office. Acutely aware that most Americans already knew about the fall of the Berlin Wall and German reunification, they were, however, concerned that most were unfamiliar with the corresponding regime changes in neighboring Eastern European nations. Austria, Serbia, Kosovo, Albania, Hungary, Ukraine, Belarus, Montenegro, former Yugoslavia, Czechoslovakia, Latvia, Moldova, Croatia, and Bosnia-Herzegovina headed the list. Of the lot, the situation in the former Yugoslavia dominated the higher-ups' agenda.

"Which one of you wants to bring me up to date?" the president asked. "And is it still Yugoslavia, or has the situation reverted to what it was during pre-Russian influence?"

An exceptionally tall and handsome man in his middle forties, Fleetwood Marshall Hollingsworth was the first Black president of the United States. His family made its fortune in their Barbadian-based sugar export business, and one of his uncles was among the first Black members of Congress during the Reconstruction Era. The former Alabama congressman had engaged Priscilla's PR firm for his bid for the presidency. During that time, they both sustained gunshot wounds from assassination attempts by the SANM PG, a South African terrorist group. The assassins had come after Priscilla when they could no longer get to her former boss, Ohio state Senator Daniel P. Callahan, because he had sponsored a bill advocating South African divestiture. They had targeted the presidential candidate because he was Black. Nor did they like his foreign policy initiatives to facilitate peace between the Arabs and Israelis.

Well into the third year of his first term, the president was conscientious about dotting his "Is" and crossing his "Ts." For the moment, though, he looked from the chairman to the director, both of whom were Napoleonic in stature and zealots but for different reasons. The president had an important decision to make, so he listened attentively as each man made his pitch.

The CIA director spoke first.

"Mr. President, our sources inform us that Slobodan Milosevic has taken over leadership and is perpetrating genocide beyond anything imaginable." Jason Roberts was a nondescript-looking man in his late fifties. He was well-groomed and always impeccably dressed in a black suit and tie. From Corporate America, Roberts' background was deeply entrenched in the rapidly growing technology sector. Otherwise, he epitomized the men in his ranks: Caucasians, clean-shaven, in their late twenties, thirties, and forties, and typically recruited from Ivy League colleges, but rarely from HBCUs such as Morehouse and Howard University. In the early 1990s, the nation's prestigious intelligence-gathering agency had yet to acquire an appreciation for race, ethnicity, or gender diversity.

Joint Chiefs of Staff Chairman Christian Kennedy knew he had the president's ear, so he ignored his colleague's remarks.

The four-starred general interrupted the CIA director with a thunderous roar: "Mr. President, authorize our troops. We can easily put down those ruffians."

Otherwise, like the CIA director, General Kennedy reflected the bygone era of the nation's top leadership as far as taking orders from a Black man was new to him, too. In his early sixties, the general wore a perpetually stern expression. He relished having reached the highest rank of the preceding generations of Kennedys in a long line of distinguished military officers. Mostly, he had the backing of the congressional hawks who were hellbent on settling disputes via armed combat.

The president used the man's titles, General and Chairman, interchangeably. "Not just yet, General. Let's hear what else Director Roberts has to say."

"Thank you, Mr. President," said the CIA director, and then he expounded. "Milosevic's men have invaded Bosnia-Herzegovina, Serbia, Croatia, and other places. They have ravaged the territory and raped and maimed civilians. Also," shaking his head, he said, "Milosevic issues death warrants on anybody espousing democracy. There are mass graves everywhere." He handed out black-and-white photos depicting the territory's mass graves, mutilations, and property destruction.

The president looked at the odious images. Without raising his head, he said, "Okay, Jason, what do you propose?" The president preferred intelligence-gathering over military intervention.

"Mr. President, I propose we send in one of our top agents to glean more intel." The CIA director paused for any interruption from the trigger-happy general. When none came, he continued.

"There's a Yugoslav lieutenant, Military Intelligence Officer Zulfika Kasun. Serbian-born, highly educated, multilingual…, but despicable. He has been sending mixed messages. We're not sure if he wants asylum, to defect, or what. But he's close to Milosevic and can provide us with vital intel. It shouldn't take us long to connect with him, especially since he's already signaling his willingness to meet."

Then came his ultimate pitch: "Sir, I urge you to go this route before dispatching troops." He stared at the general and said, "Besides, earlier reports are that it's difficult to discern the players, that is, who's Christian, Muslim, Bosnian, Croatian, Serbian, et cetera in that doggone tinderbox."

The president then looked General Kennedy straight in his eyes and said, "Mr. Chairman, I'm going with Director Roberts for now. Intel is vital to make a case before the American people, after which it's all yours."

Even the Joint Chiefs of Staff chairman knew that the president needed to buy time to orient Americans about the situation in the Yugoslav tinderbox and make his case for impending military intervention as he nodded with the understanding that he would eventually engage his troops in battle, most of whom, even he knew, had not the foggiest notion of Yugoslavia.

Later that day, the CIA director sat confidently at his desk at headquarters in Langley, Virginia. He reflected on his meeting with the president as he looked at the "Classified" file. He already knew its content. He prided himself on his agency's successes, Priscilla being among his favorite agents. He was thrilled about using her in this new mission. She was perfect for it.

After a staffer got James Froley—his most accomplished deputy director and Priscilla's handler—on the line, Jason knew this would be an even greater day. His relationship with Jim spanned many years. After all, he had encouraged him to recruit Priscilla in the first place. So, he spoke with familiarity and confidence.

"Jim! We've got a new assignment for our special agent. We need—"

Hearing the words "special agent," Jim Froley sensed he was about to have a bad day. Apart from his rapidly receding hairline, which gave him no relief, Jim was old-school and old-fashioned. Otherwise, the only noticeable difference between him and the TV character *Lieutenant Columbo* was the missing raincoat.

However, appearances can be deceiving; Jim Froley had not reached the rank of deputy director in the CIA for naught. He interrupted plainspokenly.

"Director Roberts, please don't go any further."

"What do you mean, Jim, 'Don't go any further?' I haven't said what I want."

Jim rubbed a stain on his polyester necktie that did not come close to matching his crumpled old suit. "Director, Ms. Austin-Bernhardt is pregnant."

"Ms. Austin-Bernhardt is *what!*"

"She's pregnant, sir. Her baby is due in late August." Jim was sweating, and his heart pounded. "Sir, I'm sorry, but—" He could hear his boss's heavy breathing and rising anger.

"But my damned derriere, Jim! How long have you known?"

"Shortly after, she knew, sir."

"Well, damn, just when the president wants us to check out the situation in the Balkans. Damn it, man, things are heating up over there." Director Roberts paused before continuing. "How long before she can take on another mission?" But he did not allow Jim to respond.

"My God, Jim. Her being pregnant doesn't make sense. According to her dossier, she had an abortion over a decade ago. And there is absolutely nothing in her MO suggesting she's even maternal. When did P. J. Austin-Bernhardt develop maternal instincts?" His voice lowered. "Damn it, Jim, I knew we shouldn't have waived the rules for her and Agent B." He was referring to Priscilla's husband, Carlton Elliott Bernhardt, a special operative in the Collective Force, the elite special ops unit of the CIA that performed covert "unauthorized" missions.

While the director expressed his disappointment in Priscilla's pregnancy, Jim almost lost his grip on his phone. Using a big, wrinkled, blue-and-black checkered cotton handkerchief, he wiped more sweat off his face and along his receding hairline when finally he got the courage to speak again.

"Director, it should be three to six months after the baby is born before she can resume her duties, give or take."

Then, just as quickly, the director changed the subject and shifted his attitude. When he began with, "Remember Jim, I told you to recruit her in the first place; her deceptive demeanor is perfect," Jim sat back in his seat and waited for his boss to recite his usual litany of accomplishments and traits of his special agent.

"You'd never know that she's in her late thirties. She could easily pass for much younger. And she's a chameleon. Her complexion and how she can wear her hair allow her to blend into most North African, Middle Eastern, and Southeast Asian societies. It's amazing! But I still don't understand why she identifies as

Black, not with all that Indian, British, Irish, and West African blood in her veins." He paused before continuing.

"And she's knowledgeable about Russian culture and politics. That's going to come in handy with her new assignment."

"And let's not forget," he continued, "she has a photographic memory, which produced a wealth of intel during her recent Middle Eastern mission."

As Jim listened to his boss touting Priscilla, he knew what was coming: "She's also conversant in French and comfortable around men and people of different cultures and ethnicities."

Jim finally interjected, "That's because of her upbringing in western New York in an unusual community of people from all over Europe, as well as her Ph.D. in political science."

Shaking his head, Director Roberts reentered the conversation. "Indeed, Ms. Austin-Bernhardt's files make for intriguing bedside reading. I still don't know how she eluded and then killed that Afrikaner commander inside that platinum mine near Pretoria. The woman is claustrophobic *and* has vertigo; she must've been scared out of her wits! And she's resourceful, too. Come on, Jim," he laughed morbidly. "She hammered a stake into the man's head!"

"And how 'bout when she shot all those crocs onboard that ferry on Lake Kariba in Zimbabwe? Ha! Ha! Ha! Jim, you can't make this stuff up."

Although the director was laughing, Jim steeled himself for his final reprimand. He knew it was coming, so while the director reminisced, he waited patiently.

"I'll never forget when she described how she tossed oil of vitriol on her assailants in that bunker in Amman."

He laughed again, then paused before continuing more seriously. "But how's she going to handle all those vicious white boys in the Yugoslav tinderbox? Ah, yes, I forgot about her tracking device. At least we'll be able to keep tabs on her."

After an uncomfortable silence, the director finally said, "Jim, I'm sending over the files for this new assignment. Meanwhile, pray both of us are still around when and if our special agent even gets the chance to take on this mission."

Without further ado, the director slammed down his phone, and Jim Froley began to pray.

By the early 1990s, most communist regimes in Eastern Europe had transitioned to some semblance of democracies. But the former Yugoslavia had taken a different, more dramatic course. While Washington diplomats and congressional leaders marshaled "limited coordination" with their Western counterparts—who maintained a wait-and-see posture—the situation in the former Yugoslavia escalated into a horrific catastrophe. Further complicating the matter, America still conducted its foreign policies from its Cold War playbook. In such a world, Priscilla J. Austin-Bernhardt—a thirty-eight-year-old Black female of mixed heritage—existed mainly as the only one of her rank, race, ethnicity, gender, and skillset in the CIA. Recruited in 1986, Priscilla never saw herself as a secret agent but as a professional who, due to her near-photographic memory, was good at collecting intel. But Priscilla possessed many other essential attributes.

When Priscilla first learned of her pregnancy, she had worried that her condition would adversely impact her work with the agency. But when she informed her supervisor, Jim Froley, he congratulated her. But that was then. This is now, and the tide has turned. So, Jim would wait until he thought the time was right to approach her about the new assignment. And because he and his boss still had their jobs when the time came, he would present Priscilla with her new mission when she least expected it.

But for now, it was time for her to focus on preparing to have her baby.

3

THE TIME IS NIGH

At Bow Lake, the following five months went by quickly.

As Priscilla settled into her new role as "a creator of life," she developed a routine of reading her favorite novels, particularly those about the nineteenth-century eccentric English family's Egyptian adventures and a few others by authors she had grown fond of, Paulo Coelho, Nelson DeMille, and Zora Neale Hurston among them. She enjoyed *Brideshead Revisited* by Evelyn Waugh and *Woman at Point Zero* by Nawal El Saadawi, whose writing styles she admired. She also watched far too much PBS television, particularly the British comedies *Are You Being Served* and *Keeping up Appearances* and, of course, the *Poirot* Masterpiece Mystery series. Priscilla's affinity to the British was due mainly to her having grown up in the Snowbelt of western New York, where there were many descendants of Europeans, though primarily Western Europeans.

As she reread her favorite books, she felt inspired and decided to outline some of her own adventures, of course, fictionalizing them. She wrote about her tenure in the Ohio Senate, her abduction to faraway early post-apartheid-Zimbabwe and apartheid-ruled South Africa, and as the chief PR consultant to the Hollingsworth Presidential Campaign. Although she thought twice before putting it on paper, she also wrote about her role as a special envoy to the Middle East and the intriguing international art fraud racket at the Metropolitan Museum of Art. Not only that, but she wrote about the escapades of the CF unit in the CIA. She had learned about the special ops from reading redacted reports and eavesdropping on "the boys." She had given this name to the CF agents who'd become like family to her. Like sleepers, they infiltrated enemy organizations—sometimes for years—and collected vital intel. Priscilla first met them as they masqueraded as high-powered lobbyists during her time in the Ohio Senate, but they were more than that; they had licenses to kill. Proficient in producing magnum opuses, they performed their work efficiently and effectively. Cosmopolitan, highly educated, multilingual, and well-traveled, "the boys" ensured Priscilla's safety when "in service to her country," only she was often unaware of it for the most part.

She had no idea what she would do with all of the material she had collected, but something told her to write about it. So, she did, and she kept it to herself. *Besides*, as she often thought, *no one would believe any of this stuff anyway.*

The time was nigh.

August 29, 1991, was the day before Priscilla's thirty-ninth birthday, nine months into her pregnancy. It was one of the hottest days of the summer, and everyone had forgotten about her birthday because they were all anticipating the baby's impending arrival.

Around 8:00 that evening, Priscilla grew antsy. She had been reading in bed. Becoming increasingly agitated, she started pacing around the room. She walked from the window back to the bed and back to the window again. After about an hour, she felt a sense of calm wash over her. She relaxed, laid back down, and fell into a deep and comfortable sleep.

Downstairs, Father and Ramses would have thought that Lady Chelsea was about to give birth; she was so anxious. After climbing the colossal marble staircase and peeping in on Priscilla, who slept peacefully, the lady of the house thought something was wrong. After all, the baby was due any moment, and Priscilla slept as though without a care in the world.

Just think, Lady Chelsea was the one who had so confidently assured Priscilla and Carlton that she knew what to expect with Priscilla's impending childbirth. But Ramses—who knew a thing or two about helping deliver a baby because he had assisted Hettie and Mavis when Lady Chelsea had given birth to Carlton and Arvana—reassured her. "Lady Chelsea, surely *you* know that expectant mothers always get like this *right* before their water breaks. Miss Prissy's experiencing the calm before the labor pains of childbirth."

"Oh, no, Ramses!" she fretted. "Is it time *already*?" Lady Chelsea was not feeling at all like herself. This refined, graceful woman of impeccable aplomb was usually calm and well-composed, but not tonight.

So, Ramses calmly explained. "I believe so. And it'll probably happen sooner than you think. But let's not let on to Miss Prissy. She thinks she has at least two more weeks. So, make sure that Nanny Hettie and Mavis stay close to her room because that 'little rascal' is ready to meet his new family."

Still a bit shaken, Lady Chelsea asked about Carlton. "He should be here." She sighed and fanned herself with a silk handkerchief, occasionally using it to dab tears from her eyes.

Father hurried over to her. "My Sweets, I realize this is our first grandchild. But we really must remain calm and let nature take its course. Ramses is right." He winked at Ramses and continued. "Come what may, PJ is going to be all right. As for Carlton, well, he's the father. And if memory serves me correctly, all he needs to do is show up."

His wife smiled and gently slapped his face.

But, hoping to reassure her, Ramses told her, "Carlton should arrive first thing in the morning." Then, he scratched his head, "I suppose I could've told him to come home a little sooner. But some things just can't be planned for, at least not precisely."

Lady Chelsea was not at all reassured. "O Ramses."

And so, just as Priscilla had paced the floor in her bedroom that night, Lady Chelsea now paced the floor in the family room. In contrast, Father and Ramses headed for the bar, where Jamison—the house manager—was already pouring them double shots of bourbon.

The following day, Priscilla woke shortly before 6:00. She felt strange. Fluids coursed through her body, the bed felt damp, and her nightgown was drenching wet. Priscilla was unaware that she was in the early stage of labor. No one was in the room with her. Her mom, Liza, was at her home in Sills Creek, Illinois, and Carlton had not yet returned from his latest assignment. In addition to his undercover role as a special op, he was also the congressional liaison for the Ohio governor. Meanwhile, he thought Priscilla was due in two weeks, but apparently, the baby had decided to speed things up.

As Priscilla hobbled to her bathroom, fluids flowed down between her thighs and legs. With each step, she stopped, stared at the puddle on the floor, and thought, *What a mess I'm making*. Then she felt a sharp stabbing pain course through her. She screamed.

The once quiet household burst into action.

Ramses, whose suite was on the first floor, was the first to react. He hurried out of bed, put on his robe and house shoes, and headed for the family room. It took Father and Lady Chelsea a few more minutes to robe, carefully descend the staircase, and join him. Jamison was already performing his usual duties, such as checking the menus for each meal, monitoring the laundry service and deliveries, and confirming appointments. After settling in the family room, they all waited for Nanny Hettie or Mavis to bring word about Priscilla's new baby.

Hettie and Mavis were already hurrying to Priscilla and Carlton's suite. These two faithful staffers had been with the Bernhardts for nearly a lifetime. Back in England, they had served as Lady Chelsea's companions. Hettie's mother had been Lady Chelsea's governess. Although Priscilla often described the two women as "matronly," they were indeed capable. Since Hettie had practically raised Carlton, Priscilla was thrilled to have her maternal touch on their firstborn.

When the two women bustled into the room, they saw Priscilla standing in a puddle of water. Her look of amazement told them that she had no idea what it was or what it meant. They watched her holding her stomach as if protecting it from whatever its fate.

Hettie hurried over, gently patted her shoulders, and said soothingly, "Madame PJ, don't worry. You're not losing your baby; you're about to bring him into the world." Even Hettie referred to the unborn child as a boy.

Nearly the same age as Hettie but not quite as thick, Mavis slipped her arm around Priscilla and offered to help. "Hettie, let's get her back in bed."

As the two women escorted Priscilla back to her bed, she screamed again.

"Does it get any worse? It hurts bad, really bad."

Priscilla was in excruciating pain and had difficulty maintaining her balance, but the two women held her firmly.

Somewhat embarrassed, she said, "I wet the bed. See?" She pointed to the wet spot on her bed and noticed her hand shaking. Priscilla was more frightened than she could ever remember. And this was no small feat for a woman who had been in as many dangerous situations as she had been.

"Oh, Madame PJ, that's just your water; it broke during the night," Hettie explained. "You're doing just fine." She did not have the heart to tell Priscilla that her labor pains were starting.

After helping Priscilla back into bed, Mavis collected an armful of fluffy towels from the bathroom. Then, like the professional she was, she casually lifted one side of Priscilla and rolled out the towels underneath her while covering the wet spot on the bed.

But Mavis quickly realized that Priscilla did not like being touched. Each time Mavis put her hands on the expectant mother, she would cringe, jerk away, or say, "What are you doing?" Priscilla had no idea that Mavis was doing her job, which Mavis soon realized she had to do despite her petulant patient.

Even after the thoughtful Mavis covered the wet spot on her bed, Priscilla tossed and turned because she could not get comfortable.

"Oh, God," she cried, "I don't think I can do this. It hurts too much," at which point Hettie offered to hold her hands.

"Squeeze my hands. That'll help reduce some of the pain."

"Don't be ridiculous! I don't want to squeeze your hands. And stop touching me!" Priscilla waved the two women away. Priscilla's parents, Nelson and Liza, had raised their children to be cautious of people touching them. Consequently, Priscilla disliked being touched affectionately or otherwise.

As Hettie and Mavis occasionally looked from one to the other, they correctly surmised that Priscilla had not paid attention to any of her Lamaze lessons.

She screamed again. And for half an hour, she tossed and turned about in agony. Her pain was so excruciating that she asked, "Can't someone just cut this thing out of me?"

As time passed, the women ignored Priscilla's pouting and began caressing her arms, hands, and legs and wiping streams of sweat from her face and neck. They also dabbed her face and chest with crushed ice to comfort her. By this point, they knew Priscilla had not learned much from her few Lamaze classes. But they realized something more: Priscilla was a persnickety patient. So, they thought it best to do their job despite her fussing.

Even though Priscilla had not adequately prepared for what she was experiencing, her labor pains would not last as long as some women's. Some lasted all day and night. Some even longer.

While Priscilla experienced excruciating labor pains and the discomfort of Hettie and Mavis touching her, Lady Chelsea, Father, and Ramses resumed a similar routine as the evening before. Father and Ramses drank bourbon, and it was well before breakfast. Then they all paced the family room floor. At one point, they even argued over names for the baby.

Shortly after six-thirty, Father held his glass of bourbon high and said proudly: "If it's a boy, and I know that it is, he should be named Emerson C. Bernhardt III. Yes, that's a good name." If Father had only known that Priscilla preferred CE for Carlton Elliott to EC.

"No," Lady Chelsea objected. "Why, everybody who is anybody knows it's a girl. Megan. That sounds nice. We'll call her Megan." But Lady Chelsea had no way of knowing about Priscilla's dislike of the name Megan, which she had to use while on the run in Harare in the summer of 1986.

Nonetheless, the sage Egyptian saw the situation quite differently. "Oh, it's a boy, for sure. Money on it." He and Father clinked glasses. However, unlike Father and Lady Chelsea, Ramses stopped short of suggesting a name, for even he knew that battle could only be waged between Carlton and Miss Prissy. But if only he had known how Priscilla felt about the name "Ramses," which she loved.

"Where the devil is Carlton?" asked Lady Chelsea for the umpteenth time.

It was nearly 7:00 when the father-to-be arrived. The tall, long-on-looks man with a full head of black hair pulled back in a ponytail magically appeared as if he had been expected—and, well, he had been. He dashed across the threshold of the family room, flinging off his tailored suit jacket and necktie.

"Am I too late?" asked the eager new father. "Has Missy already delivered our baby?"

No one responded, not even the overly anxious Lady Chelsea, after all her ranting.

Watching his parents and Ramses pacing back and forth, Carlton thought they had lost their minds, Father and Ramses throwing back bourbon while rambling and gesturing, and Lady Chelsea waving her silk hanky like she was fanning flies or something. Shaking his head, he raced out of the family room and sprinted up the stairs to his and Priscilla's suite.

He stopped at the door, peeped inside, and entered ever so cautiously as he watched Hettie and Mavis propping pillows behind Priscilla's back. He marveled at his wife. She was beet red as she thrashed and moaned while twisted locks of damp hair drooped over her face. It was as if a mysterious force was torturing her. As Priscilla struggled to get comfortable, she balanced herself on her elbows as best she could. Her legs were bent at the knees and spread apart—she was completely exposed.

Carlton stood aghast at what his eyes beheld. He had never seen a woman give birth, maybe animals like his horses and farm animals, but never a human being, not someone giving birth to his child. His mouth gaped at the sight before him. Then he heard: "You bloody bastard! I'm dying in here. The next time you want a baby, you carry it!" Priscilla then screamed so loudly that it seemed as if the windows might shatter.

Carlton, Hettie, and Mavis covered their ears with their hands. *This is it!* They all must have thought.

Back downstairs, Lady Chelsea, Father, Ramses, and Jamison also heard her scream. Father and Ramses exchanged glances, then continued throwing back bourbon and following lockstep behind Lady Chelsea, who continued waving her silk hanky as they paced the floor to the rhythm of Priscilla's screams.

The next time Priscilla screamed at the top of her lungs, the head and shoulders of precious new life emerged from her womb.

The last time she screamed, the rest of "the little rascal" thrust himself into the world full throttle. He was a boy indeed and a rather big boy at that.

Mavis expertly cut the umbilical cord and then made two knots, one on the baby and the other on the mother.

Hettie picked up the infant—held him upside down—and slapped its buttocks. The baby wailed.

Carlton could see from where he stood that the child was a male.

Hettie laid the crying baby on the bed, and Mavis helped hold him while Hettie wiped away the afterbirth.

When finally, Hettie held the crying child for Priscilla to see him, Carlton found his voice. "It's a boy, Missy!" More than once, he proclaimed it. Then he ran to their bed, leaned over, and kissed the new mother.

Meanwhile, man alive, did the baby wail!

Priscilla wept tears of joy. Or were they tears of relief? She reached feebly for her baby while Hettie kept a firm grip on him. Priscilla's hands still shook, and her body pulsated from her lingering labor pains. She smiled as she felt the warmth of God's creation in her hands. Carlton kissed her more than once, gently touched the baby's face, and kissed Priscilla again.

As he took hold of the child, Priscilla managed to say, "Oh, Carlton, My Love, our very own 'precious gift of life.'" Then she passed out.

Carlton cradled the child, held him high, and cried joyfully. "Thank you, dear God! Thank you!"

And so it was that on the morning of the hottest summer day, August 30, 1991, Carlton Elliott *Austin* Bernhardt came into this world the same day as his mother's thirty-ninth birthday!

4

THE LEGACY

It did not take long for the Bernhardts to call the new addition to the family "Austin," especially since calling the child "Carlton" confused everyone about which Carlton they meant. Specifically, whenever someone said "Carlton" in the father's presence, Carlton, the father, responded. As it turned out, no one was happier than Priscilla, who had called her son "Austin" from the start. Besides, she believed it was much simpler than saying, "Carlton, the baby."

But Priscilla was relieved about something else. Although she dreaded her parenting role, she need not have worried because Father and Lady Chelsea, Ramses, Hettie, Mavis, Jamison, Melissa, and Harry—the stable hand—all fought to take turns holding the baby. Indeed, Priscilla held him only for feeding, and she was not fond of that role. Soon, she fed him formula.

Austin was a big baby at three months old. His weight and height matched those of a six-month-old child.

Nor did it take long for most people who knew Priscilla to notice her treating the child like her nieces and favorite nephew, Germane. Even her nieces and favorite nephew said she treated Austin like them, which meant she showered her son with gifts but little of her time and affection. By the time Ramses introduced his surrogate role, Austin would have grown up believing he had a special mission in life. But it would be sometime later before Priscilla would come to terms with any of that.

As things stood, however, she was about to discover that she had just provided the Bernhardts with what they most desired.

But for now, she dreaded a party that Lady Chelsea had planned.

Shortly before Thanksgiving, the Bernhardt mansion filled with excitement. Liza, Germane, Emilia Hollingsworth (President Hollingsworth's mother), Arvana, First Lady Selena Hollingsworth, Carla McDougal (the vice president's wife), Julia Cahill (Priscilla's best friend), Macy Stoner and her husband Ron Chester (two other of Priscilla's friends); Laverne Macon and Alfrieda (Priscilla's friends and co-workers at her PR firm); "the boys" and their significant others—Tommy and Christina Wozniah, Jeremy and Laura Onslow, Angelo and Anita Delgato, and Bartholomew and Ruth Jordan—and a few others, all milled about laughing, talking, and predicting where Austin would be schooled and what his career would be.

For the first time in a long time, Priscilla was not the center of attention. For instance, whenever she reached for her son, someone else was always nearby, taking him from her. At one point, she complained, "My goodness, I can't even hold my own child. What's wrong with this picture?"

Soon, she headed off to the stables on this lovely fall day while her family and friends clamored and argued over the infant's future. She asked Harry to saddle Mystique, after which she trotted along the path to the lake and marveled at the magnificent scenery of the autumn foliage surrounding the beautiful lake for the first time in nearly a year.

The nearer she drew to the lake, the more precise the image. She saw several familiar faces: Carlton, Tommy, Angel, Jordy, and Onslow. "The boys" were on a motorboat, and there was a basket in their midst, which Priscilla thought was odd unless they were fishing. But "the boys" were not known for fishing. Boating, yes, but fishing, no.

Hmm, I wonder what's in that basket. Her curiosity peaked as she watched Carlton pick up what was undoubtedly young Austin. He held the child high. Speechless, Priscilla watched as Carlton and the others chanted something she could not make out.

What the bloody hell are those blokes up to with my son?

After they recited whatever it was, Carlton put the child back in the basket. Then Angel went to the wheel of the motorboat, turned on the ignition, and they sailed away from Priscilla's sight. But the curious mother refused to leave the embankment. She sat patiently on Mystique and waited for a long time. Then she heard the motorboat engine again.

When Jordy spotted her astride her horse, he waved and yelled. "Ahoy, there!" That he did as if all were well.

As she watched "the boys" disembark, she asked the obvious: "Okay, fellows, what was *that* all about?"

"Missy," Carlton replied, his chest puffed up with pride, "Young Austin's gonna be a *real* man."

"I'll say," each of the others echoed.

As if he had the last word, Tommy bellowed. "That's for damn sure."

Priscilla then watched as they trekked the long distance back toward the mansion—Carlton carrying the baby in the basket—as if the child were his catch of the day without uttering another word to her.

Priscilla had just glimpsed a rite of passage for her son, something that she would never be privy to, and that was where things stood.

But she had glimpsed something more disturbing.

Around the same time a year earlier, Carlton, the other boys, and Laverne Macon, also a CF agent, had been on an "unauthorized" tour in the increasingly war-torn Yugoslavia, where they had all sustained significant injuries. Carlton took a bullet to his left shoulder, in the same place where he had sustained a bullet wound during Priscilla's first time in southern Africa. Tommy's right hand was now useless from an unknown infection. Jordy walked with a cane due to a bullet wound to his right leg. Angel suffered an injury to his handsome face, a deep scar cut across his right cheek, and now, ever conscious of it, he turned his face aside when talking. Onslow sustained an injury to one of his legs, and, like Jordy, he walked with a cane. Although Laverne was not with them on the boat at Bow Lake, she had suffered the most injuries during their time in the Balkans—a broken arm and ribs and other injuries she never revealed to Priscilla. Like Priscilla's mixed ancestry, Laverne was Caucasian and Choctaw, also one of the few female special ops and the only one who identified as Native American.

As she stared at the lot of them walking away, Priscilla was acutely aware that the CF boys, Laverne included, could no longer effectively serve in their coveted roles as special ops. Their physical injuries and age, now in their mid-forties and early fifties, spoke volumes. Even so, it would be sometime later before Priscilla would appreciate the maxim: "Once an agent, always an agent."

Meanwhile, she pranced on Mystique behind Carlton and the others as they limped and strolled back to the mansion with young Austin still in the basket. Upon their approach, someone yelled to alert others inside the mansion of their return. "They're back!"

Harry ran to Priscilla, fanning his blazing red hair from his face. He helped her to dismount Mystique and then walked the horse back to the stables.

As they entered the dwelling, everyone inside cheered, and Priscilla noticed again that no one showed the slightest interest in her. All eyes were on baby Austin.

"Oh well. No problem," she shrugged and headed to the family room, where she saw Jamison approaching her. Of French ancestry, Jamison Montesquieu was the tall, handsome house manager. He cut a striking figure in his uniform of a classic dark suit and tie, a crisp white shirt, and traditionally close-cut dark hair. He seemed eager to speak to Priscilla.

"Well, Madame PJ, I'll bet you never saw any of this coming." Sensing Priscilla had no notion of what he meant, he explained: "I'm told this is exactly what happened when Carlton was born. During his formative years, his parents spent very little time with him. Bernhardts are raised to be independent, you know, straight out of the womb."

Jamison's figure of speech undid her. "You have got to be kidding me!"

"Afraid not, Miss Prissy. But you'll be lucky if they let you pick out young Austin's clothes for tomorrow." As Jamison snickered, he looked at Priscilla more intensely. "Sorry about that quick-and-coarse lesson on becoming a Bernhardt parent."

Priscilla shook her head. "You're just joshing me."

"No, Madame PJ." He explained: "You've just given the Bernhardts the one thing they needed to ensure their legacy—and it's a boy, too!"

"I don't believe you."

"Well, tell me your thoughts this time next year."

Like the CF boys, Jamison was cosmopolitan and college-educated. He had worked for the Bernhardts for over a decade and knew everything that happened in the household.

New England-born and -raised, he possessed a master's degree in business administration and attended Harvard College with Carlton. As such, Jamison managed the household budget, hired and trained staff, and oversaw the dwelling. He had taken over the managerial duties from Ramses, who now worked with Father. Although he could have his pick of corporate jobs, Jamison preferred life with the Bernhardts to Corporate America.

As he finished speaking, Priscilla was startled by a familiar voice that came from behind her.

"Well, well, well," Macy blurted out. "PJ, Girlfriend, you *really* did it this time. The Bernhardts will have you encased in 24-carat gold for this feat." She finished, confirming what Jamison had just said.

Macy Stoner was a highly regarded New England criminal defense attorney. She and Priscilla became friends at a critical time for the Bernhardts when Arvana and her personal aide Juanita faced criminal charges for conspiracy to commit terrorist acts and Arvana, separately, for narcotics abuse and possession. More

30

recently, Macy served as legal counsel for the Omiros twins during the international art fraud scandal at the Met.

Priscilla had mixed feelings about her friend's remarks. Was she angry, shocked, or both? Which she felt did not matter. Then she remembered something her mother Liza had alluded to some time ago: "The wealthy aren't like us, common folks. They live different lives. They have different sets of values, too." Priscilla was experiencing what her mother had tried to explain to her, something that Liza and Lady Chelsea had argued about in the private garden back when Priscilla recuperated at the Harlem Hospital Center from gunshot wounds she sustained when the South African assassins tried to kill her on the Columbia University campus.

The next thing she knew, Macy was tugging her back to the bar.

"Jamison," she said, "gin-n-tonic with a twist of lime, and keep them coming," adding, "Girlfriend has just received the shock of her life."

As Jamison handed Priscilla her drink, this time, he spoke apologetically. "I'm so sorry, Miss Prissy. On the one hand, you're a godsend. But, please, try not to grow bitter. Carlton meant no harm. He and the fellas were anointing the new heir, the legacy, as it were. Carlton loves you, but you've got to understand: Carlton is, first and foremost, a Bernhardt."

Jamison and Macy were New Englanders and long-time friends of the Bernhardts. They were more familiar with the family's traditions and ways than were Priscilla's other friends.

Like a tag team member, Macy followed up, elaborating, "Missy, you can have your heart's desires. But you can never take Austin away from this family, literally or figuratively. And that's that. Now, have another drink on me."

"What!"

"Listen, Missy." Macy snapped; her beautiful brunette hair came undone from the mother-of-pearl clamp. "Everything about you suggests you only got pregnant in the first place to please Carlton, anyway. You're hardly maternal and never even talked about having children." Macy didn't mince words. Born and raised in New Hampshire as a non-observant Jew, she was a third-generation attorney in her family's law firm. Formidable inside and outside the courtroom, she had no qualms about speaking her mind. She was also one of Priscilla's closest friends.

Priscilla hated that Macy spoke the truth with such candor. *Why, she's worse than Julia.* Julia was Priscilla's oldest and dearest friend. When Priscilla shouted, "Macy!" she was cut off.

"Shut up, Missy. I'm not through yet. From now on, you'll probably need an appointment to spend quality time with your own child."

"Well, Mace, as always, you certainly don't mince words." Priscilla thought about what she had just learned. *What am I so upset about? I'm not exactly excited about raising 'the little rascal,' anyway. This just might be a win-win. But I think I'll show out a bit first, give 'em a run for their money.*

But when she laughed, Macy said, "Missy, I always did think you a bit peculiar. So, I'll bite. What's so funny?"

"Oh, Mace, I was just thinking about how some things work themselves out for the best, no matter what we humans contrive. Life can be so *very* interesting." Of the friends, Priscilla was the only one whom Macy allowed to call her "Mace."

She raised her glass and clinked her friend's. "Mace, let's drink to my *interesting* life."

At that moment, Priscilla's other friends—Julia, Laverne, Ruth, Arvana, and Alfrieda—entered the family room giggling.

"So *here* you are!" Julia shouted. "Girl, we've been all over this place looking for you. Congrats, Mommy dearest!" She coughed, then laughed and said, "I never in a million years thought I'd say those words to you, Missy." At that, they all laughed.

Dryly, Priscilla said, "Thanks, guys. It's good to see you, too."

For the rest of the evening, the girlfriends drank and talked well into the wee hours until they departed one by one, save Julia, who spent the night.

When Priscilla and Julia were alone, curled up on the couch finishing off who knows which bottle of champagne, Priscilla told her about the Bernhardt legacy. But Julia was not in the least surprised.

"Well, Girlfriend, what'd you expect?" She shrugged and turned her flute upside down in a not-so-subtle request for a refill. Then, she continued her main point. "Besides, Liza tried to tell you, but you weren't exactly on friendly terms with your mother at the time."

A study in contrast, in every sense, Priscilla and Julia were opposites. Unlike Priscilla, Julia was statuesque at five feet ten with a radiant Nubian complexion and alluring black eyes, complementing her thin lips and straight nose. Julia was careful, thoughtful, and a straight arrow. In contrast, Priscilla was adventuresome, insensitive, aloof, and daring. Her parents, Nelson and Liza, believed, "That child lives too close to the edge." Moreover, Priscilla relished an occasional storm, as she often thought: *What would life be without its challenges?* Even Julia knew that about her friend because she herself had been lured into Priscilla's shenanigans during her time in the Ohio Senate and later when the Afrikaners had targeted her. But for the life of her, she never imagined Priscilla having a child. And so it was that she had teased her.

32

Priscilla filled her friend's flute again. "Oh, well, some things can only be learned by experience. At least now I know. So, tell me, Julia, what have you and Arvana been up to?"

Arvana, Carlton's older sister, recently completed a three-year prison sentence for narcotics possession. She had only just begun to turn her life around from being a jet setter. Tall, slender, and almost anorexic, she had hardly ever gotten out of bed before noon and spent most of her free time drinking excessively and snorting cocaine. With all that behind her, she and Julia had opened a rehabilitation facility in neighboring Manchester to aid abused women and women who suffered from narcotics addiction.

After Julia updated Priscilla about Arvana's new program and headed off to her bedroom, Priscilla went to her own suite and, as she often did when there was no one else she could trust with her deepest thoughts, knelt beside her bed and prayed. Upon entering their suite, Carlton saw her kneeling in prayer. So he knelt beside her, wrapped his arms around her, and said, "And keep him safe and unharmed," because he just knew she was praying for their son.

Priscilla continued, "And imbue him with the wherewithal to maneuver whatever lies ahead." Then she opened her eyes and looked lovingly into her husband's and said, "Amen."

"Amen," Carlton said and kissed his wife.

As he helped her to her feet, he asked, "Feel up to doing it tonight?"

"Why, Carlton, My Love, I've been wondering when we'd get back to the way we were."

He helped her to her feet and kissed her again. Then he undressed her and himself and eased her onto the bed. Smoothly and gently, he laid on top of her. She welcomed his warm embrace and gentle touch. Rhythmically, they glided back and forth as lovers evenly yoked. With few, if any, inhibitions, they tasted and touched whatever pleased them. He played with her twisted locks of hair, and she undid his ponytail and kissed and caressed his wounded shoulder.

As he kissed and gently sulked milk from her voluptuous breasts, he whispered, "Austin won't mind sharing."

Then, like King Solomon, he ventured into her vineyard. Priscilla gasped so loudly that anyone within hearing thought she was having labor pains again. But she was enjoying sensations like she had felt the first time they made love years ago. They had not enjoyed each other sexually like this since she conceived Austin.

But she nearly came undone when he handed her a platter of lemon wedges. "Where'd these come from?" The first time they made love, she chewed lemons like an ingredient while tasting his body.

"Oh, Missy, it's as if I've been waiting for this for ages." Carlton had been eager to return to making love to his wife. Though welcomed, Priscilla's pregnancy had dampened their sex life. But now, things were back on track.

5

EXTENDED BABYSITTING PRIVILEGES

After a night of passionate lovemaking, Carlton eventually broached a subject he knew weighed heavily on his wife's mind. "Missy, I realize some of what you've observed seems unusual, but you have no idea the joy you've brought to my folks. You've made them incredibly happy." He raised his elbows and looked down at her. "So, I hope you won't mind too much if they ask for extended babysitting privileges."

Extended babysitting privileges? Priscilla sat against the walnut headboard, holding the soft linen sheets to her chest, and said, "Carlton, are you asking me to let your folks raise our son?"

"Gee, whiz, Missy! There's no pussyfooting around with *you*."

"And right you are, My Love. Besides, we're talking about our flesh and blood, our first child, not a pet or a toy."

"Oh, Missy, no one's talking about taking our son away from us. They simply want to dote on their only grandchild." Well, that was Carlton's take on the matter. But he was unaware that Jamison and Macy had prepped Priscilla for what lay ahead.

Then, quite unexpectedly, she flung back the sheets and got out of bed. But when she said, "Come with me to the nursery, Carlton," he was so surprised that he did as she requested without a word. The couple put on their matching cashmere robes and slippers and headed to the nursery downstairs, where Hettie and Mavis watched the baby.

Bidding the ladies a good evening, Priscilla picked up her son, who was fast asleep in his crib. Then she told Carlton to get the basket that he had carried the child in earlier. When he returned, Priscilla put the slightly disturbed baby in the basket and told Carlton to bring him with them back to their bedroom.

Hettie watched the loving couple. She smiled as if she knew what they were up to, something she thought was so loving.

Until now, Hettie and Mavis had been watching over the youngster in his nursery, but not tonight. Tonight, the new parents slept with their son in their midst for the first time.

When Lady Chelsea went to the nursery the following morning, Hettie headed her off.

"Oh, Lady Chelsea," Hettie chirped, "Madame PJ and Master Carlton took Master Austin to their room last night." With each word Hettie spoke, Lady Chelsea became more and more upset.

"Oh!" exclaimed the lady of the house, as it suddenly occurred to her that Priscilla might not be so willing to let her have extended babysitting privileges after all. When she turned and stomped away, the nanny realized the lady of the house was not pleased.

When Lady Chelsea met Father in the dining room, she told him what had happened. Father arched his thick salt-and-pepper eyebrows as if he had half expected to hear something terrible had happened. Instead, Lady Chelsea said, "And Nanny Hettie said that 'Carlton was with her.'" Appalled, she elaborated. "And she said, 'Carlton carried young Austin in a *basket!*'"

Dumbfounded, or was he? Father knew his dear wife missed having Carlton and Arvana in their home. Her many charities for children were another way of parenting and being close to young people. He knew she had looked forward to being a grandparent, but he also knew that Priscilla might not so willingly relinquish her parenting role, at least not for any extended period. So, Father braced himself for how the impending scenario would play out.

Moments later, Carlton and Priscilla waltzed into the dining room, Carlton carrying Austin in the basket and Priscilla gliding like an enchanted angel.

Priscilla greeted her in-laws in her most pleasant voice. "Good morning, Lady Chelsea and Father."

While Priscilla pretended as if all were well and headed to the buffet—where the ever-vigilant Jamison stood at attention—Carlton picked up the baby from the basket and bounced him up and down on his thigh. In contrast, Father and Lady Chelsea sat utterly dumbfounded at the head of one end of the long dining room table. Well, at least Father pretended to be.

Priscilla said over her shoulders, "PJ at the bar and grill!" She winked at Jamison, who could not have been more amused at the scene, and when topping it off cheerfully, she said, "Carlton, My Darling and the father of our child, please place your order."

"The usual, Missy. Bring me the usual," he answered, still bouncing young Austin. Although he had no idea what his wife was up to, he played the role of the doting father while his parents turned from him and then to Priscilla as if they were watching a tennis match.

"Jamison," Priscilla said, "please prepare a bountiful plate for my darling husband. He's starving, you know, up all night with the baby." Then she picked up her plate and sat beside her husband and their son.

As if there was no one other than her, Carlton, and their baby in the room, she then said, "Listen, Love," brushing errant strands of hair from his face, "I carried him for nine months. The least you can do is hold him for nine minutes while I have breakfast. My goodness, I'm famished." She dug into her food as if she had not eaten in days.

Seeing his parents' expressions, it took Carlton's control to keep from laughing. Instead, he placed a kiss on Priscilla's cheek.

The lady of the house, Father, and Jamison had never seen Priscilla and Carlton displaying such affection in their midst. For sure, no one had ever seen Priscilla behaving as if she were a nurturing mother. More than anything else, Father and Lady Chelsea now knew it would take much prodding to get her permission for extended babysitting privileges. If only they knew that neither Priscilla nor Carlton knew what they would do now that they had a child. Even so, they need not have fretted because Priscilla and Carlton's honeymoon with the new baby would peak sooner rather than later.

The growing tension in the room was effectively halted when Ramses and Julia entered. Ramses headed for his chair while Julia walked to Carlton and reached for the child.

Julia's plea to hold the baby was met with relief from Carlton. He was somewhat unsure about his role as a father and was glad to hand the baby over to Julia, who seemed to struggle to hold the baby steady and raise him in the air.

"Oh, Missy," she said, "such a precious gift of life." She smiled at the baby and kissed his plump cheek, and he smiled back at her.

Priscilla ignored Julia and, instead, looked across at Ramses, who seemed quite amused. Then, to everyone's surprise, he declared: "And so it was that a man named Carlton Elliott, and a woman named PJ conceived in love—Carlton Elliott *Austin* Bernhardt—and God said, 'This is good.'"

Glancing at Lady Chelsea, Julia could not help noticing her tear-filled eyes. Yet, Julia looked down at the infant, not Lady Chelsea, when she said, "Have you already talked to Missy about helping her rear this 'little rascal?'" Since everybody knew the lady of the house's yearning to raise the child, without skipping a beat, Julia handed the child to her and did not wait for an answer. After that, she turned to Father and said, "Now would be as good a time as any."

She then headed over to Ramses and hugged him as if they had been in cahoots about something—but in a good way. Then Jamison handed her a cup of coffee, and she walked around the long table and sat on Priscilla's other side as if all were well.

Just as quickly, the dynamics in the room changed again.

Father moved closer to his wife and whispered something in her ear. After Jamison coughed to cover a laugh, Hettie and Mavis peeped in and rolled the empty carriage into the room. Then Mavis carefully reached for the baby from Lady Chelsea and put him in his carriage. But before Hettie and Mavis left, they curtsied and reminded everyone: "We're right outside the door." The two women returned to their comfortable chairs against the wall in the corridor. Unlike the younger staff, such as Harry and Melissa, Hettie and Mavis were old-school. From time to time, they bowed and curtsied and, like Ramses, were prone to say, "I remember the time when …."

When Priscilla's teenage nephew Germane and her mother Liza entered, the tension in the room was palpable.

"Are we interrupting something?" Liza asked, pushing her salt-and-pepper hair away from her face. Then, regally waving her hand, she said, "We can come back."

"Oh, Momma, no." Priscilla was in a generous mood. "We're just sorting through some minor details and loose ends about young Austin. That's all. You know, the stuff that parents and grandparents need to sort through, especially if the mother plans on returning to her day job."

Liza's surprise at Priscilla's decision to return to work was evident as she twisted her face disapprovingly and took a seat next to Julia. "Oh!" unhappily, she uttered, "So, you *are* going back to work after all."

Reacting quite the opposite, with vigorous laughter, Germane slapped his favorite aunt's back. Ginger-colored freckles accentuated his ebony complexion, and mischief filled his glowing eyes as he declared: "Ladies and Gentlemen, the time for placing your bets is over, and *I* win!" Quick-witted, and at almost fifteen, he loved to poke fun at adults. Only Jamison, Ramses, Carlton, and Julia seemed to appreciate his glee. Priscilla was unsure, but she had her suspicions that her nephew had taken bets that she would return to work. Meanwhile, Carlton, Jamison, Ramses, and Julia fought hard to hide their laughter.

As the tension eased, Liza shook her head and again spoke her mind. "I would've thought you'd take more time off to raise your son." She looked across the table at Lady Chelsea. "I tell you, these young people are so different from how you and I came up." Liza had no idea what her words meant to Lady Chelsea. However, Lady Chelsea did not get the chance to respond to her.

In an apparent air of dismissal of Liza's open pondering, Priscilla spoke to Lady Chelsea as if they were in a corporate board meeting that had momentarily been interrupted. "Now, where were we?" She paused. "Ah, yes, you were saying something about 'extended babysitting privileges.'"

When Lady Chelsea could take no more, she broke down and cried. She hadn't said anything about "extended babysitting privileges," at least not in this setting. Now she knew for sure that Carlton must have said something to Priscilla about her interest. *Otherwise, how else would she have known?*

Father embraced his sobbing wife. "Sweetheart," he said, "Master Austin is our *grandson*, not our son." Then he looked at Priscilla with what she thought was an overly dramatic plea and then at Carlton as if to say, "Do something, Son."

With the dynamics in the room changing back and forth, Poppa and Marlena, who occupied the head at the opposite end of the table, observed one scene after the other. They were happy to see so many faces. But more than anything else, they were delighted with the new addition to the family, a great-grandson at that. And even though they understood their daughter-in-law's dismay, they knew Priscilla had no intention of hurting her. So, they awaited what they anticipated would be a positive ending, and to Lady Chelsea's favor at that.

While the lady of the house sobbed, an uncomfortable silence seeped into the room.

Since only Priscilla knew what she was up to, no one else said a word. Besides, no one had heard Lady Chelsea mention anything about "extended babysitting privileges." Eventually, though, Priscilla explained herself.

"Okay, folks. Here's the deal. Lady Chelsea and I will draw up a schedule and see how the first year goes."

She sipped her coffee, then said, "But everybody knows I'm a pushover *and* can use all the help I can get with this big handsome boy. And, of course, Lady Chelsea," she paused again, pointing to her mother, "we need to leave some room in all our planning for Liza's turn with young Austin, too."

Priscilla heard her mother mumble, "At least that's something."

Then, to everyone's surprise, she made a more welcoming announcement: "Lady Chelsea, on this glorious day before Thanksgiving, I grant you *unconditional* babysitting privileges for the coming month, including Christmas, by the way." But before she could finish, Lady Chelsea welled up and dabbed her tear-filled eyes.

Priscilla ended her declaration: "Besides, that'll give Carlton and me time to sort through our crazy living accommodations, not to mention our work schedules." Father squeezed Lady Chelsea's shoulders with each word Priscilla spoke as the lady of the house now cried joyfully.

As if that scene had somehow been their cue, Germane and Julia chorused, "Hooray! Christmas at Bow Lake! Oh, My!"

"Ah, cut it out, you guys."

Priscilla was pleased that she had done what she needed to do. She might have been a tad harsh, but—as her former boss, Senator Callahan, used to say— "Sometimes you gotta do what you gotta do to get what you want."

While Germane and Julia cheered, Father walked to the side of the table where Priscilla sat and kissed her more than once. "Bless you, Sweet Child. I always knew there was something special about you." Then he patted Carlton on his shoulder as if all were well.

A moment later, Liza leaned over and asked Julia in a not-so-subtle whisper, "What was that all about?"

"Oh, nothing, Miss Liza. But you sure raised your daughter well. She definitely knows how to claim her turf *and* stand her ground." However, it was Nelson who'd taught his daughter to hold her own, but he would not have minded Julia crediting his "angel" Liza.

Carlton kissed Priscilla's cheek. Then he reminded his parents about something about her: "Surely by now you know Missy is a 'no-pussyfooting-around-type of woman.'" Even though he was a Bernhardt, Carlton had never raised a child. So, he was not exactly up on the Bernhardt protocol for childrearing. But he did sense a relatively tense moment had just been averted, and amicably, at that. So, he was happy.

While the grownups breathed relief, Germane dashed into the corridor, lifted Austin high, and proclaimed: "Hey, little man, you just earned me a bundle of cash. I knew Aunt Priscilla was going back to work. But she'll be good to you, and you'll get used to her funny ways, too." He rubbed his cheek against Austin's and held him high again. But when he said, "You sure are heavy," there was much laughter in the dining room and the corridor.

As so it was that Priscilla laid claim to her legacy and her new role as "lady of the house," at least when it came to young Austin.

6

BACK IN THE SADDLE

Priscilla, Carlton, and baby Austin spent a pleasant Thanksgiving at Bow Lake. Early that morning, Priscilla went to the nursery, got the child, and then, most uncharacteristic of her, did three things.

First, she took the baby to his great-grandparents' suite on the first floor in the far wing of the manor and knocked on their door.

When she heard, "Enter," she opened the door ever-so-gently. Poppa and Marlena sat up in bed and reached out to the baby. Marlena wore a full head of beautiful gray hair pinned in a bun at the back of her head. Poppa wore his gray hair shoulder-length, a tradition among the Bernhardt men. Priscilla noticed that they both wore matching gray flannel gowns. They rubbed Priscilla's head with their well-aged, slender, brown hands.

"Oh, bless you, Child," Marlena said as Priscilla placed the baby between the couple. They hugged her and kissed her cheeks while "oohing" and "aahing" over the baby.

Priscilla stood back and watched her grandparents-in-law enjoying quality time with the only great-grandchild they had ever seen as an infant. But Priscilla had no way of knowing that not-so-small detail.

"I'll leave him with you for a while. Ring for Nanny Hettie and Mavis when you're ready to get dressed."

A short time later, Hettie and Mavis brought Austin back to Priscilla and told her how happy Poppa and Marlena had been.

"I don't think anyone has ever done that before." Hettie's eyes glistened as she sighed. "Now what, Madame PJ?"

"'Now,' follow me upstairs to Momma's room." When Priscilla reached her mother's suite on the far end of the second floor, she knocked on her door and heard her enquiring response.

"Yes," Liza said. "Who's there?"

Without responding, Priscilla entered with Austin in her arms. Liza covered her mouth with her hands. Like Poppa and Marlena, Liza had a brown complexion from her West African and Cherokee lineage. She reckoned her high cheekbones derived from her Cherokee ancestry. She rarely acknowledged her Irish lineage. This morning, she wore her shimmering salt-and-pepper hair in two braids, which reminded Priscilla of her Cherokee connection. However, both she and her mother were mainly proud of their West African side and identified as Black Americans.

Utterly surprised, Liza said, "Oh, Missy, this is so unlike you. But I'm so happy to have the little man to myself." Priscilla stood back and watched her mother nestle her second grandson; Germane had been her first. But since the baby bore her dearly departed husband's surname, Austin, Liza was pleased Priscilla had created an homage to him. "Nelson would be so pleased." Yet, if anyone else had been in the room, they would have noticed the seeming lack of affection between the mother and her daughter. They did not hug or touch each other lovingly.

Nevertheless, Priscilla did smile at her mother when she said, "I'll leave him with you for a while, Momma. Ring for Nanny Hettie and Mavis when you're ready to get up." She also noticed how happy her mother was; she wore a big grin.

A short time later, Hettie and Mavis brought the child back to Priscilla again, telling her how happy Liza had been. "Now what?" both women asked again ever so cheerfully.

"We're off to Father and Lady Chelsea's suite," she said. When Priscilla reached their bedroom, she knocked on their door.

"Enter," said Father, somewhat curiously.

Priscilla pranced into the room carrying her baby boy in her arms. Lady Chelsea was so surprised that, like Liza and Marlena, she sat up and covered her mouth with her hands in glee. Like Poppa, Father smiled as his wife reached for the child. As it so happened, Priscilla got a glimpse of Lady Chelsea before applying her makeup. A headwrap covered her hair. Sleep masks hung down her neck. Her cheeks blushed. Early wrinkles framed her face and neck. Her pale complexion juxtaposed against Father's flawless, tan face, accentuated by his silky black hair graying at the edges hanging on his shoulders.

"Oh, PJ," said the lady of the house as Priscilla handed her the baby, "You never cease to amaze me." Then she and Father hugged her, squeezing the baby between them.

As Priscilla gently pulled away, she smiled at them and said, "Ring for Nanny Hettie and Mavis when you're ready to get up." Although she felt they needed to know they could not do as they pleased with her son, she had just gone the extra mile to be kind to them.

Still in her pajamas, she went back downstairs to the dining room, where she saw Jamison standing at his station beside the breakfast buffet. He gave her a thumbs-up as she headed toward him. "My, my, Madame Bernhardt. Pardon me, Madame *Austin*-Bernhardt, you sure pulled a fast one." Word of Priscilla's kindness had already spread among the household staff.

"Oh, never mind," she said, brushing off his compliment as she prepared a bowl of oatmeal, sliced pheasant, and a bran muffin with orange marmalade.

As she turned to walk away, she turned back around, stood on her tiptoes, and kissed Jamison's cheek.

Jamison stumbled backward. "What was *that* for?"

"Well, ole buddy, ole pal, if you and Macy hadn't prepared me, I wouldn't have known what to expect, let alone how to deal with *this* situation. At least now, I'm back in the saddle, not to mention the game."

"I'll say. And how!"

Minutes later, after Poppa, Marlena, Father, Lady Chelsea, and Ramses had come to breakfast, they all watched as Liza, Germane, and Julia rushed in as if they had missed out on something important. After Liza told the others about Priscilla's surprise visit with baby Austin to her suite, they all complimented Priscilla for her "good deed of the year."

But when Liza, Julia, and Germane learned that Priscilla had done the same with Poppa and Marlena and Father and Lady Chelsea, they were overwhelmed with joy, which Germane put into words: "Will the real Aunt Priscilla please stand up?" quickly followed by, "Happy Thanksgiving, everybody!"

Everyone laughed.

As an afterthought, Priscilla told Ramses, "Oh, Uncle Ramses, I am so sorry that I missed sharing the surprise with you."

But Ramses surprised her with his response.

"I could not be any more pleased than I am at your "good deed of the year!" Then, everyone laughed again. Whether Priscilla knew it or not, Ramses was happy seeing how happy she was. With the news about her surprise visits, he felt like she was indeed accepting the Bernhardts as family, and the Bernhardts were experiencing another side of their daughter-in-law, which was good.

During the compliments and expressions of glee, Jamison hurriedly prepared plates for everyone. No one needed to place their order because the ever-vigilant house manager knew their cuisine preferences. Liza and Julia preferred a cup of hot coffee before eating, usually a tiny portion of buttered toast, bacon, and eggs. As for Germane, Jamison put some of everything from the buffet on his plate and almost always brought him "seconds." He also thanked Germane for reminding everyone of this day of thanks.

Moments later, Hettie and Mavis rolled in Austin in his carriage. As they left, Hettie said, "We're right outside the door."

On Thanksgiving morning, everyone reveled in the cheerful atmosphere. However, what Priscilla said to Lady Chelsea caught almost everyone off guard.

"Lady Chelsea here's a heads-up: Carlton and I are heading back to the city this weekend and then to Columbus." She paused, "I hope that's all right with you and Father."

"Oh, PJ, Child, we understand," Father said while Lady Chelsea looked astonished. "You're a busy woman. And besides, you and Carlton have your own lives." He patted his wife's hands. "There, there, now, My Sweets."

Carlton heard their conversation as he hurried into the room. "Yes, Mother. But don't forget; we'll be back for the christening." He knew his mother wanted to showcase Priscilla and Austin together at the christening service.

But before Lady Chelsea could respond, Liza asked: "Will that be during our Christmas visit?"

"Why, yes, Ms. Liza," Carlton said as he turned and smiled at her. "I hope this meets with your approval."

"It does, young man. I'm just glad to hear someone talking about young Austin's baptism."

Observing Father's curiosity about what Liza meant, Ramses explained. "I think Miss Liza is saying that she's mighty glad to hear us talking about teaching the child about his faith, beginning with his baptism." He looked at Liza, who nodded approvingly at him. Then, just as quickly, he said, "Oops! I forgot! You're Methodist!"

At that point, Priscilla felt the need to enter the conversation. "Well, Momma, if you recall, Carlton and I married in the Methodist tradition at First Church in Columbus. Then, after relocating to Bow Lake, I joined my husband's church, Saint Paul Episcopal, which is where Austin will be baptized and indoctrinated." She paused at the sight of her mother's face fading. "But Momma, please understand that the Episcopalians are also Christians. So, Austin will be raised in the faith. I'm so sorry that I didn't mention this to you earlier." While Priscilla talked, Liza's heart sank at the thought of one of her grandchildren not being raised in the

Methodist tradition. Liza's parents had been Methodists, lest one forget her husband, the late Reverend James Nelson Austin.

No one said a word for a while. But then Father, who now understood Liza's sentiments, soon broke the uncomfortable silence.

"Oh, I see." He spoke matter-of-factly. "Miss Liza, we Bernhardts are Lebanese Christians. We believe in the same God as you. Surely you remember attending services with us back during PJ's stay at the Harlem Hospital Center? So you already know that we go to church. You also know our order of service is not too unlike the Methodists'." Then, more jubilantly, he said, "We can't wait to take young Austin with us. There are plenty of programs and activities for children, too. You'll see." While Father explained, Liza's glow was restored.

"Good," she said. "Now that that's all settled, I can definitely rest easier."

At the start of the next week, the couple returned to their respective day jobs, Priscilla to her Manhattan PR office and Carlton to his Congressional Liaison office in Columbus. Priscilla had waited until she was away from Bow Lake before ordering a passport for Austin. She was not sure why, but something told her the child would need one. From her experience, it was never too early to have one. Besides, she and Carlton traveled abroad often.

After Ruth, Priscilla's second-in-charge, and Laverne—a CF special op who also worked at Priscilla's PR firm—briefed her on her business affairs, Priscilla penciled in appointments for the first of the New Year and caught up with a few clients on the phone.

Before long, she was riding in a taxi across George Washington Bridge en route to LaGuardia Airport, from where she flew to Columbus.

A little over three hours later, she was taxiing to her West Third Street home office in Victorian Village. However, instead of settling in, she subcontracted nearly all her Ohio accounts to her two reliable PR associates there.

Afterward, she met with Carlton at his Columbus condo, where they discussed what to do about her Columbus-based PR firm.

"Why not lease office space downtown?" He suggested. "Then you'll have a shell of an operation. Besides, Julia has already started setting up shop for Arvana's new program in Manchester."

"Come to think of it," he continued, "do you think Ruth and Laverne can manage things on this end, too?"

"Good thinking, Carlton. Let me run the idea past each of them. And what of this condo, not to mention your work for the governor?"

He surprised her.

"Missy, I've already tendered my resignation."

"Oh?"

"Yes, Missy. I've been considering letting go of my congressional liaison appointment and taking up full-time work with the agency, sort of a combination of desk duty and fieldwork." Carlton looked at his wife to see her reaction.

"My Darling Carlton, are you *really* leaving your congressional liaison post with the governor and modifying your post with the agency?"

Priscilla had no way of knowing that Carlton would never consider leaving the agency, that is, the CF unit of the CIA. However, this was not the time to discuss his other job with his agent-wife, whom even he had wanted to leave her post. Oh, the complicated lives of not-so-secret secret agents.

Without giving her a definitive answer, he said, "I thought you'd like that. So, I'm putting this condo on the market and moving my things to our place in Georgetown." As an afterthought, he asked for clarification, "It is okay that we keep the Georgetown condo?"

"That's a wise decision, especially since we both occasionally visit the capital," which was about as close as either one came to discussing their "other job" —Priscilla, a CIA secret agent, and Carlton, a CIA special op. Talk about the elephants in the room!

She sighed. "Then, it's all settled. I'll call the movers and have them transport some of our furniture and personal effects to the Harlem brownstone. The office furniture and equipment can be delivered to the leased space, and everything else, well, it can be sold or donated." Glad to be done, she swiped her hands.

"Oh, Missy, what took us so long to reach such an easy resolution?"

"Well, for one thing, we weren't all that clear on what it meant to be married. We just never thought through any of this stuff."

Then, quite unexpectedly, she broached a subject that her husband never saw coming.

"Carlton, My Darling, what would you say if I went away for a short—" Carlton's eyebrows arched before she could complete her sentence.

"I'm sorry, but what did you just say?"

"I said, 'What would you say if I went away for a short spell?'"

"I thought that's what you said. Pray tell."

"I'd like to try my hand at writing." She paused to give him a moment to think. "Part of the plan I mapped out with Lady Chelsea allows us to have Austin for six months, beginning after Christmas. And I was thinking of going somewhere like Switzerland, the South of France or Italy, or maybe even Greece, where I can lease an apartment, a chateau, or a villa. Then, I can write uninterrupted and raise Austin at the same time. But if you insist, I can also bring Nanny Hettie or Mavis along. What do you think?"

"Well, I can't see you diving back into your day job, at least not full-time. I think it's a wonderful idea." Carlton was pleased that Priscilla was not talking about something involving government intelligence work. But he particularly liked that she was taking Austin along. He wanted to influence the child's early development, which was not what his parents had in their minds.

Then he mentioned something dear to him: "Before I consent, will I have conjugal privileges?"

Priscilla was learning to be a wife and mother while maintaining her own life. And so, too, was Carlton learning to be a husband and a father while maintaining his. They were accustomed to their private space and time alone. Neither had entered their relationship and eventual marriage, hoping to spend more time together than they already had.

The couple decided to wait until Christmas to share their latest news when both sides of their families would learn that, just as Ramses had alluded to earlier, "Priscilla and Carlton just might have plans of their own, which might not include any of us."

7

CHRISTMAS AT BOW LAKE

A month later, Priscilla and Carlton returned to Bow Lake to celebrate Christmas, where, once again, Liza, Germane, and Julia joined them. As they all bundled up to go caroling in the snow that evening, they were surprised by three other visitors. The doorbell chimed, and when Jamison opened it, he saw a boy of about eight years old standing in front of an adult couple.

"Who shall I say is calling?"

"Jules, sir. I'm called Jules McCorkle, and these here are my foster parents, Mr. and Mrs. James Scott."

Jamison invited the family inside and announced them to the others. "Ladies and Gentlemen, Jules McCorkle and his foster parents, Mr. and Mrs. James Scott."

When Priscilla looked up and saw Jules, he ran to her and hugged her tightly.

Glaringly curious, Father asked, "And who might this young man be?"

The young man pulled away from Priscilla's embrace. "Jules, sir, I'm called Jules McCorkle."

Father's bushy eyebrows arched, and a wide grin covered his face. There was much laughter behind Jules' introduction of himself.

"Allow me," Carlton spoke above the laughter. "Didn't Missy and I tell you? Jules is our other little one. He's our neighbor in Harlem." He lifted the youngster and spun him around. "We'll do formal introductions later." Then he held Jules, who was small and slender for his age, and greeted the Scotts.

Holding his hat in one hand, James Scott extended his other and said, "So good to visit you at your lovely home here in Bow Lake."

"Pleased that you and Mrs. Scott could make it," Carlton said as he shared a firm handshake with Mr. Scott and then kissed Mrs. Scott on her cheek.

At once, the Scotts could not help noticing everyone dressed for the outdoors, so they asked if they'd come at a bad time. But before anyone else could respond, Germane—who was delighted to see another youngster, at least someone he could interact with—reached out to Jules. "Hey there, little man. Do you want to join us? We're going caroling." A smile lit up the youngster's handsome face.

Carlton lowered Jules back to the floor.

"'Caroling?'"

"Yeah, little man," Germane said, "you know, singing Christmas songs and throwing snowballs."

"Don't think I know many Christmas songs."

After slapping his shoulders and taking him by the hand, Germane, who was pleased that he was no longer the youngest, boasted, "After tonight, you will."

Soon, everyone, along with Hettie and Mavis pushing Austin bundled up in his carriage, went caroling on the vast estate grounds. About half an hour later, they returned filled with good cheer. Jamison served hot drinks and light refreshments as everyone gathered in the family room in front of the fire.

The adults enjoyed the refreshments and got acquainted with Mr. and Mrs. Scott, while Germane got better acquainted with Jules. First, he introduced him to Austin, and Jules could not have been happier for Priscilla. He tickled the baby's tummy, Austin giggled, and Jules said, "Wow! He sure is a big one!"

Germane then showed Jules the impressively decorated Christmas tree. Colorfully wrapped boxes of many shapes and sizes formed a graphic groundcover for the thick pine.

Then he told Jules, "Most of these gifts are for the baby and me. But there's no way Grandma will let me take all this stuff home. Besides, I'm not a kid anymore." He picked up one of the boxes and handed it to Jules. "This one is for you." He smiled at Jules. Then, bending down on his knees, he began shoving more boxes to him, one significantly bigger than the others.

"But how'd you know I was coming?" Jules asked, still holding the unwrapped small present.

"I didn't. But I know you'll enjoy these two gifts. So have-at-it." Germane had some idea of what was in some of the boxes.

In the summer of 1990, Priscilla met and grew quite fond of Jules, who frequented her Harlem brownstone, often taking refuge from his troubles at home due to his mother's drug addiction. Then, one day, Children's Protective Services of the Manhattan Borough removed Jules from his mother's custody because of neglect. The young man was then assigned to the foster care of the Scotts. Though a trying time for Priscilla, she and Carlton visited Jules as often as possible, and Jules could not have been happier living with the Scotts.

Although no one else knew about the arrangement, everyone often wondered what had become of Jules. But as the young man interacted with the new people in his life, they all now understood why Priscilla had been so taken with him in the first place.

Jules sat on the floor and ripped open the small box. "Wow! A Rubik's Cube!" Jules had an exceptionally high IQ for his age. He liked puzzles and toys that challenged his intellect. As he twisted and turned the cubes and watched Germane unwrapping a much bigger box and pushing it toward him, he stood up, shouted, "No way!" and ran to Priscilla and hugged her. "I knew you'd remember. I knew it," he cried.

"Of course I remembered, Jules. Do you like it?" she said, knowing full well that he did.

"Like it? I *love* it. You got me an electric train set!" He pivoted from one side to another. "Beautiful Lady bought me my very own *electric* train set," he said to Germane and anyone else listening. "Beautiful Lady" was Jules' name for Priscilla, whom he did not like calling "Mrs. Austin-Bernhardt."

"What's that all about?" an inquisitive Liza asked as only she would at this time.

Carlton answered her. "Just something Missy promised the young fella a while back."

While everyone marveled at the young man's excitement, he ran to Mr. and Mrs. Scott and asked, "May I keep it?"

"Sure, young man," James Scott said, brushing Jules' cheek.

Then, Mr. Scott looked across the way at Priscilla while he talked to Liza. "The folks at Children's Services were spot-on about your daughter's sentiment for Jules and her generosity, too."

Afterward, Mrs. Scott explained their experience with the youngster. "We've been blessed with his company. Jules is such a brilliant and well-behaved young man." She paused momentarily, wringing out her hands, before continuing. "We were crushed when we learned I couldn't have children. And, well, it took me a long time to agree to adoption and foster care. But I wouldn't trade this life for anything." She finished by kissing Jules' forehead.

As the night wore on, Germane and Jules assembled the train and tracks. Soon, an oversized Figure 8 track sprawled across the floor.

Meanwhile, Mrs. Scott and Liza bonded after her unexpected revelation.

"Mrs. Austin, your daughter is so thoughtful. She didn't have to do any of this."

Careful not to offend her newfound friend, Liza did not comment about Mrs. Scott's acknowledgment of her infertility. Instead, she spoke admirably about her daughter. "You know something, Mrs. Scott; one never knows what Miss Prissy will do."

"Oh? What do you mean, Mrs. Austin?"

"Well, for one thing, please call me Liza."

"All right, Liza. And you may call me Pearl."

"You see, Pearl, that young woman has always been the odd one in the lot, always doing the unpredictable and getting into trouble, too. But sometimes she surprises everybody, like those gifts for the kids."

"I see. I see, indeed. But you must be very proud of your daughter. She's famous, you know."

"Yes, I know, but sometimes her fame gets her into trouble." Liza looked over at Priscilla and Jules, and her expression softened. "But I had no idea how much she cared for that little boy. I mean, there's nothing in her past to suggest she even likes children. Now, look at her with a child of her own."

"Well, Miss Liza, sometimes some of us bud later than others. Still, you must be proud of her for where she is now."

"I am. I am, indeed." Liza finally admitted.

As she observed the growing camaraderie, Lady Chelsea felt good about the evening. She now knew why Priscilla had been so enamored with Jules. As she listened to Liza and Pearl talking, she was filled with love for her extended family. Father soon put his wife's sentiments into words.

"Ever since PJ came into our lives, we've experienced one moment of joy after another." His eyes sparkled. "Liza, you sure raised your daughter well."

"Indeed, she did," Ramses chimed in. Then he winked at Liza, who blushed with embarrassment.

The following day, everyone woke early and hurried downstairs, Germane and Jules to the electric train in the family room and the adults to the dining room. A short time later, at breakfast, they discussed the christening, about which Jules was unfamiliar as he kicked Germane's ankle discreetly and asked, "What's a christening?"

Everyone turned their attention to the young men and listened as Germane explained.

"People who believe in God get baptized. You know, sometimes they get dunked in a tub of water inside the church, and sometimes they go to a lake or pond and get dipped. But since Austin is a baby, his parents must vow to teach him about Jesus, and the minister will sprinkle water on his forehead. At least, that's how it's usually done." Although a rudimentary explanation, it worked.

"Hmm," was Jules' only reaction.

Germane continued. "And since Father Lansberry was one of the ministers who performed Aunt Priscilla and Uncle Carlton's wedding, they're fortunate that he's also christening their son." He patted Jules's shoulder and said, "You'll see, my friend, and it'll all be over in the blink of an eye."

While Germane explained a christening to Jules, Liza and Lady Chelsea welled up. They were impressed that the youngsters shared such a precious conversation. But Pearl and James Scott must have felt as if they had overlooked something important in Jules' life as, moments later, James corrected that oversight. He looked at Jules and said, "Son, if you'd like, we can arrange your baptism when we return to Harlem."

"Really?"

"Really."

The next thing everyone knew, Father reminded them, "It's time, everyone."

8

GOSSIP IN THE SANCTUARY

As the Bernhardt extended family entered Saint Paul Episcopal Church, a cadre of young women huddled and whispered. Although they mostly talked about Priscilla, they also gossiped about the others.

Carlotta's cashmere floppy hat nearly covered her jealousy. "Kirsten, did you know that, of all the girls Carlton dated, PJ is the only one he ever brought home?"

"Yes," said Kirsten, gazing over her shoulders, "and Paige still hasn't gotten over it." The two friends glanced across the way at Paige, who sat with her parents and tried her best to appear unconcerned.

"But I wonder how PJ does it?"

"Does what?"

Carlotta pushed the brim of her hat away from her eyes and answered. "You know," she said, "carrying on so carefree as if nothing ever happened to her. I don't know what I'd do if I'd been kidnapped from the church on my wedding day, never even getting the chance to walk down the aisle." She shook her head and said disbelievingly, "And being swept away to Africa, of all places."

Meanwhile, Kirsten recalled, "Oh, that. Now, I remember. And assassins came after her, all the way from South Africa, too! Reminds me of something in a horror movie, save that it's true because we all watched it on the news."

"And after surviving all that," Carlotta continued, "they came after her again, this time, on the Columbia University campus, and she almost died. And all because of her association with that Black senator from Ohio."

"Yes, Carlotta," Kirsten noted. "And let's not forget her work with the Hollingsworth campaign. You know something, though," she said with a puzzled expression, "we just knew Sara Sorensen had that election in the bag." Then, "Oh well, who knew that PJ Austin was a high-powered PR consultant? I bet we all know that now because a relatively unknown Black congressman from Alabama is our sitting president! Go figure."

Carlotta agreed but pointed out something else. "All that may be true, but I kinda' think it's how she carries herself, so carefree and unassuming, despite all she's endured. Most people would've withdrawn, but not PJ, which is why I think the media tagged her 'America's Sweetheart.' She's not letting her hardships victimize her." She quipped. "Ah, heck, like the Energizer Bunny, PJ just keeps right on going."

While the women in the cadre jested and giggled, two of Carlton's polo friends joined them.

"Move over, you two. Make room for us." The handsome and haughty man sported a camel-hair overcoat, matching fedora, and leather gloves. "What'd we miss? I heard you saying something about 'America's Sweetheart.' So you *are* gossiping about Carlton's wife, PJ." His name was Winston.

Not giving anyone time to respond, the other man, just as vain, patted his hair, asking, "Have you already mentioned her time in Africa?"

Carlotta craned her neck and lowered her voice. "Jefferson, you're such a Johnny-come-lately."

"All right then, what about the sexual assault?" he quietly asked.

"No!" Carlotta was emphatic. "We don't care to talk about that."

Kirsten frowned, nodding in agreement.

But Jefferson spoke his mind, anyway. "The only thing I'll say about that is 'I wouldn't want to be on PJ's bad side.'"

The gossipers grew silent when the Bernhardt entourage filed into the nave. But, just as quickly, they resumed whispering. First, they talked about what the women wore.

Carlotta had approval written all over her face. "Lady Chelsea always graces us with her understated elegance. Only she can get away with wearing a full-length rabbit coat and hat with matching leather boots and not look gaudy." But Kirsten was interested in the new faces.

"And who are those two women with her? The one with the sparkling salt-and-pepper hair looks Egyptian, like Ramses, or is she an American Indian?"

"If you mean the shorter one," Winston responded confidently, "she's PJ's mother, Mrs. Austin. I remember seeing her in the news and coming to the chapel with Lady Chelsea when PJ recuperated from gunshot wounds she sustained from that attack on the Columbia University campus." More forcefully, he said, "Don't you ladies know anything? That was when the congressman was slated to give his

54

foreign policy speech." Like Carlotta, Winston recalled, "Back then, we all thought PJ was going to die. But her mother sure looks happy today. As for the other woman, I've never seen her before." The other woman was Pearl Scott, dressed in her Sunday-go-to-meeting outfit typically worn by staunch, middle-aged Black churchgoers.

"But check out PJ, will you!" Like Carlotta's approval of Lady Chelsea's attire, Kirsten spoke with admiration when she said, "That sable is to die for. And I thought she looked smashing on the Omiros's yacht back during that art fraud scandal at the Met, but she's just as glamorous today."

"I'll say," echoed Carlotta. "And we all kept getting confused because there were twins involved in that scandal, not to mention all those double sightings of PJ." She twisted her nose. "But my goodness, what happened to her gorgeous complexion? Why, she's almost as pale as Lady Chelsea!" The gossiping women were unaware that Priscilla's complexion faded during her relative seclusion during her pregnancy.

When he had heard enough, Jefferson snapped. "Will you two stop it? This is, after all, a christening, not a debutante ball."

"Party pooper," Carlotta said while Kirsten tried hard not to laugh.

But Winston ignored Jefferson's insistence that they stop gossiping. "Check out EC No. 2, will you? I envy him. At least he doesn't have to bake in the sun like the rest of us. And he looks like the *gazillionaire* that he is. Only he doesn't wear his wealth on his sleeves. And Ramses, always so distinguished. I'll never forget my father telling us about how, when he first met the family, he assumed Ramses was the head of the household. He carries himself with such dignity."

"And there's Carlton, bringing it up from the rear, speaking of which," Winston paused and tittered, "EC No. 2 and Lady Chelsea are carrying on as if the baby is theirs, and PJ and Carlton, well, they're tagging along like extras in their own child's christening."

While the others snickered, Jefferson wanted to know, "Who're the two young fellas?"

Sensing she could get another word in edgewise, Kirsten responded. "The teenager is PJ's nephew, Germane. He was only a child when those assassins bombed his bungalow at that Ohio resort, and he and his grandmother barely survived. But look at how he's grown. And he's handsome too!"

Carlotta's hat fanned Winston's face. When he shoved it aside, she behaved as if what she had to say was far more critical than her hat having fanned his face. "How sad. That family sure has gone through a lot. Small wonder Carlton's attracted to PJ. My goodness, she's done more impressive work in her short life than most people do in a lifetime." Carlotta shook her head again, this time away from Winston's face, and mused, "You know something? Her life is so interesting; she ought to write a book."

"I hear you, Carlotta," Kirsten cut in, "and I envy her, too. But I'm wondering what's down the road for her. You know, what else can possibly happen in her life?"

"Speaking of which," Winston interrupted and asked, "which of you would like to be in the shoes of the woman who gave birth to the Bernhardt legacy?" He nudged Jefferson, and together, they smirked.

"I would, Winston. I sure would," said Carlotta without missing a beat.

After that, the fourth- and fifth-generation New England high society buffs quieted down. If Priscilla had witnessed the gossipers, she might have likened them to those depicted in Varnette P. Honeywood's painting, *Gossip in the Sanctuary*.

Meanwhile, after nodding and speaking to the other parishioners, the Bernhardt entourage took their places on the pews reserved for them upfront.

The service began with the processional.

Father Absalom Lansberry soon delivered his homily, and the congregants sang "Hark the Herald Angels Sing."

Then came the long-awaited moment.

The priest called the Bernhardts to come forward. The congregation watched, enraptured. Poppa and Marlena were escorted to the altar first, where Poppa anchored behind Marlena in her wheelchair, nearest the baby's carriage, with Hettie and Mavis on opposite ends. Then came Father, Lady Chelsea, Ramses, and Liza to the right, followed by Julia, Germane, Jules, Jamison, Shelton, Melissa, and Harry flanking to the left. By the time Priscilla and Carlton reached the altar, they stopped in front of the carriage, where they tried to leave a wee bit of space between them for others to see the ceremony.

But given their proximity to the carriage, a stranger might have mistaken Father and Lady Chelsea for the child's parents. Why, even Liza, Julia, and Germane could see that much. Still, no one commented.

Priscilla could not see the congregants' faces when the priest sprinkled water on her baby's forehead. But she could hear them "oohing" and "aahing." When Austin raised his chubby hands to his wet forehead, and Father Lansberry said, "And he's a heavy rascal, too," there was much laughter.

After the service, Jules was surprised at all the attention focused on Priscilla. He was unaware that many had been unable to speak to her during her pregnancy because she had grown increasingly anxious about people touching her. So, the Bernhardts would arrive early enough to be seated near the front of the chapel and

56

then dash out the side door immediately after the benediction. Now that she had given birth and seemed like her old self again, the eager congregants crowded around her.

"Oh, Ms. Austin-Bernhardt, we could hardly wait to meet you."

"PJ, we read about your coming-out ball this time last year?"

"How're you enjoying life as a Bernhardt?"

"Will you and Carlton settle here?"

"You are as beautiful in person as you are in pictures."

Priscilla was not pleased being in the limelight. But she managed to cope. "Pleased to make your acquaintance." "So very glad to meet you." "Thank you." "You're so very kind." "The Bernhardts are a wonderful family." "Isn't this a glorious day!"

That was also the first time Jules noticed Priscilla's popularity. But Germane quickly orientated him when he saw the young man's amazement. "Yeah, my man, I forgot to tell you. My Aunt Priscilla is famous. But you'll get used to it. I did."

"I had no idea!" exclaimed Jules as he watched people clamoring to meet her and taking pictures with the woman he knew only as "Beautiful Lady."

Back at the manor, everyone went to their rooms and changed into casual clothing. Germane and Jules returned to the family room to play with the electric train while the adults relaxed and chatted about how well the morning service had gone; Jamison greeted them with light refreshments.

It was time for Priscilla and Carlton to bring everyone up to speed about their plans.

There was no comment following Carlton's announcement of his resignation from his congressional liaison post and that he would perform desk duty at the "agency." Of course, he didn't mention the acronym C-I-A. Instead, he talked about the "agency" as if it were a corporation. Nor did he mention that he and Priscilla had consolidated their living quarters. But when he announced Priscilla's plan to go on a writing excursion to the South of France and take Hettie and Austin with her, one could have heard a church mouse sneeze.

Uncharacteristically, "What!" Father shouted.

Lady Chelsea covered her mouth with a cloth napkin to conceal her shock. "I'm sorry. What did you say?"

"Nah, you can't be serious!" Liza said, and she meant what she said.

Ramses wore a smirk.

"Drink orders?" Jamison bellowed above the others.

Except for the occasional whistleblowing of the electric train, silence permeated the room until Ramses finally spoke.

"Lady Chelsea, you've just had extended babysitting privileges with PJ and Carlton's only child. Perhaps it's *their* turn to tend to the rearing of their son. At least for a little while."

Why, even Father relented as he strolled to Priscilla and kissed her. "Ramses is right. I suppose. We just got a little beyond ourselves." Then, just as quickly, he added, "But I sure hope we can pop in for a short visit!"

Priscilla and Carlton looked at each other and responded as one, "As long as it's just a *short* visit.'"

With the tension finally broken, everyone chuckled.

Before the conversation ended, the lady of the house volunteered Priscilla's personal assistant, Melissa, and Father volunteered Shelton—the family chauffeur and bodyguard—to accompany Priscilla, Austin, and Nanny Hettie on their trip.

Liza was the only one who remained disheartened by the announcement that Priscilla was going away. "I can't stop worrying about all that terrorism. I mean, what if those bloody fools come after you again?"

"Oh, Momma, please don't fret. Besides, bad people can harm anybody anywhere, not just far away from home. But I'll be careful. Honest, I will."

Liza persisted, but to no avail. "I know I can't stop you, but I wish you wouldn't go *so* far away." She would never get used to her daughter's adventuresome nature. Or was that her "living too close to the edge?"

9

NEW WRITER FRIEND

In January 1992, the weather forecast called for more cold weather and snow in the South of France.

"That's as good as it gets," Priscilla said to her in-laws as she bid them farewell at Merrimack Airport.

Her five-party entourage—Shelton, Hettie, Melissa, Austin, and she— boarded the Bernhardt private jetliner en route to JFK International Airport. From there, they caught a British Airways flight and landed in Paris at Orly Airport nearly half a day later. Priscilla rented a van, and Shelton drove them over four hours to their destination.

Priscilla had leased a villa in Marmande. The brochure described "a quaint town in the Lot-et-Garonne département in south-western France. At fewer than 20,000 inhabitants, the town was forty miles southeast of Bordeaux, sixty-two miles east of the Bay of Biscay, and over 300 miles southwest of Paris. Marmande hosted an annual tomato celebration in July." Priscilla liked the description of the villa, particularly its location. She thought it all so quaint.

The rustic two-story structure, with a handsome dormer, was probably built in the late nineteenth century. It did not appear to have been inhabited for some time. Two welcoming gables accentuated the front entrance, all of which fascinated Priscilla.

"They just don't make houses like this anymore."

At first sight of the villa, the household staff sensed Priscilla's love for it, even though a wooden gate badly in need of painting seemed somewhat unimpressive. Yet, they watched her watching Shelton examine the broken latch that hung from its hinges and knew he would have no problem fixing it.

Standing on the snow-covered cobblestone walkway, they saw snow-covered vines concealing much of the front of the property. Along the sides, snow-covered shrubs, heaps of dead-headed rosebushes, and other perennials created an aura of mystique.

While Hettie, Melissa, and Shelton talked about the condition of the landscape, they were amazed at Priscilla's expression: "My, my, folks! Looks like I'll be getting my hands dirty pulling weeds, after all." Unaware of Priscilla's love for doing such work—which she would not get the chance to do—they would soon learn lots more about their Madame PJ.

Finally, they went inside.

Before their arrival, Priscilla had instructed the realtor to purchase an array of throw rugs and cover as much of the floors as possible. Shelton and Melissa would cover the many windows with bed linen until Hettie and Melissa went shopping for drapes and curtains. There were four bedrooms upstairs and two on the main floor.

Mindful that her in-laws might pop in on them when least expected, she said, "These should suit us perfectly, not to mention our future guests." Priscilla loved the beds, which reminded her of her childhood in Canton, Mississippi. As she bounced on the overly stuffed mattresses, she remembered that her Uncle Charlie and Aunt Ida's beds sat high enough from the floor for her to play hide-and-seek, and the beds were comfortable, too.

Meanwhile, Hettie got busy setting up the nursery in one of the bedrooms on the main floor, and Shelton claimed the other one for himself.

There was also an unfinished basement that would be used primarily for storage.

Shelton, Hettie, and Melissa each quickly realized Priscilla was not in the least interested in decorating the place because she liked its rustic features, broken hinges, and all. So, they decided who would do what among their many other chores. "Fixing up the place," they called it.

Priscilla had traveled to Marmande to write, and that was what she would do. Well, that was not the only thing she would do, but she was not yet aware of what lay ahead.

After exploring her Marmande villa, she eventually entered her study, walked behind the desk, and sat in the leather swivel chair. She ran her hands across the top of the heavy wooden desk and noticed Shelton had already opened one of the boxes on the floor nearby. She pulled out the first item: her *Merriam-Webster's Collegiate Dictionary*. Then she pulled out her *Roget's Thesaurus*, her *Chicago Manual of Style*, and her *English Grammar* book. She laughed as she tugged at her oversized *National Geographic Atlas of the World* and felt good that she had even remembered to pack her reference materials.

Yet she had no problem visiting libraries where she enjoyed conducting research—a habit acquired during college and graduate school—leafing through old, tattered books and journals and examining microfiche and other reference material. Some people like the smell of a new car. Priscilla liked the smell of books, old and new. And she liked being around other writers and scholars in their quest for enlightenment about whatever they studied. She did not possess a Ph.D. in political science for naught. However, in early 1992, she thought her academic colleagues would snub her writing because it was "creative," not empirical or scientific. *So be it*, she thought.

Near the bottom of the box were six or seven legal pads; she had handwritten so much that she had lost count. She, therefore, had plenty of notes to start writing her first novel, whether about her adventures and escapades as a secret agent or her coming-of-age years. It did not matter to her. She just needed to start writing about something. Hidden at the bottom of the box were four journals that contained the kinds of stuff best described as "Classified," "For Your Eyes Only," or "Top Secret." Well, quite a bit of that stuff had been redacted. Otherwise, CIA Deputy Director Froley would never have authorized her clearance in the first place.

In preparation for Priscilla to start writing, Shelton and Melissa had also unpacked and placed her IBM desktop computer on the pull-out wing of her desk; the iMac and other versions had yet to be commercialized. They had put her laser printer and scanner on a shelf at a similar level as her desk. Since the floor-to-ceiling bookshelf was behind her desk, they had stacked two reams of printer paper on the shelf closest to the printer and scanner.

While Priscilla was lost in her thoughts about starting to write, Melissa asked from the doorway, "Madame PJ, are you all set to go?" When Priscilla nodded, Melissa left her alone in her study.

Priscilla was now "all set" to write her very first novel.

Meanwhile, Shelton and Melissa began unpacking boxes of bed linen, clothing, and cooking utensils. Although Melissa continued as Priscilla's personal assistant, she also did most of the housekeeping, such as cooking, cleaning, and other chores, which she enjoyed immensely. She did her best at cooking, but she was not always the best at it, and her menu was not varied. Otherwise, Shelton assisted her with cleaning, shopping, and heavy lifting.

As for Hettie, she missed Mavis, but she quickly grew accustomed to Marmande. In the afternoons, she would bundle up and push Austin in his carriage along the narrow, snow-covered passageway, familiarizing herself with their neighbors and even learning conversational French.

A few days later, Priscilla decided to take some time off from her writing. She wanted to get acquainted with her new neighborhood. But she was hardly interested in meeting any of its inhabitants. As she strolled along the narrow, cobblestone passageway, playfully kicking chunks of snow and ice out of her path, she noticed most of the homes were situated on half-acre lots, only a few were fenced in, and there was the occasional one-acre lot or more with its structure situated farther back from the street than the others. But just as she walked past one such massive home, she thought she saw someone watching her from an upstairs window, but she shrugged the thought off. *Nah,* she reckoned. *I've been cooped up in that villa too long.* So, she continued on her way as happy as she could be.

But as she rounded the corner, she sensed someone following her. A short while later, she slowed her stride and spun around to confront whoever it was. She was somewhat surprised to see a tall, middle-aged man.

Instinctively, she reverted to her confrontational New York attitude.

"Who the devil are you? And why are you following me?"

The man responded calmly. "American?"

"Oui, 'American.' Et vous?"

"Vous parlez Français. Our new neighbor? Speak English."

Priscilla was uncertain what he was asking or telling her, but she noticed something else. The man did not speak with a French accent. His was a hoarse and heavy accent, strange and unfamiliar to her. She thought he might be from one of the East European countries.

"But you are *not* Français." Her tone carried a distinct demand that he explain himself.

He stepped closer to her and held out his hand.

"Zulfika Kasun. Émigré Sarajevo. I write." Then, just as quickly, he said, "Make friend?"

Zulfika Kasun spoke in an abbreviated version of English, with few adjectives, conjunctions, and pronouns, which many narrow-minded people called "broken English." Yet Priscilla had no problem understanding him. Besides, she was in France, speaking broken French.

Even so, she wondered if he was flirting with her. But she accepted his greeting and shook his hand just the same. Although she wore gloves, his hand was icy cold as she shook it.

The next thing she knew, they walked together down the cobblestone passageway. When they headed back, Zulfika invited her to his villa and offered her "a cup of tea, or something else?"

It was bad enough to accept tea from a stranger, but since Priscilla never accepted "or something else" from anybody, she said, "Tea, please."

Before long, she was reading Zulfika's manuscript about the atrocities in his hometown of Sarajevo, of which Priscilla was only vaguely familiar from the news. Despite her encounters with war-time criminals and terrorists, Priscilla, like many Americans, still did not realize the extent of the violence, terrorism, genocide, and other atrocities elsewhere.

"Good grief!" she said to Zulfika, who no longer frightened her. "This is a firsthand account of some of the worst cases of mass genocide I've ever read!"

"Yes, yes, I know. Going on now years. But difficult getting word to international community. Reporters afraid to go unprotected places."

"Surely you know at least one editor, reporter, or media outlet?"

"Hard at first, but BBC take stories."

Zulfika mentioned one British publication, *The Guardian,* and three French newspapers. When he sensed she did not understand him, he handed her some newspapers. The English translation of the masthead on one read *International Herald Tribune.* Another read *Republican*; yet another, *The Humanity.*

While Priscilla leafed through the newspapers, Zulfika told her about his difficulty getting settled and how his contact with the BBC had introduced him to a realtor who helped him get situated in his new home. Although she believed his account in the manuscript, she felt something about the man—and his story—did not altogether ring true. But she brushed it off as being overly cautious. Before long, she would regret not following her instincts.

Although Priscilla and Zulfika became friendly, even popping in on each other, Shelton, Hettie, and Melissa did not find favor in their relationship. To say they were guarded with the man puts it mildly; they did not like nor trust him.

The next time Priscilla spoke to Carlton over the telephone, she told him about her neighbor. She called him her "new writer friend, Zulfika Kasun from Sarajevo." However, like Shelton, Hettie, and Melissa, Carlton was cautious.

"Now, Missy, for all you know, this Zulfika Kasun fella could be secretly hiding out on the run." He did not tell his wife that he was running a background check to get the bill of goods on Kasun, whom he was reasonably sure was hardly the man he pretended to be.

10

ONCE AN AGENT, ALWAYS AN AGENT

An hour later, Carlton sat across from CIA Deputy Director James Froley at the agency headquarters in Langley, where they compared notes on Zulfika Kasun.

"My God, Jim, Kasun is one of the most notorious criminals in Eastern Europe and parts of Western Europe!"

At the time, East Germany was among the first to dismantle its communist regime. Then, it reunited with its democratic Western side—followed by the former Soviet Union, which devised an outlandish version of a democratic regime.

Although by the summer of 1991, nearly all the communist regimes of Eastern Europe had begun transitioning to some semblance of democratic regimes, the world soon realized that changes in political systems, structures, constitutions, and laws did not necessarily correspond to changes in attitudes or behaviors, especially since some of the same politicians who had ruled the communist regimes found ways to worm themselves into the new political systems.

Earlier, in the late fall of 1990, while Priscilla and Julia had helped Lady Chelsea prepare for the bi-annual fundraiser (a masquerade ball) for the Children's Hospital—that had also served as Priscilla's coming out—Laverne and "the boys" undertook an "unauthorized" secret mission in the former Yugoslavia, more precisely Croatia. Although posed as "observers," they performed as American special ops.

The CF unit had been deployed to Bosnia-Herzegovina and Croatia on the eve of what ultimately developed into a full-scale war. They collected photos and vital intel of the commonplace atrocities, among which were numerous accounts of civilians-turned-soldiers vying for favor with the notorious Slobodan Milosevic.

Some Yugoslav soldiers burned, bombed, and plundered property, maimed and raped people from different ethnic groups, and slaughtered and buried others in unmarked mass graves. Such atrocities were labeled as "genocide" and regarded as "crimes against humanity."

Unfortunately, to be labeled an anticommunist was a death warrant.

During their time in Croatia, the American special ops were challenged to discern which ethnic group was which. What they experienced was like none they had ever before. So profoundly deep-rooted were the historical and religious differences among the different ethnic groups, and who knew what else, that no one from outside the territory could mediate an acceptable resolution, hence the label "the Yugoslav tinderbox."

Nevertheless, Laverne and "the boys" would never have imagined Priscilla would find herself neighbors with one of the military officers known to have authorized such atrocities. It all seemed too coincidental.

Bottom line: Priscilla was in the South of France at the inception of one of the most devastating crises in Eastern Europe, not far from what was rapidly becoming war-torn Yugoslavia.

Back at Langley, "Carlton," said the CIA deputy director, who often used the agent's first name, last initial, and title interchangeably, "no one would suspect that a Yugoslav military intelligence officer, whatever his ethnicity, would venture into the South of France to defect or exile or whatever he's up to."

"Damn it, Jim. Surely, there's something we can do. Kasun is a ruthless killer." Carlton's charming complexion faded at the thought of Priscilla having anything to do with the likes of the implacable Zulfika Kasun. "How soon can we get her out of there? There's no way their meeting was coincidental."

Jim suddenly realized that he and Carlton were at cross purposes.

"Sorry, Agent B, but we don't want her 'out of there.' We've already scheduled an impromptu visit for the first of next week."

"No!" Carlton snapped, standing up from his chair so quickly that he almost knocked it over.

"*Yes*, Agent B. The higher-ups and top brass think this is one of our best opportunities to collect vital intel right from the source! Until now, we've let them fight it out amongst themselves. But now that the situation has gotten out of hand, we can, at the least, send in observers, real ones this time."

"*Observers? Again!*" The expression on Carlton's face was priceless.

But Jim wore a poker face. "Yeah, well, so now you know."

Carlton slid back down heavily in his seat. With each word Jim spoke, Carlton's heart sank deeper. *My God, Missy has no idea who she's dealing with, and she's got our only child with her.*

This time, it was the deputy director who snapped. "Damn it, man! Are you even listening to me?"

"Okay, Jim. What's the game plan?" Carlton knew the deputy director couldn't share that information with him. But he had to ask.

So, when Jim said, "You know I can't share that with you," he was not the least angered.

"But I *can* tell you that she'll carry on as usual. You know, 'an ordinary American citizen away on an extended holiday,' in her case, to write a novel. And since she has no idea what's *really* going on, she can't blow her cover. That's all I'm telling you, Agent B."

Carlton was grateful Jim had told him that much. Now he knew for sure that Priscilla was being recommissioned as a special envoy, or so he thought.

Shortly after Carlton left, Jim called his boss, CIA Director Jason Roberts.

"Yes, sir, it's done. Yes, Agent B knows we're calling PJ back into action and is understandably outraged. But he understands."

Jim continued. "Besides, he knows how much we've bent the rules for the two of them." Then he said no more. Neither did the CIA director, who knew his agency had not only bent but broken the rules, first, by allowing Priscilla and Carlton to maintain their rank despite rules prohibiting agents from fraternizing, especially from marrying. But the folks at Langley had their reasons for allowing Priscilla and Carlton untold privileges.

Director Roberts then asked, "Are there other agents on the scene?"

"Yes, sir. We've already infiltrated the surrounding neighborhood, and we're monitoring Kasun's financial accounts and embedded messages to his cronies via his press releases about the escalating atrocities in his homeland and elsewhere." He concluded. "Additional agents will arrive in Marmande early next week."

"Good job, Jim. Damn, good work."

"Thank you, sir."

"Get back to me after you make contact." The director knew Priscilla had never turned down an assignment "in service to her country," nor would she this time. However, company rules were company rules; agency officials needed her express consent for the record. There was no such thing as a tacit agreement. Moreover, with this new assignment, Priscilla was now a full-fledged secret agent: like "the boys" and Laverne in the CF unit, once an agent, always an agent.

11

FROM SPECIAL ENVOY TO SPECIAL AGENT

By early February, Priscilla had reached a comfortable stride with her writing. She wrote hard and fast. The substance of all those notes on her legal pads, coupled with her vivid and highly-charged imagination, aided in her creation of a credible character: closely bound to her father—a Methodist minister and consummate politician—she had been raised like a son. Her unnamed character had her flaws, And how! She could be picayune and obdurate at the most inopportune times. That was Priscilla, all right. She created a character based on her own persona, which she knew well. She used her name until she came up with one for her character. "Ah, heck," she often said to herself, "who the hell would believe any of this stuff, anyway?"

A moment later, someone knocked on the door to her study.

"Enter."

It was Melissa.

"Sorry to disturb you, Madame PJ, but you have a visitor, and it's *not* Mr. Kasun…. It's someone we haven't seen in a while…. It's Mr. Froley."

Priscilla lifted her fingers from her keyboard and stared at the computer screen. "Did I forget to write that she can be easily peeved? Bummer!" she muttered. Then, she stood and calmly said, "Show him in."

The CIA deputy director entered, wiping melting snow off his face and uncovered receding-hair lined head. Otherwise, the only difference in his standard appearance was the woolen zipped-in lining in his trench coat and the galoshes covering his well-worn Oxfords. But it was cold and snowing in the South of France, so Jim had dressed accordingly. Still, he gave new meaning to "old-fashioned" and "old-school" and did not care what anybody thought about him either. As he looked around, admiring the room, Priscilla greeted him as if she had expected him. But it did not take long for him to sense her discontent. Yet, regardless of her attitude toward him, Priscilla liked and respected Jim Froley.

Dryly, she said, "Gee, Jim. How good of you to visit. Shall I ask Nanny Hettie to bring in young Austin?"

"You do know it's business before pleasure?"

"And you know it's common courtesy to ring ahead. I know you weren't *just* in the neighborhood."

"All right, already. Enough with the small talk. PJ, your country needs you." A straight arrow, Jim Froley got to the point.

"This time, it's a run-of-the-mill assignment. There's no need to change your cover as a novelist," he said to a somewhat baffled Priscilla.

"All right, Jim, you just lost me. There's usually a target for me to dance around with."

"My God, lady. They sure pegged you correctly: 'There's no pussyfooting around with you!'"

"Now that that's all-clear, answer my frigging question."

Before Jim could respond, Melissa knocked again.

"Enter."

"Sorry to disturb you again, Madame PJ. Just checking to see if Mr. Froley is joining us for dinner?"

"Well, Jim, hungry?" Priscilla asked again dryly.

"Heck, yeah, if that's all right with you?" Though he half-expected her to refuse him, Priscilla was silent as Melissa closed the door behind her.

The CIA deputy director continued his spiel. "On the one hand, you come across as an ordinary person. On the other, your lifestyle is nothing of the sort." He alluded to the household staff and the expensive villa that Priscilla had leased. Then again, she was married to a Bernhardt, New England royalty.

While her intelligence agency handler mused about her lifestyle and was reminded there was nothing ordinary about her, she forced him to answer her question: "All right, Jim, then find someone else to befriend whomever it is you want to be followed."

He stared her down. "It's your new writer friend up the street. Dance around with him for a while, and tell us what you observe. There's no need to change your routine but do use that photographic memory of yours. It was very effective during your mission to the Middle East."

Priscilla was unconvinced.

"Jim, I selected this place pretty much unseen, and as for my 'new writer friend,' well, he's just some strange Eastern European fella trying to bring attention to the atrocities in his homeland." Well, that's what she had been led to believe.

But Jim Froley knew that was not the case. He was, however, unaware that he had just substantiated her earlier discomfort with Zulfika Kasun, that she already suspected that he was not who he pretended to be. *But how* she wondered, *did Zulfika know I'd be here, of all the places in the world?* Then she remembered there had been much publicity about her new baby and later about her trip abroad to try her hand at writing. *My goodness! Word sure travels fast.* Nevertheless, she was still unaware of the significance of her relationship with the man.

"Is there anything else? Do you know how long I have to keep a keen eye on the situation? 'Cause my lease here ends the latter part of June," which was insignificant as far as Jim Froley and the top brass were concerned. They had commissioned her for as long as it took to complete her mission.

"Oh, Madame PJ," he said, reverting to the Bernhardt staff's title for her. "We should have all the intel we need by then. And if my suspicions serve me correctly, there should be minimal interference with your writing, if any."

One might regard Priscilla's acquiescence as an unbridled allegiance, like men who enlist in the military to prove their patriotism. Others might regard it as carefree. Yet others might label it as suicidal. But with Priscilla, no one knew for sure. Interestingly, as a new parent, she could have refused this assignment, but she would not give her male colleagues any grounds to suggest that her gender made her less of an agent than any of them. Even Jim Froley knew that much.

"All right, then, Jim. Let's change the subject."

"So, what do you want to talk about?"

"I don't want *to talk about* anything. Follow me. I want to show you someone." She walked out of her study without waiting for him to react.

She went into the nursery and picked up her baby boy. "Mommie is going to be a little distracted for a while. But Nanny Hettie, Melissa, and Shelton will be here for you."

Then, she lashed out at Jim. "A mean ole bogeyman wants Mommie to hang out with a neighbor for a while. So be a good boy, and Mommie will bring you a nice gift." She put the child back in his crib, turned to face Jim, and said, "God be with us, you cold-blooded wretched soul. How could you?"

For the first time, the deputy director surmised that Priscilla was upset that she had been called back "into service to her country." But he surmised incorrectly. He would learn later that she was upset, mainly because he had asked her to do something that interfered with her writing streak.

More than that, Priscilla now knew she was not merely a special envoy couriering and transmitting messages. Instead, she was a secret agent—for the American government.

Then she said something that startled her handler even more: "I should have had that damn tracking device removed."

Some time ago, CIA staffers implanted a tracking device in Priscilla's lower back when the Afrikaner assassins came after her on American soil and then almost killed her at Columbia University. Although she felt no discomfort, she did not like knowing that someone at Langley knew her every move. She now fully understood the concept of "once an agent, always an agent." She had long assumed such was the case with Laverne and "the boys." But now, that cold reality slapped her in the face, and when she least expected it, too.

That evening, Jim Froley dined with Priscilla's entourage. Priscilla was hungry. Sitting down at the table, she noticed bowls on top of plates. *Soup*, she thought; *Melissa will surprise us with an appetizer*. But Priscilla was undone when Melissa removed the top of the big-bellied dish, whereas Jim spoke before she could express her disappointment.

"Beef stew! How'd you know? It's one of my favorite dishes."

Priscilla bit her lip and pretended not to be disappointed. But Melissa, Shelton, and Hettie knew otherwise, especially Melissa, who thought Priscilla needed some nourishment.

"Oh, Madame PJ, stew is good for you. And it's cold outside, too." Melissa did not know how to tell Priscilla about her limited cooking skills.

Jim ignored Melissa's comments and Priscilla's disappointment. "Well, I love this stuff." He held his bowl high. "Fill 'er up."

Priscilla forced herself to eat four or five spoons of the stew, and then she turned to Shelton.

"Listen, Shelton. If you have time, suppose you could take Jim for a spin around the neighborhood?"

"Sure. I can do that, Madame PJ," he said as he welcomed something exciting and more substantial. Although Hettie and Melissa did not know it, Shelton had long since known that Jim Froley was C-I-A.

"I'd appreciate it, young man," said Jim as if Shelton had needed prodding.

Then, unexpectedly, "Mr. Froley," Shelton asked inquisitively, "where're you staying?"

"Uh, oh, well …."

"Ah, come on, Jim," Priscilla's attitude was glaring. "Please tell me that you have a room." Judging by his reaction, she knew otherwise. So, she instructed Melissa to prepare one for him.

Wrongly assuming that her supervisor had been caught unawares, Priscilla offered to accommodate him, whom she knew had known better. But Jim Froley had his reasons for wanting to hang out at her villa. He wanted to learn what the household staff knew about Zulfika Kasun. He also wanted to enjoy one night in the lap of luxury, especially since Melissa and Shelton both liked him and went out of their way to make him comfortable. Unlike Priscilla, however, Jim Froley spent every waking moment on the job.

"No problem, Madame PJ," Melissa said, "Mr. Froley can have the spare room. I'll make up the bed."

Then, Melissa, Hettie, and Shelton all shared amused glances while the noticeably peeved Priscilla finished a meal she did not like and prepared to lodge her boss, whom she wished had not come.

After they had eaten the main course, Melissa surprised them with a tray of dessert bowls overflowing with orange sherbert and pound cake. Priscilla's spirit lifted. "Now that's what I'm talking about!"

Shortly after dining, Shelton and Jim were off, cruising through the neighborhood and wherever else Jim might have wanted to glean while Priscilla and Hettie played with Austin.

Austin did not cry much. He was precocious for his six months of age. But he was so big that he looked close in age to a one-year-old child. Regardless, what Priscilla wanted most was for the youngster to walk when they returned to Bow Lake. She thought that would make for a great surprise for her in-laws. Then, for the first time since she had given birth, she thought about what would happen to Austin if something terrible happened to her.

If Zulfika Kasun is other than whom he pretends, I pray it doesn't affect our short spell here. Never mind her reflections; Priscilla was in for another challenging adventure, and so were the others.

By accepting this assignment, Priscilla's rank had automatically ratcheted up from special envoy to special (secret) agent. She was fully aware that she was doing the work of a secret agent, so when Jim Froley eventually broke the news to her, she merely pretended to be surprised. Whether anyone knew it, Priscilla loved the sheer rush of a storm or two, which her work with the C-I-A provided in abundance.

12

ZULFIKA KASUN OF SARAJEVO

Priscilla awoke shortly after 6:00 A.M. and headed downstairs to the kitchen to remind Melissa to prepare breakfast for their guest, Jim Froley.

Melissa greeted her as if it were midday. "Sleep well, Madame PJ?" she asked as she poured her a cup of coffee.

"Like a baby. But I was wondering, did you pop in on Mr. Froley?"

Delighted to give an update from someone as important as their house guest, "Oh, Madame PJ," Melissa reported, "Mr. Froley was up at 4:30. He hired a taxi to the airport and said to tell you that he 'enjoyed our hospitality' and that he and Shelton 'really hit it off.'"

"I see," Priscilla said somewhat distractedly. She was sure that Carlton knew of the deputy director's visit, not because they were colleagues but because Shelton reported everything that happened to him. Yet, as she sipped her coffee and pretended her boss had never been there, it did not occur to her that Shelton and Melissa might have been unlikely sources of vital intel about Zulfika Kasun to the CIA deputy director.

After breakfast, she needed some fresh air, so she decided to go for a walk. As she closed the front gate behind her, she turned in the opposite direction of her usual walk and headed down the passageway opposite Kasun's villa. So distraught was she that she kicked a chunk of snow as if she wanted to hit someone. Then, she heard, "Bonjour!"

Startled, she spun around.

"Oh, Zulfika!" She was so surprised to see the man she was trying to avoid that she almost lost her balance.

Zulfika held her arm to help her regain her composure. "Did not mean to startle you." He lied.

Priscilla pulled away from him. "You didn't startle me." She lied. "My mind was somewhere else."

On her "other job" now, she examined the man's face, particularly his eyes. Whatever she had sensed earlier during her first visit to his villa returned. Seeing his puzzled expression, she quickly said, "Sorry about that. But I have this thing about people touching me."

"Hmm," Zulfika raised an eyebrow quizzically. But she was being truthful.

"Was just starting my walk. But if you're done—"

"No, no. Join you. Okay?"

"Sure. Why not?" Another lie. Zulfika Kasun was the last person Priscilla wanted to see, let alone walk with. As they walked, she told him about the character she had created for her first novel. "What do you think?"

"Strong young woman. Raised like son by father. Good," Zulfika lied again. "Conflict? Romance?" He chuckled.

Priscilla had already sensed Zulfika's shrewdness. For one thing, an Eastern European man from a socialist society hardly appreciated gender equality. Indeed, from a patriarchal society, he would not appreciate a man raising his daughter to think like a man. For sure, he would not appreciate a self-assured Black woman as the main character. She chuckled back at him.

They grew silent as they turned the corner and headed down another passageway, at which point Priscilla challenged herself to see which of them lasted the longest in silence. They walked the long length of one Marmande-country block when, eventually, Zulfika said, "Beautiful country. Eh?"

Priscilla stopped walking, turned around as if examining her surroundings, smiled at him, and spoke pleasantly. "It certainly is."

When Zulfika smiled back at her, she asked, "Any family or friends here?" That was the first personal question she had asked him.

"Two brothers, one sister back home. Here, two neighbors make friends, then you."

Priscilla did not adequately address the fact that Zulfika Kasun was not who he pretended to be. Maybe she would have if she had known about his background and true identity.

Zulfika Kasun was born one year after World War II on the outskirts of Sarajevo in the Kingdom of Serbia. The Kasuns had been among what many Europeans regarded as the propertied class. Serbia was landlocked, surrounded by seven other nations: Italy, Austria, Hungary, Romania, Bulgaria, Greece, and Albania, all territories that had undergone more foreign invasions and occupations than one could reasonably explain. The Kingdom of Serbia became the Socialist Republic of Serbia from 1963 to 1990, then the Republic of Serbia during Priscilla's time there, and that's just the twentieth-century version of the territory's storied history. But as one foreign nation after another invaded Serbia and as one ethnic group outnumbered all the others, in his early twenties, one day, Zulfika returned home from vacation in the Romanija Mountains and found his family's estate burned to the ground. His parents' remains hung on trees on the once-lush green lawn. His heart hardened, especially when the surviving neighbors told him Bosniaks were responsible for those horrific deeds.

Until that gruesome incident, Zulfika—like his parents—had not given much attention to the many changes to the territory. However, the Kasuns were prejudiced against the Bosniaks, primarily because one of them had assassinated Archduke Franz Ferdinand of Austria-Hungary, which led that nation to declare war on Serbia, which led to the deaths of over half the Serbian male population. Otherwise, the Kasuns obligingly paid homage to whichever politician and ethnic group ruled. But the early 1970s produced unsettling complications that no one had anticipated. After that, Zulfika joined one revolutionary force after another for the ensuing twenty-odd years until he heard of an ambitious communist politician on the rise. Zulfika was endeared to the man primarily because he was not Muslim. And since, by that point, Zulfika would destroy anything and anybody he thought was Muslim, more precisely, Bosniak, he was enamored with the new leader.

He'd told Priscilla that he had two brothers and one sister. But not only had he found the remains of his parents on that fateful day, his siblings had been killed and dismembered, their bodies tossed about the grounds of the property. The memories of his family's demise were etched in his mind, as was his belief that Bosniak Muslims had been the perpetrators.

Regarding his faith, Zulfika only believed in himself, despite his family's practice of Christianity. But Zulfika was no more a Christian than anything else. Over time, he had grown from agnostic to outright disbelief, an atheist.

As such, Zulfika Kasun had been ripe for the communist leader's pickings. Radicalization came easily. It did not take long for him to grow colder and more ruthless. Watching Muslims of any ethnicity beg for their lives fueled his blood-thirsty appetite to avenge the death of his family.

However, Priscilla had yet to learn about the real man or his true history.

Dear me. The nerve of that scoundrel counting me among his friends. Oh well. She picked up her pace.

As he watched Priscilla walk away, he grew curious and asked, "Hurry?"

"Yes. I just had a good idea to incorporate into my plot. Hope you don't mind, but I walk for exercise and to refresh my mind." She hurried ahead, rounding the next corner until she was nearly out of his reach. Before long, she was unlatching her front gate and walking up the walkway to her villa, Kasun nowhere in sight.

She exhaled, removed her overcoat and other outerwear, entered her study, and sat in front of her computer. Her cold fingers warmed as they raced across the keyboard. Her thoughts about Kasun filled the following three pages. Priscilla felt she was on a roll, and, well, she was.

After emptying her mind on her computer of whatever details from her walk, she opened a desk drawer and took out a hand-held tape recorder. She pressed the "record" button and emptied her memory bank about Zulfika Kasun there as well.

"This morning, I ran into my new writer friend on my new walking route. For the first time, I saw his discomfort in me. He said he has two brothers and one sister back home, two neighbor friends here, and me."

She also recorded how Kasun reacted to keywords she had used, particularly when she said, "plot," "His irises enlarged when he talked about his family and friends," and "His hands balled up into fists" when she said, "family and friends," all indications that he had rehearsed that information which, she aptly surmised, therefore, was not valid. Priscilla took for granted her expertise at discerning psychological traits such as twitching eyelids and lips, pretentious smiles, wrinkled foreheads, and expressions such as smirks.

She put her tape recorder back in her desk drawer and took a break.

13

BREAKING HER ROUTINE

The next day, Priscilla made her move.

Contrary to what Deputy Director Froley had instructed, she knew she needed to break with her routine periodically. Well into her second month in Marmande, she did not know why she chose this day. At breakfast, she told her household staff she wanted to take them to Paris.

She looked at Shelton. "Think you could drive us there?"

"Yes, of course, Madame PJ. I'll get the map out of the glove compartment and reverse our route here."

While Shelton went to get the map, Priscilla told Melissa and Hettie more about the trip. "Apart from the typical sites, I think we might also catch an opera I saw advertised in the newspaper."

"Wow! Miss Prissy." Hettie exclaimed. Embarrassed, she quickly followed up with, "I'm so sorry. I mean, *Madame PJ.*"

"Oh, Nanny Hettie, please." Priscilla excused her informality. "How many times do I have to tell you and Melissa to call me 'PJ?'"

Although Hettie had slipped and called her "Miss Prissy," that would be the first and last time she would speak in such familiar terms. Hettie and Melissa were Bernhardt household staff, which would be the protocol they would follow. And that was that.

"Anyhow," Priscilla continued, "I thought some fresh air and a different environment would be good for all of us. Besides, who's ever heard of coming to France and not visiting Paris?" But then she shocked them when she asked, "Do you think our neighbor Zulfika Kasun might like to join us?"

Hettie and Melissa were both shocked. Neither knew what to make of her suggestion, but Melissa soon spoke.

"Madame PJ, we have no preference. We do as you ask."

But since Hettie had turned a ghastly color, Priscilla asked the obvious: "Was it something I said? Or you don't care for Mr. Kasun?"

Hettie turned to Melissa but remained silent. When Melissa nudged her to speak, she said, "Oh, Madame PJ. That man makes me cringe. I don't know what it is about him, but something does not feel right."

"Nanny Hettie, why didn't you say something sooner?"

"You seem so happy to have made friends with another writer."

"I'm so sorry, Nanny Hettie. From now on, I'll lessen his presence here." There was a strange irony in Priscilla's asking her staff's opinion about inviting Zulfika Kasun on their outing. But now, she knew she was not the only one who experienced discomfort with the man.

Shelton returned and stood in the doorway. At over six feet tall, his thatch of red hair nearly touched the top of the doorframe. Priscilla suspected he had overheard much of Hettie's confession, which he confirmed when he said, "What's this about your 'new writer friend?'"

"Nanny Hettie told me about her discomfort with Mr. Kasun, and I assured her his visits here would be less frequent."

"Hmm," he said and made no further comment.

Then Priscilla asked about the map. "That was fast, Shelton. Have you got our route all planned out?"

"Oh, yes, Madame PJ. It should take around the same time it took us to drive from Orly Airport.

"So, we can leave *now! Today!*"

"Yes. 'Now' and 'today.'" *Sometimes*, Shelton must have thought, *Madame PJ behaved like a schoolgirl.* As it happened, he, Melissa, and Hettie saw a side of Priscilla that they realized must have endeared Master Carlton to her; she could be so easygoing and down-to-Earth.

Around 10:30 that morning, as Shelton drove the entourage to Paris, Zulfika Kasun knocked on the front door of their villa. He stood there for nearly five minutes, knocking several more times. Since he thought it was unusual for no one to be home, he walked around the side and peeped through the windows. There were no lights on, nor did he see anybody. He went to the rear and peered into the patio. Seeing no lights or signs of life, he walked around to the other side and peered into one of the bedroom windows, where he spotted young Austin's empty crib. At that point, Kasun was confident no one was home. So, he walked back to the front, up the walkway, and back out the front gate. He latched the gate and continued his way.

On day two of their Parisian trip, Kasun returned to Priscilla's villa at the same time as the day before. Again, he knocked on her front door at different intervals for nearly five minutes. But this time, he dispensed with peeping through the windows. He instinctively knew no one was home. His mind raced. *Has she left town? Is she suspicious?* Before his curiosity got the better of him, he returned to his villa.

While in Paris, Priscilla nixed her plans to attend the opera after she learned that neither Hettie, Melissa, nor Shelton had ever been there. So, they instead toured the City of Light. They were excited about seeing the Eiffel Tower, which Priscilla had seen more times than she could remember. She was happy she could do something pleasurable for them. And even though he was too young to know what was happening, Austin could someday boast that he had been to the internationally famous tower. But when she took them to Maxim's, she knew for sure she would never live down that treat. So even though they had gone to Paris on a whim, that trip was "the best time ever" for Hettie, Melissa, and Shelton.

Late at night on the third day of their outing, they returned to their Marmande villa at nearly 11:00. Priscilla had fallen asleep during the return trip. After waking her, Shelton unlatched the front gate and led them up the walkway. He then unlocked the front door, went inside, examined room after room, and turned on some lights. Then, he beckoned them to enter. While Priscilla and Melissa freshened up and Hettie put Austin to bed, Shelton brought in their luggage and shopping bags. He then drove the van to the back, re-entered through the patio, and joined the others, who had since gathered in the kitchen, where Melissa took their orders for light refreshments. Shortly after that, they all retired for the night.

As far as Priscilla knew, the following two days went by uneventfully, save for Shelton, Melissa, and Hettie talking endlessly about their time in Paris. As for Priscilla, she resumed her writing streak.

On the third morning, for whatever reason, Shelton decided to inspect the grounds. As he neared one of the windows to Priscilla's study, he noticed footprints in the snow beneath it. The footprints trailed to the patio and around to the other side of the house, where someone must have stood a while beneath the window overlooking Austin's crib. Shelton was gravely concerned. *Should I tell Madame*

PJ or call Master Carlton? He took out his cell phone, called Carlton, and told him what he had discovered.

"Shelton, something's not right. Get the hell out of there, pronto. Do you hear me?" Carlton was furious.

"I hear you, Master Carlton. I can take them back to Paris if you wish."

"Take them anywhere; just get them the hell out of *there*. I'll check with you later."

As Shelton finished his conversation, his cell phone was snatched from his hand. Shelton looked into the piercing eyes of a man who looked startlingly out of place in Marmande. He wore a black turtleneck, cargo pants, a parka, and black lace-up leather boots. Seeing a gun in the opening of the man's parka, Shelton leveled his spine against the wall, his hands held high in surrender.

But when the man pointed to the front entrance and said, "Inside, Shelton. We need to get you all outta' here," his fears were allayed. He did, however, wonder how the man knew his name. "And, by the way," the man continued, "you're gonna have to cease using your phone. All you're doing is feeding them intel. They know precisely where you are, and by now, they also know that you know about them, too." When he pulled Shelton's hands down, Shelton's adrenalin pumped, but this time, it was not out of fear but instead in anticipation of whatever lay ahead.

Although still startled and somewhat confused, Shelton demanded, "And who the hell are you?"

"Calm down, young man; all will be explained in due time. For now, we need to get you all to safety."

14

THE GETAWAY

The front door to the Marmande villa swung open. Three people—one woman and two men—and Shelton entered. The woman and the man accompanying her rushed down the corridor to the dining room. The other man and Shelton went elsewhere in the villa.

Priscilla and Melissa were in the dining room. Priscilla looked at Melissa and said, "Is it me? Or is there a—" They both heard rapid footsteps approaching. Priscilla stopped talking, stood up, and felt her heart pounding. When the woman and one of the men reached the threshold, Priscilla found her voice: "Hell no! This *cannot* be happening."

The woman—whom Priscilla recognized—and the man rushed into the room. "Sorry, Missy," the woman said, "but we've got to get you all out of here."

Someone somewhere else screamed. More rapid footsteps headed their way.

Moments later, a frightened Hettie waddled across the threshold, wiping tears from her eyes. "Master Aus—! Gone!" Hettie sobbed.

Priscilla turned to the woman, not Hettie, the other one, and said, "What the hell is going on? And where's my son?

"Calm down, Missy," the woman said." *We've* got your son."

The woman turned to Hettie and then to Melissa. "No time to lose. Grab some necessities and meet us back here in ten minutes." Melissa ran out first.

But when, as if in a stupor, Hettie did not move, the woman slapped her. "Lives are at stake. Move, damn it!"

As Hettie felt the sting of the woman's hand, perhaps out of shock, she steadied herself.

Upset that the woman had slapped Hettie, Priscilla lashed out. "That was *not* necessary. Nanny Hettie speaks English. And keep in mind these are my household staff, not the rough sort you're used to hanging out with."

"Screw you, Missy," said the woman.

Priscilla backed down because she knew something crucial was afoot. But she wanted her staff, who were like family to her, to be treated with dignity.

As it turned out, Priscilla was not the only one who recognized the woman. The household servants also recognized her. They knew her as Priscilla's friend and associate from her PR firm in Manhattan. So they were all shocked at her forceful demeanor as well as her unexpected visit. But they noticed something else: Save for the pistol she wore in a holster around her waist, she closely resembled their mistress. The woman they knew as Laverne Macon was known as "Sally" in the CIA. Priscilla had recruited her to work at her Manhattan-based PR firm over a year ago. But Priscilla and Laverne's relationship had begun long before that. Nevertheless, Laverne was, first and foremost, a special op in the CF unit; "Sally" was her alias.

The man with her now spoke.

"Ms. Austin-Bernhardt, we have orders to relocate you. You've got ten minutes. Then, we're moving out. Got that?"

Priscilla had heard similar orders before. She did not need to be told twice. Besides, she did not want the man or Laverne to slap her.

Breakfast forgotten, she sprinted out of the dining room and up the stairs to her bedroom, where she put on a pair of jeans, a sweater, and her over-the-knee high-heel leather boots. She reached under her bed and pulled out a leather case, opened it, removed her Glock, and snapped the magazine into place. She grabbed her holster, attached to a spring under her mattress, and inserted her weapon. Then she snatched a woolen hat from the dresser and pulled it over her head. She was glad she wore twisted locks. The last thing she did was to get her duffel, which contained pretty much all she needed anyway, and her shoulder bag. Then she ran back down the stairwell, lugging her duffel behind her.

As she approached her study, the man who had walked in with Shelton headed her off. He held a Ziploc bag; it contained floppy disks. Thumb drives and the cloud had not yet been commercialized. When he handed her the plastic bag, she asked, "My novel?"

"Yes, Ms. Austin-Bernhardt. Your novel." While Priscilla stowed the Ziploc bag in her shoulder bag, the man took something else out of his coat pocket. "We've already transmitted your recordings. But if you want to keep the record—" Priscilla took her tape recorder and tucked it into her shoulder bag as well.

In short order, Priscilla, Melissa, and Hettie assembled in the family room. When the others saw Priscilla all suited up, they panicked. "Oh, no! Is that a gun?" Melissa shrieked. She and Hettie held each other close. Priscilla pretended not to notice their discomfort.

But when Shelton appeared, unlike Melissa and Hettie, he looked approvingly at her weapon. "Nice touch." He nodded at the gun. Then he remembered the footprints outside the villa. "I'm so sorry, Miss Prissy," as he was the only one among the household staff who often spoke to her in familiar terms, "but someone's been watching us."

Then came a booming voice from the front of the house: "Is everybody ready? We're cutting it mighty close."

Everyone hurried to the foyer, where Priscilla stopped abruptly. "Before I go anywhere, I need to *see* my son."

As the man who had arrived with Laverne beckoned to her, Priscilla followed him. He spoke into an electronic device concealed in his coat sleeve near his wrist. "Show us the heavyweight." Priscilla did not mind that he referred to her son as "the heavyweight" because almost everyone who picked up the baby commented on his weight. She breathed a sigh of relief when she saw Austin's face in the open window of a black bulletproof sedan—the kind the White House security force used to escort the American president.

While being escorted out of the villa, Priscilla felt a sudden rush. Whether the others knew it, she relished an occasional storm, so she psyched herself for whatever lay ahead. She did, however, regret that she had so many civilians with her. Yet, she knew she would think of something to lessen their fear and harm, and she would only have a short time to devise a plan. Otherwise, she trusted Laverne, so there was no need to panic.

Priscilla sat alone in the back of her black bulletproof sedan and peered out the tinted windows. The plan was for what turned out to be for the three vehicles to split away from one another and reconnect at the first of three safe houses, a forty-five-minute drive away from the Marmande villa. They would be at the first safe house for only part of the day. After that, they would move twice more under Laverne and her team's protection, which now included the French Directorate-General for Interior Intelligence and two MI6 agents, who tailed the so-called bad guys who tailed Priscilla's entourage. Priscilla never knew which French intelligence agency it was because France—one of the most policed nations in the world—had a complicated intelligence system.

While she held onto the edge of her seat and peered out the window of her vehicle, Shelton and Melissa held onto each other in the backseat of their sedan, where Melissa voiced her concerns. "I don't believe this. Who are these people? And where are they taking us?"

Shelton patted her hands and said, "Melissa, I think it's safe to assume that whoever they are, they're here to help." Then he smiled far more confidently than he felt and squeezed her hands.

Laverne sat beside Hettie in the backseat of the third sedan, trying to console the frightened woman and brief her on some of what lay ahead. Meanwhile, unlike some babies who might cry at all the commotion, Austin giggled, causing his pacifier to fall from his mouth. To say Nanny Hettie had her hands full would be an understatement. Trying to keep the heavy infant comfortable and listen to the woman who slapped her only moments ago was not easy, not to mention she was frightened out of her wits.

"Ma'am," Laverne said to Hettie, "I'm sorry to tell you this, but some bad men are interested in your Madame PJ. And, well, they'll stop at nothing to get her attention." Aghast, the nanny held Austin as tightly as she could with one hand while she covered her mouth with the other. "Nanny Hettie, things might get a little topsy-turvy, but you must be strong for young Austin. Got that?" Hettie shook her head. She understood.

As she stared out the tinted windows of the sedan, Laverne knew there was no way to fully prepare Hettie, Melissa, or Shelton for what lay ahead. After all, they were civilians who lived storybook lifestyles with the Bernhardts of Bow Lake on a 100-acre estate in the rolling hills of New Hampshire. As their vehicle veered off the main thoroughfare onto an alternate route away from the others, Laverne shook her head at the thought that something terrible was in the offing regarding the child.

Around 10:30 that same morning, Zulfika Kasun sat at his desk in his study, where three men of the unsavory type sat across from him.

"Cannot lose the woman," he said as he balled up his fist and banged on his desk. "Find her," he shouted as if the three men did not sit within hearing range when another one reported what he knew Zulfika did not wish to hear.

"Sir," he spoke in an accent like Zulfika's, "some men took new writer friend and servants." He paused and watched Zulfika's face darken. "Well, sir, gone. Villa vacant."

"When did that happen? They just returned the other day."

"Early morning, sir. Black bulletproof vehicles. Pick up early."

"Find them. Cannot lose them. Our only hope," Zulfika said, shook his head, balled up his fist again, and repeated himself. "Only hope."

Another of the men addressed something more appealing to him.

"Sir, onto them. Tracked fifty-seven kilometers headed north." But the man did not tell his boss that there were three vehicles, that the three vehicles had separated, and that he had no idea which vehicle his new writer friend was in.

"Good job, Sergei." Then he turned back to the first man who had reported and shouted in poor command of English. "Get out! Come back after find her."

If Priscilla had been there, she would have known something was wrong; the Zulfika Kasun she knew spoke English more fluently. But Priscilla was not there.

At CIA headquarters at Langley, Agent B was in a heated conversation with the deputy director. "You bloody bastard. This isn't the first time you used an untrained civilian to conduct critical intelligence-gathering. Why, I tell you, if—"

Carlton was unaware that his wife was, in fact, "trained," maybe not like special ops. However, she was indeed highly trained to do her particular job, posing as an ordinary American citizen conducting whatever business it was "in service to her country," which Jim Froley knew but could not say and which he knew Priscilla was pretty darn good at doing, too. For the moment, though, he had to find a way to assuage her disgruntled but ill-informed agent-husband.

"Pull it together, man. Our people are on the case. And Agent Macon is with her." Even though he was not supposed to pass on any intel to CF Agent B, he thought it would be okay to let that slip. Carlton was, after all, Priscilla's husband. Indeed, the deputy director, Carlton, and Priscilla shared an unusual relationship. Since Carlton knew that Laverne served as Priscilla's double, he was grateful to have learned that much. However, sometime later, he would question Laverne's role because of all her injuries sustained during their stint in the Balkans.

Jim Froley had worked with Agent B and the other CF boys for years. His promotion to deputy director followed the recruiting of Priscilla. Since then, he and Priscilla shared a tight bond that solidified over the years, from her abduction to southern Africa in the mid-1980s to her recovery from gunshot wounds she sustained when the South African assassins attacked her on the Columbia University campus to her recent special envoy mission in the Middle East, and more. Only once did their relationship suffer a tiny crack; that was when she served as special envoy to the Middle East for outgoing President James Farrington. At the time, the lines of authority over her role as a special envoy were blurred among the CIA, the National Security Agency, and the State Department.

Later, when she worked on the international art fraud racket at the Metropolitan Museum of Art and threatened to leave the agency, Jim Froley found a way to reinforce their relationship: He subcontracted minor investigative and security-related jobs for "the boys" through Priscilla's Manhattan-based PR consultancy. At the time, Priscilla wanted Carlton to resign from his work at the CIA, which she now knew was hardly going to happen.

But this assignment came directly from the top brass. CIA Director Roberts had explicitly instructed the deputy director: "Assign Special Agent P. J. Austin-Bernhardt as the conduit between the American government and one Zulfika Kasun of Sarajevo." And, of course, the CIA director took his orders from the president. But for this particular assignment, neither Carlton nor Priscilla was aware of that not-so-small detail.

15

IDENTITY NOT YET CONFIRMED

As Laverne and the other agents drove the entourage to what they believed would be the first of three safe houses, they knew they were being followed. So they only stayed there long enough for them to reunite and stretch their legs before heading out for the nearly three-hour drive to their next stop. Although Zulfika Kasun's men followed them, five international intelligence agents—three Gendarmerie Nationale, DCRI agents, and two MI6 agents—trailed them.

As the agents moved about the first safe house, Hettie and Melissa grew increasingly uncomfortable, mainly because the guards looked like what they were: highly trained special ops. They wore camouflage uniforms, carried high-caliber rifles, and sported pistols visible in their shoulder holsters. Although Priscilla and Shelton were relieved at the sight of the heavy weaponry, Shelton regretted that he was also not suited up or packing heat, as it were.

While Hettie tended to young Austin with Melissa's assistance, Laverne took Shelton to a backroom and strapped him into a bulletproof vest. But when she handed him a Glock 38, along with its holster, Shelton almost hugged her. He was familiar with guns in his dual role as the Bernhardts' chauffeur and bodyguard. He knew this weapon was conducive for concealed carry users because of its ease of use and performance, and it had eight rounds, unlike a traditional six-shooter. Proud to be suited up and ready to protect his charges, Shelton wore his weapon exposed.

"Well, it's about time," he said to Laverne. Shelton, like Priscilla, felt much better armed.

The folks at Langley knew about Shelton's reputation for slugging people and pulling his weapons, particularly on the paparazzi. He was a fierce protector, which was evident on many occasions. He had sprung into action before, most notably when the Bernhardt estate was under siege, during the murder trial of South African Nationalists Movement's Patrol Guardsman Hans Verwoerd, and when the SANM PG almost killed Priscilla at Columbia University. But little did he know he would not be using his weapon at any time during this adventure.

When Priscilla and Shelton joined the others, Melissa and Hettie were shocked again. In fact, the usually well-poised Melissa momentarily lost all poise as she stared at them, her mouth agape.

"Oh, no! I would never have pegged Madame PJ as someone who knew about guns," as if she had not already said that. As for Hettie, she squeezed young Austin tighter and started sobbing again.

Since the two women had already seen their mistress suited up, Priscilla wondered why Melissa did not comment similarly about Shelton. She then attributed the apparent distinction to Melissa's limited worldview; she refused to believe Melissa was a sexist. Nevertheless, she tried to reassure them.

"Melissa, Nanny Hettie, this is all for show." She smiled, put on her coat, hat, and gloves, and headed for the door. But then she turned back around, looked at the stunned women, and pointed to Shelton, saying, "But ole bro' here is the one you need to keep your eyes on." She winked at Shelton and strutted out the door.

As Priscilla sat in the sedan's backseat, alone again, she spotted a folder not there before. It contained dossiers of the CIA agents accompanying them. "Ah," she recognized names other than Laverne's.

When she tapped the window separating her from the driver, he said, "Yes?" as if asking what she wanted.

"Okay, Sam, so we meet again."

Sam chuckled.

Priscilla first met Sam during her second time in southern Africa. She and another CIA agent, Melanie, were with NSA Counterintelligence Agent Harry Middleton and CIA Agent Sam on a weather-beaten ferry on Lake Kariba, where Sam was bitten by a crocodile and sent home, presumably out of commission. As it turned out, Sam's leg was not as severely wounded as Priscilla had thought because here he was, driving the sedan she rode across the French countryside.

Although she did not recognize the other agents' names, who were identified only as "Stephen" and "Henry," at least now she knew what to call them. She was pleased to learn they were proficient in Russian and Bosnian. She needed to comprehend what Zulfika Kasun and his cronies said or wrote. However, she need not have worried because the three French intelligence agents and the two MI6 agents—who tailed Zulfika Kasun's men who tailed Priscilla's entourage—were fluent in the languages of their Eastern European neighbors.

But when she read that the international intelligence community had "not yet confirmed Zulfika Kasun's identity or his intentions," she cringed. She was horrified at the atrocities that Kasun and his cronies had already committed at the behest of Slobodan Milosevic's generals.

"Bummer! Bummer!" she muttered. "How the hell am I supposed to engage with someone I can't identify?" Now, for sure, she knew her instincts about the man she met in Marmande had been correct; he was not who he pretended to be.

She also learned that the implacable Yugoslav leader and one of his generals had disapproved of some of Kasun's actions, particularly his travels to France. But what caught her attention was his official title: *Lieutenant* Zulfika Kasun, *Military Intelligence Officer* to the Yugoslav Regime, and that he "has been sending mixed messages to the international intelligence community and is wanted alive, if at all possible." However, she was not surprised to learn that he had been the one perpetrating those horrific crimes he had written about to the Western media. It was only his title that surprised her.

Priscilla now understood the nature of the man with whom she had had tea and, in his home, no less. She thought about Melissa, Hettie, Shelton, and young Austin and said, "He wouldn't *dare*."

More significantly, she was now entirely sure that Zulfika Kasun intended to use her internationally recognized persona as a conduit to the West and, not only that but that he was clearly willing to use young Austin and anyone else she cared about as a bargaining chip. Zulfika Kasun was indeed a nasty piece of work.

16

GENEVA! WHERE'S *THAT?*

Closing in on three hours without any stops, the three-vehicle caravan—in which Priscilla's led the way—slowed its speed by ten to fifteen miles per hour from what seemed to her to have been ninety miles per hour. Priscilla also noticed that the road signage was in different languages.

"Why, that's French and—" At that, she slid to the edge of her seat and tapped the window that separated her and Sam.

"I should've mentioned the intercom button earlier," he said.

Priscilla examined the buttons on the overhead panel and pressed the intercom button. "Where the devil are we? Is that Swiss, German, or French?"

"And right you are. That's Swiss, German, and French. And we're pulling in here." Sam took care not to say her name. The most seasoned intelligence agents have a healthy dose of precaution. Or is that paranoia?

As the vehicle halted, a man—Priscilla assumed he was an agent— opened her door. "Bonjour," he said as he looked inside and held out his hand. Priscilla reached for it, got out of the vehicle, and stared at him. He resembled one of the CF boys, tall and handsome, with a full head of blond hair. Since most of the men Priscilla knew were tall and handsome, it did not hurt that this one also had a pleasant disposition. Yet, it was hard for her not to notice the bulge in his leather jacket; he carried a big pistol. As she sized him up, she felt his hand on her shoulder. He pointed to what looked like a small and rather quaint roadside diner and said, "The others are gathering to go inside." But when he stared at her exposed weapon, she put it under the back seat.

Then, she hurried to Melissa and Hettie, both holding on tight to Austin's carriage. So bundled up was the child that Priscilla could barely make out his face. When she rubbed his head, he smiled.

Shelton, who had also removed his weapon, joined them.

The three French and British agents led the way inside the diner to a table for ten. Once seated, one of the British agents took everyone's orders and placed them. As soon as the waitstaff left, Melissa asked about their whereabouts.

"Where are we?"

Before Shelton could respond, one of the agents said, "We're in Geneva."

"Geneva?" Melissa queried with a schoolgirl's naïveté. "Where's *that?*"

Nearly everyone looked at her as if she were joking.

But Melissa's insistence put an end to such thinking. "Well, where *is* this 'Geneva?'"

Uncharacteristically quiet since their departure from Marmande, Priscilla responded, "Melissa, we're in Switzerland."

"Switzerland! You have got to be kidding me! *Why!* This is crazy." Her blue eyes opened wide under her overlong brunette bangs.

Priscilla remembered a time in her not-so-distant past when she had uttered almost the exact words, except hers were about Harare, Zimbabwe.

At twenty-eight years old, Melissa was a small-town girl who had not gone to college and, indeed, had not traveled abroad before the Bernhardts hired her. *Surely*—Priscilla thought—*living with the Bernhardts, she's familiar with internationally recognized cities.* But Priscilla thought wrong. Melissa had never heard of Geneva. She did not know it was home to over 200 international organizations, such as the Red Cross, or the birthplace of the Protestant Reformation, which Priscilla was unaware of until she studied the New and Old Testaments. It was also where the Geneva Conventions, which outlined the terms of treatment of prisoners of war, were drafted. But Geneva was known for much more, such as organizing international humanitarian efforts, and the birthplace of political philosopher Jean-Jacques Rousseau, who Priscilla once assumed was French. But Geneva and Switzerland per se were known most for producing well-engineered watches, delectable chocolates, and finance, particularly as a haven for large sums of money.

To everyone's relief, the agent who had placed their meal orders said, "Well, young lady, I guess we owe you an explanation."

"I'll say," Melissa huffed.

"Under the apparent circumstances—"

"Humph! *What* 'apparent circumstances?'" Melissa was beside herself. But when she noticed Priscilla's expression, she apologized. "Oh, Madame PJ, I'm so sorry. I don't know what came over me."

"Melissa, you're understandably confused and upset. But let's try not to make things worse if that's at all possible."

Shelton put his arms around Melissa. He could see that she and Hettie were frightened. But whatever their "apparent circumstances," he, Melissa, and Hettie needed to be strong for Priscilla and Austin. He squeezed Melissa's shoulders and said, "Don't fret, Melissa. Let's hear him out."

The British agent nodded at Shelton, looked around, and said, "Please call me Thomas," who was an MI6 commander. He spoke with a crisp British accent, "It's not my real name, of course, but it will do." Thomas commanded the British and French agents and the special ops combined forces, including Laverne and her CIA colleagues. He lowered his voice and leaned closer to the table to avoid being overheard. "You've all met Zulfika Kasun, your neighbor at the Marmande villa. But he is not who he pretended to be and, for some reason, has latched onto Madame Austin-Bernhardt." He looked around the table before continuing. "We believe it has something to do with her being a celebrity and her high-profile network. She is internationally known, after all." He wiggled to the edge of his seat and continued in a whisper. "Until we know more, it's best to keep you away from him." Seeing the fear on Hettie's face, he said, "At this point, there's no reason to suspect any harm will come to any of you." He finished by looking intensely at Melissa. "I hope that answers your questions and calms your concerns."

Melissa only nodded.

Priscilla broke the tension at the table, or so she thought when she said, "Anybody else hungry? I'm starving."

"Oh, Madame PJ," Hettie finally spoke. "How can you be so calm?"

"Well, Nanny Hettie, when you live the life I have, you grow paranoid if *no one* is after you. Usually, it's some doggone reporter or the paparazzi poking around. However, I wondered how long before somebody would come a-calling over here. At least now, we're all together and safe."

Hettie did not feel safe as she remembered how Priscilla had almost died from gunshot wounds sustained from that incident on the Columbia University campus. She also recalled the family discussion about Priscilla's plan to travel to the South of France to try her hand at writing. It was Christmas, and they had just returned from the christening service for baby Austin. If she recalled correctly, Priscilla's mother, Liza, had expressed concern for her daughter's safety. Otherwise, she thought, *What married woman travels alone and this far away from home for whatever reason?* Still, she remained silent.

After that, no one else knew what to say. So they were all relieved when two waiters arrived with their meals. Then, everyone delved into their food as if they had not eaten in a long while. In fact, nobody talked except for the occasional "Pass the salt" or "More bread, please."

Meanwhile, outside the diner, Laverne and her colleagues substituted the three black bulletproof sedans for three high-riding bulletproof Hummers—one taupe, one black, and one camouflage—waiting for them behind the diner. Afterward, they went inside, sat at a separate table, and ordered their meals.

At one point, Priscilla bounced young Austin up and down on her lap while one of the French agents said in English, "He is a big boy, no?"

"Yes," she said. "That's what everybody says." Then, everyone at the table laughed for the first time since they had left Marmande. As Priscilla listened to the laughter, she realized their road trip was far from over. But she knew better than to ask where they were headed, not to mention how long it would take to get there. So she just waited for an opportune time to approach Laverne, needle it out of Sam, or wait for one of the other agents to brief her.

No sooner than everyone seemed to have relaxed, MI6 Commander Thomas told them, "Finish up. We're heading out in a minute. And we'll be in different vehicles. Just another precaution," he said with a smile. "This time, though, try to get some sleep. It's going to be a while before we get to our destination." By this time, even Melissa knew not to ask when and where that might be.

Priscilla glanced across the way at Laverne and the other agents. She wanted to join them but knew she could not because Laverne's team pretended that they were a separate party. So Priscilla played with her son and waited for an opportune time to talk to Laverne or another agent.

If only she could have heard their conversation. Zulfika Kasun's men were tailing them, and they were close. Laverne and the other agents had rightly assumed Shelton's open cell phone had put them on their trail. Why no one relieved him of his phone remains a mystery.

This time, when they departed, they drove around in circles. Shelton and Melissa's vehicle eventually lost the Sarajevo men as they rode through a roundabout, veered off to a narrow roadway, and then headed south in the direction from which they had originated. Then, they turned back around in the right direction and eventually reconnected with the other two vehicles, after which the caravan resumed its trek relatively unimpeded northeast.

As Priscilla's entourage made haste with their getaway, one of Zulfika Kasun's men reported to him at his Marmande villa sometime later.

"Sorry, sir. Lost 'em. Lost track of electronic device. Now too dark. Different vehicles. Lots of Hummers here." He paused and held the phone away from his ear. "Better luck in morning. By now, resting somewhere. Not many fit new writer-friend descriptions. Find in morning."

Of course, he intimated that the tan-complexioned Priscilla, with her long twisted locks of light brown hair, would stand out among the French and Swiss population. He also noted that few people traveled with a nanny, a baby in a carriage, and two household staff.

Priscilla rode in the back of the black Hummer, leading the caravan upcountry in Switzerland. She could not hear her driver, MI6 Commander Thomas, as he communicated with the other drivers. Since the drivers occasionally switched to lessen familiarity with their wards, Sam now drove Laverne, Hettie, and the baby in the camouflage-colored vehicle. At one point, the Frenchman driving Shelton and Melissa radioed to Thomas that he had finally lost Kasun's men. So, Thomas slowed his speed, allowing them to catch back up. After that, the three vehicles resumed at the higher speed of ninety miles per hour, and Priscilla fell fast asleep.

Since he did not wish to talk to her anyway, particularly not to respond to her many questions, Thomas was pleased to see she had fallen asleep. *The sooner we can get this woman and her household staff and that 'heavyweight' someplace secure, the better*, he thought. Then, *My God, how much more can she take? And for her to admit to expecting someone to come after her has become a way of life; what an awful way to live.* Thomas, an MI6 commander, should have looked at himself in the rearview mirror because he lived a similar life in Her Majesty's Secret Service as Priscilla's "in service to her country."

17

THE LUZERN SAFE HOUSE

Over four hours after departing the diner in Geneva, the three-vehicle caravan veered off the main thoroughfare onto a highway that led to a suburban community outside Zurich. After that, they rode for forty minutes until they reached a semi-rural village similar to the one in Marmande. Their second and final safe house, which they were unaware of at the time, was in a German-speaking community near Luzern or "Lucerne."

The caravan halted.

It was cold outside, and now it was snowing.

The lights in the villa came on, and suddenly, seven heavily armed guardsmen came into full view. The men all sported tattoos of snakes crawling up the trunks of trees on their necks, and the tattoos seemed to continue down to their shoulders and arms, which were covered by camouflage parkas.

Laverne opened the door to Priscilla's vehicle and noticed she was slumped in her seatbelt, fast asleep, and snoring. She called her name, and when Priscilla did not respond, Laverne shook her.

"Nah, nah, let me sleep," Priscilla grumbled. "Please, let me sleep."

"Wake up, Missy. We're here." When she fell back to sleep, Laverne slapped her.

Priscilla awoke. "What the—" She rubbed her sore cheek and looked at Laverne in shock. She could not believe she had just slapped her.

"Come on, Girlfriend. Snap out of it. Lives are at stake."

Even though Laverne and Priscilla had grown close over the past two years, Laverne took her work as a CF special op seriously. The petite Caucasian woman of Choctaw ancestry with a tan complexion like Priscilla's could pass as her twin.

The only difference was their hair: Priscilla's was naturally curly, and Laverne's naturally straight. The only person of Choctaw lineage in the CIA and one of the few women in the CF unit, Laverne, like Priscilla, was an asset to the agency. More importantly, as in their previous missions together, her role as Priscilla's decoy was paramount to all else.

Still rubbing her sore cheek, "Ah, crap," Priscilla said, "and I was having such a good dream." Stepping out of the vehicle, she stumbled. She had forgotten how high up she was. As her feet touched down, she looked around in confusion. "Where the hell are we, anyway? Looks like we're back at our place in Marmande."

"Zurich, Missy. Well, actually, Luzern," Laverne said, "your second safe house."

"Are we really *this* far north?"

"Indeed, we are," Laverne said as she walked Priscilla inside their new home for the duration, but they were not yet aware of it.

Priscilla was exhausted and just wanted to curl up in bed, but when she saw Melissa and Hettie's expressions, she knew she had to pull herself together for their sake.

"Okay, folks," she said as cheerfully as she could muster. "Welcome to our new home!" She rubbed her eyes, yawned, and winked at Laverne and the agents who escorted them inside. "Our new home," she repeated as if convincing herself—*our goddamn new home.*

It had been a while since Priscilla prayed for anything other than to give thanks. But as she observed the seven heavily-armed tattooed guardsmen moving about the villa and the grounds, conferring with Laverne, her CIA colleagues, and the five French and British agents, it suddenly occurred to her that this time, her "red arse" —as her Aunt Ida in Canton, Mississippi used to describe her—was on the line, for sure.

Laverne's voice pulled her out of her thoughts. "Here's the deal, folks. You will be split up from time to time. That way, we're less easy to track." She looked at her colleagues before continuing. "Do not park all three vehicles in the same place at any given time and, if possible, try to separate our five wards. The more confusion we create, the better. Got that?" Then she noticed Priscilla had zonked out. "Damn it, Missy; you haven't heard a word I said."

Commander Thomas entered the drawing room at the tail end of Laverne's briefing. "No problem, Sally," he used her agency name. "I'll catch Ms. Austin-Bernhardt up on the details."

He peered into her puffy, red, sleepy eyes. "Looks like she needs some rest."

Priscilla stared back at him. "I sure could use a smoke. I'm headed to the patio. This place *does* have a patio like the one in Marmande. Doesn't it?"

The British commander nodded.

One of the guardsmen beckoned Priscilla to follow him, and Thomas told her that he would bring her a drink and brief her on the patio later.

Meanwhile, Laverne continued briefing the household staff on their new "apparent circumstances." All the while, Melissa and Hettie trembled and clung to each other at the sight of the tattooed guardsmen with their automatic rifles and the big knives and pistols protruding from their holsters. In contrast, Shelton was starting to think he was in for the adventure of his life.

Before long, the similarities between the two villas enabled Priscilla, her staff, and young Austin to settle in quickly. They even got used to the tattooed guardsmen and the agents milling about the place. Priscilla resumed her writing streak, incorporating plots related to her new circumstances even though she continued thinking no *one would ever believe any of this stuff anyway.*

She also eventually realized that the Hollingsworth administration had wanted the Yugoslav lieutenant to play for his card. However, apart from the vital intel he could share with them and their Western allies, he was not someone the Americans—nor their Western allies—regarded at a premium. And since he sent mixed messages, the Americans continued sending him mixed messages, one of which involved Priscilla's whereabouts. So, it would not be easy if he wanted to collaborate with the Americans and their Western allies. For now, however, Kasun and his cronies needed to find Priscilla. Then he had darn better have something concrete and credible to share with her since she blamed him for interrupting her writing streak, and lest one forgets disrupting the lives of her staff.

As things stood, Zulfika Kasun had a more pressing problem. One of Milosevic's generals demanded that he return to war-torn Bosnia and Herzegovina. He did not know the general believed that he, that is, Zulfika Kasun, was up to something and that something, whatever it was, did not bode well with the Yugoslav president, either. For one thing, there were rumors about his doubles, of which he had a few, but no one was able to validate them. The general also suspected his lieutenant was feeding the Western media more than false information; instead, he was preparing a path to exile. Yet, whenever the general thought he had caught the lieutenant red-handed, he discovered he was dealing with another of his decoys.

Eventually, though, Zulfika Kasun, or one of the men posing as him, returned to Marmande. At the same time, the real one (or was it another decoy) remained in Bosnia and Herzegovina for the most part against his will. He needed to pay homage to the Yugoslav president, so he did as he was ordered and led untold executions, rapes, and maiming, even burying some alive in mass graves. As reports of the atrocities reached the American "observers" and their Western allies, they grew more dubious about collaborating with the increasingly nefarious Zulfika Kasun. With the mounting atrocities, the international community would soon turn its back on the Yugoslav president, who denied that he had authorized or even committed the atrocities himself.

Meanwhile, the general put the lieutenant in a tenuous position as he determined whether he was plotting to turn against the president. The general knew of the lieutenant's background and tendency to change his stripes with the wind. Yet Kasun chanced to convince him otherwise, as he stressed, "I must return to France where I can work directly with the Western media." But he did not tell the general that he needed to find P. J. Austin-Bernhardt—his "only hope" —though for what was still unclear.

Kasun knew his time was running out because Priscilla was scheduled to depart sometime in June. So intent on collecting intel on the American special envoy, he dispatched another decoy to the South of France.

While in Luzern, the international intelligence agents devised a stratagem to confuse Kasun, or whoever he was, and his men. Although the real Priscilla remained at the Luzern villa, she needed to be relatively visible from time to time. Therefore, the agents arranged for Laverne, accompanied by Shelton and Melissa, to temporarily relocate to the lavish Styles Luzern City Hotel, situated in central Switzerland, lying on the Reuss River where it issues from the northwestern branch of Lake Lucerne and from where CF Agent Laverne Macon played her role as Priscilla. Consequently, whenever Kasun's men reported to him, they almost always sent conflicting messages about Priscilla's whereabouts.

"How," Kasun asked his men, "can she be in two places at once?" One might ask the same question of the real Zulfika Kasun.

As it turned out, the French and British agents, and Laverne and the CIA agents, knew that Kasun, whichever one he was, was back in Bosnia and Herzegovina, but Priscilla did not know that. Nor did she know that when Kasun and his men returned, she and her staff's new apparent precarious circumstances would change dramatically, yet again.

Meanwhile, Hettie was relieved when Melissa, Shelton, and Laverne returned from their stay at the Styles Luzern City Hotel. She had felt somewhat alone without Melissa and Shelton, her closest connections to the Bernhardt family.

After a brief greeting, Melissa went to her room, unpacked, returned downstairs, and headed to the kitchen, where she saw one of the guardsmen standing over the sink. "Ahem." She got his attention. "I can take over from here."

The man turned around and smiled at her. He picked up his rifle, pulled its strap over his shoulder, and turned back around to face her.

"You can call me 'Ronnie.'"

Melissa could not quite place his accent. At five feet nine, he was slightly taller than her five feet seven inches but twice as broad. He had long brown hair, and standing so close to him, she could see his hazel eyes. Apart from the snake and lion tattoos on his neck and shoulders, he seemed almost approachable when he smiled.

"Sure glad you're back. Kitchen detail is not my thing," he said and then left.

As Ronnie headed up the corridor just past the dining room, Shelton caught up with him as if he had been waiting. The two then headed for the front door. Shelton was very much in his element with the guardsmen who so vigilantly protected them. Mostly, though, Shelton knew he was getting some insight into the other life that his Master Carlton lived in secret, not to mention his growing suspicions about Madame PJ.

Shortly after Shelton and Ronnie departed, Priscilla caught up with Laverne and greeted her with a warm embrace. However, Laverne unexpectedly pulled away. At that, Priscilla sensed that her friend had not fully recovered from the wounds she'd suffered during her time in the Balkans. So she stepped back and pretended not to have noticed her reaction.

"Girlfriend," Priscilla chuckled. "You really could be my twin, save for the hair, of course." Wanting to deflect attention away from Laverne's apparent discomfort from her having touched her sore spots, she joked about their hair.

"Why, thank you, PJ. I think."

Priscilla casually sat down and listened as Laverne talked about her time with Melissa and Shelton in the City of Luzern and about how, when they ventured into restaurants and designer shops, the paparazzi clamored to ask her questions and take pictures of her because they thought she was P. J. Austin-Bernhardt. Priscilla was amused by what Laverne told her.

At one point, the two women overheard Melissa and Hettie laughing in the kitchen about something they must have found amusing. Then they both heard Melissa saying, "Now I can add Luzern to my list, right behind Paris!"

Priscilla so relished the cheer permeating throughout the villa.

For much of their time at the Luzern safe house, the guardsmen, the French and British agents, and Laverne and the CIA agents mostly played cards when not on their shifts guarding the entourage and overseeing the villa. Sometimes, the men boarded vehicles and drove away as if they were leaving. They did almost anything to confuse Kasun's men, whom they knew were vigorously on the prowl for Priscilla. Sometimes, they played sports on the snow-covered grounds. Nearly all of them exercised, sparred with each other, jumped rope, or ran on the grounds to keep in shape. Mostly, they remained alert because they did not know when their hideout would be discovered or by whom.

One evening, Priscilla crossed her fingers while waiting for dinner. She prayed silently: *Please, Lord, no more beef stew or tuna casseroles.*

When Melissa and Ronnie—the guardsman who performed most of the kitchen detail—rolled two carts into the dining room and put plates before the hungry group, everyone scooted to the edge of their seats. Some even said under their breath, "Our prayers have been answered." They could not believe their eyes as they looked at the cuisine on the plates put before them. Apparently, Priscilla was not the only one anticipating something other than beef stew or tuna casserole.

Surprised, Priscilla yelled out, "Cod!"

"Baked potato with sour crème and chives!" said Commander Thomas.

"And kale, too? It's a miracle!" Sam said.

Although he had gone grocery shopping with Ronnie, Shelton also pretended to be surprised by the menu. Since he was familiar with Priscilla's preferred cuisine, he had decided that treating the somewhat disgruntled entourage and their protectors to a good meal would be an excellent way to create some calm and good cheer, and he was right.

Even Melissa understood that much. Although she enjoyed doing it, cooking was not Melissa's forté. She knew how to cook only a few dishes, mainly beef stew and tuna casserole. But Ronnie had prepared this meal tonight and several other nights, and he and Shelton kept that secret.

Later that evening, Priscilla played Blackjack with the French and British agents. But when the others opted to switch to poker, she bowed out. "Never could play that one."

"Ah, come on, Madame PJ," René, one of the French agents, called her by the title the household staff used. "Want to learn?"

She shook her head. "Not one of my strengths. Deal me out." She stood up to leave. "Too damn revealing for me, anyway." Priscilla thought that people learned a lot about others by observing their behavior during games, particularly table games. And she felt she had already revealed enough of herself at her hands at Blackjack.

18

THE INVITATION

Almost two months into their stay in Luzern, CF Agent Laverne and MI6 Commander Thomas became antsy. Things were going almost too well. And since no one mentioned moving the entourage to the third safe house, Priscilla, who had settled comfortably in this one, would hardly ask anyone about it.

"So, how close to France is that bastard Kasun?" Laverne asked.

"He's expected back sometime tomorrow. But we have our orders to wait until Kasun approaches before our next move."

"I know," she said. "Talk about a crazy cat-and-mouse game. This has got to be one of the most uneventful details I've ever had."

"Yeah, well, hold your horses, kiddo," the commander cautioned. "After what he and his men did back in their homeland, something tells me he's tasted too much blood to stop now. I've told my people to gear up for the worst. Trust me; a storm is definitely brewing. And this is just the calm before it hits."

Laverne jerked, gave Thomas a knowing look, and said, "Ah, hell!"

What the MI6 commander and the other agents did not know was that Kasun's men had queried residents in nearly every hamlet, village, and town from Marmande to Paris and then to Luzern about whether they had seen the likes of a woman fitting Priscilla's description traveling with a matronly woman and a big baby boy. It took nearly four weeks for them to finally catch up with the entourage. Finally, they spotted the villa and began monitoring the intelligence agents' and the guardsmen's routines. But Kasun's men were unaware that, by this time, the intelligence agents and the guardsmen wanted them to catch up to them, after which they would continue their trek to their third and last safe house, or so was the plan. For the time being, though, even Priscilla questioned the agents' strategy.

That night, after everyone had enjoyed another delicious meal, Priscilla and her household staff slept soundly until around 3:00 A.M., when Priscilla instinctively awoke with dread. As she got out of bed, she heard gunshots outside the villa. She hurriedly slipped into jeans, a sweater, and boots, reached under her bed, and grabbed her holster with the Glock securely fastened in it. She then headed toward the stairs, where Thomas, Laverne, and several other agents stood at the base, holding up their hands, signaling her to halt.

When she said, "Where's Austin? I've got to get to my son," the front door swung open. One of the guardsmen strode across the threshold with what looked like a heavy package. Whatever he carried wiggled and cried like a baby. Priscilla could hardly believe her eyes and ears. It was young Austin wrapped in his blanket. Priscilla almost fell down the stairwell. She saw two more guardsmen escorting someone who looked like Nanny Hettie. Priscilla was torn between crying and laughing. She recognized the nightclothes, bedroom slippers, and beautiful head of thick, long, salt-n-pepper hair. It was indeed Hettie. Her hands were tied, and her mouth gagged.

"My God!" Priscilla shouted. "How the devil did that happen?"

But there was more.

She then saw two hard-life-looking men and another who looked out of place being shoved into the dimly lit foyer, their hands held high. They were followed by three guardsmen, their rifles raised to the ready, one of whom spoke to Thomas and Laverne: "Fell right into our trap. Should I stash 'em in the cellar?"

"For the time being," Thomas said, waving them away.

At that point, Laverne beckoned Priscilla to come down the stairs. Then she and Priscilla caught up with the guardsmen who carried Austin and escorted Hettie.

Laverne spoke out of the corner of her mouth. "With this little maneuver of theirs, it looks like we're gonna have to push up our clock a bit."

Walking hurriedly alongside her, Priscilla's remarks confirmed Laverne's earlier suspicions. "I was wondering when we'd make our move 'cause this little rattrap has just gotten outta' hand."

Laverne stopped in her tracks, and before she knew it, she said, "What'd you just say?"

"I said, 'I was wondering—'"

"I thought that was what you said." For the first time, Laverne questioned how Priscilla knew about their game plan. Indeed, she thought Priscilla talked like an agent. And before the night would end, she would be so enlightened.

After entering the dining room, Thomas and Laverne removed the gag from Hettie's mouth and untied her hands. They allowed her time to collect herself. She

102

was, after all, mildly sedated. As she regained consciousness, she sobbed. Melissa handed her a cup of tea, which Hettie almost spilled as she reached for it. Like most people, Hettie had never been abducted. Nor had she ever been tied up and gagged. For sure, she had never been in the company of the type of men who had just tried to abduct her and baby Austin. Hettie had spent her adult life in the comfort, the serenity, and the safety of the Bernhardts of Bow Lake. But all of that had changed for her, Melissa, and Shelton, too, for that matter. While Hettie sat nervously sipping her tea, Laverne asked her to tell her what had happened.

"I was almost asleep across from Master Austin's crib when suddenly, out of nowhere, a strange man was leaning over me. I closed my eyes because I thought I was having a nightmare. Then I smelt something awful on my face, and rough hands pulled me out of bed. I felt groggy when I tried to open my eyes again, like I'd taken sleeping pills or something." Her hands shook so uncontrollably at the memory that her teacup rattled in its saucer.

Laverne tried to calm her. "It's all right, Nanny Hettie. Take your time. You're doing just fine."

Given what Hettie said, Laverne and Thomas looked at each other. *Chloroform*, they must have thought.

"My dear Nanny Hettie, do try to pull yourself together," Thomas said, not unkindly. Then he asked her, "What happened next? Do you remember?"

Hettie smiled at him and spoke more confidently. "I remember being taken somewhere. But my legs were so weak, and I was so groggy." She looked around as if searching for someone. She spotted Priscilla holding Austin. "Oh, Madame PJ, I'm so sorry. I honestly don't know what else happened." Priscilla smiled and waved Austin's chubby hands at her. Hettie seemed relieved that the child was fine and that Priscilla was not upset with her.

"Hmm," Thomas muttered as he thought about what Nanny Hettie had said.

Laverne asked her British colleague, "Now, what's that supposed to mean?"

"Well, it appears to me that our perps are astute enough to know that if they take the baby, they also need the nanny. And I suppose you can deduce the rest on your own." Then, the two agents looked at Priscilla because they now knew for sure that Zulfika Kasun's strategy had involved her and Austin all along. But Priscilla had long since figured out that much on her own.

As the agents relived the events of the wee hours, no one bothered to ask how Kasun's cronies had gotten past the guardsmen in the first place. That was because they had set a trap for precisely what had happened.

But Priscilla was troubled, as she pretended to play with her son, that some dangerous men, other than Kasun's cronies at his Marmande villa, were on the hunt for her. They were hardly likely to treat her, her son, or her household staff like Kasun's other men had treated them thus far. Priscilla was also keenly aware that the situation in Bosnia and Herzegovina was beyond that of a tinderbox and that even the American "observers" and their Western allies were uncertain about what else to expect. Mostly, though, she knew that Kasun would stop at nothing to get her to help him carry out his plan, whatever it was.

But she did not know that the Yugoslav general had ordered three dangerous men to accompany Kasun, or his decoy, on his return trip to France and that those men were much more despicable than the hard-life-looking ones that the guardsmen at the Luzern safe house had just apprehended.

When Priscilla had heard enough, she stood with Austin straddled on her hip and spoke matter-of-factly: "Okay, folks. I'm game. Since it is I whom he seeks, serve me up."

"What!" Laverne shouted. Holding her chest, she could not believe what Priscilla had just said.

Priscilla stared Laverne down and snapped back. "You heard me. Get Melissa, Shelton, Nanny Hettie, and my son out of here. Then, invite the bloody bastard to come here and state his business. I'll take it from there."

Outraged, Laverne shouted, "Have you lost your right mind!"

"Yes, I have."

"Missy, why—we can't just serve you up like a lobster on a platter!"

"Oh, but you can, and you will. Besides, I'm already the bait, so let's stop pretending and end this little charade. Kasun already knows my deadline is the latter part of June. And with time running out, we need some idea of his game plan." She turned around, and this time, she stared Thomas down and asserted, "Don't you agree?"

To Laverne's dismay, the MI6 commander agreed with Priscilla. "I do indeed," adding, "but you do realize you're taking some serious risks."

"I do," she said, handing a cheerful Austin back to the guardsman. "Put my baby back in his crib. I think he'll be safe there for now." The man hefted the baby boy and headed out of the room; Austin was as playful as if riding his favorite pony.

Laverne resumed trying to talk her out of it, but Priscilla raised her hand, silencing her.

Laverne stopped talking.

"Then it's decided." Priscilla looked at Thomas and the others. "Now, here's what I propose...."

Laverne suddenly realized Priscilla was not behaving like a courier or special envoy but rather a secret agent, mainly because she offered her own life "in service to her country," if necessary. Laverne and the others still did not know that Priscilla was, in fact, one of them, only that she suddenly behaved like them. Still, she and Thomas had their growing suspicions.

Then came Melissa's surprise: "Where my mistress goes, I go."

Shelton piped up next. "That goes for me, too. The Bernhardts entrusted me to protect Madame PJ, and I fully intend to do just that."

The agents and guardsmen all looked back and forth from Melissa to Shelton and at one another in astonishment.

"Now, mind you, I'm scared as hell," Melissa said. "But I will not return to Bow Lake and face Master EC and Lady Chelsea without Madame PJ."

"Roger that," Shelton echoed. "Master Carlton told me there would be days like this. Besides, when the terrorists raided our estate, Master EC took a bullet, and the assassins killed my friend, Ace Witherspoon. Nah, I'm not cutting bait and running. Whatever you want me to do, I'll do it."

At that, Laverne, Thomas, and the others witnessed how tightly knit the Bernhardt household staff were.

But everyone was taken aback when Hettie accidentally knocked her teacup over and when, in a cracked voice, she said, "And don't leave me out. How can I ever raise Master Austin if I tell him I ran out on his mother?"

With the strength of her convictions reinforced, Priscilla readied herself for whatever lay ahead. In the words of the CF boys, "Game on."

A few minutes later, she sat at her computer typing a simple message. During a crash training session at Langley some time ago, she learned that whenever an agent is unaware of the circumstances or what to expect, to be as simple as possible with whatever one does. Since Priscilla already knew she was the conduit between Zulfika Kasun and the American government, she invited him to play for whatever he wanted. Her message read:

> To: Zulfika Kasun
> From: New Writer Friend
> Re: Dinner Invitation
> Date: 9 April 1992

> The honor of your company is requested for an afternoon of fine dining at my humble abode in Luzern on Friday, 12 April, at 3:00.
>   Your choice of cuisine.

> Two chefs will be on hand at all times. You may
> bring two chefs, as well, but no more. We have a
> saying, "Too many chefs spoil the broth."

PJAB

After she printed her invitation (encrypted message) to Kasun, she showed it to Laverne, who read it and, in turn, showed it to the other agents.

"He's fluent in English," Priscilla said. "So there's no need for translation."

The MI6 commander looked at Priscilla. "So, I take it you're allowing him to establish the ground rules?"

"Yes."

When Priscilla thought she had made herself clear, she told them, "Bring up one of his men from the cellar, preferably the one who looked out of place. No need putting any of our guys on the line."

Then, quite unexpectedly, Commander Thomas told her, "When Kasun returned from Sarajevo, he was accompanied by three loathsome men who rape, maim, and murder anybody anywhere without conscience. We're certain they will accompany him to your dinner invitation. Do you understand what I'm saying?"

"I do."

Priscilla's mind flashed back to some loathsome men she had encountered over the years: Moses Cameron in the dungeon of the Anglican Cathedral in Harare, Damien Escoffery in the Rustenburg Platinum mine near Pretoria, and the Arab Islamic man in the bunker in Amman. So, this would not be the first time she would face despicable men. But Thomas and the others had no way of knowing about those encounters or any others. Although Laverne knew about Priscilla's encounter with Damien Escoffery, that was about all she knew.

Commander Thomas was emphatic.

"Do you also understand that you'll likely have undesirable company until sometime in June, maybe longer, and that it is also highly likely you'll find yourself traipsing throughout war-torn Bosnia and Herzegovina, not to mention other parts of that tinderbox?" He arched an eyebrow and stared at her intensely.

"I understand."

Laverne disagreed again.

"I object. Do you hear me? I object to this—" But she piped down when she remembered her role as Priscilla's double.

After those exchanges, Commander Thomas sent an agent to deliver Priscilla's invitation to the man sequestered in the cellar who looked out of place.

They freed him and watched as he headed back to Kasun's villa in Marmande, and they put a tail on him, too. The man's name was Afan Kljujic. He was a middle-aged man of refined comportment, standing about six feet tall. His well-trimmed black hair was parted down the middle, and he wore fashionable silver spectacles. Although dressed in the same dark clothing as the other men, it was clear that he was out of place. He did not even carry a weapon. The agents questioned his role in the bungled attempt to abduct the baby and Hettie. So, they agreed with Priscilla to allow him to deliver her invitation.

After Afan Kljujic left, the agents all went into a room on the other side of the villa, where they devised a strategy to support Priscilla's plan and to counteract any counter-play Kasun might contrive. They also interrogated the other two captives before driving them to a nearby village and leaving them to fend for themselves.

19

ONTO THEIR TRAIL

If Afan Kljujic thought his recent experience with the hard-life-looking men who had attempted to abduct Hettie and baby Austin was traumatic, he was about to experience something more traumatizing. As he entered the foyer of Zulfika Kasun's Marmande villa—his home for the past several months—he saw three heavily armed men he did not know but immediately recognized as evil. Like the guardsmen at Priscilla's Luzern villa, they carried heavy weaponry; pistols protruded from their underarm holsters, and knives were strapped onto their leather waistbands. Yet, unlike the guardsmen at Priscilla's Luzern villa, these men were loathsome. They raped, maimed, and murdered without conscience. Nor did they practice proper hygiene. Most significantly, as far as Afan knew, none of these men were here when he had set out with the others for Luzern the other day.

It took him a moment to muster the courage to speak.

"I'm Afan Kljujic, the lieutenant's assistant. I have a message from the American, his 'new writer friend.'" Why he introduced himself was curious because he was Kasun's manservant. But Afan was confused and unnerved by the three men and wondered why they were there, and he was too afraid to ask.

One of them led him down the hall. They stopped at the door to the lieutenant's study. When Afan reached for the doorknob, the man pushed him aside. Then he banged on the door, which Afan found odd.

"Enter," someone said.

The man opened the door and shoved Afan inside. By this point, Afan was even more confused and frightened because he had always had direct access to the lieutenant and had never been manhandled. He walked cautiously to the man seated at the desk, who he thought was Zulfika Kasun. Afan was so sure it was Kasun that he did not even look at his face. He kept his eyes down as he hurried across the room. He could barely speak, partly out of fear at the presence of the despicable men and from his lingering distressing experience at the Luzern villa, until finally, he said, "Sir, I bring a message from your 'new writer friend.' It's an invitation."

As it turned out, the Yugoslav lieutenant was so paranoid that he had more than one decoy—which one this was was anybody's guess. If only he had known that the despicable men—who now occupied the Marmande villa—took their orders from someone else—the general—who had ordered them to escort the lieutenant, whichever one he was, back to France and report his every move to him. But the general had done more.

Earlier, when the hard-life-looking men told the second Kasun decoy that they had an errand and needed Afan as their guide, he had had little choice but to consent. But they did not tell him they required Afan's assistance to help identify Priscilla, whom Afan had only seen from a distance once when she had visited the first Kasun impersonator. Nevertheless, none of them knew the agents at the Luzern safe house had anticipated their attempted abduction of young Austin, so the first part of the general's plan had backfired.

The second Kasun impersonator snatched the invitation from Afan's hand. He had wracked his brain trying to devise a scheme to get close to Priscilla but to no avail. But in his hand was a message from the person who had hitherto eluded him. Over the past six weeks, he had grown despondent about locating the elusive American special envoy. But he was mostly distressed about circumventing the despicable replacements the general had recruited. For sure, he was unaware of their orders. As he read the invitation, a smile came over his face, after which he flicked a cigarette lighter and burned it in an ashtray. He did not want anyone else to see it. He had already devised a scheme that involved a trip up North for a secret meeting with an American reporter, which he had told the general about shortly before he departed from Bosnia and Herzegovina, "where I will feed the Americans and their Western allies news that the Bosniak leader, not Milosevic, is perpetrating those atrocities that the biased Western media have attributed to our side."

For now, however, he instructed Afan to prepare for his trip to Luzern on the day and time specified in Priscilla's invitation. Then he waved him away. Although Afan had no way of knowing it, that would be his last significant conversation with the man he believed was Zulfika Kasun.

Back at the Luzern safe house, Priscilla busied herself thinking of all kinds of stories she suspected Kasun would feed her about the escalating atrocities in the

Yugoslav tinderbox. She psyched herself to focus primarily on what she thought he wanted her to convey to the authorities in Washington. Although Kasun was unaware of her work as a secret agent, he played off her highly recognized persona, which was equally bad from her perspective. But not even she anticipated what the loathsome men now stationed at Kasun's Marmande villa would do, for they operated by an entirely different set of rules, protocols, and modus operandi than she. Nevertheless, Priscilla was about to learn how to play poker, something she was less than enthused about, primarily because she had yet to acquire patience for playing the game, but not for long.

At CIA headquarters in Langley, Deputy Director Froley paced the floor of his office. He had second thoughts about using Priscilla as the conduit to Yugoslav Lieutenant Zulfika Kasun, a military intelligence officer, someone he suspected would break under insurmountable pressure from the notorious Serbian leader and his generals. But each time he thought about it, something told him that Priscilla could handle this assignment as effectively as she had handled all her prior ones. But as he pictured her new baby boy, his mind drifted into horrible ruminations.

His thoughts were interrupted by someone banging on his door.

"Come in."

It was Agent B.

"Jim!" shouted the unwelcome visitor, "I've given you more than enough rope. Now, out with it. Where exactly is Missy? And what are your plans to get her the hell outta there?" Carlton knew Priscilla's whereabouts precisely. Besides Shelton's routine updates, he knew Priscilla wore a tracking device. But Carlton wanted the deputy director to confirm her whereabouts.

Jim Froley finally came clean with the disgruntled agent, who was not impressed with what he learned. Nevertheless, Carlton made a few discreet phone calls and put his people onto the trail of Priscilla, baby Austin, and the household staff. However, he was unaware that his contacts were the very people the deputy director had in mind, the CF boys, of which he was one.

Back at Bow Lake, Father, Lady Chelsea, Ramses, and Jamison quarreled because they had not heard from Priscilla or any of the household staff who accompanied her. It had now been six weeks.

Lady Chelsea fretted. "Something's not right, I tell you. This is so unlike all of them."

"I hear you, My Sweets." Father struggled to find something positive to say. "But someone will contact us soon. So, let's try to be more patient. Besides, they're probably having the time of their lives." He smiled at her.

Also smiling, "My point precisely," Ramses said. "Whenever any of them are having fun, we almost always get a phone call in the middle of the night or early in the morning because they forget about the differences in the time zones."

But Ramses' tone quickly shifted. "But EC, old man," he spoke this time more soberly, "it's been six weeks, and we haven't heard a single word from any of them. At the very least, one of the staff would've checked in. I'm with Lady Chelsea on this one. We need to put some of our people on this."

On the same wavelength as Ramses, Father nodded. Like Carlton, Ramses made several discreet telephone calls and put some of his people onto Priscilla, young Austin, and the household staff's trail, and they were not the CF boys.

In Sills Creek, Illinois, Liza and Cousin Myrtle were having a similar discussion.

"But I tell you, Myrt, something's wrong. Terribly wrong. It's been six weeks and not a word from Priscilla. This is so unlike her," Liza insisted. Frown lines etched across her forehead. At age sixty-three and under five feet tall, Liza was an attractive woman who, like her daughters, looked younger than she was. The only thing giving away her age was her salt-and-pepper hair, which she now anxiously ran her fingers through.

To soothe her, Cousin Myrtle said, "All right, Liza, what do you suggest we do? Should we call her in-laws in Bow Lake? And, well, should we tell her about Helen? You know," Myrtle paused, "about her condition?"

"Not yet, Myrt." Liza shook her head vigorously. This was not the time to bring up Helen. Like all her daughters, Helen was unique. Attractive like Priscilla, but Helen was taller. And because of her pale complexion, ginger freckles, hazel eyes, and long sandy brown hair with blond streaks, she was often mistaken to be Caucasian. Highly intelligent but emotionally unstable, Helen struggled with mental illness.

Liza, like Priscilla, sometimes compartmentalized different aspects of her life, but not this time. When she could get a private moment away from Cousin Myrtle, she would call her friend, FBI Agent Marvin Rothschild, and tell him about her missing daughter and grandson, after which he would make discreet calls and put some of his people onto their trail. Liza and Agent Rothschild's relationship spanned many years, beginning with Priscilla's abduction to southern Africa in the summer of 1986. Liza valued their relationship. She only called her friend when she needed him. When she called him, Agent Rothschild was on the case.

112

20

THE PLOY

Priscilla was in Switzerland during the collapse of communism in Eastern Europe, notably the collapse of the former Soviet Union, which precipitated the collapse of the tenuously unified Yugoslav state. The latter's collapse was sparked by the death of Josip Broz Tito, who unified the country at the end of World War II after breaking away from the Soviet sphere and establishing a less repressive communist regime. But when Tito died, the regime unraveled, and American interest in the state waned.

Enter Slobodan Milosevic.

As head of the Serbian Communist Party, Milosevic was in the right place at the right time when he addressed some disgruntled Serbians in Albanian-controlled Kosovo. When he stripped Kosovo and Vojvodina of their constitutionally guaranteed autonomy within Serbia, the local leaders resigned. Shortly after that, the Montenegro leadership was replaced with Milosevic supporters, and Milosevic gained influence with the Western media, which was nonsensical.

Almost simultaneously, Slovenia and Croatia gave pro-democracy political parties control of their governments, taking precedence over Yugoslav law. However, the transfer of power, especially political power, does not always happen smoothly, such as in Bosnia and Herzegovina, where a civil war ensued.

As it turned out, the Yugoslav tinderbox erupted while the Americans marshaled "limited coordination," and the Western Europeans maintained a wait-and-see attitude. As such, inter-republic relations spiraled out of control, enabling Milosevic's ascension into power.

Something even more unexpected happened as if it were possible. Unbeknown to Lieutenant Zulfika Kasun, the hard-life-looking and loathsome men sent to accompany his second decoy to the Marmande villa had their orders.

While Priscilla busied herself imagining all kinds of stories that she suspected the Yugoslav lieutenant would feed her, her "new writer friend," or whoever he was, began his trip to meet with her at her Luzern villa.

The second Kasun decoy was happy to have departed the Marmande villa, where he had felt like a prisoner. Apart from the driver and himself, two other men sat in the back of the gray Mercedes turbo sedan. When they came within twenty-seven kilometers of Luzern, he spotted a flock of beautiful birds swarming about the snowcapped treetops. Just as he turned to get a better look at them, one of the men in the backseat removed something from his coat pocket and wrapped it around the decoy's neck, choking him to death. Regrettably, the decoy never once thought that the general would issue a kill order on him. How wrong he was.

The driver exited the highway along a snow-covered road to an out-of-the-way farm, where the other men tossed the remains of the second Kasun impersonator onto the snow-covered ground like roadkill. Then, they continued to Luzern. But why? What did the men hope to gain without Kasun—the real one or another decoy? Priscilla and the others at the Luzern safe house were about to find out.

Back in the States at Langley, CIA Deputy Director Froley thought about how America sometimes mistakenly granted asylum or accepted defectors who were decoys, doubles, and impersonators, not the persons they claimed to be. One would have thought they had learned their lesson, particularly from the numerous Germans and Japanese who had defected or sought asylum following World War II, lest one forget the Russians and military officers and scientists from many other countries. Along those lines, neither Priscilla nor her colleagues had thought much about that possibility, but not much longer. Whether she knew it, validating the man's identity was one of the primary reasons the deputy director had assigned her to this mission in the first place. Since Priscilla was adept at discerning minor discrepancies, her main task was to weed him out, that is, to determine whether he was even a suitable commodity to grant asylum.

Friday, April 12, at the appointed time, 3:00 P.M., Priscilla was on edge; something was wrong.

"Something's not right, I tell you. That man is a stickler for time. For one thing, he would come early or call," she said to Laverne and the other agents who sat with her in her study.

When there was no phone call, and it was now 3:15, Priscilla and the others knew something was wrong for sure.

Close to 3:30, someone banged on the front door of the Luzern villa. Hamish, one of the British agents, opened it. When he asked, "Who's calling?" one of the loathsome men who had just killed the Kasun decoy shoved his way past him.

The other two followed him inside when one of them shouted, "Where is he? Lieutenant Kasun came ahead. Where is he?" the man repeated himself.

"Excuse me!" Hamish bellowed, gripping his pistol handle. "Folks," he yelled, "we have a situation on our hands!"

Then, Hamish, his hand still on his pistol handle, and the three loathsome men watched as Thomas and the other British and French agents, Priscilla, and the CIA agents without Laverne—because Priscilla and Laverne rarely appeared together—assembled in the foyer where they were as baffled by the three despicable men pretending to be baffled and accusing them of hiding Kasun.

Seeing the men, Priscilla cringed and thought, *Dangerous, despicable, evil, and loathsome, all rolled up into one.* She had never seen men like these up close and personal, not in southern Africa, the United Arab Emirates, among people experiencing homelessness on the streets of New York, or anywhere else she could recall. The men were dressed in tattered, drab-colored coats and well-worn boots. Unclean fingers stuck out from the holes in their gloves. Although unshaven, gashes and pot marks were visible. Mostly, though, they carried themselves like they were ready for mêlée. At the time, Priscilla was unaware of the extent of the devastation in the neighboring Eastern European countries, where people starved and struggled to survive amid civil war and untold acts of violence wrought by the likes of Milosevic. So, these men, the sight of whom made Priscilla cringe, worked in whatever capacity to generate income, including raping, maiming, and murdering for a livelihood. Save for the missing Yugoslav Army uniform, such was the crux of the Yugoslav Army.

"Hmm," Priscilla said as Commander Thomas and the others looked on.

Then she whispered. "Never saw this one coming. So-o, what do ya suppose happened to Kasun?"

"Don't know for sure," Thomas whispered back. "But I have my suspicions." He paused. "But these, Madame PJ, are the kinds of men I forewarned you about."

Priscilla did not comment.

There was a time in her life when, if someone called her out, she would charge full speed ahead. However, life circumstances and her time with the CIA had taught her otherwise. So, when one of the men fingered her and said, "*You*, Missus Austin-Bernhardt, where hide him?" she snubbed him.

"To hell with you, blokes. I don't know any of you, anyway. So, get the hell outta my house." She turned away and headed back to her study as if she had been rudely interrupted.

As she walked away, the three loathsome men rushed at her, only to be stopped by the agents who had gathered in the foyer. The loathsome men were outnumbered three to one as some agents grabbed them while the others pointed their weapons at them. At that, they knew they could not get to Priscilla. So they held their hands in surrender, turned around, and slowly walked back out.

But they had seen Priscilla, and she wore a weapon and hardly behaved like an ordinary woman or a writer or a special envoy, at that. So when they got a chance, they would report what they had observed about P. J. Austin-Bernhardt to the general, who reported to the president. Score one for the bad guys.

Shortly after the three loathsome men departed the Luzern safe house, Laverne and Thomas received messages from their colleagues in the field who had tailed Afan Kljujic back to Kasun's villa in Marmande and who had then tailed the three men as they had driven the second Kasun-decoy to that farm, watched as they had disposed of his remains, and then as they had come to the Luzern villa.

"What!" Laverne yelled into her phone.

"What!" Thomas yelled into his.

Alternatively, "Yes," both callers said.

Again, alternatively, both callers said: "We examined the corpse, took photos, extracted DNA samples, and transmitted it to Langley, MI6, and Interpol."

After that update, Laverne, Thomas, and the other agents assembled in Priscilla's study. When they told her what they had just learned, she knew something more sinister was afoot, and she feared her worst nightmare: that it had something to do with young Austin. If she had only known that that part of the ploy had nothing to do with her son. Indeed, the general was sending Kasun a message that he was aware of his decoys. Otherwise, the ploy, which was, in fact, conceived by the real Zulfika Kasun—but valuable to the general as well—was to obtain vital intel on Priscilla, which she eventually figured out. But before she could put her thoughts into words, Laverne spoke.

"I wonder where the real Kasun is? Or is *he* the dead man?"

Ignoring Laverne's question, Priscilla said, "Has it occurred to anyone that that little ploy was their way of finding out the extent to which this place is secured? To see how many of us there are *and* to see *me* up close and personal."

The telephone rang, which was odd because virtually no one knew the number to the Luzern villa—well, except the intelligence agents and the second Kasun impersonator who had received Priscilla's invitation. Melissa answered the call.

"Madame PJ, it's for you."

Priscilla took the phone. "Yes, PJ here. Who's calling, please?"

The caller introduced himself: "Madame Austin-Bernhardt, Afan Kljujic speaking, Monsieur Kasun's assistant. I delivered your invitation to him." He paused, unsure how to proceed, and then blurted out, "Has Monsieur Kasun arrived? Something's not right. He usually checks in periodically, especially when he arrives at his appointments."

As it so happened, not even Afan knew that the man whose face he had not seen may not have been who he pretended to be.

"Oh, dear me." Priscilla put her hand over the mouthpiece and looked at Laverne. "It's Afan Kljujic, the man who delivered my invitation to Kasun or whoever the devil he was. He wants to know if Kasun has arrived."

Laverne snatched the phone from Priscilla's hand. "Afan, Zulfika Kasun has not yet arrived." She slammed the phone down. Then, she watched Priscilla walk out of the study without as much as "Excuse me" or "I'll return shortly."

She headed to her son's nursery, where she soon stood over his crib and said, "I'm not sure what's happening, but I declare it's you they want. I only wish I knew how to protect you." She felt her legs give way. Just as quickly, she grabbed the crib railing and held on as if for dear life. Her hands shook. She had just shafted a dangerous man, knowing he would retaliate.

On her knees now, she prayed. "O thou, in whose presence my soul takes delight, On whom in affliction I call, My comfort by day, and my song in the night, My hope, my salvation, my all!"

Priscilla was a preacher's kid and often prayed for guidance. One big difference was that while most people asked God to do their bidding, Priscilla asked God to give her the wherewithal to do what was necessary.

Finished praying, she stood back up and looked lovingly at her son, who slept soundly in his crib. Feeling more at peace, she was nonetheless fully aware that Austin was targeted to coerce her to negotiate whatever terms the Yugoslav lieutenant wanted from the Americans. Beyond the shadow of a doubt, Priscilla knew that her life, her son's life, and the lives of the others with her were in grave danger. She prepared herself for whatever lay ahead. She had not only asked God to protect her son; she had girded herself to engage the enemy.

21

SHEDDING LIGHT ON THE SITUATION

Everyone noticed Priscilla's absence at dinner.

The atmosphere was tense following the three loathsome men's unwelcome and baffling visit, especially after everyone learned that Kasun, or his decoy, had been murdered by his own men. Even though MI6 Commander Thomas had doubled the agents on the inside and outside, Priscilla's absence at dinner was quite disturbing, particularly for Melissa.

"And when I offered to bring her meal to her room," Melissa told all those gathered at the dinner table, "she waved me away. I'm worried about Madame PJ."

But Laverne, Thomas, and the others knew Priscilla was mentally preparing herself for whatever lay ahead.

While they all sat silently, Sam—who knew Priscilla quite well and had been listening at the door—limped inside the room.

"Ahem. I believe I can shed some light on the situation." Though no one knew how he had come about his injury, no one asked because they somehow knew Sam had sustained it in the line of duty. He pulled a chair from under the table and slid down in it, after which Laverne, Thomas, and the others asked questions. Lots of questions. Sam raised his hand to silence them.

Massaging his limp leg, he looked around the massive table and spoke matter-of-factly. "First of all, sequestering herself away isn't unusual for PJ. She needs her quiet time and space to think. And by now, you're acutely aware her looks are deceiving. But you already know that. Now, don't you?"

Sam became animated. "Her petite and youthful appearance is an excellent camouflage for her because her marks don't take her seriously." He chuckled. "She looks twenty-something but is in her late thirties, maybe older."

"Really!" Thomas exclaimed.

Sam nodded. "And she's a bit of a chameleon, isn't she?" He looked from one side to the other and noticed everyone's anticipation. Then he shared similar information that CIA Director Roberts called "intriguing bedside reading."

"Who among us is pure in whatever you think your ethnicity or race? Well, PJ is West African on both sides of her family. But she's British on her paternal side and Irish on her maternal side. Added to that, she's Choctaw on her paternal side and Cherokee on her maternal side."

While Sam talked, the others all leaned forward.

"Back home in America, PJ is classified as Black or African American. But there's no way a multicultural or multiracial person can properly identify themselves on census forms. At least," he paused and said, "I don't think so."

"Our girl brings all that and her talents to the table."

He snickered as he explained: "She can wear her hair in all kinds of styles. Sometimes, it's curly, Afro, straight, buzz-cut…. I've even seen her with a Marine-style haircut. Ha! Ha! Ha!" Little did Sam know the significance of the tidbits about Priscilla's hairstyles.

"So that's why she looks the way she does!" Thomas said as if he had reached a remarkable conclusion.

While Sam explained how well he knew Priscilla, Laverne thought she had been the one who knew her best. But she was learning that was not the case. Even though many around the table suspected she posed as Priscilla's decoy, no one dared comment about that obvious observation.

Not liking that Sam knew more about her ward than she knew, Laverne asked, "And how is it *you* know all that?"

"I have my sources."

Sam's assignment was to share information about Priscilla with the others, which he now does.

"Don't think she's sporting that Glock for a fashion statement. She's as good a marksman as any of us."

Laverne spoke up again. "And you know that how?"

"Some time ago, I was with her on a weather-beaten ferry on Lake Kariba in Zimbabwe," he paused and looked around him again, "where I watched her shoot and kill crocodiles." Sam paused long enough for his words to sink in.

Meanwhile, learning all of this about their mistress for the first time, Melissa, standing against the wall, flinched. "Oh, no! Crocodiles?"

Hettie clung to the agent seated beside her.

Shelton leaned forward for more.

Sam continued briefing them.

"That's where I almost lost my leg," he patted it and noted, "PJ tended to my wounds against my screams and bawling at the thought of losing it, not to mention the piercing pain. As you've noticed, she's good under pressure, too."

Sam paused again while everyone absorbed this new information.

"And," he told his attentive audience, "she has an incredibly high threshold for pain. One time, a man as big as any of us brutally beat her. But PJ got the last laugh because she tossed a vial of oil of vitriol in the man's face."

At that point, everyone noticed Melissa's curiosity, so someone elaborated, "An acid." But that frightened her more as she clung to the wall behind her.

"Oh, my goodness!" Hettie said, her hand at her mouth.

"And then?" Shelton said, eager to learn more.

Sam stunned everyone when he recited the names of notorious criminals that Priscilla had either helped to apprehend or executed herself. Afrikaners Damien Escoffery, Moses Cameron, and Ian Saunders (Saperstein) led the list.

"Wow!" and "No kidding!" said the typically poker-faced agents.

But Melissa wanted to know, "What's an Afrikaner?"

"White South Africans," someone said matter-of-factly, hoping to move Sam's report along. And roll along, he did.

Sam told them about when Priscilla served as a special envoy with the emirs of the United Arab Emirates. "All that royalty," he said, shaking his head. "A plum assignment. A whole lot of senior State Department staffers were outraged that she was chosen over them."

"Wow!"

"My, My!"

"As for her photographic memory, which she takes for granted," Sam pointed out, "there is no need for cameras or tape recorders if she's around. PJ captures it all in her mind."

"Photographic memory! Who knew?" someone said.

Sam laughed again as if he enjoyed himself. Then, "Oh, yeah," he said, "She's ambidextrous, too."

"But she also has some well-known weaknesses: vertigo tops the list. And lest I forget," he added, as if this were an important point: "She's got this thing about people touching her."

Laverne, Melissa, Hettie, and Shelton were all well aware of that last bit.

So entranced, the room was dead silent as they waited for Sam to share more. But he was almost done.

Meanwhile, Laverne expressed her not-so-subtle dismay.

"Apart from PJ's race and ethnicity, bouts with vertigo, and dislike of people touching her, this is all news to me." One would have thought Priscilla's decoy already knew much of what Sam was saying, but Laverne was not privy to Priscilla's dossier or the bill of goods in more common parlance. More significantly, Laverne and the others now knew Priscilla was no ordinary special envoy but rather, like them, a secret agent.

Sam could have shared more. Instead, he twisted his lips and concluded. "But I gotta tell you, I'm not so sure what to expect in this situation."

"Thank you, Sam," MI6 Commander Thomas said with a stern expression. "This is useful intel … all of tremendous value. But now, we need to get our hands on a photo, some DNA, or something about the real Lieutenant Kasun. The man is a ghost; he rarely appears in photographs. Can't say that about his boss, though, not the general; I mean the president." They all laughed but soon grew silent again.

Stephen, one of the CIA agents, broke the silence. "So it's true. We have no idea what the target really looks like."

"No problem," Thomas explained, "PJ has long since known she's dealing with someone in the shadows."

Still, Stephen expressed his concern. "So we're basically grasping at the shadows," then quickly speculated, "My God, folks, he could've been one of the assailants who burst into this villa the other day." He stopped talking.

While the agents all pondered what Sam told them and what Thomas had just said, the household staff turned from one to the other, listening and learning about the secret life of their ever-mysterious Madame PJ. They now realized that Priscilla was more than the ordinary woman she portrayed, more than a PR consultant, and more than Master Carlton's wife. They felt immense pride in her; their resolve to stay with her strengthened.

But leave it to Melissa to ask the obvious.

"What I don't understand is what you all mean when you say that Zulfika Kasun was not, or is not, the man you thought he was. Are you saying the man in Marmande wasn't the real Zulfika Kasun?" Then, more forcefully, she said, "But we all saw him. We know what he looks like."

At that point, Laverne explained what she and her colleagues knew about the real Zulfika Kasun. "So you see, Melissa, we have a bit of a problem on our hands."

"I'll say." Then Melissa shocked everyone again when she said, "I always thought people did that kind of stuff in the movies, you know, like Ethan Hunt in *Mission Impossible*. I never imagined people actually doing that for real." While Melissa talked, the others in the room wondered why she did not question what she had learned about Priscilla, which, in their minds, was far more intriguing than Zulfika Kasun's doubles or Ethan Hunt, for that matter.

But Laverne—who knew the Bernhardts and their household staff better than the others—eventually addressed what the other agents suddenly realized: They had been discussing vital intel in the company of civilians. Upon the realization of that not-so-small leak by the buckets, "Let me be clear," she asserted, looking from Melissa to Shelton and then to Hettie. "You can never divulge what you're learning about your Madame PJ. Besides," she said with an air of authority, "no one will believe you anyway."

Then, the MI6 commander put a lid on the matter, or so he thought.

"You don't know anyone named Zulfika Kasun either. And none of us is here, not any of you either. For the record, you're all with your Madame PJ on her writing excursion in the South of France. Full stop."

Although Shelton, Hettie, and Melissa could not fully grasp what they had just learned about their Madame PJ, they would not forget any of it.

Melissa was the only household staffer who had spoken. Hettie fidgeted with her hands and periodically clung to the agent beside her. As for Shelton, he was not in the least concerned about the unwritten disclaimer or non-disclosure agreement. All the same, they were excited and scared out of their wits altogether. Perhaps they were naïve or, more likely, foolhardy. Nevertheless, frightened as they were, they were committed to doing whatever needed to be done to protect Priscilla and Austin. But unlike Melissa and Hettie, Shelton yearned for adventure and intrigue. He was willing to enter the fight in a much more physical way than Melissa or Hettie could. And he would. If Priscilla had only known what her household staff were up to, she would have insisted they return home immediately. She thought they merely wanted to demonstrate their loyalty to her. She had no idea how far they were willing to go.

The subject of their conversation sat at her dresser in her bedroom upstairs. She had a rush of thoughts. Her pen chased her thoughts as she recorded the events of the past six weeks. In intricate detail, she wrote about the getaway from her Marmande villa, what Laverne, Shelton, and Melissa told her about their trip to the City of Luzern, and the three loathsome men's baffling visit, which was clearly a ploy. She ended with: Who is Zulfika Kasun? Where is he? And what does he want from me?

Around 3:30 in the morning, Priscilla went downstairs, passing two agents doing night security duty. For the sheer fun of it, she said, "Gee fellas, you're sure up late." She entered her study, turned on her computer, and commenced typing where she had left off earlier.

As if having prepared herself to battle with someone in the shadows was not enough, she had no idea that she was about to experience one of those seemingly unbearable circumstances that she had never imagined, one that her wits and faith would provide the fortitude necessary to endure, at least for the time being.

While in Luzern, Switzerland, where Sam shed light on Priscilla's prowess to fulfill her mission with her colleagues—back in the States, in Sills Creek—Liza struggled with how she would shed light on Helen's declining mental health condition with Priscilla. It was late in the evening when she sat alone at her kitchen table and fidgeted with her hands, much as she had done on the evening when her husband Nelson died. Meanwhile, she had not heard from Priscilla in six weeks, and she needed to tell her about Helen, Priscilla's younger sister, too.

"Oh, Nelson, I wish you were here."

Liza had known for quite some time that Helen was not at herself. Helen rarely held a job for more than two or three years. Priscilla never understood her sister's work. A mathematical wizard and technologically savvy, similar to how the Black women at NASA created the computer program enabling John Glenn to orbit the Earth, Helen could calculate numbers in her head and program computers. More recently, she'd received a promotion at the Bennington Hutton Corporation, where she had worked for nearly five years. But then she abruptly left and brought Germane to Sills Creek and asked Liza to take care of him while she set about finding another job and home. Priscilla never questioned why her sister left so many jobs, especially since she always earned more income than she did as a college professor and sometimes even more in her work as a PR consultant. Instead, she assumed Helen possessed skills that were in high demand, and, well, she did.

Yet, since they did not live together, Priscilla did not know that Helen had hoarded things, such as clothes, furniture, books, and papers. She was also unaware of her sister's paranoia, thinking that people did not like her. As for her paranoia, the Austin clan had brushed off her "unusual" behavior. "She's always been different," "a bit high-strung," and "That's just Helen" were often their responses when word reached them that Helen had been acting strangely.

But this time, a few days after Helen and Germane moved in with her, Liza had happened upon her daughter, who was alone in her bedroom but carrying on a conversation as if someone else were present.

Some three weeks later, it was all made plain to her. Since she was listed as Helen's next of kin, Liza received a phone call informing her that Helen was in the mental health ward of the local hospital. She almost dropped the telephone.

After she pulled herself together, she met with Helen's primary care physician and two psychiatrists at the hospital. The doctors told her that although Helen was in good physical health, she suffered from several mental illnesses. Topping the list were bipolar disorder, psychoses, paranoia, delusion, early Alzheimer's, and something else Liza could not recall. Although it was a well-known fact that many doctors misdiagnosed Black people as "bipolar," Helen was, indeed, bipolar. The doctors also told Liza that Helen's condition would worsen. They said something else about psychotherapy and neurology. Most revealing to Liza was the news that Helen had "suffered these mental abnormalities all of her life and that some of it was genetic."

"My goodness! How on Earth could I have missed all that?" As Liza thought about it, she had no idea what could have "triggered" Helen's "breakdown," all terms the doctors had used.

The doctors surmised that Liza and the rest of the Austin family had been in denial about Helen's apparent mental disorders for years. "Most families," one of the doctors said, "tend to attribute such symptoms to 'sibling rivalries,' or maybe even that she was 'just different,' common misconceptions and excuses that many families attribute to the 'unusual' or inexplicable behavior by a loved one."

But when one of the physicians told Liza to "look into legal guardianship, arrange temporary in-home healthcare support services, and find an assisted-living accommodation for your daughter," she had nearly come undone.

Ordinarily, Liza would have called Cousin Myrtle, but not this time. Instead, she kept the intricate details about Helen's mental health disorders in her immediate family. She would inform Cousin Myrtle later.

Her first call was to her two other daughters, Harriet and Camille. When she told them, neither could believe their ears. Shortly, the siblings visited, and they, like Liza, fretted over how and when to break the news to Priscilla, who they thought was in Marmande, France, on holiday with her son Austin, "trying her hand at writing."

Then, one night after Harriet and Camille had returned to their respective homes, Liza called FBI Agent Rothschild again, and this time, she told him everything. Agent Rothschild understood the significance of Helen's well-being to Priscilla. The sisters were almost as close as twins. So he set about putting plans into place that would put people on Priscilla's trail.

As Liza sat at her kitchen table and thought about her conversation with the FBI agent, her grandson Germane entered. The young man knew she was deeply worried about his mother.

"Grandma, I already knew about Momma. She's acted a little off as far back as I can remember." Having spent much time with adults, Germane was immensely grown up for his nearly fifteen years of age.

"Oh, Son," Liza started crying, covering her face with her hands.

Germane wrapped his arms around her.

"Don't cry, Grandma. Everything will work itself out. Momma will be taken care of. Besides, she's got you and me. And when Aunt Priscilla finds out, she'll come through. But you already know that. Don't you?"

Germane and Liza then held each other for a long time.

22

UNEXPECTED GUESTS

After his second, more detailed conversation with Liza, FBI Agent Rothschild shared the information about Priscilla's sister with his longtime friend, CIA Deputy Director Froley. It had been that very information that provided Froley with a way to bring the CF agents into Priscilla's mission. And so it was that he, in turn, had shared it with "the boys." Therefore, if Priscilla kept her commission, which the deputy director knew she would, the CF's new orders were to facilitate her mission primarily as a backup, which was risky because of their increased age and the physical injuries they sustained from their time in the Balkans. Nevertheless, the deputy director was aware of their desire for at least one more mission before being relieved of their duties as special ops. Otherwise—save for the presence of the British and French secret agents—only Carlton and Angelo Delgato (called Angel) still qualified. On the other hand, however, no one knew how Laverne had gotten her assignment, especially since her injuries were more severe than the others.

Five senior CF special operatives were Priscilla's friends—Angel, Jeremy Onslow (called Onslow), Bartholomew Jordan (called Jordy), Laverne, and Tommy Wozniah (called Tommy) — "the boys." The other member of the tight-knit group was her husband, Carlton, whose role was limited, given their relationship. If, after hearing the news about her sister, Priscilla chose to relinquish her commission, Carlton would escort her home. Although each of "the boys" knew her somewhat differently, they assumed that after learning about her sister's illness, she would relinquish her commission. However, they did not know Priscilla was as entrenched in her work as they were. For sure, they were unaware of her rank as a secret agent. They knew her as a special envoy, whereas CIA Deputy Director Froley knew her as an exceptional special agent.

On a cold and snowy night, someone knocked on the front door of the Luzern safe house. When it was opened, five tall, handsome men, two leaning on canes, entered the foyer. They took off their hats, gloves, and ski jackets as if they had been expected.

While Henry, one of the night security officers, called MI6 Commander Thomas on his SAT phone, the visitors talked among themselves.

Pushing strands of black hair behind his ears and leaning on a cane he used because of a bullet wound sustained to his leg, Jordy asked his CF associates in a whisper, "So, what's the game plan if she refuses to leave?"

"Beats the hell out of me. I'll cross that bridge when I get there," Carlton said as he wrestled with how to convey the news about Helen's illness to his wife.

But Tommy, the CF commander, who almost always had the last word, declared, "If she doesn't take the news well, then all bets are off."

Their musings ended at the sight of the MI6 commander at the top of the stairwell—his blond hair disheveled. An unbuttoned shirt revealed his long johns. His brown leather boots were unlaced. His eyes were puffy and red. He had just managed to fall asleep and was not happy about being awakened.

While Thomas headed down the stairs, buttoning his shirt, the door to Priscilla's study opened. She was awake and dressed, her Glock clearly exposed. She did not carry the standard government-issued pistol. She preferred the G40 Gen4, which combined a full 6-inch barrel for improved velocity with a magazine capacity of 15 rounds, a powerful yet easily carried weapon.

During her first time in southern Africa, Onslow, a guardsman at the time, taught Priscilla survival skills. But Charlie, a.k.a. CF Commander Wozniah's manservant, taught her how to handle various firearms. It was following her recruitment into the CIA that she declared her preference for the G40 Gen4, which has since been her weapon of choice.

Priscilla and Thomas reached the five unexpected guests in the foyer at pretty much the same time. When she spotted Carlton, she ran to him and embraced him. She was so happy to see him. But she welled up as she held him. Then, because he had surprised her with his unexpected visit, she pulled away and gently slapped him. She hugged the others and did not even ask what they were doing there. Priscilla was no dummy; she knew they were up to something, and she would soon learn what. Nonetheless, she was so glad to see them. Although she still did not like people touching her, she had grown accustomed to touching or being touched by people she loved. So, "the boys" were pleased to see how much she had changed from being once distant and aloof to hugging them.

While an elated Priscilla greeted them, the sleep-deprived MI6 commander approached his American counterpart, CF Commander Wozniah, whom he already knew. The two men hugged and slapped shoulders, and then Tommy introduced the others to him.

After the greetings, the CF commander told Carlton—out of Priscilla's earshot—what Thomas had confirmed—that their sources had yet to confirm the identity of Zulfika Kasun, that Priscilla had offered herself up as bait, and that she had scheduled a meeting with the man presumed to be Zulfika Kasun, which did not happen. Agent B was not happy. But what could he do? Priscilla had her orders, and so too did he.

During their brief encounter with Priscilla and Thomas in the foyer, "the boys," including Carlton, pretended not to notice Priscilla wore a weapon, and she seemed comfortable wearing it, too.

Thomas and Priscilla led the CF agents to the dining room. Then Thomas ordered Ronnie, the guardsman who often served kitchen detail, to prepare a meal for their guests.

While Priscilla, Thomas, and the five visitors settled at the dinner table, the front door to the Luzern villa swung open again.

This time, five tall, handsome men of Mediterranean complexion—mainly dressed in Arab Islamic attire—entered. They removed their red-and-white keffiyehs, gloves, and woolen kanduras that covered their Western wear and stood at attention as if they had been expected.

Once again, while Henry called for Commander Thomas, the second group of unexpected guests talked among themselves while waiting.

"Why all the fuss for a writer?" Omar asked.

"Not just any writer," explained Commander Elias, "not only is she *PJ Austin*, but she's married to a *Bernhardt*. That's Lebanese *and* New England royalty!"

Only Commander Elias—the leader of the Lebanese agents in the General Directorate of General Security, a.k.a. "first bureau"—was aware of Priscilla's role "in service to her country."

Meanwhile, he reminded his team about Ramses' instructions: "'Check up on our girl. Confirm the circumstances of her, the child, and the household staff. But whatever you do, do not let on to her that her family is checking up on her.'" Although these five men from the Lebanese "first bureau," the General Intelligence Service (GIS) —the Egyptian intelligence agency—and the Mossad—the Israeli intelligence agency—were there to check on Priscilla, they were there for much more. Most people would be surprised to learn the extent of cooperation among the various international intelligence agencies, even in the Middle East.

Before anyone could respond to Elias's comment, they spotted Commander Thomas approaching.

Just like the MI6 commander already knew the CF commander, so, too, did he know Commander Elias of the Lebanese "first bureau." So, the two men hugged and slapped each other's shoulders.

Thomas then led the second group of visitors to the dining room. Seeing them, Commander Wozniah and the others rallied because they recognized their Middle Eastern counterparts. Observing their revelry, Priscilla suspected that the presence of so many not-so-secret secret agents and special ops from different agencies had something to do with the elusive Zulfika Kasun, but certainly not that it had anything to do with her sister Helen or anybody checking up on her entourage, for that matter.

But when Ronnie saw ten new faces seated at the dinner table, he fussed, "Ah, come on, folks! How many *more* will there be?"

And so it was that Priscilla enjoyed her time with her husband, the other CF boys, and the five Middle Eastern visitors, the latter of whom she met for the first time. Her revelry would dissolve, however, but not just yet. Her agent-husband wanted her to experience joy before telling her the unpleasant news about her sister.

23

NEWS FROM HOME
AND
THE NOT-SO-SECRET
SECRET AGENTS' REVELRY

Carlton went to Priscilla's bedroom in the wee hours. She'd left the revelry earlier and was sitting up in bed. He sat on the edge of her bed and reached for her hand.

"Missy, there's something I need to tell you. I have some unpleasant news from back home in Sills Creek."

Priscilla could not recall when her husband spoke in such a somber tone, and rarely was he the bearer of "unpleasant news." She suspected it was about her mom or her favorite nephew. As her heart pounded and her pulse quickened, she blurted out, "Oh, no! Not Momma! Not Germane!"

"No, Missy. It's Helen." Carlton spoke slowly and calmly.

Priscilla's eyes watered as she covered her mouth with her hands.

Carlton elaborated. "Helen has been diagnosed with mental illnesses, one of which she is not expected to recover."

"You've got that all wrong. You can't be serious. What happened? Did she have a nervous breakdown or something? Helen has always been a little fragile. I mean, is it something from her past? Is it that man she was married to for a split second?"

Priscilla rambled a while longer.

"Carlton, Helen has always talked about people being out to get her, and she talks a lot about people not liking her, too. But we all thought she was trying to get attention."

"You know, Missy, much of that kind of talk by Helen has been diagnosed by her doctors as 'paranoia.' Helen has some other illnesses, too, like bipolar disorder. But I won't say anything more because I don't know anymore. The question is: Do you want to visit your sister now or sometime later?" He was careful not to mention relinquishing her special envoy mission.

"Oh, Carlton." Her watery eyes were red now, and tears rolled down her cheeks. She grew silent. That was when Carlton sat her on his lap and rocked her back and forth. He watched as her once cheerful smile faded. Anger and then sadness engulfed her. She stared off into space. Carlton felt Priscilla slipping away from him, so he pleaded with her.

"Missy, Helen needs you to be strong for her. Please don't go into the abyss."

Although Priscilla stopped crying, Carlton himself now shed tears. He loved Priscilla, and he felt her pain. Although he fretted, it was best that Priscilla went through her grief, sadness, and anger sooner rather than later. She would need her strength to go forward, help her sister, and cope with the situation ahead with the elusive Zulfika Kasun. Priscilla did not know for sure, but she reckoned that Carlton had already dispatched mental health specialists to Helen's care and authorized someone to secure suitable accommodations for her. And she was right. She and Carlton were evenly yoked.

Priscilla somehow found a second wind, pulled herself together, and headed to the hallway. Her bedroom was across the hall from Melissa's. Two guest rooms were on the opposite end of the hallway. Midway was a small sofa, a table with a lamp, and a telephone.

When she stopped midway, Carlton, who'd followed her out of curiosity, asked, "Where are you going? What are you looking for?"

"I'm calling Momma."

He wisely supposed she would need a shoulder to lean on, so he stood beside her and occasionally stroked her hair and hands while she talked to her mother. Carlton was Priscilla's anchor, her rock, her all.

Delighted to hear her daughter's voice, Liza said tearfully, "It's early evening here in Sills Creek, and you would like that it's snowing, too."

While Liza talked about everything but Helen's illnesses, Priscilla's first words were apologetic. "O Momma. I'm so sorry that I haven't been in touch. Carlton told me about Helen. Is it true? Is she really, you know?" Priscilla could not say the words "mentally ill."

"I'm afraid so, Missy." Liza choked. "Unfortunately, your sister is suffering from several mental illnesses."

"Oh, Momma. It'll probably take me a couple of weeks to get there. Will that be okay?" Priscilla hoped her desperate request did not seem insensitive.

"Child, please." Liza was happy to hear her mention visiting, but she was hardly interested in the timeframe. She felt someone pulling at her. It was Helen.

"Let me talk to Priscilla."

"Missy," Liza said, "Helen knows it's you I'm talking to. Let me hand her the phone." The next voice Priscilla heard was Helen's.

"Priscilla, girl! Is it really you?"

"Yes, Helen," Priscilla choked over the massive lump in her throat. Yet, she managed to say, "I'm so glad to hear your voice."

"Me, too," cried Helen.

"Don't cry, Helen. You'll make me cry, too. Anyway, I just called to let you know I'm coming to see you in a couple of weeks."

"Okay, Missy, I'll hold on until then." Helen hung up the phone.

Unfamiliar with mental illness, Priscilla did not know how to interpret Helen's statement. So, she was determined to visit sooner than she had said.

Priscilla looked at her husband tearfully. "Sorry about that, but Helen hung up before I could say 'goodbye' to Momma."

"That's all right, Missy. Liza understands. The point is that you all talked."

Moments later, exhausted from her emotions but relieved to have spoken to her mom and sister, Priscilla fell asleep in her husband's arms. But he had mixed feelings as he removed her weapon. His role was to be her husband and protector, yet he was pleased to see she could fend for herself. Mainly, he knew she would cope with the news about Helen's mental health, although she had been shocked.

After putting her weapon atop the chiffonier, he disrobed her. Then, as he pulled the bed linen over her, he noticed that she was sleeping soundly. Priscilla was calm again—stoic was more like it. *She's accepted Helen's condition*, he reckoned. Yet, he did not fully understand Priscilla's propensity to shut down, particularly when faced with seemingly unbearable circumstances. She had already compartmentalized the unpleasant news, which she would deal with later.

After he tucked his wife in, he knelt beside her bed and prayed to God to imbue her with the strength necessary to go forth and that she did not slip away from him. When he got up, he felt much relief. Then he headed back downstairs, searching for their son's nursery.

Carlton's entry disturbed the light-sleeping Hettie. Seeing a man walking into the room, she got out of bed and hurried to the crib to confront the intruder. When the man laughed, her demeanor relaxed. As he came into full view, she held open her arms, and Carlton gladly embraced her. Just as Ramses was his surrogate father,

Hettie was his surrogate mother. But Hettie's glee turned into sadness when Carlton told her the unpleasant news about Helen and how hard Priscilla had taken it. Like the rest of the Bernhardt household, Hettie had come to love Priscilla.

Carlton reached into the crib and picked up his son. Austin whined from having been disturbed. His eyes were still shut as he rubbed his chubby hands across his father's face and pulled at his nose and long hair. Carlton smiled.

Just then, Carlton heard someone outside the nursery, so he handed Austin back to Hettie. It was Stephen, one of the CIA agents.

"Say, Carlton, my man, are you coming back?"

Carlton wished Hettie a good night and followed Stephen back to the dining room, where the gathering had grown to twenty not-so-secret secret agents and special ops, including Laverne, her CIA colleagues, and the British and French agents. Carlton heard the revelry as he approached. But it all simmered when he appeared on the threshold.

He could not help noticing CF Commander Wozniah seated at one end of the massive table; his eyebrows arched in a not-so-subtle demand for an update on Priscilla's reaction to the news about her sister.

"Let's have it, bro'. Is Missy packing or what?"

"No, Tommy," Carlton called the CF commander by his first name. "Missy won't be leaving for another two weeks."

"Pardon me," the CF commander said just as calmly.

"Yes," MI6 Commander Thomas chimed in, asking, "Why's she waiting so long?

When Carlton had had enough, he made his position plain.

"Okay, fellas, back off. First, Missy took the news hard. Then, after she thought about it, she realized there was not much that her immediate presence could do to improve Helen's situation anyway. When she called her mother, Liza was thrilled to hear her voice and said so. But she also spoke to Helen, who was equally pleased." Then Carlton said more.

"Missy says she has some other business to deal with right now, and she'll be less constrained in about two weeks."

But the domineering Commander Wozniah persisted. "Oh well. One would think she'd be on the next available flight back to the States. I know if it were—"

Before he could complete his sentence, Carton cut him off. "But Helen's not your sister. She's Missy's." He looked around the tightly seated table and asserted, "And Missy will deal with the situation when she's good and ready."

Leave it to Jordy to smooth things over.

"Fellas, the good news is that Priscilla knows about Helen's mental health and has already spoken to her and her mother. I vote we raise our glasses to PJ and offer good wishes and prayers for Helen." Jordy was the only agent who knew Priscilla and Helen from their Prendergast, New York upbringing. They had attended high school together. Ah, heck, even Jordy's CF associates knew he used to have a thing for Helen.

Seated at the other end of the table, "Hear! Hear!" Commander Thomas said eventually and raised his glass.

Even Commander Wozniah relented, stood, nodded at Carlton, and raised his glass with all the others.

But when Carlton asked Ronnie, who struggled frantically to serve the growing number of unexpected guests, "What've you got for us to eat?" everyone but Ronnie laughed.

At that point, Ronnie—overwhelmed by his kitchen duties and trying to prepare food for the ever-increasing group—sought Melissa and Shelton's assistance. Frustrated, he snapped, "Ah, hell, this is madness! Sheer madness!"

The dining room was bursting at the seams with intelligence agents and special ops carrying on as if they were at a family reunion. Even the intelligence realm has its underground where agents and special ops share, sell or otherwise exchange vital intel. Among those who survive "in service to their country," many become cohorts of a sort because one never knows when one will require the assistance of another, regardless of their government or politics.

Along those lines, the Bernhardts, especially Ramses, had long arms in the Middle Eastern espionage realm, which was why the Egyptian, Israeli, and Lebanese officers were at the Luzern safe house in the first place. As for FBI Agent Rothschild, he had a leg up with CIA Deputy Director Froley and the folks at Langley primarily due to his relationship with Liza and Germane from Priscilla's early experience in southern Africa. And so it was that some twenty not-so-secret secret agents and special ops gathered at the Luzern safe house and reveled in their reunion.

Before daybreak and while Priscilla slept, the unexpected guests would transmit messages back to Liza and Ramses. Although Priscilla had already spoken to her mom and her sister, Agent Rothschild would, in turn, get word to Liza that "all is indeed well with Priscilla, the household staff, and young Austin."

Meanwhile, the remaining not-so-secret secret agents and special ops would devise a plan or two to snare the elusive Zulfika Kasun, and Priscilla would be none the wiser.

Most of the visitors had departed early the following day. However, CF Commander Wozniah, Agent B, and Commander Elias remained. Agent B would soon join the Middle Eastern group in executing Plan A. Because Priscilla was integral to all their plans, her husband was prohibited from direct involvement in her mission. Company rules may be company rules, but "the boys" were known for bending or ignoring them altogether, albeit discreetly.

Shortly after 9:00 A.M., Agent B strolled across the threshold into his wife's bedroom with a silver breakfast tray.

When she saw him, she stretched her arms and yawned. "I must have overslept." Although a covered dish concealed her breakfast, she saw two cups of steaming hot coffee. "Oh, my darling husband. You shouldn't have. Besides, I haven't even freshened up."

When Carlton noticed she was in a pleasant mood, he opted not to engage her in any serious conversation, mainly about Helen. "Miss Prissy, you need your strength. You can freshen up later." But he had something else on his mind.

As she began eating, Carlton plopped down on the bed beside her. He sipped from one of the coffee cups, casually pulled at her twisted locks, and said, "Have I told you how much I like this hairstyle?"

"More than once," she muttered between bites of poached eggs, sausage links, and toast.

After she had eaten most of her food, Carlton said, "Hmm, somebody was hungry."

"I didn't eat much last night. And this coffee is good and hot, too." As she took another sip, she was surprised at his next comment.

"I like my coffee hot too, really hot, just like my woman."

Priscilla looked up from her plate at her husband. She lightly slapped his face. "Why, you ole scoundrel. I should've known." She handed him her breakfast tray; he sat it on the floor beside her bed. Then they made love as if for the first time, for it had been months since they had been together intimately.

"Mm, that was good." he sighed.

"Magnificent was more like it," she said, snuggling in his arms.

After a short while, Carlton said, "You sure were delicious, but I could use some more hot coffee."

Priscilla radiated. "And so were you delicious." But then, as she got out of bed, she looked herself over and said, "I'd love another cup of coffee, but I need to shower before joining the others downstairs."

"Roger that, Missy."

They both laughed.

But her husband surprised her again when he lightly pushed her aside and rushed into the bathroom to shower before her. When he returned, she watched him get dressed, pick up the breakfast tray, and leave, blowing her a kiss on the way out.

As it turned out, Carlton did not revisit the subject of Helen's mental health, and he certainly did not broach the subject of Zulfika Kasun. He knew Priscilla would deal with both situations in her own way. As was her penchant, she would tell him pretty much everything anyway— "when she is good and ready" —as Liza and her friend Julia often said of her.

As things stood, Priscilla still needed to develop a plan to tackle her new assignment. So she opted to remain at the Luzern villa until she did, after which she would return to the States to visit her sister and meet with a colleague essential to her mission. Carlton and the others were not privy to the details of her mission or her association with another agent who was not among them. As such, Priscilla's business was none of theirs.

24

BACK IN GAME MODE AND THE MAKEOVER

Later that morning, when Priscilla entered the dining room of the Luzern safe house, she was surprised to see that—except for CF Commander Wozniah, Commander Elias, Ronnie, and her husband, Carlton (Agent B) —most of the other guests were gone, along with Laverne, her CIA colleagues, and a few others.

"Say, Tommy, where'd the others go?"

"On a little errand." CF Commander Wozniah said though he was not being entirely honest.

Acutely aware of the commander's ways, "Sure they are," she said, "And I'm Bette Midler." She continued. "And Jordy, Onslow, and Angel? Come on, Tommy. Let me guess; they're all in the men's room."

The indomitable Tommy Wozniah would hardly tell Priscilla what she wanted to know. He was not the CF commander for naught.

Priscilla looked over at her agent-husband—who was already back in game mode and who even she knew not to provoke. She switched tactics.

"All right, then, Carlton. Can you at least tell me when *you* plan on leaving?"

"Sure, Missy. As soon as Tommy and I clear up a few more details and schedule a flight out."

But seeing her puzzled expression, he added, "But I'll be back, and I promise you that we'll have more quality time together, maybe as you're writing the final chapters of your novel." Then he pierced her ego by saying, "It is a novel, isn't it?" Carlton had found ways of coping with his lingering frustration over the fact that his wife had essentially become one of "the boys," as it were.

At that point, Melissa, who wisely sensed a bit of tension, asked, "Would Madame PJ like me to get her something else? Perhaps freshen her coffee?"

Melissa knew her mistress was amid something more sinister than previously thought because—apart from the recent ploy by the men who had attempted to abduct Hettie and baby Austin and the unexpected arrival of the ten visitors—she and Shelton had been duly instructed to stay close to her and watch over Hettie and the baby boy. But they need not have worried. They had grown accustomed to the tattooed guardsmen who had become like family to them, especially Ronnie, whom Melissa spent much time with because of their shared kitchen duties.

Priscilla shook her head and waved Melissa away. She knew the drill. Looking around the room, she saw that everyone was back in game mode. But she was unaware of their plans to snare Kasun and that all the unexpected guests had roles to play. For sure, she was unaware that they'd all been there to check up on her.

As she left the dining room, she ran into Hettie with Austin in a stroller. She stopped and played with her son. She picked up a colorful plastic rattler and shook it over the youngster's head. Austin reached for it and took it from her hand. Then he did what many infants do; he tried to bite it. When Priscilla did not let that happen, he reached for the colorful trinkets that were strung along a loop overhead. Priscilla laughed as she played with him. Young Austin was a well-adjusted and happy child.

While she tended to her son, she overheard tidbits of a conversation among the CF commander, Carlton, Commander Elias, and Ronnie. But Priscilla had long since mastered the art of ignoring much of what other agents said within her hearing, mainly "the boys," much of which, she figured, was intended to mislead her, anyway. She once overheard them discussing "something vital" they would do on a particular day at a particular place and time. They repeated the terms of that mission several times, all within her hearing. But when she arrived at the place on the day and time, she became undone because no one there knew about a meeting or anything else planned for that day and time. What irked her most about that incident was that when she returned to the CF central command center, "the boys" had already gone to wherever they had planned to go in the first place. They did not wish to include her. So, this time, she ignored them altogether.

Besides, she already suspected that when she returned, none of them, including the CF commander and her agent-husband, would be there anyway, and she was right.

After CF Commander Wozniah, Carlton, Commander Elias, and Ronnie departed, Priscilla sprang into action. She was ready to implement her plan.

She took out a pair of scissors from her dresser drawer. Then she removed her sweater and went into the bathroom, snatched a damp towel from the rack, and covered her shoulders. Then she sat at her dresser, stared at her face in the mirror, and began sectioning her twisted locks. She cut her hair section by section until it was half an inch long.

As she cut her hair, she remembered her disguise during her first time in southern Africa: She wore a Marine-style haircut, a loose-fitting top, masculine-style harem trousers, or sarongs, as they are called in some societies, and brown leather sandals. "The boys" wanted her to look like a Middle Eastern boy or young man. She also remembered how Charlie had instructed her to conceal her feminine ways and speak as little as possible.

Looking at her haircut in the mirror, she saw that it needed a trim. Unmindful of how she was dressed and that she had just cut off her hair, she went downstairs to look for Shelton, who was shocked when he saw her.

While Shelton stared at her, she asked, sounding like one of "the boys," "Say, bro', think you can find some hair clippers and help me finish this job?"

Shelton regained his composure after being startled by Priscilla's new look and her calling him "bro." He told her to follow him to his room. He picked up a pair of hair clippers from his dresser. She sat in a chair. Then he trimmed her hair even shorter.

Shelton double-checked his work. He handed her a hand-held mirror and asked her, "How's that, Madame PJ?"

Looking at her haircut from one side to another, she exclaimed, "Great job, Shelton! You're a good man, Charlie Brown." Charlie Brown was the name she used affectionately with men she liked. She winked at Shelton and said, "By golly, I think we did it."

As they left his room, Shelton said, "I'm serious, PJ; if there is anything else, holler. OK?" Shelton felt a bit of a rush. This was one of those rare times he was with Priscilla when she went into game mode, and Shelton could not have been more excited than at this moment. For he and most everyone else in the Bernhardt household already knew Carlton was an agent; as for Priscilla, they all had their growing suspicions. But now, for sure, he was onto her. As he walked her back to the staircase, he hoped she would ask him to help in other, more substantial ways.

Back in her room, she pulled out her over-the-knee high-heel leather boots. As she inspected them, she decided to pack them away. Then she grabbed her duffel from under her bed. She had chosen this duffel because it was reversible. One side had red-and-crème stripes on rollers. The other side was taupe, without rollers. For this mission, she kept it on the taupe side. Also, both sides had handles and straps that allowed her to easily carry it over her shoulders or tug it under her arms.

After tossing stuff from the duffel onto the floor, she said, "Ah-ha! I wondered where I'd put those." She held up two berets; one was red, the other black.

Near the bottom of the duffel was one of her company-issued uniforms, a pair of cargo pants, and a thermal top in brown-and-black camouflage. She pulled them out and slipped into them. A pair of dark brown lace-up leather boots was at the bottom of the duffel. She had opted for dark brown because, as she had told the CIA staffer who issued her the uniform, "Those black ones remind me of the Nazis." She put on her boots, laced them up, and walked around her room. Although she had not worn that outfit in a while, she was pleased it still fit. She stood on her toes and felt around the top of the chiffonier where she knew her ever-cautious agent-husband had put her weapon. She pulled it down and strapped it on.

Standing before the floor-length mirror, "Now what?" she asked herself as if half-expecting her to answer.

"Uh, oh! I need to get rid of this makeup and jewelry," including her wedding ring, which she replaced with a masculine-looking one, covering the pale section made by her wedding ban. When she remembered some men wore earrings, she located a pair of small gold hoops, put them on, and returned to the floor-length mirror. "Ah, now. That's more like it. I could be a man or a woman."

She also chose not to wear anything that suggested she was a Westerner, particularly an American. She dispensed with wearing a baseball cap, a hat, or a helmet. Again, she sorted through items on the floor until she noticed her turban, which "the boys" had used to create her Middle Eastern disguise some time ago.

Another thought crossed her mind. *Muslims are in Yugoslavia, lots of 'em. It seems like this little scheme of mine might work after all.*

She also thought *I could easily be anyone from any country except the good ole U.S. of A.*

"Voila!" she said, admiring herself in the mirror.

Priscilla was now ready to play her role as a man while having fun as she deceived people, especially "the boys," who had no reason to believe she had kept those garments from her first time in southern Africa. Since her inability to outwit them at their little shenanigans had always infuriated her, this would be her chance. But she mostly wanted Zulfika Kasun to play for whatever card she held. *After all,* she thought, *the bloody bloke needs me more than I need him.*

25

STRAY CAT

While Priscilla put the finishing touches on her disguise, the doors to Zulfika Kasun's Marmande villa opened. Two men and a woman entered. The two men—Egyptian GIS agents—took off their heavy overcoats, hats, and gloves and waited as if they had been expected. Shivering, the woman did not remove her floor-length Russian sable coat, matching hat, or leather gloves. The guard who greeted them was one of the loathsome men who had killed Kasun—or was he another double? —and had gone to the Luzern safe house pretending to search for Kasun but had since returned. Not knowing why the visitors were there, the guard called for someone to get Afan. Indeed, the loathsome men at the Marmande villa were unaware that the agents at the Luzern safe house knew that they had murdered Zulfika Kasun or the man who had posed as him.

As it turned out, the three loathsome men who had garroted and disposed of the remains of the second Zulfika Kasun impersonator had made at least one mistake. They had not eliminated the one person who had last seen them with the victim, the one who had delivered Priscilla's invitation, Afan Kljujic.

A moment later, Afan entered the foyer. He wore a light gray cardigan sweater over a pristine white shirt and black trousers with a razor-sharp crease. He was soft-spoken and proper in manner. But his greeting did not match his calm appearance, for Afan seemed far from calm.

"Hello, I'm Afan Kljujic. How may I help you?" he asked, looking a bit perplexed.

The woman extended a gloved hand, smiled, and said, "Why, hello to you, Afan. I'm P. J. Austin-Bernhardt. We spoke over the telephone."

But the woman was not Priscilla. Nor did she remember she had abruptly ended their telephone conversation when Afan had called the Luzern villa to see if the lieutenant had arrived. Nevertheless, Afan had since recovered from her curt response.

Under her slightly open fur coat, he could see she wore a cream-colored shawl over a peach-colored turtleneck sweater, fitted jeans, and over-the-knee high-heel leather boots—Priscilla's signature trademarks, while on her writing excursion in the South of France.

While CF Agent Laverne Macon waited for Afan to react, she and the GIS agents noticed how well he spoke English and the uneasiness in his demeanor as he nervously glanced around as if he expected someone else to appear. Since he had only glimpsed Priscilla in the dimly lighted foyer of the Luzern safe house, he had no reason to doubt Laverne was who she pretended to be. Moreover, Afan never even met Priscilla during her stay at the Marmande villa. Otherwise, he had only seen her once from a distance when she walked with Kasun and when, at the time, her head was covered with a hat. So he had not seen her hair.

So why the uneasiness?

"Why, Madame Austin-Bernhardt, we thought the appointment was at your villa in Luzern." He smiled at her and noted, "A few days ago at that."

"And right you are. But I decided to surprise my 'new writer friend' and save him the journey north."

Laverne waited for Afan's reaction. It would soon become apparent that Afan had no notion of what had happened, and that was despite the fact he had been forced to accompany the men who had attempted to abduct young Austin and Nanny Hettie. For sure, he was unaware that three other men—the loathsome ones who now occupied the Marmande villa—had murdered Kasun, or perhaps it was another of his doubles.

Since Afan was speechless, Laverne spoke again, more sternly this time.

"Is Monsieur Kasun here? Or is the surprise on me?"

"Er, I'm not sure. He… he does not seem like himself." Afan was flustered and began telling them about the strange behavior of the man he believed was Zulfika Kasun. "He talks and acts quite differently. And, oh, how short-tempered he has become." Afan's rambling surprised Laverne and the two GIS agents. He leaned closer and whispered. "Why, before he left for your villa the other day, he was so pleasant. And, never, ever, was he mean to me. But that has all changed." He stepped back, glanced around, and stopped talking. At that, Laverne and the two GIS agents realized that Afan was unaware that Zulfika Kasun, or the man who had pretended to be him, was dead and that another man had replaced him.

After a moment of uncomfortable silence, Afan continued.

"Since his return, he hasn't paid any attention to his attire, cuisine, or hygiene. The man I know enjoys fine dining and outings to cultural events and such."

Like Laverne, Maalik and Omar—the two GIS agents—were equally baffled when Afan said, "And he hasn't written a single word."

While Afan talked, Laverne and the other agents pretended to be surprised. But they appreciated all the intel he provided.

"Nor has he read a single newspaper. He used to call news editors and chat endlessly, but not anymore." Nervously wringing out his hands, he said, "I tell you, something's not right."

He shook his head and muttered. "And all these *men!* Where'd they come from?" He meant the loathsome men who carried heavy weaponry, had a very poor command of English and poor hygiene, and killed the other Kasun impersonator.

Cutting to the chase, Omar asked him point–blank, "Afan, are you asking for asylum or something of that nature?"

The expression on Afan's face said it all.

"Or are you considering defecting to the West?"

Afan knew the real Zulfika Kasun was a Yugoslav military intelligence officer closely associated with the perpetrator of the most heinous crimes imaginable. As such, anyone remotely associated with him would also be deemed a war criminal as well.

As it turned out, the loathsome men had spared Afan's life because he had been the only one who could facilitate circumstances involving P. J. Austin-Bernhardt and who knew how to relate to Westerners, not to mention his fluency in English. Therefore, Afan had been essential, particularly to the Kasun doubles, maybe even the real one himself. Sometimes, a stray cat brings more to the table than one might think, and so it was for Afan Kljujic.

Afan's voice trembled. Yet he managed to state his plea clearly.

"Yes, please," he whispered. "Can you help me?"

While Omar engaged Afan in conversation, Maalik spoke into a concealed electronic device. "Folks, we've got a live one for special delivery. That would be *now.*"

When Maalik reached for the door handle, someone from outside pushed the door open. One of the other Middle Eastern special ops executing Plan A entered. He grabbed Afan and whisked him outside, "Hurry!"

As the special op shut the door behind him, the three agents inside looked at one another. "Now what?" Omar asked Laverne and Maalik.

Before anyone could respond, the same guard who had greeted them returned.

144

"Stray cat, Afan?" Like his fellow loathsome henchmen, he was not fluent in English. Neither were Laverne and the GIS agents fluent in any Slavic language, such as Bosniak or Bosnian, spoken primarily by Bosnian Muslims.

Acutely aware of the linguistic differences, Omar tempered his English to match the guard's manner of speech. "Quick errand. Back soon." Then he looked around as if searching for someone, waved his hands, and said, "Master of the house? We surprise him."

Pointing to Laverne, he said, "Madame P. J. Austin-Bernhardt, 'new writer friend.'"

At that moment, Laverne and the two agents noticed that the guard had done a double take; looking from Omar to Laverne, he almost dropped his rifle. Quickly composing himself, he led them to the study, where he walked inside and, after signaling for them to enter, did not even make introductions.

As Laverne and the two agents entered—as if they had been expected—the Zulfika Kasun decoy abruptly stood from his chair behind his desk. He had heard the front door open but assumed it was some of his men coming or going. He never imagined his "new writer friend" was one of those coming to meet him.

Laverne and the two agents saw a man who resembled the one Priscilla had met. But that man was well over six feet tall; this one was barely six feet. Although he was around the same age and had a full head of hair, his was brown, not sandy. He also wore an untrimmed mustache, unlike the first Kasun. Otherwise, the frame of his face was the only likeness between the two men.

The first Kasun decoy was multilingual, including fluency in French. He was comfortable discussing literature, writing, and Western European media. But there were not any legal pads, paper, or pens, particularly a typewriter, not even a desktop PC, most of which a serious writer would possess in their study. Even though plenty of books were on the shelves, there were no magazines or daily newspapers. So, Laverne and the two agents surmised that—like Laverne doubled for Priscilla—so, too, were their doubles for Zulfika Kasun.

"Why, Madame Aus—sorry, PJ," he quickly corrected himself. "Was not expecting you." Whether he spoke English poorly on purpose was beside the point. But Laverne and the GIS agents knew that the first decoy spoke English more fluently. By this time, though, they noticed another similarity: both men had difficulty with adjectives, conjunctions, and pronouns.

Nevertheless, Laverne continued acting out her role as Priscilla.

"No, darling," she said, mimicking Priscilla's more classy style as she strutted toward him. He turned to face her when she reached the backside of his desk. She gently squeezed his shoulders, pressed her cheek against his, and felt a revolting sensation; the man needed a bath. Regardless, after that bold move, she said, "You needn't apologize." She continued since she already knew the other impersonator had been eliminated, and this one had never seen the real Priscilla. But Laverne was unaware that the loathsome men who had killed Kasun, or his decoy, had seen the real Priscilla when they came to the Luzern safe house, and they had since shared that intel with this impersonator.

"All right, now, Zulfika," Laverne said as she fidgeted with papers on his desk. "You promised to show me your latest work. Are you experiencing writer's block? Because I haven't seen any of your articles in *The Guardian*, the *International Herald Tribune,* the *Republican,* or *The Humanity*."

But when she said, "Things heating up back home in Bosnia and Herzegovina?" the man blinked and stumbled. The Zulfika Kasun that Priscilla met had mentioned Sarajevo as his hometown. Laverne pretended she had not noticed him blink and stumble and that she had not mentioned Sarajevo. She stepped back. *It's time for the bastard to start acting like he knows the real PJ.* It never occurred to her that he did not believe she was who she pretended to be, either.

"Well, I, uh. PJ," he stuttered, "make arrangements to eat. Then, sit and, as Americans say, 'we catch up, eh?'"

As the guard escorted Laverne and the two GIS agents out of the office, they overheard the Kasun impersonator shouting: "Where the hell is Afan? Find the damn stray cat!"

While Laverne and the two GIS agents settled in Marmande with yet another Zulfika Kasun decoy, the very real Afan Kljujic sat in the backseat of a black bulletproof Hummer. But he was not alone. CF Agent B, Commander Elias, and Ariel were with him. Before they made their "special delivery," it seemed to Afan as if they drilled him endlessly.

Beyond any doubt, in exchange for diplomatic immunity and sanctuary in the West, Afan Kljujic demonstrated a remarkable singing voice. He was an invaluable source of intel about Zulfika Kasun—whichever one(s) he knew and the ongoing situation in the Yugoslav tinderbox—which only an insider could have known, all of which Interpol, the CIA, MI6, the "first bureau," the GIS, the Mossad, and a few other international intelligence agencies had so desired.

While Plan A was being executed under the command of CF Agent B, Laverne and the two GIS agents inside the Marmande villa were not alone. Another GIS agent and the four CIA agents assigned to them had remained on the grounds. And although the international intelligence agents got an unexpected bonus with the "special delivery," they had no idea what was happening inside the villa. Yet, they were so confident that they had not plotted a backup plan.

In contrast, although the Kasun-impersonator was unaware that the heavily armed loathsome men who had guarded the grounds were either dead or captured, at least he had a backup plan, and it would soon reveal itself.

And so it was that Plan A to snare the elusive Zulfika Kasun had already begun, and Priscilla was still none the wiser.

Everyone was so sure that their plan was perfect that no one had bothered devising a backup plan. Priscilla, on the other hand, had yet to complete hers.

26

ENTER PHILLIPE WINSARAH

At the Luzern safe house—still unaware of the identity of the real Zulfika Kasun and that Laverne and two GIS agents were in Marmande—Priscilla mapped out her plan. It was now clear to her that she needed to meet Lieutenant Zulfika Kasun on his turf right smack in the Yugoslav tinderbox. She had already deduced that, like herself, the lieutenant had a decoy or two, and she was anxious to meet the real one. Since she had spent much time amid secret agents, mercenaries, and vicious villains of pretty much all types, she was undisturbed and unafraid, merely anxious to get on with it. As her fingers scrolled across a map of Switzerland and Italy, she knew hers would be an arduous and dangerous trek, and once in the belly of tumultuous Eastern Europe, she would pretty much be on her own, or so she thought.

Even though she had considerable leeway to fulfill her mission, there was one critical condition: Unbeknownst to her, CIA Deputy Director Froley had matched her up with CF Commander Wozniah and "the boys," a somewhat problematic working relationship at best. Priscilla and Tommy often clashed and had difficulty taking orders from each other. But, before Priscilla signed on to this mission, Froley had assured her, "This one is yours, PJ. We'll only send in backup on an as-needed basis." He did not tell her anything specific about her backup except that it would "be easily recognizable." Priscilla was about to make rough with people she loved and treated like family, that is, "the boys," one of whom it seemed as if she had prepared to match wits over a lifetime, not to mention put the lives of her son and household staff in jeopardy. But for now, her mind was set on Zulfika Kasun, no one else.

As she studied her map, committing it to memory, her fingers scrolled to Slovenia, then Croatia. Her index finger stopped when it touched Bosnia and Herzegovina.

"Ah, crap!" she said to herself, "I know nothing about the people over there." But she was wrong. Priscilla did know something "about the people over there," and since she had yet to come upon a particular group, she was unaware of just how much she knew.

Confident she had a plan in place, she looked up from the map and out the window of her study. She smiled at the sight of the falling snow and the sun shining overhead. *Ah, what the hell. What would life be without a bit of adventure?*

She was glad she had called her mom and assured her she would visit. But if only she'd known that Liza was simply happy to hear her voice? Although her mother knew there was nothing Priscilla could do to improve Helen's mental health condition, she knew there was no way Priscilla would not visit her sister, who was also the mother of her favorite nephew. Liza was mainly relieved to know that Priscilla was indeed safe.

As Priscilla's thoughts returned to her mission, someone tapped her shoulder. It was Shelton. His usual jovial face looked worried.

"Say, Madame PJ, I realize something's up with the makeover and all. But when are you going to let me in on what you're up to?"

"Oh, Shelton. If only I could. You see—"

"Never mind, Madame PJ. Master Carlton used to act the same way whenever he had something unmentionable to do. But please don't go and disappear on me. Why, Melissa, Nanny Hettie, and I promised those guys that we'd keep close watch over you and young Austin." By now, Shelton also knew "those guys" were not-so-secret secret agents because Deputy Director Froley had enlightened him when they cruised through the Marmande neighborhood some time ago.

"Don't worry, Shelton. I don't think anything will be happening anytime soon, at least nothing bad. Still, I might need to disappear for a few days alone."

"Absolutely not, PJ! The guys made me promise to keep an eye on you."

"I know, Shelton. But some things can't be helped."

There now, at least I've prepared Shelton for my unexpected absence. But she had no notion of how concerned he was and what it might lead him to do.

That was not all she did not know.

She was unaware of Plan B, which called for CF Commander Tommy Wozniah, "the boys," the French, and the MI6 agents to follow her. But unbeknownst to Wozniah and the others, Secret Agent P. J. Austin-Bernhardt was about to match wits with them, especially the CF commander. About the only thing

Tommy and the others knew for sure was Priscilla's propensity to call out her prey and on his own turf, at that. However, the most critical factor, at least from Tommy's standpoint, was that he and Priscilla sought a common prey, Zulfika Kasun. So, while he and the others waited for her to make her move, Tommy relished it when Priscilla realized that he commanded her backup, and they were both on the prowl for the same quarry. Even Deputy Director Froley was uncertain how all that would play out.

She was also unaware that, under Plan C, Sam commanded the guardsmen who protected Melissa, Hettie, Shelton, and young Austin.

However, neither Commander Wozniah nor Sam nor Agent B knew that Shelton was about to poke a few holes in Priscilla's carefully made plan.

Back to the moment. Priscilla had not anticipated the reactions to her makeover. Almost everyone was shocked when they saw her new hairstyle.

When she walked into the kitchen, Melissa's blue eyes opened wide, and her mouth gaped. "Oh, my! What'd you do to your hair, Madame PJ?"

"I cut it off," Priscilla said matter-of-factly. "Besides," she continued, "I got tired of washing and twisting all those locks."

"But your hair was so pretty. I'm sure glad Master Carlton isn't here."

When Hettie saw her from a distance, she merely assumed she was looking at one of the smaller guardsmen. But as Priscilla drew closer, Hettie almost fainted.

"No! It can't be!" She raised her hands to her mouth.

However, one of the guardsmen was quite impressed and said as much.

"My, my," Erik said, nodding approvingly. "Look who's come over to our side. I wasn't expecting that, but it suits you. You'd make a good guardsman."

"Well, it's about time someone agreed with me. I like my new look, too," Priscilla said, patting her short hair.

Although she was unaware of plans A, B, and C, she awaited the opportune time to disappear while Laverne and the others, including her agent-husband, were away. Her only problem, or so she thought, was Shelton, whom she figured she could easily elude.

Around 4:00 on a cold, snowy morning in Luzern, Priscilla waited until everyone was fast asleep or out of sight. Then, she sorted through her duffel and found her ski suits. One was a striking powder-blue color, but she opted instead to wear the more masculine black-and-brown one. She wore her ski suit over her long johns and company-issued camouflage uniform. She wrapped her turban around her head and put on her small gold hoop earrings. Lastly, she stepped into her snow boots.

Well-layered and warm, she walked to her dresser, looked at herself in the mirror, and practiced her greetings: "Yoa, man." "Bonjour." "No problem." "Excusez moi." She spoke in a deep, gravelly voice. "Good to go, man."

Reasonably satisfied with her transformation, she stuffed a paperback in the pocket of her ski jacket. She would read it to ward off people who wanted to talk. She patted a pocket on her pants and felt for her currency. She had British pounds, Swiss francs, and Yugoslavian dinars. The euro had yet to take effect. She felt her breast pocket for her British, Swiss, and Yugoslavian passports. The name inscribed on each was "Phillipe Winsarah."

She stood before her floor-length mirror and thought, *I sure hope I don't forget to use the men's room.* She chuckled. Then she remembered that Europe has unisex facilities.

She checked the contents of her duffel. It contained her holster—her Glock securely fastened in it—her toiletries, an extra company-issued camouflage uniform, her dark brown lace-up leather boots, two bulky sweaters, two pairs of men's woolen slacks, an extra pair of long johns, and other items such as her two berets, a pair of men's dress pants, a beige haute couture woman's cashmere outfit and her over-the-knee high-heel leather boots.

She hoisted her duffel, which was not heavy, slid her arms through the straps, and pulled it over her shoulders. Next, she checked to see if anyone lurked in the corridor outside her bedroom. *You never can tell with that nosey Shelton.* She peeped inside Melissa's suite across from hers. Melissa was sound asleep. Then she quietly made her way down the stairs where she should have checked Shelton's suite—a not-so-small mistake.

When she did not see either of the two agents on night patrol, she headed down the corridor toward the kitchen where she had a habit of going out onto the patio— sometimes in the wee hours—ostensibly for a late-night cigarette—but really to study the routines of the guards on night patrol. As such, she knew when to make her move. The guards patrolling the property, especially out front, were about to be relieved of their watch; others would come on duty in a few minutes. The changing of the guards would give her a small window of opportunity to leave unnoticed. Since numerous footprints already covered the snow-covered yard and walkway, hers would hardly be noticed. When Priscilla saw her chance, she made a mad dash for the front gate, making sure to stay in the shadows.

Around 4:30 A.M., Priscilla—now walking with a masculine stride—looked like an avid skier in the area. She had devised the first part of her plan at her Marmande villa and completed it at the Luzern safe house, where she had observed the habits of skiers on their way to the slopes. *After all*, she thought, *no one would find it odd that a skier carried a duffel in the wee hours en route to catch a tram.* She had also learned about the tram and intercontinental train service and had presumably plotted her plan to shake anyone following her off her tail. The nearest tramcar station was just under two kilometers from the Luzern safe house. She would have to think of mileage in terms of kilometers for the rest of her journey. But she needed to be mindful of something else: the tracking device that had been surgically implanted in her lower back. She had worn it for so long that she often forgot about it.

As for the rest, she would figure it out along the way.

She might not have been so self-assured if she had known CF Commander Wozniah's men were already tracking her every move.

But what she nor the commander knew was that Shelton had also been keeping an eye on her. And thinking she might be planning her getaway, he had hidden behind the snow-covered shrubbery at the front gate. When he saw Priscilla dressed in her ski suit with a duffel hoisted over her shoulder, casually strolling up the street, he knew he had been right. But when he noticed that she was being followed by two men trailing her and the others inconspicuously, he came out from hiding and followed the lot of them. But the lot of them, Shelton included, were unsuspecting of anyone else who might have followed them.

As Priscilla—disguised as Phillipe Winsarah—and the skiers assembled, awaiting the arrival of the tram, some sipped mugs of hot chocolate or hot tea-and-rum. But Priscilla waited patiently without drinking or talking to anyone. More importantly, she was unaware that two men tailed her, that Shelton hid amid the skiers, and that some other men tailing the lot of them lurked nearby.

Then came the bells ringing, signaling that a tram was approaching. Priscilla and the others grabbed their duffels and skis and eagerly awaited boarding. Since there was no fee for transport, most travelers, particularly the skiers, dropped tokens or Swiss francs into a bucket on the floor at the conductor's feet. The local government, called a canton, had long since realized that the honor system generated far more income than fees. When Priscilla observed most travelers pulling out Swiss fivers, she did likewise. Then she boarded the nearly capacity-filled tram, walked to the rear, dropped her duffel on the floor between her legs, and grabbed the overhead handrail. She rode, standing, all the way to Luzern, where she and most skiers disembarked. Afterward, they would take a train upcountry to the ski resorts in and near Zurich.

27

THE WAYWARD CHAUFFEUR

Back at the Luzern safe house, around 6:00 that same morning, Sam got word from CF Commander Wozniah via radio transmission that Priscilla had "snuck out in the wee hours, presumably on a skiing trip."

Sam laughed. "Sure, boss. Roger that."

To Sam's surprise, though, Commander Wozniah, as impassive as Priscilla, also laughed. The Priscilla he knew was not a strong swimmer, feared heights, close quarters, and people touching her, and suffered from acrophobia, claustrophobia, and vertigo. Wozniah was confident she could not ski. So, like the other intelligence agents, he laughed heartily at the thought of Priscilla skiing.

As the commander scoffed, "I think she could've come up with a better disguise than as a skier," CF Agent Jordan did not join in the ridicule. Knowing Priscilla from their time in the Snowbelt of western New York, he knew she had grown up in a community where many skied on the city streets, parks, and hills on the city's outskirts. Some residents also traveled to nearby Sinclairville and skied on the magnificent slopes there. Although Jordy could not validate Priscilla's skiing prowess, it was not out of the question that she could ski and was probably no slouch. Still, he kept quiet while the others laughed.

The CF commander then asked Sam if he had seen Shelton.

But when Sam said, "One of my men could swear he saw Shelton board a tramcar at 0500, around the same time that 'our girl' boarded," one could have heard a pin drop.

After a moment of uncomfortable silence, "Ah, heck, man!" Sam blurted out. "I forgot how close-knit that family was."

"Don't worry, Sam. My boys will deliver him back like a rabbit in a hat," said the CF commander, shaking his head.

When Sam conveyed the CF commander's message to Ronnie, Ronnie asked, "What should I tell the other staff?"

"Tell them that Madame PJ didn't want to disturb them so early, but she wanted to go skiing, and she'll return soon."

"And what's the line for Shelton's absence?"

"He dutifully accompanied his mistress. And say, 'they'll return shortly in a day or so.'" Sam added that last part to allay concerns about Priscilla's safety.

"Anything else?" Ronnie asked.

"Oh yeah. Ask Melissa if she has any more of that cod or shrimp. And, if you can, try to get her to ease up on those casseroles."

Then Sam and Ronnie both laughed.

Melissa was already in the kitchen when Ronnie arrived. As soon as she saw him, she peppered him with questions.

"Have you seen Madame PJ?" she demanded. "She's not in her room, not in her study, not even on the patio."

Ronnie barely had time to answer one question before Melissa asked many more.

"And what of Shelton? Come to think about it, I haven't seen him at all this morning." She crossed her arms and asked, "Is something happening that nobody has told me about?"

While Melissa ranted, Ronnie patiently waited for her to stop talking. He had a surprise—actually one of many—in store for her.

"They've gone skiing," he finally answered.

Speechless. Melissa unfolded her arms and stared at him. Although she did not know whether Priscilla could ski, she was not surprised to hear she had gone skiing because she was, after all, from the Snowbelt of western New York. But Melissa was surprised to hear that Shelton had gone skiing with her, someone whom Melissa knew did not ski. That was true; Priscilla did as she pleased, but it was not like Shelton not telling her or Hettie that he would be away for the day. *And why leave secretly in the middle of the night?* Deep in her thoughts, Melissa suddenly realized that Ronnie was talking to her and, in a most unusual way, at that. The whole time she had known him, he had barely said more than a few sentences to her and was usually far more gruff than genteel.

"Come. Have a seat, Miss Melissa. Let me wait on you this morning. OK?" He led her to a chair. "How about a cup of coffee?" When he noticed Melissa's stunned reaction, he smiled and gently patted her shoulder.

Melissa watched as he carefully put his ever-present rifle in a corner. Then he picked up the coffee pot from the kitchen table, carried it to the sink, filled it with water, and said, "Now, where'd we put the ground coffee?"

Still stunned, when Melissa regained her voice, she stood, put her hands on her hips, and said, "Humph! Why, Ronnie, what took you so long?" Melissa liked this Ronnie, and he liked her, too.

Back in Marmande, after CF Agent B, Commander Elias, and Ariel finally completed interrogating Afan Kljujic, who sang like a bird and gave them vital intel, they arranged for his "special delivery" to Interpol and Langley. After that, they transmitted reports to their headquarters and then briefed CF Commander Wozniah, who relayed the intel down the line. As for Priscilla, she would be briefed later, as Jim Froley had told her, "by someone she would recognize."

Meanwhile, Priscilla—disguised as Phillipe Winsarah—the skiers, the two men tracking Priscilla and Shelton, and the men who followed the lot of them all assembled in separate spaces in the Luzern Train Station. Some stood and talked among themselves. Some sat and relaxed. Yet others leaned impatiently against the walls—their skis—like loyal companions—propped vertically alongside them. Almost everyone glanced periodically at the clocks displaying international time zones. They also kept looking at the meter boards for the gates and the arrival and departure times for their trains. Priscilla—who stood out from everyone else, primarily because of the turban she wore—sat patiently on her duffel near one of the walls, reading her book.

The announcement came at 6:00 A.M.: "The train for Zurich and all points North is now ready for boarding." The voiceover repeated the announcement in French, German, Italian, and English. Since Priscilla, like most travelers, understood the first announcement, which had been in Swiss—and since most travelers had already purchased tickets—no one hurried as they casually queued and waited their turn to board. Priscilla followed suit by shoving her duffel into the designated compartment, locating her assigned seat, and shedding her ski jacket.

Moments later, an attendant arrived to collect the passengers' tickets. Priscilla held her breath and hoped she had completed the form correctly with the month and date European style, which was the date followed by the month, not the month followed by the date, American style.

The attendant examined Priscilla's ticket, tore off the needed section, and returned the other portion to her.

"Bon voyage, Monsieur Winsarah."

Priscilla was, however, somewhat surprised that he did not ask for her passport. Then she remembered that it was not an international trip. They were traveling upcountry. Even so, she knew many tourists, which included many Swiss, had grown accustomed to the increasingly diverse society, such as men wearing turbans, even keffiyeh, something that Priscilla—who had spent the more significant part of her life in smalltown western New York and the American Midwest—rarely saw. Nor did she see many men wearing turbans or keffiyeh in Bow Lake. But she had seen such in New York City.

Something else surprised her. Many passengers, especially the young women, smiled and nodded at her when she entered her compartment. Priscilla did not realize how much she, disguised as Phillipe Winsarah, resembled a "pretty boy," as people of many cultures considered handsome young men with delicate features. Already, Phillipe had attracted the attention of a few young women, an affirmation of Priscilla's disguise.

Seated several rows behind her, Shelton watched as the attendant stood beside the only passenger wearing a turban. His curiosity was heightened when the attendant called Madame PJ, "Monsieur Winsarah." But he was startled as the attendant soon asked him for his ticket.

When Priscilla heard the attendant asking someone, "Monsieur, parlez-vous Français?" She assumed the passenger was a foreigner and was about to learn he was American, too.

When again he asked for the passenger's ticket in French, the man said, "Oui. Non. Ah, heck. I'm American," several passengers snickered.

"Monsieur, your ticket. S'il vous plaît." The attendant then fussed.

"You Americans think you can do as you please. This is all *wrong*." Then he explained the correct way to fill in the ticket, during which Priscilla assumed the American must have done as instructed. She did not surmise that the American was Shelton, who held his breath and prayed that she did not turn around and see him even as he was the cause of all the commotion. But Priscilla would hardly put her nose into someone else's business. Besides, she was engrossed in one of her favorite novels about the nineteenth-century eccentric English family's trek on yet another excavation in Egypt.

Shortly after the attendant completed his business with Shelton, an announcement came over the loudspeaker: "We are experiencing a slight delay to Zurich due to snow removal on the tracks up ahead. Please consider visiting the dining car. We will resume our trip shortly." The typical three-hour trip would last nearly four hours.

Somewhat disappointed, a few passengers grumbled while others headed for the dining car. It was around 6:30, and although Priscilla was hungry, she waited patiently until the aisle cleared.

As she entered the dining car, people seated at tables with empty seats raised their fingers, indicating the number of available seats, or they nodded at "him" to join them. Priscilla had long since learned to look for specific types of people, such as older couples or people who seemed unimposing and non-threatening. She spotted an older couple smiling, made a faint smile back at them, strolled over, her book prominently displayed, and took a seat at their table.

"Bonjour, Monsieur," the man said, still smiling.

His wife nudged him. "Ask if he's skiing. And don't forget to tell him this is the *end* of the ski season." She smiled at Priscilla as if she had not understood a word she had just said.

"This is the *end* of the ski season," the man said while speaking in French.

Unmoved by their conversation, Priscilla nodded and smiled, then showed them her book and continued reading.

A tad more persistent than his wife, the husband chanced to get acquainted.

"Are we British, French, from the Arab world? And do we agree it is best to ski after peak season?"

"Je suis d'accord," said Priscilla in a gruff voice without looking up from her book. But then she surprised the couple by answering the husband's first question, "I'm British."

"Well, now," the husband said, somewhat relieved, "we'll oblige and speak Anglais."

Somewhat more relaxed, Priscilla placed her book on the table, picked up the menu, and said, "I'm famished. What do you recommend?"

After the couple recommended a dish, Priscilla did not get another word in edgewise because they talked until their meals were delivered. Then they talked seemingly endlessly while she ate a breakfast of fried eggs on sourdough with Swiss chard, a bowl of Swiss muesli, a hefty serving of salmon on something that she could not pronounce, and drank a cup of steaming hot café au lait. She ate as if she had not eaten in a long time.

After finishing her meal, she wiped her mouth with a cloth napkin, took some Swiss francs from her breast pocket, and laid them on the table. Then she picked up her book, stood, nodded at the couple, and strolled away.

She sauntered down the aisle without making eye contact with the onlookers, including some young women giggling to get "his" attention. Then, right before she stepped through the sliding doors, she glimpsed a thatch of red hair on a tall, pale-complexioned man and did a double take.

"Uh, oh!" Shelton knew he had been spotted.

Priscilla looked long enough to see Shelton's face flush.

The nosey bugger, she thought and forced herself to keep walking.

Shelton had followed her from the villa. *Now, if that doesn't beat all*, she almost laughed out loud; after all, she was the secret agent, and her chauffeur had tailed her.

28

AN UNLIKELY COUPLE

After the crew removed the snow from the tracks, the train to Zurich rode smoothly, stopping intermittently at Kilchberg, Ruschlikon, and Thalwill until it reached Zurich Central Station. Priscilla did not want to miss her destination. She also wanted to avoid entering Germany, which was slightly north of Zurich and had far more stringent border controls. Nor did she want to enter Lichtenstein, slightly northeast. As they pulled into the station, she reached for the rack above for her ski jacket, slipped it on, and remained standing like most other passengers. When Priscilla, with Shelton not far behind, headed to the luggage compartment to get her duffel, she saw that Shelton was not the only one following her. She had another tail. Two overly nondescript men, their hats pulled down low over their faces and their collars up around their ears, were trying desperately to pretend not to be watching her. Yet, she did not panic because she was used to being followed. But now she needed to lose the men and Shelton, too.

She waited on the platform until she spotted her wayward chauffeur, whom she intentionally brushed up against. "Keep walking. You bloody twerp. We'll talk later."

Somewhat startled, Shelton whispered, "When are you going to tell me what you're up to?"

"You bloody bastard. Don't you know? We're being followed. So stop talking and do as I say."

"All right, already. But do you have to call me a 'bastard?'"

Priscilla ignored the question. Instead, she stopped, dropped her duffel, and took out a tourist map when she noticed Shelton was smart enough to pretend to look for something in his jacket.

"Pay attention," she said after glancing at the map. "We're headed three blocks south of here. Look for the Barabas Hostel. That's B-A-R-A-B-A-S. It's a historic building right off Lowengraben Avenue. Look for a street that begins with the letter 'L.' Now walk a step or two ahead of me, and do not look at me as if you recognize me. I'll fill you in along the way."

Priscilla had figured out how to use Shelton's unexpected presence to her advantage.

Before long, they were at the Barabas Hostel, where she told Shelton to go inside and wait in the lobby as a precautionary measure. "I've got to lose those bloodhounds on our trail; I'll be about ten minutes."

She waved down a taxi. When one pulled up to the curb, she noticed another passenger in the backseat as she got inside. Since the other passenger wore a ski suit and had skiing gear, she figured he must have caught the taxi from the train station. Priscilla nodded at the man and told the taxi driver to proceed up Loewengraben Avenue for ten blocks. She removed her ski jacket, took out a heavy woolen sweater from her duffel, and pulled it over her camouflage top. All while she did that, the other passenger ignored her. This was a society where people minded their own business. But he did watch with interest when she removed her turban and brushed her short hair.

She now wore a slightly different disguise.

But before they had ridden the ten blocks, "Arrêter ici," she said, "Stop here."

The driver was upset because of the shortened distance and subsequently reduced fare. But when Priscilla handed him the equivalent of twenty U.S. dollars in Swiss francs, he smiled and said, "N'importe quel moment, Dame!" clearly pleased with the large tip.

She slipped on her fabulous Jackie O'-style eggshell-colored sunglasses. Now, in casual attire, she resembled a movie star more than when the man who had entered the taxi earlier had first seen her.

No longer recognizable by the men who tailed her, Priscilla tucked her duffel under her arm and proceeded down another street parallel to Loewengraben Avenue. Thinking she was still inside the taxi, the men on her tail followed the taxi with the other passenger.

Priscilla was back at the hostel a few minutes later. She spotted a delivery entrance at the rear and walked through to the kitchen. The staff stared at her as she took out her map. "Is this the Barabas Hostel?" Without waiting for an answer, she continued as if she had entered the front.

"Assertive people," her father once told her, "often gain unconditional access and acceptance."

Upon entering the lobby, she saw Shelton anxiously pacing. He must have thought she had duped him. But when he saw an androgynous-looking person with a buzz haircut, which he himself had cut, and those fabulous Jackie O'-style sunglasses, he relaxed. He waited for further instructions. But Priscilla did not go straight to him. She headed to the registration desk. After receiving the key to her room, she discreetly beckoned for Shelton to follow. Priscilla had already decided that losing him would take too much energy and resources. Since he refused to return to the Luzern safe house and was adamant about looking after her, she revised her plan to allow for his companionship. But he was about to find out her terms were conditional. She had done something similar with her friend Julia during her time in the Ohio Senate years ago.

"Shelton," she said when they were in the room and the door closed, "you and I are lovers." She ignored his flummoxed expression and continued to her point. "We're gay, queer. Whatever the expression is." As such, Shelton, like Julia before him, now realized Priscilla was not above utilizing her friends to get the job done, including pretending to be gay.

Still ignoring his incredulity, she glanced around the room and noticed a cedar chest, a floor-length mirror, a small dresser, what looked like a card table, two high-back leather chairs, and a full-size bed. "Excellent. This'll do just fine." The room was more extensive and better furnished than the typical bed-and-breakfast, or hostel as it was called in Europe. Swiss proprietors in the world-famous City of Zurich offered amenities their guests appreciated. On the other hand, the facility had communal bathrooms.

After finally finding his voice, "I'm sorry, Madame PJ, but what did you just say? I must've misheard you," the wayward chauffeur said.

"Shelton, you heard me right the first time. In Switzerland, no one gives a damn about anybody's sexuality. By the way, stop calling me 'Madame PJ.' My name is Phillipe Winsarah. Practice saying, *Phillipe*."

"Are you telling me that you and I are an item, that we will share this room, and that—" He paused as he could not say the word "bed."

"Yes, yes, and yes."

"But Master Carlton will *kill* me."

"*Master Carlton* is not here. Nor will he ever know about this arrangement unless you tell him. Stop fretting, Shelton. You and I aren't actual lovers, but we will continue as lovers in public. *Got that?*"

Shelton's pale complexion turned a dark shade of red, darker than his blazing red hair. He shook his head in disbelief as he sat on the edge of the bed. When he realized it was the bed on which he had sat, he jumped up and sat on one of the chairs.

While Shelton openly pondered, "What have I gotten myself into?" Priscilla silently pondered how much he knew about her mission. She knew he and Carlton were close and often shared secrets. Shelton and Deputy Director Froley had bonded during the deputy director's unexpected visit to her Marmande villa. Shelton had also befriended Ronnie and maybe even one of the intelligence agents, probably Sam. Hence, Priscilla surmised that Shelton already knew more than he should about her mission. Why else would he tail her? At that moment, though, he seemed baffled, unsettled, and even frail. But Shelton was not a frail man or easily unsettled or baffled. He was shrewd and could handle himself in many precarious situations. As she pondered what Shelton was really up to, she decided to take the bull by its horns, as it were.

"What have *you* gotten *yourself* into? *You* haven't the foggiest idea how *you've* interfered with *my* work." Then, just as quickly, she changed the subject and her voice.

"Listen, Shelton, do you ski?"

"Ski?"

"Yeah, that's what folks do in this part of the world."

Without waiting for his answer, she began unpacking her duffel, laughed, and said, "We head over to the slopes shortly. Then we come back here, and I write. Then we head back to the slopes in the morning, then back here again, where I write some more. Then, if necessary, I sleep. And since you do not ski, you might find amusement sitting around the fireside, socializing with the tourists, sipping hot tea-and-rum, and watching us ski." Priscilla put her game plan into action because she did not possess enough energy or desire to deal with whatever seemed to unsettle Shelton. *After all*, she thought, *I never asked for his help in the first place.*

Just then, she realized that Shelton did not have any luggage. She told him they would go shopping at some point, which they did eventually.

Priscilla left the unsettled Shelton and headed to the communal bathroom. She removed her woolen sweater, kept on the camouflage uniform, and put her ski suit back on. When she returned, Shelton still sat on the chair, this time holding his head in his hands.

"Oh, yeah," she said as she removed a folded blanket from the foot of the bed and a pillow and tossed them on the floor. You can make a pallet. For sure, I'm sleeping in the bed." Then she laughed.

Shelton was more than just unsettled; he was at a loss dealing with what was now *their* precarious circumstance, not because people might perceive him as gay

162

or about whatever Madame PJ was up to. After all, his relationship with Master Carlton was not without knowledge about what secret agents did. But he now knew for sure that Priscilla was on a mission. Although he was unsettled, it was out of fear for her. As her bodyguard, he was sworn to protect her. And he would do just that. For now, however, fear was making way for another emotion: excitement.

"Are you coming, Shelton? It's ski time!"

While the unlikely couple headed to the slopes, the two men who followed the taxi soon realized the passenger who now exited the vehicle was not the person they had been tailing. They called CF Commander Wozniah to report.

"Yeah, boss. Sorry, but she duped us. And the chauffeur, Shelton, seems to be in on it. She met him on the train and left him at a hotel, but we're fairly certain that was another ruse."

"No problem," the CF commander said. "We're tracking her. They're headed over to the slopes where we suspect 'our girl' is about to try her hands, or is that her legs, at skiing." He laughed.

"Oh yeah," the agent said. "I forgot about her tracking device."

As for the men who followed the lot of them, they soon realized that they, too, had been given the slip. But unlike the two men they had followed, they did not contact their superior—the Zulfika Kasun-impersonator. As they followed the men who followed Priscilla—disguised as Phillipe—and Shelton, they observed Priscilla and Shelton carrying on like lovers, holding hands, hugging, and touching each other affectionately. Well, Priscilla did most of the affectionate touching because—terrified at what would happen after his Master Carlton got wind of this little scheme—Shelton was as stiff as a board.

29

SKIING ON BEACH-MOUNTAIN

Priscilla's goggles hung down from her neck as she and Shelton exited the hostel. She would rent her other skiing gear at the lodge.

"Are you really going to ski?" Shelton asked. "And how long will it take us to get there?"

"It'll probably take half an hour or so." She ignored his first question.

"And we get there, how?"

"A taxi."

As Priscilla hailed a taxi, she was surprised when Shelton grabbed her arm. "Hold a while, Phillipe; if we're going to be an item, *I'm* the man. Just tell me what you want to do, and *I'll* take care of it. *Got that,* Phillipe?"

Priscilla shook her head. *Even as a man, I still have to yield to another man.*

As the unlikely couple got into the taxi, Shelton told the driver, "Beach-Mountain," looked at Priscilla for confirmation, and said, "unless that tourist map of yours was incorrect."

"Seidengasse ou Niederdorfstrasse?" asked the driver.

"Niederdorfstrasse," Priscilla answered.

Nearly twenty minutes later, around 11:00 that morning, they were at the base of Beach Mountain. The taxi driver slowed and headed up the hill to the observatory. Priscilla marveled at the sight of the picturesque snow-capped mountains and the skiers—some carrying their gear, others laughing and frolicking about, while others strolled along the narrow, snow-covered lane.

Looking up at the slopes, she said, "Wow! This is gonna be fun!"

When the taxi came to a halt, Shelton paid the driver. As they got out, he held Priscilla's hand and led her to the lodge. They looked around the bustling space for the rental shop. Shelton spotted a sign that read **Magasin de Location**. Still holding Priscilla's hand, he led the way.

An eager sales attendant greeted the couple, as Shelton seemed to command rather than ask, "Do you speak English?"

"Oui, Monsieur, I speak Anglais. Will the both of you require the gear?"

"Only my partner, Phillipe."

Priscilla sidled up to the attendant, who had already asked about her boot size.

Moments later, he showed her three different pairs of boots and was surprised that his customer was so easily satisfied.

"I'll take those." She chose a black pair to match her black-and-brown ski suit. Then she removed her snow boots, stepped into the ski boots, snapped the latches into place, and walked around the room to test the fit.

When the attendant turned to the skis and pointed out three styles, Priscilla selected the black pair.

"And so, noir it is." Next, he pointed to the helmets and asked, "Would you like a helmet, or do you prefer to keep on your handsome headdress?"

Priscilla had forgotten she even wore the turban. She smiled and thought about the men who followed them. "Yeah, mon ami, I'm keeping on my turban."

The last thing the attendant did was measure her for poles. Priscilla selected a pair of lightweight but durable black aluminum poles with straps. The poles had a curvy white design, which Phillipe's feminine side liked. She held the poles and bent her knees as if ready to ski.

"What do you think, Shelton?"

"Swell, Phillipe. Just swell."

Priscilla paid for the gear and then headed to the slopes.

Shelton went upstairs and found a window seat to watch the skiers. Not knowing what to expect, he held his breath when he saw Priscilla approaching the slopes. She bent her knees and held her arms triangularly, with her poles parallel to the snow-capped terrain. When she took off down the slopes, Shelton's eyebrows rose, and his pale complexion almost matched his red hair color. "Wow! She really can ski."

As Priscilla skied seemingly effortlessly, Shelton had no way of knowing that she had been praying the whole time.

Priscilla had not been on the slopes in years, but as she felt the snow-packed terrain under her skis and the cold air brushing against her face, she felt more and more confident. She last skied on the bunny slopes in Sinclairville, New York, a decade ago. Now, here she was skiing in Zurich, Switzerland, and on world-class slopes. *No one is going to believe this.*

She swerved carefully to the right and then left, feeling more at ease. As her confidence increased, so did her speed. After a few minutes, she was whizzing down the slopes, swerving this way and that.

Then, quite unexpectedly, she welled up. Tears filled her goggles. She wedged her skis and stopped abruptly. Priscilla was thinking about Helen, who she knew had never skied and now never would because of her declining mental health.

When the other skiers noticed Priscilla had stopped seemingly suddenly, they came to her rescue. But when she realized she had drawn attention to herself, she quickly regained her composure.

An American couple stopped, and the woman asked if "he" was okay.

Priscilla spoke in a deep, masculine voice. "Oh, it's nothing. Forgot my contact lenses, and the air at this altitude is more irritating than I thought."

The woman reached inside her ski jacket and took out some tissues. "I always carry tissues with me. Then again, maybe it's a girl thing."

The man with her introduced them. "I'm David Wasserman, and this is my girlfriend, Amy Fisher. We're visiting from San Francisco."

"Phillipe Winsarah," Priscilla said. "I'm pleased to meet you. I'm here on a ski trip." She firmly shook their hands.

After the introductions, they caught a lift back to the lodge. As the lift stopped, Priscilla was surprised to see an overly anxious Shelton.

"Phillipe! What happened? Are you all right? You stopped so abruptly."

"Yes, Shelton. I'm fine. Needed a few tissues was all, which this lovely couple was kind enough to give me." Priscilla turned to her new acquaintances. "This is David Wasserman and his girlfriend, Amy Fisher. They're from San Francisco."

"Pleased to make your acquaintance, David, Amy. I'm Shelton, and Phillipe is my partner." That was the first and the last time Shelton would introduce himself as such. But for now, he did not feel too bad, especially since David and Amy had been so kind to Madame PJ.

The couples ordered drinks and got better acquainted. Then, some fifteen minutes into their conversation, Priscilla stood up and declared: "Didn't come this far for conversation. Anybody up for another run?"

David and Amy both shook their heads. "We'll sit this one out and enjoy our drinks by the fire," Amy said, smiling.

"It was a pleasure to meet you," Priscilla said as she collected her gear and headed back to the slopes.

More relaxed now, she smiled as she resumed skiing confidently and thought about how she would one day teach Austin to ski. *Then again*, she thought, *perhaps*

Carlton has already included that on his list. More importantly, Priscilla figured out how to use Shelton for the next part of her plan.

While Priscilla skied and Shelton enjoyed drinks with David and Amy by the fire at the Niederdorfstrasse observatory, the two men who followed them and the men who followed the lot of them took photos and videos and transmitted them back to their respective superiors.

CF Commander Wozniah examined the images. "Well, damn. Our girl really can ski!"

But when Angel commented that he "already knew Priscilla could ski," the commander came undone, especially when Jordy made a similar comment.

"What do you mean, Angel, you 'already knew?' And you, Jordy? What do you mean, 'You had your suspicions?'"

Angel turned the scarred side of his face away and said, "Well, Tommy, we already knew she was a pretty good outdoors person. You know, horseback riding, tennis, scuba diving, and other sports. So, why not skiing?"

Tommy turned to Jordy for his explanation.

Jordy pointed his cane at him and said, "Priscilla grew up in Prendergast at the tip of the Allegheny Mountains in a town not far from a ski resort. It makes sense that she could ski. Besides," he elaborated, "skiing and ice skating are favorite pastimes in our hometown."

"Anyhow, bro'," Angel noted, "we kinda' thought you already knew."

Then, he and Jordy nudged each other and fought hard not to laugh. They were well aware of the ongoing competition between their longtime friend Tommy Wozniah—their CF commander—and Priscilla, whom they still regarded as a special envoy. They had no idea she was one of them, a full-fledged agent.

Even so, Angel and Jordy were unaware of the extent of the differences between Priscilla and Tommy, who had been in stiff competition to outwit each other from the start. Although Priscilla had no way of knowing how Tommy fit into her mission, she took great pleasure in having already thrown the men who followed her off her scent at least once. But she was unaware that Tommy was keeping tabs and scores on everything she succeeded in doing, which included outwitting him. Now, she had just proven to him and everybody else who wondered about her skiing skills that she was no slouch in that department.

Meanwhile, the other Zulfika Kasun impersonator was taken aback when his men who followed Shelton and Priscilla reported. Yet, while he put another part of his plan into action, so, too, did Priscilla.

30

THEY WON'T TRACK ME NOW

Priscilla now carefully crafted a crucial part of her plan. This mission was complicated. Nevertheless, she was greatly relieved that she controlled the terms of her rendezvous with Zulfika Kasun. Her ski excursion not only helped her to relax and put some of the people who followed her off her trail but also gave her time to think through the execution of her plan, which she did not discuss with anyone, not even Deputy Director Froley. Now, she needed to figure out how to return to the States to visit her sister Helen and discreetly meet with her contact, an NSA counterintelligence agent.

For the next three days, Priscilla skied, wrote, and slept at odd hours, preparing herself to adjust to the difference in the time zones, particularly the time difference between New England back in the States and Croatia in Eastern Europe. She needed to be on top of her game when she met with the elusive Zulfika Kasun, or whoever he was. She also wondered who her contact in Eastern Europe would be, even though Jim Froley had said it would be "someone she would recognize."

CIA Deputy Director Froley knew of Priscilla's plan to visit her mother, Liza, and her sister, Helen, and her NSA contact. So, he waited for her update upon her return from the States. But while he waited, he took great pleasure hearing how skillful she was at eluding and matching wits with the CF commander. He got an earful and an eye-full, too, when he learned of Priscilla's skiing prowess and saw the photos and videos of her disguised as Phillipe and Shelton as an item, a gay couple, at that! But his amusement with his special agent would soon dissipate when he learned about the crucial next part of her plan.

Before Priscilla departed for the States, she kept an appointment at a local medical clinic. Shelton did not question her announcement that she was going shopping in a new disguise—as a woman. Nor did he offer to accompany her. Meanwhile, Priscilla was not sure, but she had her suspicions that Shelton was still transmitting messages about their every move to Sam back at the Luzern safe house. Also, tracking Shelton's phone made it easy for the men who followed the lot of them to stay on their trail.

Now posing as her female alias, Phyllis Winsarah, Priscilla headed out to her appointment at the Zurich Medical Center. She sported her beige haute couture cashmere outfit and matching over-the-knee high-heel tan leather boots. Her makeup, dangling earrings, and Jackie O'-style sunglasses complemented her buzz-cut hairstyle.

When the receptionist called for "Phyllis Winsarah," she approached the receptionist's station.

"The doctor will see you now."

Priscilla went into the doctor's office.

"Good morning, Mlle. Winsarah. I'm Dr. Julian Brandenberger."

"Good morning, Dr. Brandenberger."

From where Priscilla stood, the doctor was middle-aged, medium height, and slender, with a full head of thick blonde hair. His kind blue eyes contrasted against his gold-rimmed glasses. Enough certificates were on display documenting his medical credentials to make any parent proud. After sizing him up, Priscilla liked him immediately. Nevertheless, she wondered about the degree of his discretion.

"It is my understanding that you wish me to remove a small electronic device from your lower back. Correct?" Then, without waiting for a response, he told her, "Please remove your clothing, put on the dressing gown, and I will do a preliminary examination."

The doctor left the examination room, giving Priscilla enough time to change into the dressing gown. When he returned, he was accompanied by a female nurse, whom he introduced as "Nurse Fraser." Then, he asked Priscilla to show him where the electronic device was implanted. As he examined the area around the device, he asked her questions about her health and any medication she was taking and was surprised at her candor.

"Apart from meclizine and diazepam or valium tablets, I don't take any other medicine. You see, Dr. Brandenberger," she said, over her shoulders, "I have a problem with my equilibrium, hence the vertigo. I'm also acrophobic and claustrophobic."

While Priscilla talked, Dr. Brandenberger noticed a raised elongated welt on her lower back measuring an inch and a half long and one-half inch wide. He then instructed the nurse to prepare for an X-ray. The screening took only a few minutes.

The doctor soon held a dark film against a bright light. Standing beside him, Nurse Fraser said, "That's strange. Don't you think?" Both realized immediately that hers was no ordinary medical implant; it looked like an encrypted device. But since the patient had asked for its removal, the doctor would oblige.

Touching the welt, he said, "Do you feel anything? Any discomfort?" Then he surprised her by saying, "Perhaps Mademoiselle does not wish to share information about how she came to have this implant."

"I can feel your cold fingers," she said, but no more.

At that, the doctor realized his patient was hardly forthcoming about her mysterious implant. Without further discussion, he told her to lie still on her stomach as he prepared to administer anesthesia to offset any pain. "This should only take a minute."

While the anesthesia took effect, Priscilla told the doctor that the person who implanted the device had used a tool like a staple gun, which the doctor had already determined.

But before he made his first incision, he surprised her when he said, "So Mademoiselle no longer wishes to be tracked?"

Priscilla flinched.

Then, "Precisely," said she as she felt latex gloves and something like a sharp scalpel sliding across the outline of the implant. While the doctor performed the surgical procedure, Priscilla was excited to regain her freedom and privacy.

"Now for our little secret," he said.

Priscilla felt something like tweezers pulling at the tracking device. The doctor used grasping forceps to pull at it more than once because it was so snuggly implanted.

Less than a minute later, Dr. Brandenberger exclaimed, "Voila!" He dropped the tracking device into a metal pan that Nurse Fraser held. Then he said, "That wasn't so bad. Was it? Now, all we need are a few stitches, and as you young people say, 'You'll be good to go.'"

He carefully stitched the wound and covered it with a flesh-colored bandage. Now Priscilla was "good to go." The nurse could have stitched the small incision, but the doctor knew this was no ordinary patient. Ordinary people did not wear sophisticated tracking devices like the one he had just removed from this woman's lower back.

Priscilla got dressed after the doctor left the room and prepared to leave.

Shortly, Dr. Brandenberger returned alone. He held a small plastic bag in his hand, and before Priscilla could say anything, he handed it to her. "This, young lady, you might wish to dispose of yourself. I'm sure to be called upon by the authorities. And I need to tell them that I removed the electronic device and placed it back in your care. Comprenez-vous?"

"Oui, Médecin."

Dr. Brandenberger provided many services for patients from around the world, which is why Priscilla had chosen him in the first place. But this was the first time he had been asked to remove such a device. Since he knew he would have to report his work to the Swiss Medical Board, not to mention the Swiss government, he informed his one-time patient that that was what he would do.

"Oui, Médecin. Et, merci." Priscilla thanked him and bid him farewell.

She left the Zurich Medical Center a free woman, well, sort of, because she never once thought about how what she had done would impact her current or future missions, for that matter. Nor did she consider how Deputy Director Froley might regard such an action. On that note, her friend Julia could have pointed out how Priscilla rarely considered the ramifications of her actions. For sure, she gave no thought to how CF Commander Wozniah would react once he found out.

Priscilla would think about all of that later.

For now, her thoughts were clear, and her steps light. As she strolled from the Zurich Medical Center, she smirked. *Now, for sure, they won't be able to track me with that damn tracking device. Besides, none of "the boys" wear such ludicrous devices. Why me?* Priscilla was a staunch feminist. But would her philosophical viewpoint impact her work as a CIA agent? Only time would tell, and for now, time was not talking.

It was time for Priscilla to take care of some personal business.

Before she returned to the Barabas Hostel as Phyllis Winsarah, she walked along Bahnhofstrasse, a well-known street in the prominent shopping district in Zurich. She popped into an opulent boutique and tried on a leather coat, looked at herself in a mirror, and told the salesperson, "This'll do just fine." She purchased an elegant cherry-red leather coat that perfectly matched her red beret.

After being away for almost three hours, Priscilla returned to the hostel. Since she had only one shopping bag, Shelton wondered what had happened; he had expected her to return with loads of items, but she had not.

"Did you leave your other packages in the lobby? Do you need me to get them?"

"No, just this one item." She removed the red leather coat from the bag and showed it to him. Admiring her new coat, she said, "Shelton, how would you like to return to the city with me? I need to do some banking."

"Sure. But are we going as an item? Are we a regular couple? Are you a woman on your own again, or what?"

"'An item.'"

Priscilla removed her dangling earrings and wiped the makeup from her face. Then, she changed into her men's clothing to become Phillipe again and put on her turban.

As Shelton watched her change into another disguise, he said, "Nobody, I mean nobody, will ever believe any of this."

They both laughed.

When Priscilla, as Phillipe, carrying her duffel under her arm, and Shelton arrived at the Credit Swiss Bank on Seefeldstr—amid the most highly-valued real estate in Europe—neither resembled the sophisticated and wealthy clientele known to cater to the financial establishment. Indeed, the unlikely couple looked like tourists who might have gotten lost and sought directions. Yet, Priscilla carried herself assertively. She approached a customer service station, sat facing the manager without being asked to do so, removed a card from her wallet, and handed it to him. The manager examined it, and when he saw an account number, he held open his hand, and she handed him her Phillipe Winsarah British passport. The manager swiped it.

Swiss banks have exceptional security and rules governing access to accounts. Some require a finger or palm print or an iris and an account number. This bank validated a customer's identification from encryptions on their passports, but it still required a key. After validating Phillipe Winsarah's identity, the manager called for a staffer to escort "him" to "his" safe deposit box. As it turned out, the manager was accustomed to wealthy clientele who did not look the part, and so it was that Phillipe Winsarah was well-received. As Priscilla followed the staffer, she beckoned Shelton to join them.

"Well, now, let me guess," Shelton said jokingly, "We've even got a Swiss bank account." He chuckled as, for the moment, he already knew that much. Even so, what he thought he knew about Madame PJ was about to change again.

They stood before a wall of safe deposit boxes. When the staffer spotted the one associated with Phillipe's account number, he and Priscilla inserted their respective keys, and presto! The staffer then handed her the rectangular metal box and escorted the couple to a curtained space with a table and chair. He pulled the curtain behind him and left them alone.

Priscilla lifted the lid on the metal box. Then she placed her duffel on the table and removed some items. But when she started to undress, Shelton blushed and turned away. She quickly changed from the men's clothing into her beige cashmere outfit and over-the-knee high-heel leather boots. While Priscilla changed, Shelton was amazed at her calm demeanor. Just imagine changing disguises in a Swiss bank vault. Priscilla transformed yet again when she removed the tan turban and put on her red beret, the new cherry red leather coat, and her Jackie O'-style sunglasses.

Disguised again as Phyllis Winsarah, she sat at the table and examined the contents of the metal box. She removed an American passport, an American Express card, and a New York driver's license, each bearing the name Phyllis Winsarah. She counted a sum of two thousand U.S. dollars. However, she did not remove either of the two pistols, which she knew Shelton also saw. As an afterthought, she counted out loud a sum of five thousand U.S. dollars, looked at Shelton, and said, "You're buying a nice European-cut suit to wear on the next leg of our journey and some sophisticated casual wear. Got that?"

"Oh no! Madame PJ." Shelton slipped and called her by her real name. "I'm sorry. I forgot. It won't happen again. But I can't take your money."

"Oh, but you *can,* and you *will.* You see, Shelton," she explained, "You *cannot* use your credit cards on this trip because *you* are not here." She finished counting the bills, then soberly made her point: "On and off the record, you are not here. Understand?"

"Oh, I guess I see—"

"Yeah, I thought you would. None of what we are doing is even happening. I am *not* in Switzerland skiing, and neither are you." She looked into his confused brown eyes and repeated herself slowly and clearly. "Neither of us is here, Shelton." At that reminder, Shelton remembered that Laverne and MI6 Commander Thomas had likewise cautioned him, Hettie, and Melissa at the Luzern safe house. He was beginning to understand the seriousness of Priscilla's mission.

Priscilla then smiled and said, "Showtime again, my man!"

She closed the lid on the metal box, picked up her duffel, and turned it inside out, revealing its more feminine side—the red-and-beige striped side on rollers.

"Your efficiency is amazing," Shelton said as he helped her collect the items and put them back into her duffel.

"Time to get you into a nice suit, you dashing fella."

"I sure hope I don't call you Phillipe instead of Phyllis, and to think, I was warming up to Phillipe."

Then they dramatically pulled back the curtain and handed the metal box back to the staffer, who was astonished at the sight of an attractive, stylishly dressed

174

woman mysteriously having replaced the man he had only moments ago handed the safe deposit box to, but whom Priscilla and Shelton pretended not even to notice.

As the couple headed toward the exit of the Credit Swiss Bank, the manager who had assisted them, the security guards, and customers who had seen them earlier did double takes at the couple strolling through the lobby, especially at Phillipe, who now looked like a fashionista.

But no one was as astonished as the two men who followed the couple and the men who followed the lot of them because they had all seen the couple when they first entered the bank and then when they had exited. Then, one of the men said, "No one is going to believe any of this. No one."

Later that afternoon, Priscilla and Shelton, now in his European-cut suit, made for an eye-catching couple as they sipped cocktails in the VIP lounge of an American Airlines gate at the Flughafen Zürich AG. There, they waited for the announcement of their flight departure to JFK Airport, from where they would catch a connecting flight to St. Louis, Missouri, and rent a car for Shelton to drive the short distance to Sills Creek, Illinois.

Several hours later, after an exceptionally long flight from Zurich to New York and another flight to St. Louis, Priscilla and Shelton rented a car using Phyllis Winsarah's American Express card. That was one of the first discrepancies Deputy Director Froley noticed as he and his men at Langley tracked Priscilla's movements. "How," they all queried, "can she be in two places at the same time?" As it so happened, no matter how many scenarios they considered, they could not fathom how that could be the case. It never occurred to any of them that Priscilla had been bold enough to remove her tracking device, which she had stashed in a trash receptacle outside the Barabas Hostel. The cold reality would eventually come to them, but not just yet. For now, the deputy director made a calculated guess and correctly assumed that Priscilla—using her alias as Phyllis Winsarah—had indeed flown to New York and then to St. Louis en route to Sills Creek, one week ahead of her scheduled visit at that!

31

THE SURPRISE VISIT

It was cold and snowing in southern Illinois. When Shelton opened the door of the black Cadillac in which he chauffeured Priscilla as herself—she stepped out in her haute couture beige cashmere outfit, cherry red leather coat, red beret, over-the-knee high-heel leather boots, and, of course, her Jackie O'-style sunglasses—more than a few people stared from their windows and the street. *Who*, they must have wondered, *is that fabulous-looking woman? And that dashing man!*

Sitting in her front room, Liza could not help noticing through the window the black Cadillac parked curbside in front of her home. When she saw a fashionably dressed woman, she thought momentarily that a movie star was visiting, but soon realized the woman was her beloved Priscilla. *But Priscilla said that she'd be visiting in two weeks. And it's only been one!* As Liza's eyes filled with tears at the surprise visit, she patted her hair into place and smoothed out the wrinkles on her dress. Happy tears rolled down her cheeks as she opened her door to greet Priscilla and the dashing man, who looked somewhat familiar.

Seeing her mother, Priscilla rushed up the steps and, uncharacteristically, hugged her tightly. Circumstances being what they were, she knew her mother needed it, and at this moment, so did she.

"Momma. I'm so sorry I didn't come sooner."

"Oh, Priscilla, Child. It's so good to see you." Liza stood back and looked at her daughter up and down. "My, my, how we've changed. Are you in a movie or something else you haven't told me about?"

When Priscilla did not respond, Shelton stepped up on the porch and interjected: "Hello, Mrs. Austin. I'm Shelton. Remember me?"

"Yes, young man!" Liza indeed remembered him from her visits to Bow Lake. "I certainly do." She held her arms wide to embrace him.

Pulling away from his embrace, she said, "Where are my manners? Come on inside, you two. You must be cold and hungry. Besides, my doorbell is going to ring real soon. So too will my telephone." That she said because she knew her nosey neighbors and relatives were sure to come a-calling.

As they walked through Liza's front room, Shelton noticed several large pictures on the walls: an image of The Last Supper and one of Jesus, the Christ, adorned one wall; and an image of Martin Luther King, Jr., President John F. Kennedy, and President Fleetwood Marshall Hollingsworth hung prominently on another wall. He had heard tell of Black people displaying such images on their living room walls, but now he saw that it was true.

When they reached the den, Liza told him, "This is our family room. Some call it a drawing room. But it's nothing like the one in your great big mansion back in Bow Lake."

"Oh, but Mrs. Austin," Shelton corrected her, "this house is just like my parent's home, well, except for the pictures on the walls. And, by the way, I'm not a Bernhardt; I'm their chauffeur. But your daughter, Madame PJ, is married to the owner's son. So, one day, 'that great big mansion' will belong to her. Otherwise, I'm just like you and most other people."

Shelton sat on the sofa and watched Priscilla enter the kitchen. Then, he and Liza continued their conversation.

As Priscilla entered, she saw Helen seated at the small table. She seemed listless and stared straight ahead at nothing. Priscilla, not known for being emotional, at least not in public, welled up as she pulled out a chair to sit next to her. She tried hard not to stare at her sister's pale face, which looked like life had been sucked out of it. Helen had always been thin, but now she was rail thin. All that aside, her eyes twinkled at the sight of her beloved sister.

"Ah, Priscilla, it's you. When did you get in? And what's with the short haircut?" Despite her waning mental health, Helen had moments of clarity, like now, as she admired her sister's new look.

Priscilla took off her beret and rubbed her short hair. Her sad tears turned into tears of joy. "Oh, this," she said, finally thinking, "*Thank you, Lord, for creating a clever segue.* "Helen, I'm playing the part of a young man. So I cut my hair." It was the truth, at least partly.

Just as she asked how things were with Helen, she almost regretted it, but Helen responded unexpectedly.

"Well, Missy, since you asked. I suppose Momma already told you what the doctors said about me. But they don't know what they're talking about."

"Oh?"

"I told them about the time that you and I rode the train as twins and how Momma used to dress us in the same outfits. But they claim that something is wrong with me." Helen grew silent and stared into space again.

Priscilla felt a big lump in her throat that she could not swallow. She fought back tears. Then she remembered how she and Helen used to comb and brush each other's hair. So she went into Helen's bedroom and got a comb and brush, returned to the kitchen, loosened Helen's braids, and began combing and brushing her hair. Again, Helen regained clarity. "I knew you remembered."

Shelton and Liza heard some of their conversations, and Shelton thought Madame PJ might need some assistance. So, he got up from the sofa and went into the kitchen. The resemblance between the sisters struck him. But Helen was nearly a foot taller and more slender-framed, and she wore her shoulder-length sandy-brown hair in two braids parted down the middle. Helen resented that she had some Caucasian features, such as her thin nose, freckles, and traces of blonde hair. When Shelton leaned over and kissed her pale, freckled face, he noticed she blushed a bright, peachy color.

He was, however, a tad taken aback when she asked, "Who're you? And what brought that on?"

"Helen, I'm a friend of your sister PJ. I'm also the Bernhardt chauffeur. Everybody back home in Bow Lake wishes you the best." This time, he kissed her forehead and returned to the den, where he rejoined Liza.

"You're such a kind young man," Liza said, holding back tears.

Shelton changed the subject and filled her in on the goings-on at Bow Lake. But when he said, "And Lady Chelsea is having the time of her life redecorating," he and Liza laughed. Liza laughed because she thought the Bernhardt mansion was a tad old-fashioned, and Shelton laughed because he agreed with her.

Following Priscilla's revealing conversation with Helen, in which she realized her sister was not the same person she had last seen, she left the kitchen and joined Shelton and Liza, who could see the disbelief on her face.

"Oh, Momma, I had no idea. Helen, well, she's not even in the present. She talks to me as if we were in our youth. When I brushed her hair, she talked about when we behaved as twins."

Shelton noticed Priscilla was far away in her thoughts, and he wanted to comfort her. He did, however, wonder why Liza had not done so. As he stood, Liza pulled at his wrist. "No. Don't even think about it."

178

Shocked, Shelton dropped back to his seat. "But she needs comforting."

"Perhaps. But Son, that child is her father's daughter, and Austins do not break down in the presence of anybody but family, and certainly not in public. Do you understand me?"

"My God! You've got to be kidding me!"

There was no need for Liza to elaborate on the ways of the Austins to Shelton or anybody else. But when she could hold her peace no longer, she reminded him, "Surely you've witnessed similar behavior among the Bernhardts?" Thus, ended that part of their conversation.

When Priscilla seemed to return to the moment, Liza told her about "the nice nursing home that someone has provided for Helen," at which point Priscilla knew that "someone" was her darling Carlton. But Liza thought that "someone" was Priscilla. Priscilla did not comment, nor did she ask who that "someone" was. Therefore, Liza continued talking as if her line of reasoning were correct. "The folks from the nursing home are coming in the morning to pick her up. So, your timing was perfect: you got to see your sister at home for probably the last time."

Liza then excused herself and went into the kitchen to prepare a meal.

Thirty minutes later, they were eating spaghetti and meatballs when the doorbell rang. Just as Liza had predicted, Cousin Myrtle and Liza's other relatives and friends soon filled the house as word had spread about the glamorous visitors. They now knew that Priscilla was the "movie star" who had stepped out of the black Cadillac, and "the dashing man" was not her husband Carlton but the Bernhardt chauffeur Shelton.

"Oh, we have so much to tell the others," Cousin Myrtle bragged. Then she stopped to take in Priscilla's new hairstyle. "Why, Miss Prissy! You cut your hair!"

That was when Priscilla heard her favorite nephew's voice.

"I knew you'd come. Oh, Aunt Priscilla!" Germane shouted as he elbowed through the crowded rooms. "I'm so glad to see you." When he looked her over, he ran his hands through her short hair and said, "I see you cut your hair again." The first time he had seen her hair this way had been at the military intelligence facility during the press conference in Germany following Priscilla's first time in southern Africa. As he hugged his favorite aunt, he heard a familiar voice.

"Hey, young fella, what about me?"

Germane walked over to Shelton and held out his hand. Ignoring it, Shelton hugged him, which Germane happily returned.

At least the young man is comfortable demonstrating affection, Shelton thought. Then, he said, "My goodness, Germane, how we've grown!" Germane was almost fifteen and only a smidgen taller than when Shelton last saw him over the holidays. "And you're so handsome. You've got your mother and Auntie's good looks."

"Ah, cut it out," Germane said, punching him lightly on the shoulder.

That night, after the guests had finally left, Liza arranged for Shelton to stay with her older brother Jasper's family, who lived two short blocks away.

Priscilla slept with Helen for the first and last time since they were raised as twins. As the night wore on, she wept and prayed for her sister.

In her bedroom, Liza felt the power of her daughter's prayer to God to look after her younger sister. She knew Priscilla was learning the hard way that there are some things that even money cannot buy.

More importantly, Priscilla had finally come to terms with her sister's mental health condition. The question was no longer whether Helen would recover but rather how long before she succumbed to the rapid deterioration of her brain.

Early the following day, Priscilla and Shelton bid Helen farewell. They watched as two uniformed staffers helped her into the nursing home's van. Priscilla knew the next time she would see her sister, she might not recognize her. Then she and Shelton bid Liza, Germane, and Cousin Myrtle farewell, but not before Cousin Myrtle asked Germane to take pictures of her with the "movie star" P. J. Austin-Bernhardt and "the dashing" Bernhardt chauffeur Shelton.

32

THE WAFFLE HOUSE ON K STREET

Not until Priscilla—disguised as Phyllis Winsarah—and Shelton returned to the Lambert International Airport did Shelton learn they were not headed back to Zurich. "At least not right away," Priscilla said, which was not the whole truth.

"First, I have a pit stop in D.C."

For the time being, Shelton did not argue with her. Nor did he ask about the pit stop as they caught a flight to the nation's capital.

A couple of hours later, Priscilla, Shelton, and the other passengers felt the aircraft slow down substantially.

"Folks, we're coming up on the nation's capital," the captain informed them. "You'll see the Washington Mall is coming into view."

Looking out the window, Priscilla and Shelton saw the Lincoln Memorial at one end of the mall, the towering 555-foot marble obelisk of the Washington Monument at its center, and the U.S. Capitol at its other end.

The captain rambled on like a tour guide. "Most of you recognize the White House and several other historic structures such as the Smithsonian, the Thomas Jefferson Memorial, the Vietnam Veterans Memorial, and many others. Isn't it a spectacular site? There's no other like it in the world."

A few moments later, he said, "Welcome to the United States capital!"

While the captain spoke ever so proudly about the historic sites in the nation's capital and as the aircraft hovered over the federal district, Priscilla felt her heart skip a beat. *Yes, it's good to be an American.* Her mind returned to her mission "in service to her country."

The aircraft began its descent. Minutes later, the landing gear released, and they taxied to the gate. The gate announcement came next, and they were finally allowed to release their seatbelts, retrieve their personal effects, and exit the plane.

The unlikely couple maneuvered through the crowded Washington Dulles International Airport in search of the nearest exit. Priscilla took charge because Shelton had no idea of the pit stop. Soon, they stood in a growing line outside the terminal, waiting for a taxi.

The line moved quickly. When their turn came, the taxi driver asked for their destination. "To the Waffle House on K Street!" Priscilla said cheerfully.

After they got inside the taxi, the driver repeated their destination: "'To the Waffle House on K Street,' it is."

A waffle house is the pit stop? Or are we going to have breakfast? Shelton wondered as he sat back in his seat.

"We'll talk later," Priscilla whispered as she got comfortable. "But from this point forward, I need your complete confidence. I mean it, Shelton, no more leaks to the folks back at the Luzern villa or anywhere else. Got that?"

Shelton "got that," all right. However, he was somewhat embarrassed to learn that Priscilla knew he had been sending messages to Carlton and the folks back in Luzern. But he had been doing it to protect her. He certainly could not protect her on his own. It still had not occurred to him that she could protect herself and him just fine.

The taxi stopped at their destination some twenty-five minutes later. Priscilla allowed Shelton to pay the fare, "In cash," she whispered in his ear.

They entered the glass-paneled restaurant, where the regular customers were accustomed to seeing all sorts of prominent people like themselves: lawmakers, lobbyists, celebrities, prominent residents, and movie stars. And so it was that no one turned around or even looked at them as the chic couple entered. Priscilla spotted a booth facing the front entrance. They sat there.

Comfortably seated, they watched an attractive Black woman waltz over, holding an aluminum carafe in one hand and two menus in the other hand. "How 'bout some steaming hot coffee to start your day?"

When they nodded, the waitress poured coffee into their cups.

Priscilla savored the aroma and smiled at her.

"Now, what can I get you this lovely morning?" the waitress asked, pointing to her name tag. "My name is Samantha, but you can call me Sam."

Not another Sam! Priscilla thought and smiled.

But Priscilla smiled, not so much at the woman but at the realization that aside from her family, she had not been around Black people in a long time, not really

182

since she lived in Harlem. Otherwise, her primary interaction with Black people had been intermittent. They were usually staff or workers—waitstaff, salespeople, flight attendants, maintenance workers, and taxi drivers. She was delighted to be amid a multicultural gathering, which included many Black people. Looking around appreciatively, she soaked up the ambiance and continued savoring the aroma of her steaming hot coffee.

But when she said, "I'm ready to order, Sam," Sam looked surprised. Without looking at the menu, Priscilla said, "I'll have a couple of sunny-side-up eggs, an English muffin with orange marmalade, a couple of sausage patties burnt, and a bowl of oatmeal."

Then, Shelton placed his order. "And I'd love a Johnsonville Bratwurst and a plate-size Belgian waffle if you have that?" When Sam nodded and winked at him, Shelton blushed and stammered, "Why… thanks…, Sam."

Sam knew she would earn a tip much bigger than the price of their orders. As she strolled away, she shouted at the cooks behind the counter: "An English *and* the American Special!" But since neither Priscilla nor Shelton had read their menus, they had no idea there was even a name for their meal orders.

Sam returned with their meals in short order, and just as she turned her attention to another table, the door to the restaurant opened. A medium-height, handsome man with traditionally cut dark hair entered. But he had a bit of trouble navigating the door with the aid of his two canes.

The man hurriedly made his way to their booth—as if he were expected—and sat next to Priscilla, who noticed his canes but made no comment about them. Sometimes, the work of special agents from different agencies intersects. During her time in the Middle East, Priscilla learned this when she first met NSA Counterintelligence Agent Harry Middleton. Harry sustained the injuries to his legs when Priscilla served her first commission as a special envoy. At the time, she, Melanie—a CIA agent known to Priscilla only by her first name—and Harry fought Arab Islamic extremists in a bunker in Amman. The men beat Harry with metal chairs and broke his legs. However, it was clear that Harry would hardly let broken legs end his career in the spy business. The ease with which he meticulously folded his canes and shoved them aside indicated to Priscilla and anyone else watching that Harry's physical impairments were just that, physical. Otherwise, there was nothing else about him to suggest he could not do what anyone else could do.

Looking across the table at Shelton, who had already dug into his food, Harry said matter-of-factly, "Shelton Ablewhite, I presume?"

Shelton nodded, covered his mouth, and swallowed hard. "Yes, I am he. How do you do?" Then, he continued eating. Though he was interested in what their guest had to say, he pretended not to be.

"All right, then," Harry said as he returned his attention to Priscilla, who was also enjoying her breakfast.

Again, he spoke matter-of-factly when he said, "PJ, you'll find your gear in a locker at Dulles."

It would be another duffel. But this one differed from the red-and-beige striped one on rollers that Priscilla had left in the locker at the airport in Zurich. Weather-beaten and taupe colored, this one contained two sets of company-issued camouflage uniforms—which included a pair of dark brown leather lace-up boots—some men's and women's clothing, her holster and Glock, and a few other items pertinent to the next leg of her mission about which Priscilla was not quite ready to share with Shelton. She waited to tell him later when he could not do much about it, anyway.

Although he appeared to be focused only on his meal, Shelton saw Harry slide a manila envelope beside Priscilla's plate. He also noticed Priscilla kept eating as if she had not seen what Harry did. Then he watched Harry squeeze Priscilla's hand and say, "And may the Force be with you."

Harry Middleton served his country through the Department of State, sometimes the National Security Agency, and who knew which other agencies? Like many of his counterparts, particularly the CF boys in the CIA, Harry was a man of faith. Even though they all worked for different and sometimes competing agencies, Harry genuinely prayed for the success of Priscilla's mission.

Unlike "the boys," however, Harry had long since regarded Priscilla as an outstanding special agent. He was also acutely aware that she wanted to prove that she was as good on her own as "the boys."

His thoughts returned to the moment.

Harry knew that when it came to mission assignments, Priscilla was always paired up with another agent, such as himself, Sam, or Laverne, or sometimes with an agency specialist, such as Melanie, but never with a civilian like Shelton, another reason for his prayer.

Meanwhile, Shelton's curiosity got the better of him, so he asked, "Can you tell me how you two met? Are you a Buckeye? Did you work together in the Ohio Senate? Or are you a PR client?"

"Oh? So he speaks!" Harry exclaimed. Then, without skipping a beat, he said, "PJ and I are business acquaintances. You *are* aware that Miss Prissy is a PR consultant extraordinaire?"

"A darn good one, too," Shelton said.

Then, in her customary way of letting people know when she has been rudely interrupted, Priscilla stared at Shelton intensely and said, "Finish your breakfast, my friend," staving off his not-so-subtle attempt to learn who this seemingly mysterious man was. "This man is on a tight schedule."

"No problem," Shelton said, "Was just trying to be friendly," which neither Priscilla nor Harry knew was the case. Nevertheless, as Shelton finished his breakfast, he surmised that Harry was anything but a PR client.

With no segue whatsoever, Harry used the name adopted by the Bernhardt staff when he said, "Madame PJ, I know what you did. But I'll leave you to explain that to the deputy director."

By then, Shelton's curiosity ripened when Priscilla's only response was her customary smirk. *Hmm*, he wondered, *now what has she done?*

After Harry finished his business, Priscilla put down her knife and fork, slid the manila envelope into her shoulder bag, winked at him, and said, "You're a good man, Charlie Brown. But tell me. Are you the new quartermaster?" She teased Harry for doing something she attributed to underlings. But Harry delivered more than the message about her duffel. Besides, an underling would hardly have known what she had done with her tracking device.

Harry smiled at her, nodded at Shelton, unlatched his canes, and left the diner as if he were late for another appointment.

As for Priscilla, she picked up her knife and fork and finished eating her breakfast as if Harry had never been there.

A moment later, Shelton said, "My goodness, I didn't even get his name."

Priscilla leveled a stern look at him. "Whose name, Shelton? There was no one else here."

She winked at Shelton, who now realized the Waffle House on K Street had been their pit stop after all, and neither of them was even there.

33
THE YUGOSLAV *WHAT!*

Priscilla and Shelton were back at Washington Dulles International Airport, where, again, Shelton assumed they would catch a flight back to Zurich. He and Priscilla—still disguised as Phyllis Winsarah—stood before a locker, where he watched, utterly amazed, as she casually removed a different duffel from the locker than the red-and-beige stripped one and enlightened him about their destination.

"Sorry, ole buddy, ole pal. But our next flight is to *Venice* or Venezia, as the Italians call it. And then, mon ami, we head into what Westerners call 'enemy territory.'"

Shelton was so stunned by her words that he just stared at her. He did not even offer to help her to remove the duffel. He stood like a blazing red-capped tower, juxtaposed against her five feet four and a half inches. When finally finding his voice, he said, "I'm sorry, Madame PJ, Phyllis, Phillipe, or whoever you are this time, but what'd you just say?"

"Shelton, you made your first mistake when you followed me from the Luzern villa. Now I'm stuck with you, so brace yourself. You're in for a grand adventure. But first, we need to shed these flashy clothes."

Still dressed in her exquisite outfit and lugging her duffel, Priscilla led the still-stunned Shelton down the concourse. Ignoring the onlookers, she pulled items from her duffel at the men's restroom entrance. Experienced travelers are used to people changing clothes as they travel from one place to another, especially as they leave or enter different climate zones. Priscilla and Shelton would be traveling to colder, drearier climates where it snowed more than in the American capital.

"Here you go, Shelton. These should fit you." She handed him a brown-and-beige striped shirt, a long-sleeved brown sweater, and dark brown trousers. Then, she said, "Back shortly."

She turned toward the women's restroom and went inside with the duffel. Standing at one of the walls, she removed her cashmere outfit and put on an off-white silk blouse, a light blue sweater, and dark gray slacks. She exchanged her over-the-knee high-heel leather boots for her dark brown leather lace-ups. Then she pulled a dark gray skull cap over her short hair. Since she wore small gold hoop earrings, she could have passed for a male or a female.

When she noticed a woman staring at her a moment too long, she picked up the cashmere outfit, held it up against her, and said, "How 'bout it, Girlfriend? This should fit you just fine."

The woman took the garment and looked incredulously at Priscilla. "My goodness," she said. "Are you sure? I mean, this must've cost a fortune!"

"Yeah, well, you're quite right about that. But you deserve it."

Back in her disguise as Phillipe Winsarah—though she could have passed as an androgynous person—Priscilla picked up the duffel and walked out of the women's restroom where Shelton waited impatiently, holding his European-cut suit as though he did not know what to do with it.

"Say, Shelton, you like your suit, eh?"

"Well, yeah. Of course, It's very well made."

"It is indeed," she said, folding it and stuffing it inside the duffel.

She shoved the duffel to him. "It's time you earned your keep." He smiled. He knew better than to argue.

But Shelton surprised her as they headed toward the departure gate.

"Not so fast, Madame PJ, Phyllis, Phillipe, or whoever you are right now. Not another step until you tell me what you're *really* up to."

"What do you mean, Shelton?"

"Well? You are, after all, a *married* woman, *and* you have a baby, not to mention you're supposed to be in the South of France, writing, not traipsing about the globe like James Bond."

Priscilla sighed, turned to face him, and beckoned him to follow her to the window that overlooked the tarmac.

"Shelton, I'll be clear. Now that you've stuck your nose into a beehive of sorts, and although I cannot tell you precisely what I'm up to, I can say that our lives might be jeopardized. I have something that someone wants, and until I get answers, I really don't know what to tell you or anybody else, for that matter," which was only partly true. Priscilla was a secret agent; she knew how to create a yarn with enough credibility and hope to string someone along.

"All right, I'll play along," Shelton said. "After all, the reason I'm here in the first place is to be of service, to protect you, or both. That's why I followed you. But can you at least tell me what you meant by 'enemy territory?'"

"I can only tell you we're headed into the Yugoslav tinderbox."

"'The Yugoslav' *what!*"

"The Yugoslav tinderbox." She repeated, adding, "After a spell in Venice, we head to Rijeka, which is right inside enemy territory."

Then she said no more about what she was really up to. Having mentioned "enemy territory" and "the Yugoslav tinderbox," she had hoped Shelton would back off. But she soon realized his excitement grew as the mission's description grew more dangerous. As much as she did not want to take him behind enemy lines, she would draw unnecessary attention if she had him apprehended by the CIA in D.C. Losing him once they were in enemy territory would be much easier, but she would not do that.

Although she refused to elaborate further, Shelton was satisfied that she had at least told him where they were going, although, with Priscilla, that could change at any time. Regardless, Shelton was going wherever she was going. Like the rest of the Bernhardt household staff, he would do everything he could to protect her, even if she thought she did not need his help. As they headed to their departure gate to await their flight to Venice, Shelton continued thinking about precisely what Madame PJ was really up to.

Meanwhile, Madame PJ was thinking about precisely what the folks back at the Luzern safe house were really up to, lest one forget precisely what the elusive Zulfika Kasun—or whoever he was—was really up to. She also wondered precisely what Laverne and the two GIS agents had encountered at the Marmande villa where the other Zulfika Kasun decoy—or Kasun himself—kept house. Mostly, though, she wondered precisely what CF Commander Wozniah and "the boys" were really up to because she knew they had not just happened at the Luzern safe house in the wee hours of that cold, snowy night—as if they had been expected. But she did not think for one moment about how Deputy Director Froley or anybody else, for that matter, would react when they learned she had discarded that doggone tracking device.

34

THE MEN WHO FOLLOWED THE LOT OF THEM

While Priscilla—disguised as Phillipe Winsarah—had skied at Beach-Mountain in Switzerland, visited her mother and sister Helen in Sills Creek as herself, and connected with NSA Counterintelligence Agent Harry Middleton at the Waffle House on K Street in Washington, D.C. —the two men who had followed her and Shelton and the men who had followed the lot of them transmitted intel to their respective superiors: the CF commander, the Zulfika Kasun decoy, and the real Zulfika Kasun—all of whom were wise enough to know that not even the illustrious P. J. Austin-Bernhardt could have been in more than one place at a time. Although it would take a while for the lot of them to figure out how she had put them off her trail, the real Zulfika Kasun had analyzed his intel more thoroughly, after which he had dispatched two reserve units totaling fourteen loathsome men, one reserve unit to Switzerland and the second to rescue his double, who he thought was being held by the CF agents at the Marmande villa. But that was not all he had ordered.

While Priscilla had been skiing in Zurich, Kasun's first reserve unit had descended on the Marmande villa, where they surprised Laverne and GIS Agents Omar and Maalik. When the men cornered Laverne's team inside the parlor with their weapons aimed and ready to fire, the Kasun double shouted, "No! We need her alive until we verify the real one." Then he walked closer to the trio and demanded to know, "Who *are* you, people? Do you think we are fools? There's something not quite right about you." He stared at Omar and Maalik and declared, "PJ Austin-Bernhardt is not Egyptian." Then he stared at Laverne more intensely and said, "And I can't put my finger on it, but I *know* you're not her." It was then that Omar and Maalik had traded knowing looks; then, as if on cue, they lunged at the men and soon traded blows.

Seeing what she believed was her chance, Laverne went for the Kasun decoy, hoping to subdue him and use him as a hostage so she and the GIS agents could escape. Laverne was in no shape for hand-to-hand combat. What was she thinking? Deputy Director Froley had commissioned her to serve as Priscilla's look-alike, nothing more. For sure, he did not authorize her to engage in hand-to-hand combat, not in her condition. Then, before she knew anything else, more loathsome men rushed in and quickly overpowered her and the two GIS agents. When word reached Jim Froley, he would be outraged with Laverne.

Kasun's men dragged the three captives down to the villa's cold and damp lower level, where they tied them up and gagged them.

"Where is P. J. Austin-Bernhardt?" one of the men asked again but was greeted with silence. "If you answer, we'll give you food and water." It had been two days since they dragged them into the basement. Omar, Laverne, and Maalik were exhausted, hungry, and thirsty, and they had been badly beaten.

Nevertheless, food is not an incentive to an agent. The only incentive is a promise to spare family and loved ones, but none of these agents had immediate family and loved ones. So, their captors resorted to torture.

One of the men removed a cigar cutter from his pocket, walked over to Omar, and grabbed his hand, which was tied above his head. He placed the cutter over Omar's thumb and shouted for the umpteenth time, "Tell us what we want to know! Where is she!" When Omar did not tell him what he wanted to know, the loathsome man whacked off his thumb mercilessly. Unafraid, even as he screamed in agony, Omar still did not yield.

As Omar screamed, one of the other men snatched Laverne's sable coat and hat. "We can get plenty of cash for these furs on the black market." He laughed at Laverne, who shivered on the damp, cold cement floor. Turning away, he spun back around and said, "Now I remember. It's your hair! P. J. Austin-Bernhardt wears her hair differently than yours."

After years of being Priscilla's double, this was the first time anyone had ever mentioned the difference between the two women's hair.

Kasun's second reserve unit had executed their mission at the Luzern safe house four hours earlier. Pretending to be neighbors and delivery men, they had kept keen eyes on Melissa and Hettie's routines. One day, as Hettie casually pushed Austin in his carriage along the familiar path, the men she had met during her earlier walks approached. Hettie smiled and was about to return to the villa when another man snuck up from behind and covered her face with a chloroform-drenched cloth. Hettie's eyes rolled back in her head. She fell limp in the man's arms. Then, one of the men grabbed the carriage while the other two lugged Hettie into a waiting van and pulled away, all within the blink of an eye. Hettie and Austin were out of sight of the guardsmen for only a moment, but that was all it took.

Inside the back of the van sat a tall, lean, otherwise ordinary Eastern European woman. Boxes of diapers and milk containers were piled beside her. The woman attended to the child for their journey while Hettie lay unconscious.

A day later, when Hettie came out of her drug-indued state, she soon realized that she was no longer in Switzerland but in a cabin in a snow-covered forest somewhere unknown to her. She was on the outskirts of Sarajevo.

As it so happened, when CF Agent B, Commander Elias, Ariel, and the four CIA agents who were on the grounds surrounding the villa had gotten word of the abduction, they hurried back to Luzern, leaving the Marmande villa unprotected. So, Kasun's first reserve unit captured Laverne and the two GIS agents effortlessly. Meanwhile, the second reserve unit eluded Sam and his guardsmen at the Luzern safehouse and abducted Hettie and baby Austin.

Not far from the Luzern safe house, CF Commander Wozniah was in a fit of violent wrath. Not only had Laverne and the two GIS agents been captured and held hostage, but Hettie and Austin had been abducted again, this time for real, and the agents had no idea where they were being held.

"How much damn worse can things get?"

That was when one of the two men that he had assigned to follow Priscilla and Shelton arrived to give him a report.

"Two people fitting the description of Ms. Austin-Bernhardt and her chauffeur were last seen in Zurich somewhere near a hostel and then downtown shopping, but no trace of either of them since then." The commander almost lost his temper again when the man said, "Are you *sure* we're not dealing with another decoy, sir?"

As it so happened, the CF commander's men lost track of the unlikely couple after Priscilla removed her tracking device and Shelton finally turned off his cell phone, which the CF commander was not yet privy to. For all Tommy knew, they were at the hotel in Zurich; at least, that was what the technology showed about the tracking device.

After listening to the report and observing the commander's reaction, CF Agents Jordan and Onslow attempted to ease his concerns. But Agent B was angry;

the mission had suddenly become personal. Red-faced, errant strands of hair fanned his face as he paced the floor. He yelled a lot, too.

"For heaven's sake, Tommy, this was a simple babysitting assignment. How the devil did you let them snatch my nanny *and* my son?"

Attempting to calm the situation, Jordy suggested something: "Listen, Tommy. We need to figure out *how* to track our girl. You know, we've located lots of missing people before. Why not now?" Jordy was assuming that the child's abduction was somehow related to Priscilla's absence.

Like Jordy, but not quite on the same wavelength, Onslow assumed the child's abduction was intended as a bargaining chip for the Yugoslav lieutenant. So he focused on *why* they needed to find Priscilla and maybe even Zulfika Kasun himself. "And I think I know just how to do it." Yet, no one seemed the least interested in his point of view.

Although the CF commander had his hands full, he still tried to allay his friend's concerns.

"Carlton, listen to me. I apologize. I really do. But even you know that sometimes circumstances, well, they get beyond us." *As if I didn't have enough on my plate*, Tommy sighed. *Now, how the devil do I tell him that his wife and the chauffeur have been masquerading as a couple?*

This time, Jordy attempted to bring closure to the matter. "Okay, fellas. Okay," he repeated and, turning to Carlton, suggested, "I understand you're worried about your son, but you need to keep a cool head. We all do. Priscilla is on the case, and she's more than capable." There now, Jordy was finally seeing the matter from Onslow's perspective.

Onslow recounted Priscilla's efficacy with hammers, chisels, and stakes and her effective use of the oil of vitriol. But he remembered something else. "And she's darn good at a point–blank shooting range, too." Then, frustrated that no one listened, he snapped. "Ah, the heck with you all. PJ's an agent. Remember? She can handle herself."

After Onslow dropped that bombshell, Tommy asked for clarification while the others wore stunned expressions. "Do you know something that we don't know?" as all attention now focused on him.

"Well, she's not exactly a damsel in distress. Now, is she? It's as if you still don't respect her as our equal." Onslow stomped away on his cane as he, like Jordy, sustained an injury to one of his legs.

And so it was that Onslow was the only one among "the boys," including Priscilla's agent-husband Carlton, who thought they did not give her credit for her little gray cells, not to mention her prowess as an agent. Onslow was with Priscilla

192

when she pushed past her vertigo and descended three levels into that Anglican Cathedral dungeon in Harare, where she lived among the bishops' crypts, fought Moses Cameron, and survived the brutal attack from the SANM PG at the Mwenezi River. However, as the newest member of the CF unit, he was unaware of the extent of the commander's influence over the others, including Carlton. Mostly, though, he did not know that the commander had allowed his personal feelings to get in the way of business in that he secretly kept score on the times Priscilla outwitted him and her unsuspecting agent-husband, too, for that matter. As things stood, Onslow was the only one who regarded Priscilla as one of them. It would take some time before the others came to terms with his perspective.

Back at CIA headquarters at Langley, Deputy Director Froley could not tell what he was more concerned about, that Priscilla had once again shirked CF Commander Wozniah and the other CF boys or of her impending encounter with the real Zulfika Kasun or that Hettie and Austin had been abducted, or that Laverne and two GIS agents had been captured, or that Priscilla had removed her tracking device. Or was it all of the above? His only consolation was knowing that Priscilla had outwitted Tommy more times than he could count, yet another indication she was darn good at her job.

Jim Froley was reaching for his telephone, which rang just as he was about to pick it up.

"Yeah, Jim. How's it going?" NSA Counterintelligence Agent Middleton knew full well how it was going for the CIA deputy director. So he poured salt in the man's wounds just the same when he said, "Jim, are you *sure* you're all right?"

"Come on, man," Jim snapped. "Did you or didn't you get word to her?"

"Affirmative," Harry said and paused. "But you don't sound so chipper to me. Are you sure you're alright?" He finished with a chuckle.

"Screw you, Harry." Jim slammed the receiver back down.

CIA Deputy Director Froley did not appreciate working with the NSA counterintelligence agent—the one agent he did not command but with whom he had been ordered to cooperate on this case. For the orders had come straight from the White House to the CIA director's office on down the line, accordingly:

> All relevant parties—the CIA, the State Department, and the NSA—must be civil and cooperate to bring about a successful conclusion to the situation involving Zulfika Kasun of Sarajevo.

Meanwhile, back in Luzern, Melissa and Ronnie had grown close. Ronnie shared Melissa's concern that something awful might happen to her Madame PJ, especially if she did not do whatever that Kasun fellow, or whoever he was, wanted. But Ronnie and Melissa shared another concern: "What was to come of Nanny Hettie and young Austin?" Each time either of them looked at the other, they had to turn away so as not to make the other sense their concern.

Interestingly, even though Priscilla and Shelton had been away for at least one week, presumably skiing, neither Melissa nor Ronnie seemed the least concerned about their prolonged absence.

35

ENTERING ENEMY TERRITORY

Priscilla and Shelton met their first tour guide at Venice Marco Polo International Airport. After riding in an open jeep in silence for about fifteen minutes, they stopped at the Gulf of Venice waterfront between Italy and Yugoslavia. It was dusk, so it was difficult for Priscilla to determine the exact type of ship the guide directed them to, but it was a spectacular Azimut model.

"What's going on?" Shelton asked as they followed the man. "Is someone going to tell me where we're headed?" When they stopped at an impressive ship, Shelton then asked, "And why're we boarding a yacht?"

"Come aboard, mate." Priscilla waved him onto the impressive vessel.

The guide, already stepping under the Bimini to the cockpit, turned to Shelton and said, "Welcome aboard. My name is Maximillian."

"So, you *do* speak English, after all," Shelton said as he tossed the duffel on the deck near the bow and continued fussing. "Please tell me we're not already headed into 'enemy territory?'"

Priscilla, not the tour guide, kindly obliged, "We're not already headed into enemy territory," which was not true.

Shelton sat confounded, staring into the darkness of the night. He had no idea what was happening or about the enemy territory they were sailing into.

A short time later, Priscilla took the duffel to one of the cabins below deck, where she changed into her camouflage uniform and strapped on her weapon. But she did something else. For some time, she thought she did not look masculine enough, so she put on a thin mustache. "There now," she said to herself. "That's more like it." She wanted as little curiosity about her gender as possible, especially among the loathsome men she anticipated encountering in the Yugoslav tinderbox.

She found her red beret and put it on, too. She had no idea the significance of its red color to her mission. She picked over other items, pulled out another uniform, went to the door, and yelled, "Shelton, it's showtime!"

Still peeved, Shelton stomped below deck because he had no idea where they were headed.

"Okay, now, Madame PJ, ready to tell me where we're really headed?"

"But Shelton, I already told you. And stop calling me PJ. We've already gone to Venice, well, sort of. Now we're on our way to Rijeka, by way of Koper, where, well, I'm not so sure how to say this—"

"Out with it!" he demanded.

"Well, this time, you get to be yourself. You'll be doing most of the driving."

"Well, now, if that don't beat all." He shook his head and asked again, "Will I know where we're going?"

"Don't worry. Our tour guide will direct you."

Shelton crossed his arms, frowned, and said, "Did we forget something?"

"Oh, yeah. My mistake." She pulled out his weapon and handed it to him.

But then he said, "My goodness, PJ, Phillipe, whoever you are this time, there's something different about you." He stared at her face. She pointed to her mustache. He shook his head, and then they both laughed.

Nevertheless, Shelton was ready to become the Bernhardt chauffeur-bodyguard once again. He nodded his thanks to Priscilla. Besides, Priscilla thought the best way to use him on this mission was in his primary capacity as chauffeur, a role he would play for the duration, well, at least part of it.

And so it was that Priscilla and Shelton were all suited up as they headed into enemy territory.

Only NSA Counterintelligence Agent Middleton, CIA Deputy Director Froley, and CF Commander Wozniah now knew Priscilla's whereabouts. Everyone else had lost track of the unlikely couple, which was how Priscilla had planned it in the first place. Well, she did not exactly want the CF commander to know, but such are the lives of secret agents on the same team.

A couple of hours later, after cruising comfortably on the Azimut slightly northeast on the Gulf of Venice along the triangular peninsula of Istria, Maximillian reduced his speed almost to a halt and shouted, "We're here!"

Priscilla ran upstairs with Shelton, carrying the duffel, right behind her.

"Over there." Maximillian pointed. "See those lights?"

They looked out into the darkness over the water at the flashing lights in the distance. Since the yacht was too big to dock along the shoreline, Maximillian anchored some distance away in deeper water and lowered a raft for them.

196

Shelton went first. He swung his long legs over the edge; his feet felt the roped ladder. After descending far enough, he dropped the duffel, stepped onto the raft, and waited for Priscilla. But he grew alarmed when he looked up and saw her dangling from the ladder. So, he climbed back up and reached out for her as she swung against the side of the yacht. Shelton pulled her down in panic. He was relieved when she regained her composure, sat up, reached into one of her pants pockets, took out a small medicine bottle, popped the cap, and flung back some tablets. While Priscilla chewed the meclizine tablets, she held fast to the raft's sides to steady herself. When Shelton tried to help, she pushed him away.

"I'm all right, Shelton. I forgot to take my meds. Bloody stupid of me." But she was not alright, far from it. Her head was spinning. And the rocking of the raft in the wavy water was not helping.

"What's wrong?" he asked.

"Oh, it's nothing. Just a bit of an equilibrium problem."

"You have got to be kidding me!"

"Not this time, Shelton. Now you know one of my weaknesses."

His memory of Sam's briefing about Priscilla's phobias was no consolation as he thought about it. When Shelton thought Priscilla had regained her composure, he picked up the oars and began rowing slowly, trying not to rock the boat too much. Even though the raft swayed on the wind-tossed water and did not bode well with Priscilla's vertigo, the medication would eventually take effect. Meanwhile, they were silent and watchful as they both realized they were headed into enemy territory. Yet Shelton wondered how they would accomplish the mission if Priscilla suffered from bouts of vertigo.

As they neared the shoreline, Priscilla spotted a man walking toward them.

"Welcome to Koper! I'm Tyler, your tour guide," he yelled. There would be one more. The CIA, in conjunction with the NSA, had made all the arrangements. After meeting Maximillian and now Tyler, Shelton now knew that "tour guide" was merely a code, and their names were aliases, too. So, he kept quiet.

Tyler waded in the water and steadied the raft while they got out. Then, he and Shelton pulled the raft onto the shore, and Shelton picked up the duffel.

Still unsteady, Priscilla stood as best as she could on the shoreline and watched Maximillian rev the engine in the Azimut, motor away, and disappear into the darkness of the night as if he had never been there. She reckoned they were on their own now and was not so sure that she liked their new precarious circumstance.

She turned to the guide, "All right, mate. What're we looking at?"

Tyler was clear: "We have a ways to go before we get to our ride. A short trek on foot. Then, about twenty-five kilometers over some rugged roadways. All set?"

After a quick calculation, Priscilla figured they were looking at over fifteen miles, which would take quite a while since they would be riding on rugged roads. She assumed that they would be riding in a modern vehicle like a jeep. Otherwise, she had no idea what type of vehicle awaited them.

Neither Priscilla nor Shelton introduced themselves. Nor did Tyler ask their names. He just started walking briskly, Priscilla and Shelton in tow.

While the threesome headed to their next stop, Tyler briefed them on the situation in the Yugoslav tinderbox and cautioned them: "Be on the lookout for bandits and thugs who take advantage of unsuspecting tourists—petty spies and thieves—people who work for a pittance to appease Milosevic and his cronies." Hearing the name "Milosevic," Priscilla and Shelton suddenly realized they were indeed in enemy territory.

But the Yugoslav tinderbox was not unique in that respect. Similar circumstances existed elsewhere. *Ah heck,* Priscilla thought, *such was the case on the streets in America—nothing unique along those lines.*

Nevertheless, she knew danger lay ahead and what that might mean. Each time she started to think about Carlton, Austin, Helen, her in-laws, and other family and loved ones, she pushed the thoughts back down deep into the recesses of her mind. She needed a clear head. She had to be sharp.

While Priscilla cleared her thoughts, Shelton's anticipation mounted. He was far more comfortable in his role as driver and bodyguard and not as Phillipe's partner. He relished the holster's weight under his arm and prepared himself for what lay ahead. *However,* again, he reasoned, *nobody back home at Bow Lake would believe any of this.* But Shelton was unfamiliar with the lives of the Bernhardts before coming to America.

Precisely twelve minutes had passed when Priscilla saw an old-fashioned farmer's truck ahead. She knew the time because she had glanced at her wristwatch when they started walking. Still dizzy, though, she wondered when the meclizine would take effect. She was mainly surprised at the sight of the old-fashioned vehicle.

Tyler slapped Shelton's shoulders. "How 'bout it, young man? Isn't she a beauty?" He meant the old truck.

"You can't be serious! That can't possibly be our ride. I mean, will it even get us where we need to go?" Shelton was beside him, but not for long.

Priscilla startled Shelton when she took the duffel from him and said, "I'm riding shotgun in the back." Her vertigo would eventually subside; besides, she wanted to stretch out a bit and maybe get a little shuteye.

Tyler was also caught somewhat off guard when the more petite man told him, "Ride upfront, Tyler. Guide the driver."

Their marching orders intact, neither Shelton nor Tyler objected. Tyler now realized the short man was in charge. He could only discern in the darkness that the man calling the shots was short and small-framed. Since Tyler's job was to meet them at the shoreline and guide them to their next stop, that was what he would do.

Slouched on the floor in the back of the truck, Priscilla recalled some historical conflicts in the Yugoslav tinderbox. The territory had undergone many changes in sovereignty, including France, Rome, Austria, Italy, the Habsburg, the Ottoman Empire, and Yugoslavia. There were three primary ethnic groups: the Bosnians—called Bosniaks—the Croats, and the Serbians. The Bosniaks were primarily Muslim, but many others were Eastern Orthodox and Roman Catholic. The Croats were traditionally Christian, primarily Catholic. The Serbians tended to be Christian Orthodox, Muslim, Roman Catholic, Protestant, Jewish, and others. That was just part of the scenario. Of all the foreign invaders, perhaps the Ottomans had the most significant influence, hence the presence of the Islamic faith and the architecture of many historic structures. There was also the role of the Germans, particularly during World War I, with whom Croatia and Slovenia had aligned, whereas Serbia had joined forces with the Western Allies. Then came Tito, whose ancestry included Croat and Slovene, credited with holding the various ethnic groups together, though tenuously. Unlike Tito, however, Milosevic, a.k.a. the Butcher of the Balkans, had taken advantage of the ethnic tensions, eventually leading to war. Though not the whole story, that much Priscilla recounted.

But what disturbed her most was the phrase "ethnic cleansing," which many politicians and media representatives used. The Balkan War was not the first time that people of different ethnicities fought civil wars, nor would it be the last. Such wars and skirmishes have occurred since the beginning of time under the mantra of "Ridding the Earth of its wretched or other unwanted people."

Since Priscilla was in excellent physical shape and conditioned to be awake at night, she had no problem riding in the back. Sitting comfortably crouched against the rearview window on raggedy blankets and straw, feet resting on the duffel, she smoked a cigarette or two. She did not mind the cold. Nor did she fear bandits, thugs, petty spies, or thieves. What mattered most was that her vertigo had finally subsided. Meanwhile, she kept an old rifle that had been hidden underneath some raggedy old rugs and straw in plain view. She rode shotgun in the back to protect them from potential attackers.

As for Shelton, there was no fear of him dozing off or being afraid of bandits, petty spies, and thieves either. Not only that but his complaints about the truck had turned into fascinations. Even in the darkness of the night, he felt the well-worn seat—rugged was more like it. There were no electronics either, not even a working radio. The roll-up windows and the sham of a dashboard were utterly unlike anything he usually drove Madame PJ and the Bernhardts in. What a fantastic experience! Shelton enjoyed driving the old truck. Naïve or foolish, he rejoiced as he drove deeper into enemy territory.

They traveled slowly along the Dalmatia mountainous coastal range on the triangular peninsula's interior. At the base of the Dinaric Alps, Priscilla and Shelton, led by their guide Tyler, occasioned numerous drowned valleys, during which time Priscilla prayed that nothing unexpected would happen to the truck. She got used to a strange odor, too; it was limestone, plentiful in the territory. Dense forests and wide-open areas looked like abandoned territory. Even in the darkness, she could make out the ravages of massive deforestation. Although she could not see the forests clearly, she did notice what looked like and smelled like fruit orchids of figs and lemons. She even saw olive groves, though no olives were on the trees. As the truck bounced up and down on the unpaved snow-covered muddy road, she shed her jacket because, unlike the climate back in Luzern and Zurich, Istria was in the Mediterranean climate. Though the weather was reasonably mild, in early May, it still snowed.

As they continued along the rugged road, up and down mounds and steep hills, and around sharp curves across the interior of the triangular peninsula, Shelton and Priscilla got used to the bumpy ride, which they likened to a roller–coaster ride of sorts, only slower and steadier.

36
WELCOME TO RIJEKA!

No sooner than Priscilla and Shelton got used to the slow, steady, and sometimes bumpy roller–coaster ride and the occasional changes in the scents and scenery along the Dalmatia mountainous coastal range, the old truck jerked and stopped abruptly amid what Priscilla regarded as a dozen "interesting-looking people."

She was about to raise the rifle when she heard Tyler announcing, "Welcome to Rijeka!"

Just as quickly, Shelton screamed, "Rijeka!"

Hearing "Rijeka," both Shelton and Priscilla knew for a certainty they were in enemy territory, though not precisely, but they were in northwestern Croatia.

"Now," Tyler said quite seriously, "whatever you do, do not move or say anything until someone speaks to you." He did not need to repeat that advice to Priscilla, who prayed Shelton would likewise heed.

But Priscilla had already stood and squinted at the "interesting-looking people." They reminded her of gypsies, not the loathsome type she had expected to see. Their attire caught her attention: floppy, old leather hats, finely tailored dark and loosely fitted clothing, and leather shoes and boots from another era. They did not appear to be armed or dangerous, which did not mean they were unarmed or not dangerous. But it was still quite dark out, so she could not make out much more. Two of the men pounded on the truck and pointed at her. When one of them spoke, she did not understand him or recognize his accent or dialect. But she heard Tyler yelling something from the passenger's side of the truck. Then she watched as the two men hurried to Tyler's window and carried on what sounded like a friendly chat.

Eventually, Tyler said, "Okay, folks, this is where my tour ends. These men will take you to your destination."

"Alright, Tyler," Priscilla roared in a deep, masculine voice from the back. "But do any of them speak English? How 'bout French?"

"Yes, for English. But they will not speak directly to you until you meet their leader, your next tour guide. Collect your belongings."

Well, damn, thought Priscilla. *How much more vetting will there be?* She picked up the duffel and jumped out of the truck with her Glock in plain sight.

Shelton had already gotten out, his weapon also exposed. When he reached for the duffel, Priscilla said, "I've got this, mate." They nodded farewell to Tyler and followed behind "the interesting-looking people," who were already walking away briskly.

They traveled off the beaten path, not along the roadway. Occasionally, Priscilla and Shelton stumbled, stepping into unseen ditches and holes. They also fought back snow-covered tree branches slapping their faces, but the guides did not pause or take a break. They did, however, often laugh at their unsuspecting customers.

Twenty minutes into their brisk trek, Priscilla heard music, string instruments like banjos or guitars. Or were they violins? As she and Shelton drew nearer, they saw campfires and more "interesting-looking people." There were more old trucks and even horse-drawn wagons.

As Priscilla scoped out the camp, she knew where she was geographically, in a forest on the outskirts of Rijeka. Earlier, she had spotted the city on her map. The place was also identified in the notes Harry had given her at the Waffle House on K Street as the place where she would meet her contact, whom Jim Froley assured her she would recognize. Otherwise, her only awareness of Rijeka was as a principal Yugoslav seaport, certainly not part of the soon-to-be Croatian state. She had no idea how close she was to a naval base, major shipyards, or oil refineries, nor where Englishman Robert Whitehead had invented the torpedo. None of that information was on her map or the notes that Harry had given her. However, she did remember the rail system connected Rijeka to Western Europe via Trieste. *That'll come in handy later*. Otherwise, she felt she was in no man's land.

After examining their surroundings, the unlikely couple was escorted through an opening in a dark tent. Not thinking much about who or what was inside, Priscilla and Shelton both blinked at the sight of a familiar face.

They stared at the man who sat cross-legged on the rug-covered ground. He wore dark clothing, a colorful headdress, and a handsome Mediterranean complexion. Sitting next to him were several other men, like the ones who had just escorted the couple. But unlike the other men, the headdress worn by the man sitting cross-legged was pulled across his face, partially covering an unmistakable deep scar that he tried to conceal.

"Nah, it can't be," Priscilla peered into his charming dark eyes. "Angel! What are *you* doing here?"

It was none other than CF Agent Angelo Delgato.

"Good to see you too, *Phillipe*. Welcome to the ROM camp!"

"You're my contact! Well, I'm sure glad Jim sent you. What news have you for me?" Her delight that Angel was her contact overshadowed her curiosity about the "interesting-looking people," which she would revisit later.

Shelton was also surprised but kept quiet, relieved to see someone he knew in such an unlikely place. He knew Angel as one of Carlton's friends, not as the special op he was. Although his curiosity heightened, he remembered how Priscilla staved off his questioning of Harry at the Waffle House. So, he knew better than to ask Angel anything. He found a spot on the rug-covered ground and sat in silence.

Angel began with good news.

"The identity of the Yugoslav lieutenant has been confirmed, and he has consented to a meeting with you."

Priscilla had already learned of Lieutenant Kasun's identity from the papers Harry slipped to her at the Waffle House. But Angel was unaware of Priscilla's pit stop in D.C. Not only that, but the location he gave her for the rendezvous was contrary to the one she had in mind.

After pausing to let his next words register, he then said, "And it's clear that he intends to use a certain 'heavyweight' as an asset. A bargaining chip."

Before the CF agent could say more, Priscilla tensed. "Bummer! Bummer! Bummer! What are you saying?" she asked in disbelief as if she had not already anticipated such.

"Sorry, Phillipe, but the lieutenant's cronies have already taken the youngster and his nanny, too." Across the way, Shelton flinched, but still, he kept quiet.

As Priscilla nearly came undone, Shelton pretended not to be concerned. He was beginning to get the big picture from what he had just heard—lest one forget his recollection of the earlier failed abduction.

But Priscilla fought to control herself. Once again, composed as Phillipe, she took a deep breath and faced Angel. "All right, what *exactly* is our game plan?" Then again, she mistakenly assumed their game plan included Phillipe Winsarah. However, Angel had alluded to the CF commander, the other CF boys, and the British and French agents, which did not include Priscilla disguised as Phillipe.

With Priscilla's undivided attention, he continued. "The CF commander, "the boys," and the British and French fellas are already en route to Sarajevo, where they plan to escort the real Zulfika Kasun to Rijeka, where you'll finally meet him." But was their intel correct?

Regardless, Angel was about to find out that Priscilla had an alternative plan.

"Sorry, Angel, but I have my own plans. Our rendezvous will be in Bihać."

Outraged, Angel countered.

"My orders were to brief you on the current circumstances and ensure your availability. That's why I've arranged with the ROM to escort you accordingly. The meeting will occur *here* in Rijeka, not some God-forsaken hellhole like *Bihać*." Situated on Una, Bihać, Bosnia-Herzegovina, was landlocked inside Serbian-controlled territory 195 kilometers south of Rijeka.

Priscilla was unaware that she was being embedded among the "interesting-looking people" who had recently traveled three arduous long days from Bihać—much deeper in enemy territory—and would have to alter their itinerary to accommodate her plan. Neither was she aware that the price for their service as her tour guide had just doubled, but Angel was fully aware of all that and more. While Angel thought about all that, Priscilla exercised her authority.

"Well, you can follow your *bloody* plan without me. Besides, why the hell should we concede to Kasun's every wish? Remember, *he* called *us*." Priscilla took another deep breath and lowered her voice, which had started to rise. "I say we meet the bloody bastard head-on on his turf. That'll show 'im." *Besides*, she thought, *I want to make him pay for abducting my son and Nanny Hettie.*

As it turned out, NSA Counterintelligence Agent Middleton's sources indicated that some of Milosevic's men were near Bihać, which included some of his best officers, like Lieutenant Zulfika Kasun. Yet, for whatever reason, CF Commander Wozniah and the international military unit were stationed in Fojnica, near Sarajevo. But Kasun was last seen in Krajina, northwest of Bihać. Therefore, Harry had given Priscilla the best intel, hence her decision to rendezvous with Kasun on his own turf.

Notwithstanding, Angel now understood some of the CF commander's frustration with Priscilla. *She really is something else.* But Angel did not possess the intel that Priscilla had. So, he wrongly assumed she was trying to outwit the commander, which was not the case this time.

Priscilla elaborated: "All right, now, Angel, here's the deal. First, I camp out here for a couple of days and put out the word that 'some American observers are headed to an undisclosed location upcountry.' But I," she stopped abruptly, looked across the way at Shelton, and said, "*we,* wait for the bloody bastard to cross our path midway."

Was Priscilla gunning for Kasun, or was she trying to outwit Wozniah? Angel could not be sure, but he had his suspicions. Regardless, Deputy Director Froley had assured Priscilla this was her call, so she exercised her authority and disregarded the CF commander's game plan altogether.

With business out of the way, she glanced around the tent and eventually asked Angel, "Who are these people? You mentioned the word Rohm. Is that an acronym? What does it stand for? They look 'interesting' to me." Then, looking at the men sitting with Angel more intensely, she said, "They remind me of gypsies." She did not know that the word "gypsy" was offensive.

"And right you are. Welcome to the ROM camp."

"Are you saying, R-O-H-M?"

Angel corrected her. "These 'interesting-looking people,' as you call them, are the R-O-M. ROM is the name for refugees and other immigrants, often mistaken as gypsies, as it were, traveling in Eastern Europe. Sometimes, they're called ROMA, but ROM is the more common term. There are different sects of ROM. These ROMs are Falasha. They know these areas like the back of their hands, which makes them great guides."

Then, seemingly from out of nowhere, two of the Falasha women appeared. They scooted next to Priscilla, patting her and tugging at her clothing.

While the women flirted with Priscilla disguised as Phillipe, Shelton—uncharacteristically quiet until now—joined Angel in laughter while the others in the tent ignored them.

"They find *you* 'interesting-looking,' too. Kinda' small and cute for a man. Don't you agree?" Angel pointed to her mustache and laughed even harder.

As Priscilla pushed the two women away, she asked, "How do you say 'stop' in ROM?"

"Stop," Angel said, still laughing.

Then he said, "You know, Phillipe, some of them do speak English."

37

RAID AT FOJNICA

Back at the central command station near Luzern, CF Commander Wozniah had had enough of being outwitted by Zulfika Kasun, his decoys, his reserve units, and, last but not least, Priscilla. So he ordered Sam and the guardsmen to seize the Marmande villa, rescue Laverne and the two GIS agents, eliminate Kasun's first reserve unit, and, if necessary, the Kasun double.

"Get Laverne and her team outta there. And when you return, I want you to track down Kasun's other reserve unit holding Nanny Hettie and Austin hostage and handle them once and for all." Wozniah sighed heavily. "'Cause Lord knows, I owe Carlton big time."

Sam had his orders as he and his guardsmen set out with a vengeance for the South of France. But it would not be that easy. They assumed the nanny and the infant were also held somewhere in Switzerland, but they were entirely wrong.

⸙

In the wee hours, having driven straight through the day from Switzerland to the South of France, Sam, Ronnie, and the rest of his guardsmen descended on the grounds of Kasun's Marmande villa, their weapons raining bullets like a hailstorm cutting down the night security detail. Caught off guard, the Kasun double, his first reserve unit, and all the neighbors in the small village must have thought the violence in Yugoslavia had reached their doorsteps.

Moments later, the front door to the villa swung open. Sam, Ronnie, and the guardsmen burst in and shot anything and anybody moving on the main floor, including the Kasun double, who had staggered, half asleep, into the corridor, directly into the line of fire.

Sam then ordered four of his men upstairs, where they encountered more of Kasun's men. The guardsmen took them out one by one.

At the same time, Sam, Ronnie, and the other guardsmen headed down the corridor past the study on the main floor. When they heard muffled sounds coming from the cellar, Sam pointed his rifle at the keyhole on the door, shattering the hardwood that held the lock in place. Ronnie then kicked the door open, and they hurried down the stairwell, where they found Laverne and the two GIS agents battered, gagged, and tied up on the cold, damp floor.

As their rescuers untied them and removed their gags, the pain-stricken and exhausted Laverne asked, "What took you so long?"

Sam smiled, helped her get to her feet, and gave her a pistol. "Will you be able to walk out of here?" he asked because he knew she was not at her peak performance. She cocked the gun and nodded.

While Ronnie bandaged Omar's injured hand, Sam turned to Maalik and asked, "Are you hurt?"

"Mostly my pride." Looking across the way at his friend holding his bandaged hand. He said, "Omar got the worst of it. Give me a gun. I want to make those bastards pay."

While Ronnie handed Maalik a weapon, Laverne said, "The Kasun double is mine."

But to her dismay, Sam told her, "He's been handled already, and his men along with him. But there might be stragglers. So, everyone, keep your head on the swivel. We're not losing anyone tonight."

They raced back up the stairs and joined the others who had already swept the upstairs. Then they ransacked the study for anything helpful in finding Hettie and Austin. They picked up maps and strips of paper that contained notes they did not comprehend because they were in Bosniak. Although they were reasonably sure the man was another imposter, they still rifled about the villa, collecting clothing, combs, brushes, and toothbrushes to analyze the DNA.

Finally, they hurried outside, got into the bulletproof Hummers, and headed back to Luzern at lightning speed. By the time the local French police arrived at the scene—apart from the dead loathsome men—there was no trace of anyone, or anything remotely affiliated with the CF unit of the American CIA.

When Sam, Ronnie, and the other guardsmen arrived back at the central command post near Luzern, they were stunned to learn that CF Commander Wozniah, "the boys," and the British and French agents had all departed. As for Agent B, he had been called back to Langley for the ongoing interrogation of Afan

Kljujic, who was also now at Langley. But Sam, Ronnie, and the other guardsmen were mainly stunned to find only Melissa, Commander Elias, Ariel, and CF Agent Jordan at the safe house.

"And since Carlton's nanny and child were abducted," Jordy told them, "You can't imagine how upset he was when he received his new orders."

Ever so disquieted about the missing nanny and the baby, Laverne asked, "So, what's our game plan now to rescue Nanny Hettie and Austin? And does PJ even know about any of this?" None of them knew that Priscilla was very much aware of it. Angel had told her about the abduction back at the ROM camp.

While the remaining CIA agents and guardsmen argued about how to find Hettie and baby Austin, Melissa waved Ronnie into the hallway. She had been eavesdropping on their conversation.

"Oh Ronnie, I'm so glad you're back safely, but where are Nanny Hettie and Austin?"

Ronnie took Melissa's arm and walked her to the kitchen, out of earshot of the agents and other guardsmen.

"You know, Miss Melissa, I probably shouldn't be telling you this, but it's not going to be easy rescuing the nanny and the child."

"Oh? What do you mean?"

"We have reason to believe the real Kasun plans to use the baby boy as a bargaining chip."

Melissa covered her mouth and stumbled backward onto a chair at the kitchen table. When she found her voice again, she said, "This can't be happening." She shook her head. "Does Madame PJ even know what's going on? Is she still skiing, and is Shelton still with her? Where are they, anyway?" She rambled on and on.

From her reaction, Ronnie knew he had already told her more than he should have. So, instead of answering her, he abruptly ended the conversation and left her wondering how they had all ended up in this predicament in the first place.

Simultaneous to Sam's team's operation, CF Commander Wozniah, "the boys," and the British and the French agents were flying in unmarked military helicopters deep into the Yugoslav tinderbox, where they landed in an open field in the village of Fojnica, slightly northwest of Sarajevo, where, Zulfika Kasun or one of his decoys believed that, apart from dispatching "observers," America had yet to enter the war officially. Since the Yugoslav lieutenant had no reason to anticipate American forces or undercover agents, he and his troops wrongly assumed the helicopters they heard were their own.

The Yugoslav lieutenant, whichever one he was, was also unaware that the international intelligence agents knew he held Hettie and Austin hostage. For sure, he was unaware that no matter what deal he planned to cut with the American special envoy, there would be no deal without the safe return of the nanny and the child. Even he thought Priscilla was a special envoy, a representative of the American government who would treat him gingerly. He had no idea she was a secret agent, gleaning vital intel on him. Nor did he know she would stop at nothing to rescue her son and his nanny.

Meanwhile, the CF commander and his men set about proficiently doing what they did. Rarely did they come upon a situation that could be overtaken so effortlessly. Yet, they were about to do just that inside the Yugoslav tinderbox. The CF commander's quarry was still at large. The prize was Kasun, and Wozniah was hardly leaving without him, or so he thought.

When his helicopter landed, a scout greeted him and reported about the enemy encampment: "Commander Wozniah, Sir," he said, "Lieutenant Kasun and his troops have just returned from ravaging Fojnica, where they raped, maimed, and killed nearly all its inhabitants. They buried the corpses in a mass grave and then returned to the home of an elderly couple, whose property they seized and turned into a central command post." The scout lowered his head in sadness and said, "They put the couple out into the cold to fend for themselves."

It was still cold and snowing in early May in Bosnia and Herzegovina.

As the commander and his men approached the village, they saw freshly turned soil that barely covered the victims' remains. In a fit of rage, Wozniah then ordered his men to raid the enemy's camp, which was ten kilometers away.

His men had never heard him shout so loudly: "Seize the property! Hunt down Kasun's men! If they resist, shoot them and toss their remains into the woods!"

One of the French agents radioed in a report, something he knew Wozniah would be pleased to hear. One of Lieutenant Kasun's soldiers, whom he held at gunpoint, told him where to find him: "He says the lieutenant took off into the woods when he heard the gunshots." But that was not true.

Even the CF commander found that message strange. *Officers don't run away from battle; they run into it.*

"Whatever," the CF commander said, "he won't get far." Then he motioned to MI6 Commander Thomas, "You go east, I'll go west. We'll radio in when we've found him."

His men had their orders.

The closer they came to the cabin, the more Yugoslav soldiers they encountered. When it was all over, they shot and killed forty-one of them, then dumped their bodies into the forest. In the meantime, a few other men came upon the elderly couple wandering in the woods.

Around the same time, after traipsing through the woods for far too long and without any trace of the Yugoslav lieutenant or anyone else, the CF commander told his men, "Double back. I think our prey is at the elderly couple's home, where he least expects anyone to find him."

The CF commander knew that Zulfika Kasun was a military officer of a rank similar to his, so if any fighting ensued, he would be the one who would take him on. Even so, something kept telling him that the Yugoslav soldier who had given the Frenchman the message had done so to take them off Kasun's tail.

The commander and his men approached the cabin cautiously. When one of them reported that seven Yugoslav soldiers guarded the cabin's front and back, the commander ordered them to "Take them out, one by one," and they did. Since the CF soldiers and the British and French agents muzzled their weapons, no one inside the cabin heard the gunshots. By that point, a horde of CF soldiers and British and French agents surrounded the place.

But when, for whatever reason, the Yugoslav lieutenant —Or was he another decoy? —ordered one of the four men with him inside the cabin, "Check outside. It's too quiet," no sooner than he opened the door, one of the CF sharpshooters shot him dead.

The Yugoslav lieutenant, or the man who pretended to be him, prepared to shoot until his death or surrender. That was particularly the case when he heard CF Commander Wozniah yelling, "Come out with your hands in the air! We've got the place surrounded!" Fluent in English, the Yugoslav lieutenant understood the commander's orders loudly and clearly. But was he the real lieutenant or another decoy? The CF commander was not sure.

In short order, as the Yugoslav lieutenant and his remaining three soldiers surrendered, exiting the cabin with their hands held high, the CF commander said, "Well, damn, where's the glory in this?" Then, he thought *I would've come out firing. The Yugoslav lieutenant that I know of would fight to the very end. And his uniform is odd. Where are the pendants and medals on his breast pocket and collar?* The CF commander also knew that military officers identified themselves when surrendering, which this one did not do. Still, he did not follow his instincts.

The CF commander could easily have shot and killed Lieutenant Kasun on the spot. But he had already determined, "There is no glory in such a feat." Besides, his primary role was to deliver Kasun for his rendezvous with the American special envoy—nothing more. So that was what he prepared to do.

Ironically, the Yugoslav lieutenant, or the man who pretended to be him, was unaware that a one-handed man, CF Commander Wozniah, had just captured him.

"Get a move on it. I'm on a tight schedule," the CF commander said when he heard someone slushing hurriedly through the muddy, snow-covered Earth. It was MI6 Commander Thomas who had doubled back.

Seeing Zulfika Kasun, whom he believed to be, in surrender mode, the MI6 commander asked in disbelief, "All clear, Commander?"

"Roger that, Commander Thomas. Tell our men to make room on the cold floor of that luxury airliner for our catch of the day." Then, using his good hand, he whacked Lieutenant Kasun, or his decoy, across his forehead with the butt of his rifle.

The two commanders and their men then rifled the cabin for anything that they thought might be helpful.

Before the international team departed, they gave the elderly couple a paper bag filled with dinars to cover the damage to their property by Kasun's soldiers. Enough to care for the couple for a long time. The elderly couple, both noticeably short in stature, wore dark-colored, worn-out clothing, not even coats or blankets. It was a miracle they had survived the outdoors. As they peeped inside the paper bag, they could not believe their eyes. But after accidentally dropping it and some of the currency spilled out, the couple hugged each other and the soldier who had handed it to them.

After the international team's successful raid at Fojnica, they returned to Sarajevo with the man they believed was the real Yugoslav lieutenant and three of his soldiers handcuffed and gagged beside him on the cold floor of the aircraft that Tommy described as "that luxury airliner." As was often the case, the CF commander almost always considered the usefulness of his catch. *One never knows what good intel they might provide, whether the real lieutenant or another decoy.*

Two hours later, CF Commander Wozniah, "the boys," and the British and French agents interrogated the man they believed to be the Yugoslav lieutenant before escorting him to meet with his "new writer friend" at Rijeka.

In addition to capturing the man who he believed was the real Yugoslav Lieutenant Zulfika Kasun, Wozniah, without losing any of his men, was also pleased with the favorable report that Sam had radioed in about their raid on the Marmande villa, exterminating the Kasun imposter and rescuing Laverne and the two GIS agents. He was about to ask about the nanny and the baby boy when another CF agent turned up to report. It was Agent Delgato.

In a good mood, the CF Commander said, "All right, Angel. What have you got for me?"

Angel had long since known that the best way to convey unwelcome news to his longtime friend and CF commander was to tell it to him straight the first time and then get out of his line of fire.

"Commander, Miss Prissy's no longer in Rijeka. She's on her way to Bihać." Angel then quickly stepped out of the commander's line of fire.

CF Commander Wozniah roared plangently. *"What!"*

$$38$$

EMBEDDED IN THE FALASHA CAMP

Priscilla did not know when CF Agent Delgato departed the Falasha camp, only that he was gone. Before departing, he had arranged for Phillipe to meet "his" last tour guide—Menilek—who headed the Falasha sect. They were Ethiopian Jews in exile on the outskirts of Rijeka. But Menilek was a priest and did not interact with Gentiles, "the impure and unclean." Consequently, Agent Delgato was introduced to the priest's representative, Absalom, whom he eventually introduced to Phillipe.

Absalom was in his early sixties, about five feet ten, with a radiant ebony complexion and a full head of henna-streaked dreadlocks. Agent Delgato had previously told Priscilla that Absalom was fluent in English and reasonably conversant in Bosniak. Ever mindful of the multi-ethnic community, Priscilla probed Absalom about his ethnicity, specifically whether he was Jewish.

"Any relatives in the area?"

Priscilla had no way of knowing that tour guides in this neck of the woods did so at their peril. Many were on the lam or seeking refuge from some extraordinary situation back home. To earn income, they often served as guides for travelers near their camp, which was also an added precaution. Exceedingly cautious about getting acquainted with their customers, the Falasha already had the bill of goods on Phillipe and Shelton. They had even created nicknames for them, calling Phillipe "Monsieur Petit" and Shelton "Monsieur Grand" behind their backs.

"Oui, Monsieur," Absalom said in response to Priscilla's probing as he tactfully referred to his wife and children. Otherwise, he said nothing specific about other relatives, his point of origin, or his faith, which he assumed was somewhat evident.

Likewise, CF Agent Delgato had not revealed Priscilla and Shelton's names or origins, primarily for security reasons. There was no need to discuss their faith, as even Absalom had figured that out himself.

Priscilla met Absalom's wife, whose name she never knew, over breakfast in the family's tent. She sent her husband away. She wanted a moment alone with the stranger Menilek had agreed to harbor and provide protection for "his" journey to Bihać. Apart from her discernment that Phillipe was, in fact, a woman, she also noticed that this woman who pretended to be a man was religious because Priscilla instinctively closed her eyes, bowed her head, and quietly blessed her meal before eating. Eventually, the wife said, "Good disguise. Your secret will be kept. And my husband, well, even he suspects, but he would never betray a confidence." Added to that, since the Falasha followed the international news, they had already recognized, through her disguise, one P. J. Austin-Bernhardt, a.k.a. "America's Sweetheart."

When Absalom returned, his wife ordered him, unbeknownst to Priscilla, "Find a strong, confident male escort for Monsieur Petit," for reasons that would be made clear to Priscilla later.

For the time being, it was readily apparent to Absalom and his wife that Shelton may have been an excellent chauffeur and bodyguard back in the States; however, he was no match for the shrewd and ruthless war criminals in the Yugoslav tinderbox. The couple knew Yugoslav scouts searched the forests for the Falasha, foreign observers, and opponents of the Milosevic régime as they dared venture deeper into enemy territory. Moreover, the two women who seemingly flirted with Phillipe did not go away; they continued popping up here and there while Absalom showed Phillipe and Shelton the camp. And so it was that Absalom and his wife had taken added precautions to fulfill CF Agent Delgato's revised request to escort Phillipe to "his" destination, Bihać.

Mainly, they were acutely aware of the ways of the ultraconservative communists, the race-conscious, not to mention the homophobic communist sympathizers. So, they did their best to blend Phillipe into their community.

As for Shelton, the couple figured out early on that although he sported a weapon, Shelton was hardly in the espionage business. So, they kept him occupied and out of Priscilla's way, assisting the men who prepared for skirmishes with Lieutenant Kasun's scouts, not to mention soldiers who often pillaged the territory near their camp. In his element, Shelton enjoyed cleaning and repairing guns and pistols, sharpening blades and machetes, changing the oil and belts on the old trucks, changing and pumping air into tires, and replacing worn-out horseshoes.

Throughout it all, Shelton believed that he would see action. If only he had known that that was not going to happen.

Presently in Rijeka, the Falasha were closer to Italy—the destination for many—than to Bihać, which was further south. Consequently, given their new agreement with CF Agent Delgato, the priest ordered Absalom to assign fifty strong men, four horse-drawn covered wagons, a few farm animals, and a few women, including Olga and her companion (the two women who flirted with Phillipe) to backtrack to Bihać, a not-so-small favor to facilitate Priscilla's rendezvous with the Yugoslav lieutenant. However, the remaining Falasha would stay in the relatively safer Rijeka until the others returned. Plainly, Menilek was hardly going to risk the lives of all his contingency.

Most significantly, the priest authorized Absalom to take as many weapons as possible in case action occurred.

Sometime later, Priscilla researched the Falasha sect. She learned about their disputed origins: They were descendants of Abraham, the first Jew, and Terah, Abraham's father, who had originated from the land of Ur of the Chaldees, a Kushite tribe. Priscilla liked that Kushite meant "black" and that the Kushite descended from Kush, a son of Ham. She learned the name "Menilek," derived from the son of the Queen of Sheba and King Solomon. Quite surprisingly, she learned that Emperor Haile Selassie was a descendant of the Solomonic Dynasty. Priscilla admired the Falasha mainly because they knew who they were and did not hide their identity.

She learned that although the Falasha did not practice Talmudic laws, their preservation of and adherence to Jewish traditions was undeniable: They observed the Sabbath, practiced circumcision and synagogue services, and adhered to Judaism's dietary laws.

Most Falasha had long since fled the drought-stricken and war-torn Ethiopia. Many had immigrated to Israel, where their presence was tenuous at best. But some continued into Eastern Europe, moving from one countryside to another. During Priscilla's time there, Israel had already airlifted nearly 14,000 Falasha from Ethiopia following the mass migration in 1980. Priscilla marveled at the similarity between the Falasha and the Black Americans—some of whom, during African enslavement, escaped the American South and sought refuge in the North; some even continued to Canada, whereas a few others, as far away as Europe, and fewer still, back to Africa. Mostly, she liked that Ethiopia had never been colonized.

Yet these Ethiopians had broken the tradition of not marrying outside their tribe, primarily because there were so few in Europe. Therefore, they intermarried, mainly with Italians and Croats, as evidenced by the fairer complexion of some of the children. Whether they were Jews, Priscilla did not know for sure, but she had her suspicions. She and Helen visited Israel when they were younger and saw the original Jews. They had distinct Ethiopian features, like the ones in the Falasha camp on the outskirts of Rijeka. Even though Priscilla never met Menilek—nor had any desire or need to meet him—what mattered was that the priest had countenanced Phillipe being embedded among his people so that "he" might rendezvous with the very person that his people also regarded as the enemy: Zulfika Kasun who served Slobodan Milosevic, and Slobodan Milosevic was no friend of Falasha or any other ROM sect.

On the eve of Priscilla and Shelton's last night in the ROM camp in Rijeka, Olga asked her, "Do you have any rouge garments?"

When she put her hands around Priscilla's neck, Priscilla was still uncomfortable with the romantic advances of the two women, so she pushed Olga away. But Olga persisted.

"No, no. Here, I show you." Olga untied a red bandana from around her neck, rubbed it, and said, with an expression of understanding, "Rouge, red."

Priscilla finally understood what she meant. She opened her duffel, poked around, and pulled out her red beret.

Olga grabbed it and said, "Yes!" Then she and the other woman clapped their hands gleefully.

Olga then put the beret on Priscilla's head, tilted it slightly to the right, and stood back to get a better look. "Perfect!"

"Yes! Yes!" the other woman said.

Someone else was coming.

Somewhat startled, they faced the tent's opening. A tall, muscular, and confident man named Rohan entered. He sat down, took out a block of wood and a small, curved knife from a pouch, and began carving. Olga left, only to return shortly with a carpetbag filled with carved wooden figurines.

"See!" Olga said, displaying a beautifully carved stallion, and Priscilla thought, *Oh, how my darling Carlton would love that one.*

The two women watched Priscilla choose more items and then take some currency from her pocket. "Francs, pounds, dinars?" Priscilla behaved like an unsuspecting tourist, revealing all that money in plain sight.

Olga snatched the currency from Priscilla's hands. "Twenty francs, twenty pounds, twenty dinars. Merci, Monsieur Phillipe." She handed Rohan twenty dinars, her female companion twenty francs, and kept the twenty pounds for herself. Priscilla did not mind that the women took advantage of her because she enjoyed her time with them.

After that, Olga said, "We will tell you when to wear the rouge beret."

Throughout her stay, only once did Priscilla nearly slip from her disguise. She often gazed at Olga's colorful, handmade leather boots. One time, she even pointed to them and gave Olga a thumbs-up. At the time, however, she had no idea how much she had reverted to her more feminine self, as she had even smiled. It was then that Olga had all the confirmation that she needed.

Throughout her stay, the Falasha believed that Priscilla was more familiar with Slobodan Milosevic than she had let on, but that was not the case. Priscilla had only a rudimentary knowledge of communism, not to mention the history of the Yugoslavs and their Eastern European neighbors. Although she had studied Soviet and Western European politics during her graduate studies at The Ohio State University, she was, however, less familiar with the Eastern Bloc.

She knew about the former president, Josip Tito, easing his way into leadership during World War II, resting the country from Soviet control, and that Milosevic had followed suit. She pictured Tito and Milosevic as evil, yet others regarded both men as comparatively good. "But compared to what?" Priscilla once said. "So, what are we comparing, the lesser of two evils?" She did not know at the time, nor did anyone else, just how nefarious Milosevic was. Traditionally, the Yugoslav leadership was influenced by the neighboring communist USSR, which was in the throes of its most dramatic transformation since Vladimir Lenin introduced the concept of a socialist state.

Priscilla recalled cringing during her teenage years watching the black-and-white televised news of President Nikita Khrushchev, especially at the sight of all those Russian submarines off the coast of Florida during the Cuban Missile Crisis. Then, one day, Khrushchev mysteriously disappeared from the world stage following a coup d'état, and shortly after that, Leonid Brezhnev ruled for nearly two decades.

Then came the seemingly compassionate Mikhail Gorbachev, who served as General Secretary during Priscilla's time in Eastern Europe. He instituted perestroika, liberating fifteen republics and the eventual dismantling of the communist system, or so many had thought. Back then, Priscilla welcomed the newly transformed régime. If only she had foreseen what came next. But what caused her the most discomfort was how each former Soviet leader mysteriously disappeared, never heard from again. Then again, perhaps Gorbachev was the first to resurface.

Nevertheless, Priscilla had no desire to traipse into the bowels of Russia or any Eastern European communist territory—none whatsoever. Her mission was to vet Yugoslav Lieutenant Zulfika Kasun Military Intelligence Officer, which she would do—nothing more.

39

EN ROUTE TO BIHAC AND
A BOTCHED OPERATION

Priscilla had chosen Bihać to rendezvous with the Yugoslav lieutenant because Harry's notes indicated it was in the vicinity of his last known whereabouts and because she thought she could quickly board a train "and get the hell outta here." But Bihać was deep in enemy territory, and, unfortunately, neither Priscilla nor Harry knew how rapidly circumstances were changing there. War was raging.

Nor did she know that it would take approximately three days for the Falasha to return to Bihać, not to mention the inconvenience of her mission on theirs. Throughout her time with them, no one ever told her they would be backtracking and risking their lives to facilitate her mission.

She was also unaware that CF Agent Delgato did not appreciate being the messenger of unwelcome news to the CF commander. But at least he understood her alternative plan, which the CF commander would eventually. But Agent Delgato knew more. He knew Priscilla was first and foremost a survivor, not an action heroine, and that she already knew this Kasun scumbag was hardly worth his weight in salt, as it were.

Soon after Angel delivered Priscilla's message to the CF commander, the commander received yet another unwelcome message. NSA Counterintelligence Agent Middleton thwarted the commander's objection to Priscilla's alternative plan even more: "Remember, Commander Wozniah, this is P. J. Austin-Bernhardt's mission. You may bag the prey, but everything else is her call." After serving as her protector for several years, Tommy had yet to regard Priscilla as his equal—a competent secret agent.

Early in the morning of Priscilla, Shelton, and the fifty men's departure from the ROM camp in Rijeka, Priscilla wondered why the caravan motored at such a snail's pace. Riding in the back of a horse-drawn covered wagon, she noticed, for the first time, the size of the group. Although she did not know how many people there were, she did notice two more horse-drawn covered wagons and quite a few horses and farm animals. She leaned out the back and saw people on foot and some pulling harnessed animals. But when she heard someone talking about the time it would take to reach their destination, she realized she needed to do something to occupy her time. Besides reading her novel about the nineteenth-century eccentric English family's Egyptian excavations, she needed to do something physical. Since she could ride, she jumped out of the wagon and climbed onto a horse bareback. She imagined herself in an old black-and-white Western movie rounding up cattle and horses, and man alive did she enjoy galloping about! As it turned out, Rohan, who she was unaware was her escort, was hard-pressed, keeping an eye on her.

If only she had known about Bosnia's impending secession and the heavy fighting between them and the Serbian militia, she might not have been so carefree. But Priscilla clung to a tiny consolation that Bihać connected to the European rail system that she so desperately desired. So, no matter what happens, if she somehow survived this mission, she would not have to travel all the way back to Trieste to "get the hell outta here," after all.

As she galloped about, she spotted Shelton for the first time in quite some time. He was holding the reigns of a horse-drawn covered wagon and, from her discernment, was enjoying himself.

Scrutinizing the caravan and eavesdropping on conversations, she soon realized that this sect of Falasha was not the docile wanderers or helpless refugees she once presumed. Life under Haile Selassie and the precarious circumstances in Israel had produced hard lessons in survival. The Falasha were heavily armed with knives, bows and arrows, machetes, pistols, and automatic rifles, which she glimpsed in the wagons. More significantly, the Yugoslav lieutenant's scouts never even got a chance to report any sightings of international observers or opponents, not even the Falasha, not in this neck of the woods. Why was that?

Once, while eating with Rohan, he told Priscilla that the Falasha rarely camped in lowlands or open meadows but in high altitudes, "making it easier to spot and eliminate predators. We shield ourselves in forests where we have the advantage." He also told her, "Given the large size of our community, we split up into three or more groups, rarely as a single unit, and assign sentries to guard and be on the lookout for enemies or strangers." He did not confide in her about the contingency in which they now traveled. Such was the life of the Falasha.

Neither did Rohan confide the Falasha's ulterior motive for backtracking and escorting Phillipe deeper into enemy territory. Likened to the "unwanted" that Priscilla encountered during her first time in southern Africa or the "marginalized" described by Frantz Fanon in *The Wretched of the Earth*, the Falasha were the kinds of people that the ruling elite systematically mistreated and labeled as "others." Nonetheless, they were adept at outwitting the ruling elite. Falasha were forward-thinking people. They understood politics. Not only that, but just because Priscilla never saw any electronic devices such as radios, televisions, or cell phones did not necessarily mean that there were none. The Falasha were not entirely off the grid.

More than anything else, however, the Falasha mainly reasoned that Phillipe, like CF Agent Delgato, was an American intelligence agent who would speak favorably of their bravery and facilitation of "his" mission and that, in return, the American government would kindly oblige for whatever their needs.

After three days of traveling, the Falasha finally made camp in a deeply wooded area near Bihać, where they would remain long enough for Phillipe to rendezvous with the Yugoslav lieutenant. As it turned out, one of their scouts had mysteriously reconnected with CF Agent Delgato and scheduled the meeting for the next day at 0700. When Priscilla learned the meeting with Lieutenant Kasun was finally confirmed, she was more than ready to execute her mission, do her government's bidding, and then "get the hell outta here."

Late afternoon on the eve of her rendezvous, she rested in her tent, safely embedded within the Falasha camp in the heavily wooded forest of Bihać, preparing for her mission. She silently practiced the discussion points outlined in that envelope that NSA Counterintelligence Agent Middleton had given her at the Waffle House, which now seemed like a lifetime ago. Then silently, she prayed, "Thy will be done."

As it turned out, back in Switzerland at the Luzern safe house, CF Agent Jordan, Commander Elias, Ariel, Sam, Laverne, Omar, Maalik, Ronnie and the other guardsmen, and Melissa assembled in the dining room, where they argued vehemently. The failed rescue of Nanny Hettie and baby Austin had taken its toll on everyone.

Most notably, Laverne was less spry than before; she kept holding her chest. The others were unaware of the extent of her injuries, and she would hardly talk about them. But, upon her return to the States, she would be relieved of her commission as an active field agent. Yet she held on for the duration because she desperately wanted to finish this mission and ensure the safe return of Hettie and Austin, lest one forget her friend and ward, Priscilla.

Amid these disgruntled not-so-secret secret agents, guardsmen, and special ops, now totaling fifteen, Jordy struggled to maintain a semblance of order.

"My God! Where could they be?" someone asked for the umpteenth time.

Sam turned to Laverne and fussed. "If you and your two companions hadn't gotten caught off your guard, we wouldn't have had to divert our attention and come and rescue you."

"Back off, Sam!" Jordy shouted, not that Laverne needed his help. "They were left unprotected when their backup took off for Luzern."

Laverne shouted back. "And yet you still lost Nanny Hettie and young Austin!"

Omar also ignored Jordy as he yelled at Sam, saying, "And if *you* and *your* men had not gotten caught off *your* guard, they wouldn't have been kidnapped in the first place. And I see you still have all your fingers for your troubles!"

The commotion continued.

"Wozniah will surely have our heads if we don't find 'em."

Eventually, Jordy stopped trying to douse the spontaneous brushfires. He had heard these same arguments repeatedly over the last few days. Still, he blurted out, "Stop it! Please," he pleaded again, to no avail.

"The CF commander!" Laverne yelled again, slamming her fist on the dining room table and startling everyone. "What about Agent Bernhardt? Their baby's been kidnapped! And I do not even want to think about PJ."

The fifteen-member disgruntled gathering continued ranting and accusing one another of "a botched operation."

What was believed to have been a well-thought-out rescue operation was never even executed because—while Sam and his guardsmen had gone to Marmande to rescue Laverne and the GIS agents—Kasun's second reserve unit had abducted Hettie and young Austin from the unprotected Luzern safe house.

Making matters worse, nothing from the elderly couple's cabin in Fojnica had shed any light on the nanny and baby's whereabouts, and the man believed to be Lieutenant Kasun had not broken under interrogation.

As things stood, no one there knew Hettie and Austin's whereabouts. For, the CF commander had ceased transmitting messages to them altogether.

40

THE RENDEZVOUS

At the Falasha camp near Bihać, Priscilla awoke around 0600 the following day, dressed, and headed out of her tent to the campfire. There, she ate breakfast with Olga, her companion, and Rohan, whom she had come to trust.

It had rained the night before, and although the ground was damp and muddy, there was still a substantial amount of snow. Priscilla found a tree stump to sit on as she ate sourdough bread and goat cheese, drank steaming hot coffee from a metal cup, and listened to Olga's final instructions.

"If, as you head to the oak tree and see two men coming, casually put on your rouge beret. If only one man approaches, keep walking. Either way, say nothing. Let whoever approaches talk first. No matter what the man says, you must demand to see Lieutenant Kasun. Otherwise, tell him, 'All bets are off.' Then, turn around, point in the opposite direction, and walk away." Olga did not tell Priscilla that Rohan would be with her like they were on an early morning outing. As such, anyone observing, such as Zulfika Kasun's scouts, would be none the wiser.

The more Olga talked, the more Priscilla realized that the Falasha had executed such an operation before. But what caught her attention was the role of the women, especially the two whom she thought were flighty, even loose. But it was now clear that that was their cover; they were hardly flighty women. Indeed, they were as good at their craft as she was. Most notably, she learned that Olga was more fluent in English than she had previously let on.

Rohan, who had sat in silence up to this point, stood and said, "It's time. I'm your tour guide." It was then that Priscilla realized she would not be alone. Since Rohan was comparatively European in appearance, he fit the bill for what was about to happen. Although Priscilla instinctively trusted him, she wondered about Absalom's whereabouts, who would reveal himself when she least expected.

Hidden amid the cold and dampness of the heavily wooded forest, CF Commander Wozniah, "the boys," a host of other agents, Lieutenant Zulfika Kasun, another decoy, and a yet-to-be-identified group all waited anxiously for Priscilla, disguised as Phillipe Winsarah, to arrive. They would take their cue from her when she sat underneath the designated oak tree. But unbeknownst to the CF commander, the Yugoslav lieutenant had hatched another plan. And unbeknownst to the Yugoslav lieutenant, someone else had orchestrated a plan quite like his.

When the Yugoslav lieutenant had ordered his men to kidnap Hettie and Austin and bring them to Yugoslavia, he believed that—with the child as a bargaining chip—Special Envoy P. J. Austin-Bernhardt would yield to his every wish. As a signal that his men had succeeded in kidnapping the child, two men would approach Priscilla at the appointed time of the rendezvous.

On the other hand, the CF commander had ordered Angel to approach Priscilla to facilitate the rendezvous. But would he even get the chance?

But if Priscilla followed Olga's final instructions, she would be much closer to her alternative plan of "getting the hell outta here."

Notwithstanding, neither the CF commander nor the real Zulfika Kasun, not even the yet-to-be-identified group, had considered what Priscilla would do of her own volition.

Priscilla and Rohan slushed through the muddy, snow-covered forest until they spotted a small clearing. They would reach their designated site when they spotted an oak tree and two chairs on carpets beneath it.

Along the way, Rohan admirably performed his role as a tour guide. He pointed in different directions and described the trees to Priscilla when, suddenly, two men approached them. At that point, the CF commander and the others hiding in the forest nearly came undone.

Watching from a distance, the CF commander turned to the man he thought was the Yugoslav lieutenant and said, "You double-crossing, bloody bastard!" He knew he could not trust Kasun but never expected that move. He told his men to stand down for Priscilla's safety and let the scenario play out.

As the two men approached Priscilla and Rohan, she casually pulled out her red beret and put it on.

"What's that all about?" asked the CF commander, while the other agents, not to mention the man posing as Zulfika Kasun, said nothing, especially since none of them knew what was happening either.

As the two men drew closer, Priscilla looked straight ahead. She did not know they had half-expected her to say something to them. And when it appeared as if she was ignoring them, one of them spoke.

"Aren't you, PJ Austin-Bernhardt, the 'new writer friend' to Monsieur Kasun?"

With that bold move, Priscilla knew that no one, absolutely no one, was supposed to use her real name. So, she did not respond. She shocked them and the onlookers even more when she and Rohan continued walking past the two men. Their goal was to reach the two chairs underneath the oak tree, at which point "all bets were off," well, sort of.

The two men stood in utter shock at Priscilla's outright repudiation of their presence, and so, too, did the hidden onlookers in the snow-covered forest. For sure, no one knew what to do when Priscilla sat in one of the wooden chairs because no one knew what the bloody hell was happening.

While Priscilla casually took out a pack of cigarettes, lit one, and began smoking, Rohan continued describing the trees in the area.

"Their move, whoever the hell they are," she said to herself.

After a couple of minutes of uncomfortable silence, the two men that Priscilla ignored looked at each other with confused expressions. Then they headed to the oak tree, where she sat casually smoking. When they reached her, the same man who had spoken earlier repeated himself.

"Aren't you PJ Austin-Bernhardt, 'the new writer friend' of Monsieur Kasun?"

Priscilla sat back in her chair, crossed her legs, and blew smoke rings. Without looking at the man, she said in a deep voice, "I will only speak to Zulfika Kasun. Bring him to me." She shocked everyone again when she spoke out loud, "Otherwise, *all bets are off!*" Everyone hiding heard her last words.

Then, as if the two men were not even there, she resumed talking to Rohan about the different kinds of trees in the area.

After another two minutes, which seemed much longer, when the two men still had not moved or said anything more—nor had the Yugoslav lieutenant showed up—Priscilla stood, squashed her cigarette, and turned to walk away.

As she and Rohan started walking away, the same man who had asked if she was PJ Austin-Bernhardt bellowed, "Bring out the 'heavyweight!'"

Still hidden in the cold and dampness of the forest, the CF commander balled up his good hand into a fist and punched the man, whom he now doubted was the real Yugoslav Lieutenant Kasun, in his face.

Angel and Onslow pulled Tommy off the man. Despite the commander's outrage, they did not want to disturb the situation further by deflecting attention away from what remained of the rendezvous. Nonetheless, Priscilla had no idea any of them were even there.

Then, to everyone's shock, save for Priscilla, two loathsome men escorted Nanny Hettie and young Austin into the clearing. Although they were some distance away from her, they were close enough for the nanny to recognize the small-framed, tan-complexioned person dressed in a soldier's camouflage uniform, wearing her hair in a buzz cut. But as Hettie attempted to call out to her, one of the loathsome men swung his arm across her chest, effectively holding her back. Then he dared her to move again. Hettie, who was already crying, cried more vigorously.

Otherwise, no one could believe their ears and eyes, particularly Priscilla's reaction, or rather lack thereof. But Priscilla had long since prayed over the matter, so she was hardly surprised. She was not even shocked, especially since Angel had already cracked that egg. As such, Priscilla trumped Kasun's plan to use Austin as a bargaining chip to leverage her compliance. Yet, everyone watching the scene thought that surely she would buckle under the apparent precarious circumstances and yield to the Yugoslav lieutenant's every wish.

But they were unaware of the quiet, still voice that guided and sustained Priscilla during seemingly unbearable circumstances.

"Go on the offense," said the quiet, still voice. So that was what she did.

Priscilla ignored the two men, Nanny Hettie and young Austin's wailing and shouted, "Zulfika Kasun, show yourself! If you want anything from me, now is the time. Otherwise, *all bets are off!*" Then she looked around the clearing and said: "If I don't see you in the next few seconds, I'm outta here." Again, since she spoke loudly, the onlookers hiding in the snow-covered forest all heard her.

At that, Hettie cried even more vigorously. She could not fathom why Priscilla behaved as if she did not see her and baby Austin.

Otherwise, everyone else looked from Priscilla to the two loathsome men with Hettie and Austin. Those who stood with the Kasun decoy looked from him to Priscilla. The two men nearest Priscilla looked from her to their accomplices with Hettie and the baby boy. Rohan was undisturbed by anything that was happening.

Then, everyone watched as Priscilla turned her back and began walking away briskly with Rohan in tow.

By then, Nanny Hettie had mustered the courage to speak again. She leaned forward and shouted at the top of her lungs. "No! Madame PJ, don't leave us!"

Priscilla prayed to God for the strength to continue walking away as she heard Hettie's shouting and Austin's bawling intensify. She did not know how much longer she could keep it up. But she continued putting one foot before the other as she slushed through the mud and snow.

Then, even more unexpectedly, everyone heard tree branches rustling and watched as a big, burly man stepped out into the open. His loud, hoarse, masculine voice cut through the air, overshadowing Hettie's cries and Austin's wailing: "Stop! Alright, already!"

Priscilla turned back around and, for the first time, came face to face with the real Zulfika Kasun, who, along with everyone hiding out, realized that she was undeniably someone with whom to reckon. Even the indomitable Tommy Wozniah now realized that much.

As the real Zulfika Kasun stomped toward Priscilla, he motioned to his four accomplices to stand down, which included the two men with Hettie and baby Austin. By then, the CF commander realized the extent of the Yugoslav lieutenant's deception; the man he had captured and held was indeed another decoy.

That was also when Onslow mightily declared. "I told you Agent Austin-Bernhardt could hold her own. Besides, nobody is going to believe any of this, anyway. Nobody."

Nonetheless, as things stood, Onslow surmised the situation a tad too soon.

41

THE RED BERET

At long last, American Secret Agent PJ Austin-Bernhardt and Yugoslav Military Intelligence Officer Lieutenant Zulfika Kasun were face to face. But unbeknownst to either of them, CF Commander Wozniah had ordered his men to erect a hidden camera in the oak tree. So, everything that happened would be a matter of record. Tommy Wozniah was not the CF commander for naught.

As it turned out, regardless of her disguise, the Yugoslav lieutenant already knew what Priscilla looked like. But she was shocked at his image. There, before her, sat a tall, muscular, cold-hearted, and ruthless man who, unlike his first impersonator, was refined though equally cold-hearted and ruthless. The first impersonator's face was unblemished and clean-shaven; the real one bore scars, pot marks, and an untrimmed mustache. He also had greasy chestnut brown hair. Like the third impersonator, he had poor hygiene and emitted a foul stench. His teeth were stained. His facial hair and fingernails were filthy. His boots and uniform were filthy, too. Most significantly, however, like his first decoy, the real Zulfika Kasun also spoke English fluently.

But his dissatisfaction that he had to converse with a woman, one of color, got the best of him. Or was that the worst? Thus far, NSA Counterintelligence Agent Middleton's notes about the man's identity and demeanor were spot on. So, Priscilla knew she was in the presence of the real Zulfika Kasun. Although Harry's notes mentioned the man's dislike of Muslims and his prejudice against people of color, notably Black people, Priscilla was adept at handling such personalities.

Kasun's dissatisfaction with Priscilla was apparent as soon as he sat down. He twisted his lips and turned up his nose. "Why did they send you? What do *you* know about my country? What do *you* know about negotiating or anything else, for that matter? I'm insulted." He spat.

Priscilla was undisturbed. "Lieutenant, you could have chosen someone else, but for whatever reason, you chose and pursued me. So, stop wasting my time. What do you have for us?"

When he did not respond, she switched tactics.

"For the record, I do not negotiate. I collect intel and convey it, nothing more," which was not the case. She continued to ignore his offensive remarks, and she certainly was not going to introduce herself as a secret agent, ergo the title "special envoy." Priscilla mainly needed to know what he wanted from the American government in return for vital intel about Milosevic. Full stop.

She stunned him when she said, "You've got a little under fifteen minutes to state your case."

While he stared at the small-framed, tan feminine figure disguised as a man, as if, indeed, she had confused him with someone else, she chose another angle. "All right, then. Shall we start with your defection?" But when she specifically asked about Milosevic, and he offered no intel, she filled in the blanks for him. "Perhaps sanctuary, an asylum of sorts?"

The lieutenant leaned forward and opened his eyes wide. "And?"

"And what else do you want?"

"No extradition."

"No extradition! You must take us for fools. What's in it for us? You've yet to put any cards on the table."

"I want what you Americans call 'witness protection' and a new identity, not just a new name but a new face and all."

If mine looked like yours, she thought, *I'd want a new face, too.*

Kasun then rattled on detailing his wishes, such as a condominium here and there, a bank account, and so forth. Priscilla now knew for sure that the Yugoslav lieutenant was an unacceptable commodity. Besides, he had yet to mention any vital intel about the Milosevic regime.

"Surely, you jest."

"Young lady, I'm quite serious."

At that point, the CF unit, their international intelligence associates, and one other group unknown to the others acted as if they were puzzled because they did not see a female soldier but rather a male. Although they could not hear much of the conversation, they could make out that the lieutenant called the little soldier "young lady." This was particularly puzzling since the CF commander, "the boys," and their international intelligence associates all knew of Priscilla's role in the rendezvous. Then again, they were hidden in the forest, much farther away from the oak tree than were Nanny Hettie and baby Austin. Yet, why they pretended to be puzzled remains a mystery since they had all heard the nanny call out to "Madame PJ." On the other hand, perhaps they were trying to conceal Priscilla's identity. Before it was all over, the CF commander would order the videographer to delete and redact all references to Priscilla's name and gender from the tape.

Meanwhile, Priscilla ignored the put-down, being called "young lady." Although she had undergone training to ignore insults and baiting, common tactics used by those who suspected she was thin-skinned about her race and gender, she still had a bit of a problem with that.

She carried on and continued speaking in a gruff voice, "I'm not one for repeating myself. So, please keep it simple. Now, what *exactly* do you want?"

"It's complicated, *young lady*," said the Yugoslav lieutenant, who, despite her masculine voice, already knew Priscilla, disguised as a man, was, in fact, female. But he knew more. He knew one of her weak spots was being called "young lady," so he played that card.

Though her blood boiled at his impertinence, she portrayed a poker face and, this time ignored his putdown.

"I already told you I do not like repeating myself."

"But you do not understand."

"I do not need to 'understand.' All my people want to know is what *you* have for us. Then, and only then, will I entertain what you want. By the way, I don't give a rat's ass about complications and other stuff. Got that?" She looked at her watch.

"Your fifteen minutes are almost up."

"*Fifteen minutes!*"

At this point, many onlookers quickly discerned the lieutenant's shock about the rendezvous' timeframe. They had seen Priscilla checking her watch, but no one had anticipated a time limitation. Priscilla was playing out her plan, which she was thus far fulfilling. NSA Counterintelligence Agent Middleton had written in his notes that she must "include one shocking surprise, a limitation of sorts," hence the fifteen-minute limit.

"You heard me. Besides," she noted, "You screwed yourself when you made this personal. Now, where were we? Oh, yeah, we should help you because?"

The lieutenant looked at Priscilla as if seeing her for the first time. He leaned forward and finally began answering her questions.

When she had gleaned what she thought she needed to transmit back to CIA Deputy Director Froley—the names of the Yugoslav generals and their operations, the last citing of Milosevic, and details about their military apparatus, which was not much from Priscilla's viewpoint—she stood. Puzzled, Kasun stared at her. She signaled to Rohan to collect Nanny Hettie and Austin from the men who held them.

Back when she served as a special envoy to the Middle East, she learned that it takes multiple meetings to reach amicable agreements. Yet, she hardly anticipated anything remarkable to come from a subsequent rendezvous with Kasun. Besides, there were hundreds more like him in equally tenuous situations worldwide.

Without another word or backward glance, she started walking away.

While Priscilla engaged with Kasun, everyone hidden in in the snow-covered forests remained mesmerized. No one could fathom what they witnessed—a petite five-foot-four-and-a-half-inch Black woman of diverse ancestry disguised as a man—challenging—or was that outwitting? —a despicable Yugoslav lieutenant with her child's life on the line.

But when the two remaining audiences saw how the two men who still held Nanny Hettie and Austin hostage reacted, their hearts skipped several beats. One of the men held Austin high while the other pointed his rifle at the child's head. Oh, how the baby gagged and wailed.

Then, as if on cue, Priscilla turned back around and tilted her red beret the way Olga had shown her. Hell broke loose.

The two men standing behind her and the lieutenant under the oak tree, the two men holding Nanny Hettie and pointing a rifle at the child's head, and what was now one audience hiding in the snow-covered forest all heard guns cocking and blades clanking. Swords were being drawn, too, as, seemingly from out of nowhere, a horde of "interesting-looking people" —fifty armed Falasha—leaped out into the open and encircled everyone, their weapons at the ready.

Excellent trackers, the Falasha knew those forests better than the other men. They could traverse the woods without making a sound or leaving many indentations because their survival depended on it.

When Priscilla saw the Falasha encircle the clearing and surrounding snow-covered forest with their weapons drawn, she raised her arms high, thanked God, and declared, "We did it!"

The two men holding Hettie and Austin hostage quickly and carefully released the nanny and the child into Rohan's custody.

Thunderstruck. "Well, damn," Kasun said at the realization that what he had been told about the Falasha was, in fact, valid. He also marveled at how well that woman of color performed her job.

More significantly, he and everyone else suddenly realized they were in a precarious predicament.

"Who are these people?" someone yelled out in fear.

"Interesting-looking people to me," someone else said.

Yet another one said, "Whoever they are, they've got the drop on us," at which point everyone dropped their weapons.

While the two men who once stood behind Priscilla and the lieutenant under the oak tree, the two men who once held Hettie and Austin hostage, and the CF commander, "the boys," and their international intelligence associates all pondered what was now their precarious predicament, Priscilla headed back to the ROM camp, closely followed by Rohan carrying young Austin on his shoulders and Hettie slushing swiftly through the muddy, snow-covered Earth, shuddering and weeping tears of joy and relief. The baby had already stopped wailing, mainly because, sitting astride Rohan's shoulders, he liked that the man played with him. Or was it that, as Rohan kept pushing Austin's chubby hands away from covering his eyes, the child thought he was playing with him?

While the unarmed onlookers all stood stunned, Absalom stepped out from the encircled ranks of the Falasha. No one else moved, not even the two men who once held Austin at gunpoint, nor the two men who once stood behind Priscilla and Kasun under the tree, not anyone.

Only Angel recognized Absalom, who marched gallantly in his direction. Angel, in turn, nudged the CF commander—who, like everyone else—was now unarmed and mesmerized by what had just transpired.

"Come, Commander, let me introduce you to our contact and backup."

As the two commanders shook hands, Absalom asked, "And what would you have us do with the loathsome men who held the nanny and the baby boy hostage?" He asked the same question about the two other men who had stood behind Priscilla and the lieutenant under the oak tree. Since he assumed the CF commander would take charge of the Yugoslav lieutenant, he did not ask about him.

"Take their weapons and leave them to fend for themselves," the CF commander said of the lieutenant's accomplices.

Then, as he stared at the real Zulfika Kasun—a man he loathed and wanted to eliminate—who now stood alone, he said, "Something tells me the lieutenant has something else up his sleeves. But leave him, too. Besides, let's see how he explains this little charade to his superior officer, especially after his general receives a copy of the videotape." The CF commander laughed.

As if an afterthought, though, using his good hand, he whacked the imposter, who still stood stunned next to him, across his forehead and said, "I knew there was something fishy about you other than your foul odor."

As far as Absalom was concerned, he had done what the priest had authorized.

The Yugoslav lieutenant shouted when he saw Absalom and his fifty-armed men disappearing back into the forest as if they had never even been there.

"Hey, Commander. What about me? You can't just leave me here."

But CF Commander Wozniah ignored the Yugoslav lieutenant, not to mention his decoy, now down for the count on the muddy, snow-covered ground.

Angel looked at the astonishment on the faces of his CF and international associates and said, "Well, fellas, looks like our work here is done."

The CF commander nodded. "And something also tells me that Miss Prissy is going to submit a 'No' vote on granting Kasun whatever he wants."

Onslow chuckled. "That'll teach him not to take a woman for granted." However, his comments were meant for the CF commander, but he would never have said that to his face.

It was equally notable that the CF commander and Priscilla were finally on the same page—no longer competing to outwit each other.

As for their quarry, they left the nefarious Zulfika Kasun, his double, the two men they had sent to approach Priscilla, and the two men who had held Hettie and baby Austin hostage, wondering what would become of them.

As it turned out, after Deputy Director Froley reviewed the videotape, he was hardly surprised with Priscilla's preliminary report, which was verbal.

"I'm still not sure why all the fuss over him in the first place. He's an evil man and was playing us." She continued, "Why waste precious resources on someone who gets his jollies from hurting people? We must cast our net for someone else. Besides, never once did he share any vital intel about the president. He behaved as if he were the real cheese."

"Throw this one back," she declared. "He's a nasty piece of work and would simply ruin our table setting." All right, so Priscilla had a way with words.

Even though the cunning and ruthless Yugoslav lieutenant had made similar overtures with at least three other governments, Priscilla was unaware of the dragnet one of Milosevic's generals had set for him, not to mention the videotape of the rendezvous. Come to think of it, neither was the lieutenant.

42

THE TRAIN RIDE BACK TO LUZERN

Priscilla waited until she returned to the ROM camp before displaying affection and maternal instincts. When she saw Hettie dragging her feet through the muddy, snow-covered Earth and gasping for air, she ran to her. Embracing her, she said, "Thank you for taking care of my son. You are such a brave soul. But I'm sure you know you can never tell anyone about what happened. Besides, no one would believe you, anyway." But Priscilla was hard-pressed because she knew Hettie would blabber to Father, Lady Chelsea, and Ramses. Still, she hoped they would think Hettie's stories fanciful.

Hettie stumbled backward. Her mouth gaped. Her eyes opened wide. Speechless, she was astounded by Priscilla's embrace. She thought about how Priscilla had turned and walked away briskly when the despicable man held his rifle to Austin's head. Her mind flashed back to the morning when she and Mavis helped to deliver baby Austin, and Priscilla kept pushing them away, saying, "Stop touching me!" At this moment, however, she just stood still, her arms wagging at her sides. Never had Priscilla even touched her. It was no secret that Priscilla did not like being touched. So, for her to hug Hettie so tightly was astounding, to say the least. But Priscilla was happy, thankful, and relieved that Hettie had cared for her son during what must have been a harrowing experience.

It would take time for Hettie to recover from her terrifying experience with the loathsome Serbians, not to mention Priscilla's present display of affection. But for the moment, she managed to say, "I'm just glad to see you're all right, Madame PJ. The Bernhardts would never forgive me if something bad happened to you or Master Austin."

Priscilla hugged Hettie again and then turned her attention to her son.

As she reached for young Austin, she smiled at Rohan, who towered over her. "Thank you," she said. He smiled back at her and handed her son to her.

She swung her heavy baby boy around and around and laughed. The child laughed, too, and then, to Priscilla's surprise, he said, "Down."

"What was that?"

"Down," the child said.

Priscilla had never heard Austin say anything short of "Momma" or "Da Da." She lowered the child and watched him stand up using her leg for support. He stood, wobbled, and fell. Pulling himself back up, he wobbled away from her. Priscilla laughed with glee as she watched her son walking for the first time.

"Madame PJ," Hettie said, "I wanted to tell you he's been trying to stand on his own for quite some time. But I'm so happy he finally mastered it for you." Hettie was beside herself. She knew the child was exceptionally developed and was walking ahead of most toddlers his age. But she was still shaken from that incredible experience at the oak tree, let alone the two weeks she had spent with the Serbians at a cabin in the woods where she and Austin were held hostage. But for now, she was happy at the outcome of it all.

"Oh, Nanny Hettie," Priscilla cried, "God bless you." Tears streamed down Priscilla's cheeks. She repeated. "God bless you." Hettie could not help noticing Priscilla displaying genuine gratitude, a side that Priscilla rarely, if ever, demonstrated. That she had hugged her and shed tears so freely was so unlike her.

Priscilla was not the only one joyful.

Olga and her companion appeared. They cheered and clapped because they knew Monsieur Petit—whom they already knew was a woman—had had a successful mission. Yet, instead of approaching her—seeing Austin wobbling about the snow and muddy ground—they picked up the child, tickled his chubby cheeks, and rubbed his head.

When Shelton showed up, unaware that Priscilla had completed her mission, he said, "Back so soon? Someone said Rohan took you on a tour."

Then, he seemed to have remembered something when he said, "You know something? I could swear that I'm the only man in the camp. What happened to the others?" But the missing fifty men would reappear before their entourage departed.

Priscilla smiled at him and said, "Good morning to you, too, Shelton. Believe it or not, we're leaving this morning." Then, as an afterthought, she said, "Even better news, Austin is walking!" She pointed to her son and said no more. For sure, she did not answer his question about the missing men.

At that brief report by Priscilla, Shelton then walked to Hettie because he was surprised to see her and Austin. He asked her how she came to be there. But Rohan pulled him aside and filled him in on what had happened: that he had taken Priscilla on a tour of the area "and ran into Hettie and Austin out for a walk." As such, like Absalom and his wife and the two women who befriended Priscilla, Rohan kept Priscilla's secret. Whether Shelton believed Rohan was beside the point. It would be a while before Hettie confided in him about her harrowing experience, especially since Priscilla had cautioned her against it.

Notwithstanding, for the time being, Hettie kept keen eyes on the two women playing with Austin because she had no idea who they were. Besides, she was still shaken up from her terrifying experience during Priscilla's rendezvous, her two weeks with the despicable Serbians, and the lingering shock of Priscilla hugging her. So, she ignored Shelton and kept watch over young Austin.

While Olga and her companion played with Austin under Hettie's watchful eyes, Shelton seemed like an outsider for the first time since he had injected himself into Priscilla's mission.

As for Priscilla, she went inside the tent that had been her home for the last time, where she rummaged through her duffel for a change of clothes.

When she returned, no longer disguised as a man, she still wore her red beret. But she also wore a modest amount of makeup, dangling earrings, her signature black pantsuit, a white silk blouse, and beautiful, colorful leather ankle boots. And so it was that while Priscilla had rendezvoused with Lieutenant Kasun, Olga had slipped inside her tent and put the boots on her duffel with a handwritten note that read: "Blessings, my friend, Olga."

Seeing Priscilla as the woman she was, adorned in more feminine attire, including those gorgeous handmade colorful leather boots, everyone who knew her as Monsieur Petit shouted with glee and clapped.

"Wow!"

Olga, who held Austin, waved the baby's hands at Priscilla. "Look, Austin. Your mommy is so pretty."

As if responding to her, the baby boy said, "Momma."

When Priscilla hugged Olga, Hettie and Shelton—who knew Priscilla did not like people touching her—wondered what that was all about.

As Priscilla's entourage departed, something told her not to ask about Absalom and his wife's whereabouts. They would have been there if they had wanted to see her, especially his wife. But Priscilla was not the first stranger for whom they had done a good deed. Nor would she be the last one, either.

As it turned out, Absalom had arranged transportation for Priscilla's entourage to the train station in Bihać, where, just before they boarded, Nanny Hettie said enthusiastically, "Madame PJ, I've never ridden on a train!"

Priscilla found Hettie's confession interesting, especially since she knew she had grown up in the UK, where there were lots of trains and subways. She watched as Hettie marveled at the locomotive. Then she watched Hettie's cheeks flush as she squeezed baby Austin with excitement.

Before Priscilla or Shelton could react to Hettie's confession, they watched as a conscientious porter helped her onto the platform where, with each step, Hettie looked at young Austin and said, "Well, I suppose we're in for another grand adventure." Delighted that Hettie was excited, not afraid, Priscilla and Shelton followed and settled in for the long ride back to Luzern, Switzerland.

Almost immediately after settling into her compartment, Priscilla took out a legal pad and pen and began writing about her recent escapades. Something told her that whether she drafted her story as fiction or nonfiction, no one would believe it, anyway. Yet, she wrote and wrote until Hettie peeped inside and said, "Time for dinner, Madame PJ."

As they all sat at the table in the dining car, Priscilla looked out the window into the darkness of the night. She smiled as she thought about the PBS Masterpiece Mystery *Poirot* series and how she might create her version of *Murder on the Orient Express*. But she also continued thinking that nobody would believe any of this stuff, anyway. Then, she heard Shelton saying her name.

"What was that?"

"Madame PJ, I said, 'Where is your mind?' You've been unusually quiet since we first boarded."

"Oh, Shelton, it's nothing. Just musing over how blessed we all are."

As the train's wheels rode smoothly and swiftly across the tracks, Priscilla ignored onlookers staring at her, some even asking the porters if she was who they thought she was. "You know," said a middle-aged woman of refined comportment in a French accent, "she looks like the American PJ Austin-Bernhardt. Her hair is much shorter. But she certainly looks like her."

"And right you are, Madame. But we must take care not to impose on our famous passengers." The porter had hoped his caution would lessen the woman's curiosity.

Meanwhile, restless, young Austin climbed down from Nanny Hettie's lap and clung to the edge of the seat. When his feet touched down, he wobbled up and down the aisle as if it were his very own playground. That gave the other passengers something else to discuss. When Hettie stood to go after him, Priscilla beckoned for her to be still.

"Never mind, Hettie. Let him stretch his legs." With attention primarily on her son, Priscilla realized she could enjoy her meal without all eyes on her.

Shelton and Hettie watched the youngster as everyone with an aisle seat attempted to pick him up and play with him. They passed him around from one table to another, pinching his plump cheeks and tickling his tummy. But when, occasionally, he said, "Down," they put him back down and "oohed" and "aahed" as he wobbled throughout the dining compartment.

As it happened, Austin enjoyed his time on the train, as many of the onlookers commented:

"He's so handsome."

"He's so well-behaved."

"He's so cute."

"How old is he?"

When Priscilla could take no more, she said, "Hettie, Shelton, you can take it from here. Besides, I'm not up to making small talk." Sliding out of her seat, she looked at Hettie and Shelton and then said, "Just let them know we're on vacation and thank them for their kindness. But I do need my rest."

At that, Priscilla nodded, acknowledging some passengers as she walked briskly back to her compartment, leaving Shelton and Hettie to deal with the curious onlookers and Austin.

Priscilla did not realize it, but their train had long since departed (enemy territory) Bosnia-Herzegovina and Croatia. Soon, they would reach Trieste, Italy, and spend the next day traveling through the country's northcentral sector. Her mind set on her writing, she described the scenes along the way and took care to record the correct spelling of small towns such as Monfalcone, Pontograuro, San Dona di Piave, Lido Venezia, Verona, Brescia, and Milano, where she noticed they veered north toward Switzerland.

With her mission behind her, she had no idea how exhausted she was, but sleep was calling, so she napped.

While she slept, Shelton and Hettie made friends with other passengers. They enjoyed socializing in the dining car and the lounge.

There was no mistaking that Austin was more affable and enjoyed being the center of attention, unlike his stoic and aloof mother.

When Priscilla finally awoke, the train was within three hours of their destination. She freshened up and thought about her darling Carlton for the first time in a long time, and this time, she did not push thoughts of him away. She could have used a cell phone but preferred the wire service. She thought it was a tad more romantic. So, she called for a porter to assist her in sending a wire, which read:

My Darling Carlton,

I am fine. Young Austin walks!

Am on a train with Shelton, Nanny Hettie, and our son. Will arrive back at Luzern shortly and at Bow Lake as scheduled.

Oh, yeah. I have lots of souvenirs!

Love always,

Your Miss Prissy

After sending her wire, she ordered room service. Or was that cabin service? Her order consisted of a steak with side orders of a baked potato with sour crème and chives, Swiss chards, and a bottle of red wine. She also picked up her legal pad and pen and commenced writing again.

Shortly, Austin, Hettie, and Shelton returned to her compartment.

"Good to see you back to yourself," Shelton said.

"Oh, Madame PJ!" Hettie exclaimed. "I can't remember ever having so much fun. I never imagined riding a train would be like this. The countryside is beautiful, and I've met so many wonderful people. And everybody adores Master Austin. I can't wait to tell Melissa and everybody back at Bow Lake." Already, she had overcome her harrowing experience of the past couple of weeks. Priscilla knew of few people who were that resilient.

She continued marveling at Shelton and Hettie, both radiating with glee. As for Austin, Priscilla could see he enjoyed pulling at their legs, anchoring himself. Once or twice, he fell to the floor where, almost immediately, he either fell fast asleep or was back up on his feet again.

43

NO ONE'S GONNA BELIEVE ANY OF THIS ANYWAY

After Priscilla's entourage disembarked from the train at the Luzern station, Shelton hailed two taxis back to the villa, where they were about to find out how much they had been missed. But they had missed the others dearly as well. As they pulled up to the gate, they were reminded of the security forces when the guardsmen rallied. Some even ran inside to notify the others of the entourage's return. But those inside had also seen the taxis through the windows and brushed up against the cheerful guardsmen as they rushed out to greet the returning family and loved ones.

Melissa and Ronnie led the way, holding hands.

Melissa was ecstatic. "Oh, Madame PJ, it's so very good to see you." But, knowing better than to touch her, she instead turned and hugged Hettie. "I sure missed you, Hettie."

Although Hettie was somewhat surprised to see Melissa and Ronnie holding hands, she surprised them with her news. All the while, Ronnie remained quiet.

"Melissa, I have so much to tell you. Now, we can add a train ride across Europe to our experiences. I met so many wonderful people." Hettie glowed.

Melissa could not recall seeing Hettie so excited, but she was astonished when she heard young Austin saying, "Down." After Hettie put the child down, and he started walking—wobbling was more like it—Melissa and everyone else shouted at the top of their lungs. That was the only time that Ronnie reacted. While everyone else shouted, "Wow!" he picked up the toddler and whirled him around. Then he smiled at Melissa.

Everyone expressed glee at seeing the nanny and the baby boy back home—safe and unharmed—not to mention Priscilla. But they were mainly drawn to young Austin, who wobbled about on his own.

Melissa ran to Shelton, hugged him tightly, and whispered, "Why didn't you stay in touch? I was worried something bad happened."

Shelton whispered back to her, "Melissa, my job is to look after Madame PJ, and that's what I've been doing." Then he said, "But it sure is good to be back and see how well you're doing." He looked her over, and when he said, "You look so happy," Melissa blushed. Of the lot of them, Shelton was not in the least surprised to see Melissa and Ronnie holding hands.

While Priscilla stood back and allowed Hettie and Shelton to receive the heartfelt greetings, Austin continued dazzling everyone by walking. Otherwise, the others merely nodded at her since they knew of her aversion to being touched.

Of the lot, Jordy, Sam, and Laverne bowled over to see Austin walking. Unable to contain his happiness that all was well with Austin, Hettie, and Priscilla, Jordy hefted the baby onto his shoulders. Austin held on, clasping his chubby hands around Jordy's head. Never mind that Jordy did not walk with his cane.

As for Laverne, she stood mesmerized as if she did not know which of them to approach first. Then, soberly, she said, "It's so very good to see you all back safely." But Laverne's greeting was meant primarily for Priscilla. She was so happy to see her friend and colleague safe and unharmed.

As for Sam, he slapped Priscilla's shoulders and said, "Congrats, Girlfriend, for another successful mission or two!" He added "or two" because he was confident that Priscilla had rescued her son and his nanny.

As the entourage entered, there was a chorus of "Hellos" and "It's so very good to see you all." Everyone patted Austin, hugged Hettie, and back-slapped Shelton. As for Priscilla, the not-so-secret secret agents, special ops, and guardsmen mostly nodded and smiled at her.

During what seemed like an endless homecoming, the not-so-secret secret agents, special ops, and guardsmen passed baby Austin from one to the other, earning bragging rights for a long time.

Then, Shelton and Ronnie shared a moment. "Glad to have you back from your grand adventure," Ronnie said with a smirk while Shelton grinned broadly. But when Melissa joined them and held Ronnie's hand, Shelton knew for sure why she looked so happy.

Perhaps it was the sight of Hettie and Austin—safe and unharmed—that no one bothered to ask about Priscilla's rendezvous with the Yugoslav lieutenant. Nor did they ask about any of her other escapades, which was fine by Priscilla, who was simply glad to have successfully finished her mission.

She did, however, notice something interesting. Melissa and Ronnie, the guardsman who often served kitchen detail, appeared to have bonded affectionately. She would also observe improvements in Melissa's cuisine. Melissa's repertoire now included well-prepared steaks and seafood dishes. *My, my*, Priscilla thought, *love does have its benefits*. She liked it when people around her were happy. She was delighted about Melissa's newfound love.

Meanwhile, Priscilla was sure Shelton would blabber about all that he had experienced to the not-so-secret secret agents, special ops, and guardsmen, and right she was. Shelton felt like he was finally part of the intelligence realm's inner sanctum. But he was wrong. Before long, he would be debriefed by a CIA staffer. Even so, nothing would stop him from blabbering to Carlton. Even Priscilla knew that much. But for whatever reason, she had not thought much about how Hettie would deal with her experiences.

With a little over one month on her lease at her Marmande villa, Priscilla told Laverne, the other agents, the special ops, and the guardsmen that she was returning to Marmande and completing her novel there.

She contacted the realtor and paid the lease for the next six months.

But she did more than that.

She instructed the realtor to contact the Red Cross and organizations that provide shelter and services for abuse victims to make the villa available to them. She had no idea why such thoughts entered her mind, but she needed to do something meaningful with her financial resources. She would later share this information with Julia and her sister-in-law, Arvana, who would take it from there.

After that, she submitted her official report to CIA Deputy Director Froley. Because she had completed her mission successfully, he told her they would discuss her discarded tracking device later.

In the interim, a remnant of the not-so-secret secret agents, special ops, and guardsmen remained at the Luzern villa until the five-member entourage returned to Marmande.

As Priscilla neared the completion of her first novel, she was surprised when, one day, someone knocked on the front door of her Marmande villa. *Who could that possibly be?*

She heard Melissa scream.

"Father! Lady Chelsea! And Ramses, too!"

Father broke through Melissa's excitement. With a big grin, he said, "We thought we'd take advantage of PJ's offer to visit for a short spell." Then, he, Lady Chelsea, and Ramses strolled into the foyer as if they had been expected.

When Priscilla arrived, they each hugged her but could not resist teasing her about her new hairstyle. Lady Chelsea wiped her eyes with her silk hanky and Father and Ramses with their big cotton handkerchiefs. Though shocked seeing her hair *whacked off*, as Lady Chelsea thought, Father and Ramses could not resist patting it. "Trying a new look, eh?"

As Priscilla and her in-laws reunited in the foyer, Shelton appeared, and when he saw the Bernhardts, he yelled over his shoulders, "Hettie! You had better wake Austin. Father, Lady Chelsea, and Ramses, too, are here."

Shelton did not know that when Hettie heard someone scream, she had closed the door to Austin's nursery because she did not know what was happening. So she waited until someone told her. When Shelton told her through her closed door that the Bernhardts had arrived, she could not move fast enough.

Moments later, Hettie came hurriedly pushing Austin in his carriage. She could not control her excitement.

"Father! Lady Chelsea! Ramses! Master Austin walks!" At that, the baby woke up crying, but when Hettie picked him up, he calmed down.

The excitement mounted when the toddler said, "Down." Then, one by one, Father, Lady Chelsea, and Ramses expressed utter glee.

"Oh, my!"

"I don't believe my eyes and ears!"

"My, my!"

When Austin stood, rubbed his sleepy eyes, and continued wobbling about, they were all beyond themselves.

That night at dinner, Father told Priscilla that "Lady Chelsea was homesick, so we visited her family's homestead near Leeds. That was when she suggested 'popping in' on you."

Priscilla did not care why they visited. She was delighted with their company.

"This is such a pleasant surprise." Animated, she openly pondered, "I hope you approve of our little abode." This was the first time her in-laws had visited her in a home other than Bow Lake, not even at her Harlem brownstone. As such, they noticed the rustic architecture in the Marmande villa and came to terms with her appreciation for the equally impressive architecture of the Harlem structure. That Priscilla was a down-to-Earth woman was ever so evident.

So, she was surprised when, at dinner, Lady Chelsea, dabbing her eyes with her cloth napkin, said, "I simply love this villa. It reminds me so much of my family's home. But I'm mostly pleased to see all of you enjoying yourselves and, of course, young Austin walking."

"I'll say," said Ramses, who beamed. Staring at Priscilla, he said, "You sure look good, Girlfriend," using the language of her girlfriends, then adding, "Hettie, Shelton, and Melissa look good, too. As for Austin, he looks like he can't wait to grow up." Then he laughed heartily.

"Ditto." Father raised his glass with a big grin.

"I still can't believe all this," Lady Chelsea kept saying, "It's so good seeing all of you."

Then she said something that caused much laughter. "And just think, who knew Melissa could cook!"

As the days wore on, Priscilla grew tired of chatting with her in-laws. Mostly, she grew bored talking about the property's décor and Melissa's cooking cuisine. She remembered something requiring her attention, returned to her study, and picked up where she had left off from typing her novel.

That Priscilla was hardly interested in talking about the property's décor and Melissa's cooking did not go unnoticed by Father and Ramses. So, they engaged her in conversation about something they knew interested her, or so they thought. As they approached her study, they noticed the door was open. They tapped on the panel and stepped through the threshold as if they had been expected. Priscilla was not the only one who behaved assertively.

"Got a minute?" asked Father as he strolled casually toward her.

"Father! Ramses! Come in, fellas," she said, pushing away from her desk.

"We like your study," Father said, scoping the space.

"Yes," echoed Ramses, adding, "Few, if any, distractions." But then he cut to the chase and said, "Say, PJ, my child, when last have you communicated with your friends in the Hollingsworth camp?"

"My goodness! Where'd all that come from?"

Ignoring her surprise, Father told her that President Hollingsworth was on the ballot for reelection in November 1992.

"Yes, I'm aware of that," she said, following up with a question: "Has something unexpected happened?"

"Not really," said Ramses. "However," after pausing briefly, he said, "there's growing discontentment about the situation in the Balkans, and the president is having a rough go at trying to connect it to American interests."

"Oh, I see."

244

"By the way, PJ," Father said, as if concluding their point, "the issue will probably be discussed in the presidential debate on foreign policy in October."

Father and Ramses stared at each other until one of them finally said, "PJ, someone has been calling and wants to talk to you about something important."

"Oh? Who might that be?"

"Bradley Nielson," Father said matter-of-factly. Bradley was the Secretary of State. Priscilla worked with him on the 1988 Hollingsworth Presidential Campaign.

She was unamused that Father had dropped the secretary's name so slyly.

"Bradley Nielson? What on Earth—"

"I'll bet you thought you were through with presidential campaigns," Ramses said, his eyebrows arched high.

"No, fellas. I'm not getting involved in another presidential campaign."

"Ah, come on, Girlfriend," Ramses said. "We're pretty sure they want you to create a PR campaign educating America about the situation in the Balkans."

"Ah, crap! I should have known." Priscilla had not thought about providing PR services for the Hollingsworth team again, or anybody else, for that matter, for a long time. Besides, her priorities had changed. She was hardly interested in breaking away from her writing to conduct another PR campaign, not even a presidential one.

While she thought about it, Father asked, "PJ, are you even listening to us?"

"Yes and no. Let's change the subject. I'll deal with that headache when I return. For now, I prefer to enjoy your company and wrap up my first novel. Deal?"

"Deal," both men said because they had achieved their goal. Even though Priscilla did not appreciate the way that they had broached the subject, the "two old geezers," as she sometimes called them, knew she would do an excellent job creating an information campaign to enlighten the American people on the need for America's involvement in the Balkans.

While Father and Ramses brought Priscilla up to date on the impending presidential election, she thought about Hettie and Austin's abduction and her rendezvous with the Yugoslav lieutenant not so long ago and how they had barely escaped Bihać.

Serbian forces had since sieged the Bosnian town. Blockaded by Serbian territory on all fronts, the Serbs bombed Bihać mercilessly. Bihać residents now lived in shelters without electricity, food, or water.

Priscilla also wondered whether the Falasha had escaped. It is not every day that strangers perform such honorable deeds as they had done for her. However, they'd narrowly escaped, with most eventually settling in refugee camps in Italy while others continued further north to who knows where.

At the time, no one knew the war in Bosnia and Herzegovina would last from mid-June 1992 through early August 1995. Yet Priscilla wondered why her in-laws had chosen that topic to discuss with her.

The evening before her in-laws departed, Priscilla heard someone scream. "What!"

Just as she had reckoned, Hettie could not resist blabbering about her adventures, particularly her and Austin's abduction. She told Lady Chelsea all that happened and ended whispering, "But Madame PJ and her friend Laverne said it's a secret, and nobody would believe me anyway. And," she said as an afterthought, "some men met with Shelton and me and said that we were not to discuss our experiences. Then they said precisely what Madame PJ had said, something about 'nobody believing us anyway.'" That was when Lady Chelsea had screamed.

As for Shelton, Priscilla never knew for sure, but she had her suspicions that he had brought Father and Ramses into the loop. Earlier, when he took them for a walk through the neighborhood, he told them about his adventures, about Hettie and Austin's abduction, and that "A CIA staffer said not to tell anyone what had happened 'because no one would believe me anyway.' And I can't remember how often Madame PJ said, 'We're not here, Shelton. Neither one of us is here. Got that?'" Listening to Shelton's report, Father and Ramses arched their bushy, graying eyebrows and smirked. They had long since suspected Priscilla was a government agent, and now their suspicions were confirmed.

And so it was that, as Priscilla completed her first novel, that she reckoned no one would believe anyway was not entirely the case.

ABOUT THE AUTHOR

Indie author M. J. Simms-Maddox, Ph.D., is the creator of The Priscilla Series, chronicling the coming of age and adventures of a modern-day, self-assured Black American woman of diverse ancestry. She has also published two books on creative writing and self-publishing.

The author is self-taught; she did not study creative writing in college. She began writing fiction in the late 1990s behind a recurring dream about a conversation with her father. She thought she finished after publishing her first novel, *Priscilla Engaging in the Game of Politics*. However, more came forth, hence the series.

In *Special Envoy 2: In Service to Her Country*, the sixth installment, Priscilla sets about as a secret agent collecting vital intel on a Yugoslav lieutenant amid the former Yugoslavia's transformation into a democracy. Yet, one wonders if the tide is returning to autocracies.

After colleagues encouraged the author to share advice about her creative writing and self-publishing experiences, she published *A Handbook for Emerging and Seasoned Authors: An Insider's Step-by-Step Approach to Becoming a Successful Indie Book Author and Publisher*, followed by *Creative Writing and Self-Publishing Your Way*.

Dr. Simms-Maddox earned her Ph.D. in political science from *The* Ohio State University. Her professional experience includes service as a legislative aide in the Ohio Senate, as the owner and operator of a public relations agency, and as a tenured professor of political science. As such, most plots in The Priscilla Series address political issues, and more are coming.

The author stays up to date with her writing and publishing endeavors via the African Literature Association, the Chanticleer Authors' Conference, the North Carolina Writers' Network, and the Surrey International Writers' Conference.

For further information about the author and her literary work, please visit her website at https://www.novelsbymj.com. Her books are also available at https://www.amazon.com/author/mjsimmsmaddox.

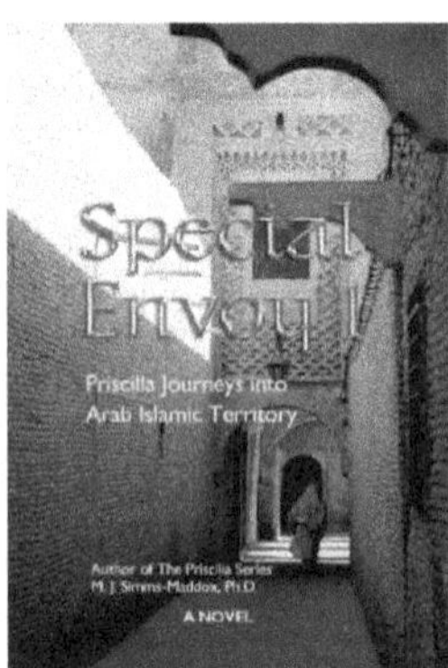

Originally published June 1, 2021, by M. J. Simms-Maddox, Inc.

Republished January 5, 2024, by Austin Macauley Publishers, LLC

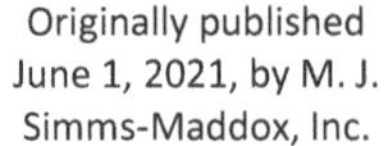

Republished December 4, 2024, by Citi of Books, Inc.

Stay tuned for more in The Priscilla Series!

www.novelsbymj.com